THE COUNTDOWN KILLER

Sam Holland is the award-winning author of the Major Crimes series, following detectives as they investigate murders committed by brutal serial killers in the south of England. Her debut, *The Echo Man*, shocked and enthralled readers and reviewers alike with its sinister depiction of a serial killer copying notorious real-life murderers of the past.

The Countdown Killer is her fourth novel.

For more information about Sam and her writing, visit samhollandbooks.com or follow her on social media at @samhollandbooks.

Also by Sam Holland

The Echo Man
The Twenty
The Puppet Master

THE COUNTDOWN KILLER

SAM HOLLAND

HEMLOCK
PRESS

Hemlock Press
An imprint of HarperCollins*Publishers* Ltd
1 London Bridge Street,
London SE1 9GF

www.harpercollins.co.uk

HarperCollins*Publishers*
Macken House, 39/40 Mayor Street Upper
Dublin 1, D01 C9W8, Ireland

First published by HarperCollins*Publishers* 2025
3

A catalogue record for this book is available from the British Library

ISBN 9780008615154

Set in Sabon LT Std by HarperCollins*Publishers* India

Printed and bound in the UK using 100% Renewable Electricity by CPI Group (UK) Ltd

This book contains FSC™ certified paper and other controlled sources to ensure responsible forest management.

For more information visit: www.harpercollins.co.uk/green

*For Queen Charlotte and King Tom Arthur.
The original Griffin and Deakin.*

Hell is empty and all the devils are here.

William Shakespeare, *The Tempest*, 1611

Prologue

The room is a box, no more than a few metres square. One door, no windows. Empty, but for a scrawny-looking man lying on the wooden floor. He's wearing ripped jeans and a football shirt. No shoes, no socks. He groans. He opens his eyes. Slowly, he lifts his head, blinking in confusion at the bright strip light on the ceiling. He gingerly touches the long, bloody gash on his forehead with dirty fingers.

His movement triggers a small red light on the camera in the corner of the room. There is a hiss, then a voice echoes from a speaker.

'Tell me your name,' it says.

The man jerks, as if stung. He frantically glances around, trying to locate the source of the sound.

'What . . .? Where . . .?'

'Tell me your name,' the voice repeats, patiently.

'Wha—? Jimmy. My name's Jimmy. Let me out of here.'

'What do you do for a living, Jimmy?'

'I . . . Who are you?'

'What do you do?' The question is shouted this time, reverberating off the brick walls.

'I'm . . . I'm unemployed.'

'And what else?' The voice reverts to monotone. 'You're a drug dealer, aren't you?'

'What? Are you the police?'

The voice chuckles, slow and deep. 'No, Jimmy. We are worse than the police.'

Jimmy jumps to his feet, whirling on the spot, frantic. His breath appears as frozen gasps; he wraps his arms around his skinny chest, trying to keep warm.

'Where am I?' he stutters.

'That isn't important. What is important is that you're here now. And we have a game to play.'

A metal bolt scrapes in a lock; the door opens. Jimmy backs away as a man appears, his bulk filling the entire doorway as he ducks to walk through. He's all in black, a balaclava over his head, obscuring everything but a pair of small, dark eyes. The man closes the door behind him, looks up to the camera, then pulls a baseball bat from behind his back. It's old, discoloured, dents visible in the wood.

'You have a choice, Jimmy,' the voice says overhead. 'Left or right?'

Jimmy gasps, his eyes wide as the man deftly twirls the bat in his right hand. Then he spots what the man has in his left: a syringe, the needle already uncapped and glistening. Jimmy's eyes dart around the room – to the man, the door, the needle, the bat, then up to the camera. The man takes a step towards Jimmy.

'What . . .? What's in there?' Jimmy stutters, backing himself into a corner. 'I've got money. Whatever you want. You can't . . .'

There's no reply. The man advances. He smells of stale sweat, and it's then that Jimmy notices the rust-coloured blotches on the floorboards. The scratches in the white painted brickwork. The almost palpable taste of desperation and fear and pain in the stale, brittle air.

His mouth open and closes, but no words come out. A dark stain blooms on the crotch of his jeans.

'Ple—' he begins, but the words are snatched away as the bat makes its swing, hitting Jimmy's right shin. The tibia shatters, splintered ends piercing the skin as Jimmy drops to the floor.

Jimmy stares in disbelief at the white bone, the blood, his ankle and foot loose and useless, bent at an unnatural angle. And then a sound draws itself up from the bottom of his lungs: a howl of pain, evolving into a high-pitched wail that bounces and distorts, turning human into animal cries.

'That's it, Jimmy,' the voice says from the speaker. 'Be a good boy. Make sure you scream.' There's a pause as the man drops the bat and grabs Jimmy's wrist, puncturing the delicate skin on his forearm with practised ease, pushing the needle deep into the vein. Jimmy can't do anything more than stare as the plunger is pressed. And as the smooth, clear liquid enters his bloodstream he continues to shriek. Knowing what's coming, how he's going to die.

A quiet chuckle comes from the speaker. And then the last words he ever hears:

'They like it when you scream.'

Part 1

DAY 1

FRIDAY

Chapter 1

These are the moments that Cara enjoys the most: a comparative calm, when the interviews have been concluded and the charging decision has been made. When the hard work of compiling evidence for the CPS has not yet begun, and Cara can convince herself that the case is over. The team has gone home, earning a well-deserved rest, and the office is empty. She should go too, but she revels in the rare moment of silence, walking around the desks, gathering festering mugs, throwing sweet wrappers in the bin and loading the dishwasher. She makes a cup of coffee in the small, cramped kitchen and carries it back to the whiteboard, removing the photographs and cleaning it off with wide, pensive strokes.

The case has been short, resolved quickly with minimum fuss. A sex worker, Joyce Hunter, reported missing by her friends. No witnesses, no body, but a horrible sinking feeling, confirmed when a member of the public called 999 about a homeless man twenty-four hours later. Ranting and raving in the middle of town, his clothes saturated in blood yet he had no wounds. Tests confirmed the blood was hers;

interviews were started and abandoned when it became clear the man needed help. And fast.

He is locked up now, in a different institution to the one they planned, justice on hold until such a time when a psychiatrist can balance his mental state. Possibly never, Cara thinks, taking the smiling photo of the missing woman down from the board and placing it in the file with the rest of the notes. The location of her body may remain a mystery, but the amount of blood confirms it: she is dead.

A phone rings; she reaches to answer it.

'DCI Elliott?' the voice says. 'Front desk. Are you the only one available?'

'At the moment.'

'It's just . . . I'm not sure this needs a DCI—'

'I'm here, how can I help?'

The woman pauses. 'Come down. I'll explain.'

Cara takes the stairs. The police station is deserted; the canteen is shut; admin staff have gone home. Only the night shift remain, their skin yellowed in the fluorescent lights, their eyes heavy. The enquiry officer waits behind reception.

'Thank you for coming,' she says as Cara draws closer. 'I would have passed it to Response and Patrol, but it's a Friday night, a full moon, and it's raining, so . . .'

'Say no more,' Cara says with a smile, imagining the bedlam in town as drunken revellers go crazy, living up to every cop superstition with abandon. 'What have you got?'

There's a worn Tesco Bag for Life on the desk, a small package inside. The whole lot has been placed in a see-through evidence bag – the officer pushes it across.

'A woman dropped this off. She wouldn't stick around

for an exhibit statement, wouldn't even give her name. Just dumped this on the counter and legged it.'

'What did she say?'

'Just that she didn't want it. No, that's not right.' She thinks for a second. '"I can't stand to be around it anymore." Yeah, that was it.'

Cara pulls the bag closer and holds it up to the light. 'Feels like a CD.'

'DVD. But one of those recordable ones. Will you take it?'

Cara looks at it, frowning. It's not her job, definitely not her paygrade. Her phone buzzes in her pocket and she pulls it out, reading the text.

Another hour, it says. *Sorry. You go without me. Cx*

Charlie, the head of the digital team, and her boyfriend of the past year. He's embroiled in a last-minute request – a child protection issue. The sexual abuse team need to see what's on a laptop, and they need it now.

Cara looks at the odd package. She replies to Charlie's text – *I'll wait x* – then picks up the bag, signs the paperwork and gives a smile to the grateful officer. She'll check out what this is, then either pass it back to Response and Patrol to deal with, or, most likely, book it into stores, along with the rest of the things crazy people drop off in the dead of night. The taxidermy badger; the papier-mâché alien spaceship; the full human skeleton (thankfully plastic). One random DVD isn't going to make a dent.

Knowing her coffee will have gone cold, she pauses in the kitchen to make a fresh mug, then carries both back to her office. She sits down next to the old computer in the corner of the room and switches it on. It's stand alone with no connection to the network, kept for just this reason; it bursts into life with a beep and a whirr. She puts on a pair of blue nitrile gloves, opens the evidence bag and carefully takes the box out.

The square case is clear with a black plastic back, the disc inside. There are no identifying markings, no writing on the spine. Nothing to indicate what it might contain. She squints at it, puzzled. Something or nothing, she's not going to know until she takes a look.

She presses a button on the front of the machine and the drawer opens. She places the disc inside – it slides back with a clunk. She waits, blowing on her coffee.

Outside, rain drips against the window, droplets stick then merge, running down the glass. The office is peaceful as she selects play.

The screen is black. The counter ticks through ten seconds, then twenty. She clicks the fast forward button, and just as she's considering giving up on it for good, an image appears. She scrolls backwards, craning forward as the picture evolves from black to a strange tableau. A room: white walls, wooden floor. A door on the far side. The video is shot from high up, from the corner of the ceiling, Cara assumes. The only sound is a low hum, as a man paces in the small box.

Cara's brow furrows. She slowly lowers her coffee, placing it on the desk. A scene plays out, and as she watches her mouth drops open; her heart thumps so loudly she can hear it in her ears. The whole video can't last longer than ten minutes, maybe fifteen, but as the film comes to an end she realises her mouth is dry.

She presses her trembling fingers against her lips, still staring at the blackened screen. And then, slowly, she picks up her mouse, rewinds to the beginning and watches it again.

Second time around it doesn't have the same shock factor, but it's still horrific. She looks for signs it's been staged, but it looks real. It *feels* real. She's transfixed by the brute force, the aggression, so when she feels a hand on her shoulder, she jumps. Reels around, her fists clenched.

'Whoa, sorry, sorry,' Charlie says, his hands out in front, defensive. 'I didn't mean to sneak up on you. Are you okay?' he adds, his voice concerned. 'You're as white as a sheet.'

'I'm fine. I'm sorry, my fault . . . I . . .' Cara's eyes drift back to the screen where the video's still playing.

'What are you watching . . .? Cara?'

Charlie quietens as he sits down next to her, his gaze locked as he leans forward, taking in the images on the screen.

Cara looks away. She feels light-headed, and realises she's barely taken a breath since the video began. With a shaking hand, she reaches out and presses pause.

'What the hell is that?' Charlie asks.

The image is frozen, a man in the middle of the shot. His body is limp. His legs are splayed, ankles at an unnatural angle. His head is tilted back, his eyes glassy. His mouth gapes, his jaw wrenched open, blood, spit, vomit, down the front of his white shirt.

'That,' Cara begins, but she can't go on, her mouth parched. She swallows and tries again. 'That is a snuff film.'

Chapter 2

An hour later, Cara and Charlie sit at Cara's kitchen table, a laptop in front of them. A man joins them from the living room, dressed in grey jogging bottoms and a black T-shirt, with bare feet and a baffled expression. He's followed by a small black cat.

'What's so important?' Griffin says, sitting down next to them. The cat jumps onto his lap and stares at Cara with resentful amber eyes.

'Were the kids okay?'

'Picked them up from school. Gave them dinner. Fed the cat. Anyone would think I was your husband rather than your brother.'

Cara ignores the unsubtle dig. 'You said you didn't mind. Besides, Frank's yours.' The cat glares, unperturbed, then climbs on the table and settles on a pile of paperwork.

'You can have him.'

'He hates me,' she replies. And he really does; the scars on her hands are testament to that.

Her brother – and his cat – have been living with her for over a year now, and she likes it for the most part. He helped her move house, settled in the spare room, pays half the rent, and shows little sign of getting a place of his own. He goes to bed far too late, can be grumpy in the mornings, and doesn't hesitate to put her in her place when she's being unreasonable, but he's sober, single, never brings women home, and babysits her two kids when needs be. Probably too often, as he himself pointed out.

'Who picked them up?'

'Sarah. About quarter past six.' Cara sighs. 'You weren't home either,' Griffin points out, to her annoyance.

'I just don't like the woman.'

'You don't like her because she's twenty-eight and engaged to your ex-husband. Isn't that right, Charlie?'

'Don't drag me into this,' Charlie replies. He'd got up to make tea and toast and now places mugs on the table, a plate in front of Cara. 'Eat that,' he instructs.

Cara scowls at Griffin. As siblings, they couldn't be more different. Her younger brother is six foot tall, has converted the garage into a gym, makes use of it every day and looks like it, while she's the wrong side of forty, and can't remember the last time she lifted anything heavier than a full mug of coffee. But they both have the same dark brown hair, the same light brown eyes. Together, they've been through a lot, and she'll forgive him anything.

She takes a bite of her peanut butter on toast. She hadn't realised how hungry she was and smiles gratefully at Charlie. He smiles back; behind his glasses the creases around his dark eyes wrinkle in a way she finds both attractive and comforting.

For a year, life has been simple and quiet. Cases solved, their small team running like clockwork, but Cara has a bad feeling about this video. Deemed free of viruses by an obedient and late-working member of the IT team, it's been transferred to the network, and now Charlie pulls the laptop around to face Griffin, the screen paused on black. Her brother's forehead furrows.

'Someone brought this to the police station this evening.' She holds up the evidence bag; he takes it, squinting at the case inside.

'And this involves Major Crimes, how?'

'You'll see.'

She leans forward and presses play. Forces herself to watch as the scene unfolds for the third time.

A small room, a man standing in the centre. Best guess: mid-thirties. Short brown hair, wearing a once smart black suit, white shirt, navy tie, all in disarray. He paces the room, shouting, clearly annoyed at being there. He rattles the locked door, then circles, his manner changing from anger to fear.

'Tell me your name.' A voice booms in the room, the speaker crackling. The man looks around, confused, then spots the camera, looking directly into the lens.

'Who are you?' he bellows.

'Tell me your name,' the voice repeats. 'Things will go a lot easier for you if you do as you're told.'

The man hesitates. 'Terry,' he says. 'Terence Gregory.'

'And what do you do for a living, Mr Gregory?'

'I'm . . . I'm a hedge fund manager.'

The crackle of the loudspeaker stops.

'Who are you?' the man shouts. 'Why am I here? It must have been days. I'm hungry. Thirsty. I demand you let me go.'

For five minutes, nothing new happens. The man paces for a bit, then stops and leans against the far wall, his eyes darting.

14

She feels Griffin glance her way, but doesn't move, doesn't take her eyes off the screen.

With a creak, the door opens. The man stands straight, his stance wide, facing the two men that enter. Big blokes, dressed all in black. One of them drags a tall, sturdy wooden chair behind him; he leaves it in the centre of the room and they advance on the man.

His eyes are frantic as he backs away, but the room is small, his options limited. They grab him, taking an arm each. He protests, shouting, screaming, feet scrabbling on the wooden floor. A shoe is lost, but his efforts are useless as he's pinned in the chair, bucking as a roll of thick silver tape secures his hands, arms behind him, low, defenceless. His feet next – to the legs of the chair. He shouts, begs, but the men are stoic as they force his skull back hard, wrapping tape around his forehead.

The man's completely immobile now, only his eyes and mouth can move as he watches the two men walk behind him. He's crying, his previous pleas going unheard.

Cara wants to look away, but she can't. She's transfixed by the scene, by this frantic victim as he weeps, sobs, completely ignored.

'What's going on?' Griffin says. 'What—'

Cara remembers her own reaction. She expected guns, knives, fists, and was confused when one of the attackers pulled a bundle of paper from his pocket.

'What's that?' Griffin says.

'Cash,' Cara replies. 'Old style paper money.'

The large man passes half the bundle to his mate, then they both look up into the camera.

'Permission granted,' the voice says over the loudspeaker.

'Permission to wha—' the victim begins, but he's silenced

as one of the men grabs his jaw, forcing it open while the other pushes a bank note into his mouth. Then another, and another. He chokes, gags, but the men are persistent; one by one, chunky fingers push the cash inside. Methodical, meticulous, not a single note dropped. The man is silent, unable to speak or cry out, but Cara can see his muscles are tight, his fingers splayed, his eyes wide with pain and fear. They have a job to do. The crunch is audible as the man's jaw cracks, breaking open to an impossible angle as the men force their hands inside, feeding bank note after bank note into his gullet.

And then the man stills. His body goes limp, his eyes stare vacantly to the ceiling, all life dimmed. The two men continue until every bank note is gone, then dust themselves down.

The men glance up to the camera, nod, then leave the room. The victim is left; nothing moves but for a trickle of blood as it runs from his nose.

'Job complete,' a voice says, and the screen goes black.

Chapter 3

The kitchen is quiet. So quiet Cara can hear the hum of the fridge, the tick of the clock. Charlie closes the lid of the laptop and Griffin lets out a long exhale.

'Fuck,' he says. 'Someone dropped this off at the station? Who?'

'That's what we need to find out.'

The men stare at her. Her brother and her boyfriend – both have seen some horrific things through their time in the police force, neither seems keen to move on this now.

'Are you sure . . .?' Charlie begins. 'I mean . . .'

'What?'

'Are you sure you want this?' Griffin finishes.

'This is murder. I'm the DCI of Major Crimes. Who else is it going to?'

'DCI Ryder? Up in Basingstoke?'

'Hell, no—'

'It's . . . Cara . . .' Charlie reaches out and takes her hands in his. He's warm, and his eyes are pleading. 'You've been through a lot. The team have been through a lot.'

'Last January we were investigating a serial killer,' Griffin says, taking over. 'The Echo Man was only a few years ago. Jamie's just been promoted—'

'To detective inspector. Which means he is more than capable—'

'The team is still small, we need to recruit—'

'We can get more staff—'

'Cara, I'm just saying. Maybe this shouldn't be ours.'

Cara softens. Her brother has endured it all: addiction, break-ups. The death of his wife at the hands of the Echo Man, the first serial killer case she ran. Only now, here, does he seem stable for the first time in years.

'I'm not going to force you to take this case,' she says. 'But we're all in better shape than we were last January. And this is straightforward. We even have the victim's name. We find the person who dropped this off at the police station, we have our killer. We move on. What could be simpler than that?'

Charlie and Griffin exchange a glance. 'Fine,' Griffin says after a moment. He rouses himself with a shake of his head, then pulls her laptop across. 'He said his name was Terry Gregory, what do we know about him?'

'That was my question,' Charlie says, pulling his own laptop out of his bag. 'We thought we'd get home first.'

'So you could share this with me? How lovely.' A pause. 'Okay, so . . . Terence Gregory,' Griffin reads. 'Reported missing by his wife on the fifth of August, 2014. Went for a job interview and was never seen again.' He turns the laptop around to show Cara; the smiling man in the photograph looks like the guy in the video, as much as they can tell. 'Hedge fund manager, as he said. Worked at Fredricks and Braverman.'

'What conclusions did the investigating officer come to?'

'That he had left of his own volition. Not much actual investigation was carried out.'

Charlie takes over, reading from his screen: 'Listen to this: "Police are searching for Terry Gregory, aged 34. At the time of his disappearance Gregory was under investigation for fraud and theft, and under suspension from work, after money and investments went missing. Police are asking the public for . . ." *blah blah blah*, you know the rest,' he concludes.

'So, Terry Gregory was being investigated in relation to fraud involving – I assume – a lot of money, then disappears after being suspended. What conclusion would you come to?'

'That he's fucked off and is living his best life on a tropical island somewhere.'

'Exactly. Meanwhile the sad truth is he's been abducted, murdered, and ten years later his body has never been found.'

'And it can't be coincidence that he's killed by having bank notes shoved into his mouth,' Griffin says. 'Feels like a revenge killing to me.'

'A perfect murder. No body, no crime.'

'Until today.'

'Until today,' Cara repeats with a sigh. 'First thing tomorrow, the investigation begins.'

'It's a Saturday,' Griffin comments.

'Saturday or not. This is murder.'

She gets up, carries her mug and plate to the dishwasher. She can feel both Charlie and Griffin watching, and turns her back. She doesn't want them to see her face; knows that indecision and worry are scoring lines across her features.

The team can't cope with another serial. One more and

the case will destroy them. Chew them up and spit them out, but she's made up her mind. She's not going to back away now.

She tries to reassure herself. This is a one-off killing. A cold case, a revenge attack where the suspects will become obvious and even the crime itself has been recorded. And the team is stronger now. They've been solving cases like clockwork, knocking them out of the park one by one. Only DCI Ryder in Basingstoke has a better solve rate than her, and she's damned if she'll give up this one.

'Call the team,' she says, closing the dishwasher with a decisive clunk. 'I'm going to bed.'

DAY 2

SATURDAY

Chapter 4

Jamie Hoxton wakes to the sound of a baby crying. The enthusiastic wail of a five-month-old that sears through even the deepest of dreams, leaving him gasping for air at the surface. He rubs his eyes and listens; already he can hear the soothing rumbles of a male voice, the cries abating to a mild bleat.

He looks at the clock and picks up his phone, surprised to see a message from DS Nate Griffin. *Come in*, it says. *Urgent.*

What could be so important? So soon after wrapping their last case. A few drinks last night – a few too many. But killers don't respect days off, and babies certainly don't care about hangovers.

He swings his legs out of bed and makes his way to the bathroom. The door to the next bedroom is ajar, and through it he can see the dim glow of the bedside light, a lump in the bedclothes. Footsteps behind him; he turns, and Adam is there, two mugs of steaming coffee in his hands, dressed only in a T-shirt and boxer shorts. Hair askew, eyes bagged from lack of sleep.

'Did Ivy wake you?' Adam half whispers.

'Nah. Work.'

'Now?' For a second, he looks interested, then his attention is diverted by the cries from the master bedroom. 'Coffee's on. Enough for you. Come round again later?'

'I can't spend every night with you guys.'

'You're always welcome.'

Jamie showers quickly and dresses in yesterday's clothes, heads downstairs. He pours the remaining stewed coffee into a mug, puts on a new pot to percolate, then takes a moment, leaning against the kitchen counter and sipping at the coffee.

He should be heading to the nick. *Cara says ASAP*, as Griffin reiterated in a follow-up message, and as the newly promoted detective inspector in the team, he has a vital role to play as Cara's second-in-command. But he needs a moment; to remind himself why he does this job, why he should care for the victim, or the latest bereaved relative.

Next to him, the bottle steriliser is going full blast, hot steam pumping out of the top. Through the door into the living room he can see a gaudy playmat, with bright yellow giraffes and orange lions. A bouncer sits next to it, empty but for a white muslin he knows will smell faintly of baby sick.

Life has changed since Ivy was born five months ago. Amending priorities, learning new routines and adjusting accordingly. Gone are the nights out, drinking until the early hours, followed by Sunday mornings in front of the TV. Replaced by broken sleep and tummy time for Adam, and a lonely bare flat for Jamie.

Because Ivy isn't Jamie's baby. This isn't his house. But it is a home of love and support, a safe haven, where he regularly claims the spare room. Adam is his closest friend, and together they've been through the best and the worst of times. A case that left Adam on the edge of death, a murderer that abducted and killed Jamie's wife, leading to a spiral of depression and attempted suicide. Adam and his wife Romilly were there for him then, and they've been a steadying constant since – never complaining about his presence, never objecting to feeding one more. And Jamie loves the noise and the bustle, arriving to a warm house full of conversation and smells, even if the aromas are baby poo and off-milk.

Contemplation over, he places his empty mug in the dishwasher and picks up his coat. Time for work.

By the time he makes it to the nick, the rest of the team is already in. DC Toby Shenton is in the kitchen making a tray of coffees; DC Alana Brody is plugging in a projector, and Griffin and Cara are in her office.

'Do you know what this is about?' he asks Brody as he dumps his bag and shucks his coat off.

But before Brody can reply, Cara emerges. She has a laptop in her hand that she places on the table in front of them.

'I have no wish to watch this video again, so I'll leave you all to your private viewings. But before you do, a quick summary.' She sits back, resting her bum on the edge of the desk. Griffin joins them, taking a seat behind Jamie and greeting him with a hearty tap on the arm. Cara continues: 'Terence Gregory, aged thirty-four. Went missing August 2014 after a suspected theft from his job as a hedge fund manager. No trace until a disc shows up at the police station last night. Dropped off by an unknown woman.' She taps a finger on the computer. 'Snuff film, detailing his last, excruciatingly painful moments.'

'Someone filmed him being murdered?' Jamie says, observing the team's disbelieving stares.

'Yes. And unfortunately, you'll all need to watch it. Look for clues about where this is, who these people are. From how Gregory is dressed, I'm assuming he was killed fairly shortly after he was abducted, but it would be good to know for sure. Charlie and his team have the disc and are looking for metadata. The case and the plastic bag it arrived in have already been taken to the lab for analysis.'

Cara pauses. Jamie knows her well enough by now to see the determination on her face, but also the concern and the fatigue. They've barely had time to rest after the last investigation.

She continues: 'We have two main lines of enquiry. Firstly, where did this disc come from? A woman dropped it off last night and you don't get in and out of a police station without being on tape. I want to know who she is and how she got here. Griffin, Brody, I'll leave that with you.

'Secondly, Jamie, I want to know about our victim. He was married when he went missing – track down his wife, ask about last movements. Where he might have been abducted from and when. Take Shenton, he needs to get out in the field more.' Jamie gives his colleague a nod, Shenton flushes. 'Plus, let's find out about this fraud. The investigation stalled when he went missing, but speak to his boss from that time. See for yourselves, but this looks like an act of revenge. Who knew about what he had done and who would want him dead in this way?'

Jamie nods, making notes on his pad. 'Should we be

looking for a body?' he asks. All faces turn his way. 'Terence Gregory is dead, we have the video, so where's his body? I'm guessing that we have his DNA on file from when he was reported missing, so any John Does found in the last ten years would have been matched to him. Can we assume his body is still out there somewhere?'

'These people were clever enough to keep this quiet for over a decade, I'm guessing they know how to hide a body. Find the killers, we'll find the corpse.' She stands up. 'Watch the film. Keep me updated. Thank you everyone.'

She claps her hands together and the meeting is adjourned. Jamie looks at the laptop, the snuff film saved inside. He glances to Brody, to Shenton – they're doing the same. They know what it shows; nobody wants to watch this thing.

Brody sighs and pulls it closer using just her fingertips, as if it will make her physically dirty.

'Come on,' she says. 'It's not going to get any better.'

Chapter 5

It takes Griffin and Brody half an hour to find the information they need. Police stations are plastered in cameras; CCTV covers every angle of the woman's visit, inside and out.

They can see from the video that she's older, with short grey hair and a stoop, wearing a long black overcoat and sensible shoes. She arrives by car, spends quarter of an hour dithering outside, then a further five minutes and forty-two seconds speaking to the enquiry officer before she leaves again. She dabs at her eyes, shakes her head at the questions and departs in a hurry.

They now know exactly what she looks like. Even better, they have a number plate. And a name.

'Gwen Morris,' Brody says, looking up from her laptop. 'Sixty-one. Lives in Sherfield English. Do you want to go?'

'Now? To the house of a murderer?'

'You saw her – she's a little old lady. You're six foot and a metre wide. But sure, call Response and Patrol for backup, everyone needs a laugh.' She looks at him, eyes sparkling mischievously. 'Truth or dare?'

'Alana . . .'

'Humour me.'

They've been playing it for a while, but what started as a game has evolved into something riskier. Griffin narrows his eyes at her. With her dyed black hair and piercings marching up her ears, Alana Brody looks unconventional, but they work well together. Griffin enjoys her no-nonsense manner and perceptive eye; Brody uses him as a foil for her more radical ideas.

And Griffin rarely turns down a challenge.

'Dare,' he replies.

'Are you sure?'

'Dare.' Because it's always a dare between them, never the truth.

'We're going.'

He sighs. 'Fine. But if she charges me with a kitchen knife, this is your fault.'

'I'll defend you, my liege,' she mocks, leading the way to the car park.

They take Griffin's battered old Land Rover, Brody giving directions from the passenger seat. It's not long until they're clear of the grey of Southampton, driving through small country roads lined with green hedgerows. Birds take flight as the clunky truck roars past in a cloud of exhaust.

'I told you we were right to go: the boss says to update her when we get there. No heroics.' Brody shows him the phone. 'She's put it in capitals, see?'

Griffin grunts. Brody's light-hearted, but she's seen the disc, she knows what they're facing. Someone killed this man, and they're heading to the source – a remote location that would serve wonderfully as a murder site. Plenty of room for dead bodies, where no one will hear you scream.

'Left here,' Brody says. 'Do you want to arrest her?'

'For murder? No, unless she gives us cause. She's more likely to talk if we're sitting with a cup of tea on her sofa. Simple chat. Let's see where it goes.'

Griffin takes a turn through a narrow gate, the Land Rover bumping over potholes and puddles as they make their way down the drive towards a grand house. But as they get closer the extent of the decay is revealed. Paint peels from the windowsills, chunks of rendering have fallen from the walls, revealing the brick underneath. Multiple tiles have fallen from the roof, the holes gaping like missing teeth. Once an extraordinary house, it has been allowed to descend into ruin.

He pulls the truck up and they get out. The garden is a similar mess – overgrown lawns stretch into fields bordered by dilapidated fences and unkempt hedgerows. The grass is long, scattered with treacherous thistles and stinging nettles branching up to the sky; the rusted remains of a swing set crumples under an impressive oak, the once bright red metal misshapen into bloody broken bones.

They approach the front door and rap the tarnished gold knocker against the wood. It echoes ominously inside.

Brody peers through the grubby windows. Griffin knocks again, and this time he hears footsteps, then bolts being pulled. The door opens a few inches and a face peers out.

'DS Nate Griffin, this is DC Alana Brody.' Griffin shows his ID. 'Can we come in?'

The door closes for a moment as the chain is removed. It opens to reveal a grey-haired woman, cowed, wearing the exact same clothing as they saw in the CCTV from last night. She looks older than her sixty-one years.

'You found me,' she says, bent in resignation as she holds the door open. 'You better come in.'

Griffin nods his thanks, stooping to get through the low doorframe. The house is dark, and he waits for his eyes to adjust to the gloom as the woman walks ahead into a kitchen. A huge space, warmed by a massive red Aga in the centre. Shelves line every wall, crockery, glassware, knick-knacks and saucepans mingling together.

'Have you lived here long?' Brody asks, although it's clear this woman has been here for years, decades even, every mark, every scratch a testament to her life.

'We moved in when we got married,' the woman says. 'It was my parents' house, and when they died we took over. We were happy here.'

'We?' Griffin asks.

'My husband and I. Edward. He died a month ago.'

'Sorry for your loss,' Griffin and Brody murmur.

The woman takes an old silver kettle to the sink, fills it up and plugs it back in. It resembles a relic from the fifties, but starts bubbling straight away. 'Tea, coffee?' she asks.

'Coffee, thank you,' Griffin replies as Brody asks for the same.

Brody takes a seat at the table, but Griffin hesitates, unsure how to proceed. Her calmness seems at odds with the frantic woman on the video from last night, and Griffin has to remind himself why they're there. This woman dropped off a snuff film detailing a horrific murder – and now she's making drinks for the police like nothing has happened?

'Mrs Morris,' Griffin begins.

'Gwen, please.' She places the chipped mugs on the table, gestures for Griffin to sit down. He reluctantly does as he's told.

'Gwen. Do you know why we're here?'

'That disc.'

'And do you know what was on it?'

She nods, and for the first time, Griffin can see emotion on her lined face. Her shoulders sag, her chin wobbles.

'Did you watch it?' he asks, gently.

'Yes,' she whispers. 'But that man, I don't know who he was.'

'That's fine. We can work that out. Where did you get it?'

She picks up her mug with shaking hands and takes a sip. 'My husband,' she says. 'I was going through his things. After he died. And . . . And . . .' Her voice trembles. 'I think I always knew,' she says so quietly Griffin has to strain to hear, 'what he was doing.'

Griffin hardly dares to ask. He opens his mouth, but she puts her hand on his, stopping him. She's cold, her skin dry like paper. She looks up, meeting his gaze.

'Do you want the rest?' she says.

'The rest?'

'Yes,' she replies, replacing her mug on the table and standing up. 'You didn't think that was the only one?'

Chapter 6

They follow Gwen Morris through the house. Down narrow
corridors smelling of damp and mould, past belongings
heaped into piles – books, clothes, an old TV.

With every step, the sense of foreboding and dread
increases. Griffin catches Brody's gaze, concern at what
they're going to find. The trophies of a serial killer? Or
worse – the bodies themselves?

They pass through a dim living room with dark
wooden furniture, once plush armchairs moth-eaten into
patchwork – and into a back room.

It's an office, with huge windows opening out onto a
paved garden. Paper covers every surface – notepads, books,
loose sheets – some fallen to the floor, but all scattered with
ducks of every shape and size. Wooden, porcelain, even
yellow rubber ones. All watching them with beady black
eyes.

Griffin raises his eyebrows, but Gwen doesn't stop,
leading them up to what looks like a cupboard door. She
takes a ball of keys out of her pocket, selects one and fits it
into the keyhole. It turns with a heavy clunk. Then a second,

the hole higher up. She can hardly reach, but manages it on tiptoes, before stepping back and turning the handle. She heaves the door open.

It's clear this is no ordinary cupboard. The door must be four inches thick, and heavy. A lock room. But what could be so valuable it needs this much security? What on earth did this man do?

Gwen moves out of the way, and Griffin takes a tentative step forward. He peers into the dark, reaches around until he finds a light switch and snaps it on.

The cupboard is lined with shelves, every one stuffed full of tapes. VHS, DVDs, CDs. Some shop bought, mostly titles Griffin recognises from the eighties – *Bergerac*, *Poirot*, *Howard's Way* and various Merchant Ivory films. Others have scrawled labels: *Christmas 89*, *Gwen's birthday*, *BAFTA ceremony DON'T DELETE*. A motley selection of home videos, nothing that sets Griffin's senses on alert.

'Griffin?' Brody says from behind him. He turns.

The bare bulb in the centre of the room swings, eerily lighting the shelf – and the row of plastic boxes. Just over a dozen, identical. No markings, anonymous discs.

Griffin looks back to the poor woman. She's standing in the doorway, shaking.

'I haven't watched them all,' she says. 'Only a few. But . . . they're real, aren't they? Those people.'

'We believe so.'

The thought that each one of these discs shows a murder is horrific. He counts them. Fourteen. Griffin can't stand to be in here any longer, the ghosts haunt him and he turns, escorting Gwen back into the main study and gesturing for her to sit behind the huge desk. He grabs a chair and pulls it up next to her.

'Tell me about your husband,' Griffin says. 'What did he do?'

'He made documentaries. Worked for the BBC for a while, but usually freelance. He was brilliant.'

'Director? Cameraman? Editor?'

'All of the above, and more.' She points to a shelf – at the top rests an iconic BAFTA mask, the gold award incongruous among the clutter and mess. 'He won that in 2004,' she continues. 'Best documentary for his film about the start of the Iraqi War. The fall of Saddam, that sort of thing.'

'Who did he work with? Was there anyone who stood out?'

'Always different, so many names. I met a few of them, but he kept me away from his work. He said that the things he'd seen . . .' Her voice trails off, lost in thought. 'He'd have nightmares, wouldn't tell me what about. He was often depressed, but his work – that was the thing he lived for. When he was buried in a project, that's when he was happiest.'

'And you didn't know those films were there?'

'No. Not until I found the keys in his desk drawer.'

'And it was just the two of you? No children?'

'We had a daughter – Siobhan. Shiv, we called her. But she was killed when she was eighteen. Nearly fifteen years ago now. Drunk driver.'

'I'm so sorry. She was your only child?'

'Yes. It was a difficult birth, we didn't want to risk it again.'

'Nieces or nephews?'

'Nobody.'

'Griffin?'

Brody calls from the doorway, gestures him over. He gets up, leaves the woman lost in her thoughts, and joins her.

'I've called Cara,' she says. 'And the SOCOs. They're on their way.' She gestures to the discs. 'Are we really saying this bloke killed fifteen people?'

'Terence Gregory was killed in 2014. Over the course of ten years? It's possible. Get in touch with Charlie Mills in digital. Someone will have to go through this lot. Document it all.'

'Will do. But Griffin, there's more.'

She steps back to the edge of the room, gestures for him to do the same, then pulls at a corner of the raggedy carpet. It comes up easily, revealing a concrete base, and in the middle, a small square metal door. Griffin crouches down, runs his finger around the edge of the keyhole.

'Floor safe?' he says, then calls Gwen into the room. She stares at the metal door with horror, as if the floor is collapsing beneath her.

'Do you have a key?'

'Key? No. I wasn't even aware.' She starts crying again, and through her tears, she says the very words Griffin has been thinking. 'What on earth is down there?'

Chapter 7

The pairing of Jamie with Toby Shenton is a new one; an idea of Cara's to get the relatively inexperienced detective constable out of the office.

'He needs to meet some people,' she'd said to Jamie. 'Show him that humans aren't just a psychological profile on a page.'

She was referring to Shenton's PhD – his part-time study into what Griffin disparagingly calls 'the woo-woo serial killer theory'. Jamie asks him about it now, desperate to break the yawning silence between them. They've been driving for nearly an hour, and Shenton has hardly spoken.

'It's going well,' Shenton replies.

'What's it on again?' Jamie asks.

'The prediction of offender personality traits based on the modus operandi of a kill.'

'Psychological profiling?'

'That's right. I'm building on the work started by the Behavioural Analysis Unit of the FBI.'

'So you spend all your free time studying serial killers?'

'What else is there to do?' He's completely serious, and

looks at Jamie for the first time, moving a wave of straight blond hair out of his face with long fingers. With his ivory, flawless skin, he looks young, but Jamie guesses his age at mid-thirties. 'What do you do when you're not at work?' Shenton continues.

'I . . . watch TV, go to the gym.' His protestations sound pathetic, even to him. Especially when he hasn't done any exercise in years, something his tubby physique makes more than obvious.

'What about last night?' Shenton asks, pointedly. 'You're wearing yesterday's clothes.'

'I stayed at a friend's house. I didn't expect to get called in this morning.'

'Oh. I thought you might have been out on a date. How long's it been since your wife died?'

His directness is distracting, and for a moment Jamie looks away from the road, straight into Shenton's piercing blue eyes.

'Just over two years.'

'Isn't that long enough? Look at Griffin. His wife was murdered, and he's out meeting new people. New women.'

Jamie feels his throat tighten. In the absence of a polite response, he keeps quiet until Shenton says, 'You missed the turn-off.'

'Yes, sorry.'

Jamie swings the car around and this time hits the right-hand junction. They drive the rest of the way in silence.

The house is the last in a row of pebble-dashed terraces. An empty pot containing the half dead remnants of an unrecognisable plant sits on the paving slabs, the street quiet.

Jamie rings the bell and Mrs Gregory answers. They had phoned ahead, so he's surprised to see her in a towelling robe and slippers, hair dishevelled.

'Mrs Gregory? We can come back later—'

'No, no, come in. Please, call me Marie. Sorry about the state of me, I'm just back from a nightshift. Don't worry about taking your shoes off. House is a pigsty.'

She shows Jamie and Shenton through to the living room. Sure enough, it's messy, seemingly random articles left where they fell – a pair of socks, a tube of mascara, a paperback book – but it's clean, with a faint air of citrus.

'Sit down, sit down.' Jamie and Shenton take a seat opposite Marie, as she pulls a bowl onto her lap and continues eating. Porridge and banana. 'How can I help?' she says through a mouthful. 'I assume it's to do with my good for nothing husband. Have you arrested him yet?'

Jamie hasn't given the reason for their visit, preferring to get her reaction as it happens. He delays the bad news a little longer.

'Mrs Gregory – Marie, sorry. Can you tell us about the day your husband disappeared?'

She chews, thinks. Swallows. 'Terry had been suspended, we assumed he was going to be fired, so he was rattling around the house. Not this house,' she adds quickly. 'Had to sell that when he went missing. He left nothing, barely a penny in our joint bank account. Back then I was a housewife. Daughter was eight, happy at school, loving husband on the fast-track to promotion, thought I was the luckiest woman alive.' She laughs, a mocking cackle. 'Little did I know. Before long, my husband is unemployed, disgraced, with a police investigation hanging over his head. And then he was gone.'

'In your initial statement, you said he was wearing a suit and tie when he disappeared, is that correct?'

'Yes, although I couldn't tell you what colour or anything now. He was dressed that way because he had an interview. New job, he told me, and I was so relieved. Of course it was all a lie. He left at ten that morning, never came back.'

'And it made sense to you that he left?'

'Not at first. I thought he loved me. Loved our daughter. But once the police explained . . .' She leans forward, places the bowl on the coffee table. 'You found his car at the airport. He'd taken his passport with him. The police said he'd stolen funds, defrauded his company.'

'I read the notes. The investigating officer said there was no record of him leaving the country.'

'Yes, but at the time they also said he could have bought fake documents. New passport, new identity. He had money, after all.' She frowns. 'I got the feeling they weren't looking very hard.'

'And your marriage was happy? You had a child together?'

'That's what I believed. Stupid cow that I was.' Her brow furrows, she nibbles on a nail. 'I think it's about time you tell me what's going on, DS Hoxton. Please.'

Jamie prepares himself for the inevitable. 'Marie, there's no easy way to tell you this, but we believe your husband didn't leave you that day. We have new evidence that suggests Terry was abducted.'

'Abducted?'

'And then murdered.'

'Oh, God.' Her hands fly to her mouth, she looks at Jamie, disbelieving. 'What sort of evidence? Have you found . . . his body?'

'No . . .'

'Then how . . .?'

'We have video footage. Of his death.'

A thousand different emotions cross Mrs Gregory's face. Confusion, devastation, maybe even relief. She starts to cry.

'Is there anyone who can be with you today?'

'Yes. My daughter. Our daughter. She's eighteen now, at university down the road. So he's been dead . . . all this time?'

'We believe so, yes. The interview he went on – do you have any information about that?'

She frowns. 'No. He didn't tell me much. But his laptop – I've still got it. It's old, and the battery's probably gone, but you're welcome to it.'

'Thank you. Yes, please.'

Mrs Gregory gets up, leaving Jamie and Shenton in silence. Shenton takes in the room, and Jamie notes what he's seeing. The tired furniture, the dated wallpaper.

'Ten years,' Shenton says in a low whisper. 'He's been gone ten years, and it never occurred to her that he was dead?'

Jamie stares at him. 'What are you saying?'

'Her husband stole millions, left her penniless with a young child. A lot of negative emotions wrapped up in that – if we want a motive, we don't have to look far.'

'I agree she'd be bitter, but to kill her husband? And like that? Pretty psychopathic.'

Shenton shrugs as Mrs Gregory comes back into the room clutching an old fat laptop. She hands it to Jamie.

'Do what you want with it. I don't want it back.'

'Thank you.' The three of them walk to the front door. 'How did you cope?' Jamie asks. 'After your husband disappeared?'

Marie Gregory sighs, leaning heavily on the wall. 'Badly. My parents were dead, no family, few friends. But people stuck by me. Got me back on my feet – helped me buy this place. Babysat my daughter while I went back to work. Now look at me. I'm a trained nurse, I do a good job. My daughter is happy and smart and studying to become a lawyer. What more can I ask for?'

'I'm glad.' Jamie gives her a warm smile. 'We'll be back in touch when we know more.'

'Thank you.' She pauses, lost in thought. 'Can I ask,' she says. 'When Terry died, did he suffer?'

'Yes,' Shenton replies before Jamie can intervene. 'Horribly.'

Jamie looks at Shenton in dismay, then at Mrs Gregory. She screws her face up. At first Jamie thinks she's going to cry, then she pulls herself up, standing straight in her doorway.

'Good,' she says, decisively. 'After everything he put us through, all those poor people he stole money from. Good.'

Chapter 8

'There's no way you can manage this whole investigation by yourself.'

Cara sits in her boss's office, surrounded by police textbooks and certificates on the walls. Even she has to admit, her detective chief superintendent has a point.

DCS Halstead leans forward, tapping her pen on the report Cara sent an hour ago. She was swiftly summoned up the two flights of stairs.

'At last count, you have fifteen videos, all of which could contain evidence of a murder. We could draft in more analysts, civilian administrators, as many PCs as Response and Patrol can spare, and you still wouldn't scratch the surface. Plus, you've still got that missing sex worker to find? Where's your main suspect?'

'Medicated up to his eyeballs at the Priory, guv,' Cara protests. 'Section 136. He'll not be talking for a while. Our case load is empty. We know the offender. And he's recently deceased. We just need to track down his accomplices—'

'Fifteen dead, Cara. Dating back at least ten years.' Halstead's face softens. 'Look, I'm not going to take you off

41

it – you're still SIO. But you need some help. Let DCI Ryder coordinate efforts from the Basingstoke nick while you hold it together from here. She's keen and eager. Take advantage of that.'

Cara huffs her annoyance.

'Why are you so against her?' Halstead asks. 'I would have thought you would be in favour of more women in senior positions in the force. You don't strike me as the sort of person to pull the ladder up behind them.'

'I'm not. It's just . . .'

'What?' Halstead adjusts the bright yellow silk scarf draped artfully around her neck. It contrasts perfectly with her navy jacket, with the leather handbag sitting on the chair next to her. Halstead is a woman who likes things just so. She doesn't tolerate sloppiness or lies.

'She gets on my tits,' Cara confesses, abandoning all professionalism in a last-ditch attempt. 'She's all young and perky. No family, no husband. All that free time she likes to wave in my face.'

'You're only forty-something yourself,' Halstead laughs.

'Forty-two,' Cara mutters.

'Forty-two! Time – and gravity – will catch up with DCI Ryder soon enough. In the meantime, enjoy her enthusiasm, and get this case closed. I'll ask her to call you. Understood?'

'Loud and clear.' But Cara doesn't get up.

'Anything else you want to tell me?'

Cara hesitates. 'No, guv.'

'Then crack on. Keep me updated.'

Cara leaves quickly, knowing that the uncertainty must show on her face. There's something about that disc, something that's created insects, squirming, in her stomach, giving her a sense of unease she can't put her finger on. And it's not just the violent murder. It's more than that.

She goes back to her office and sits down at her desk. She logs onto the system, watching as the photos slowly trickle through from the huge house that once belonged to Edward Morris, renowned documentary film-maker, winner of a BAFTA, and owner of fifteen snuff films.

Brody reports that the SOCOs have begun their process, taking the house apart bit by bit, but the whole search is going to take days, weeks even. Firstly, the contents of the lock room needs to be catalogued and examined, then the rest of the house, and that's not including the floor safe. A locksmith has been dispatched to break in – quicker than looking for a key – and Cara dreads what might be inside. What horrors could possibly earn two levels of security? What could be worse than the snuff films?

As it is, the fourteen new discs are on their way back to the nick, to be scanned, watched and catalogued by specially trained officers in the digital team. Once that's done, they'll know what this man was capable of.

They have to consider the possibility that Edward Morris had simply bought these. A man with a penchant for nasty films, no more than that, and the true killer is still out there, unknown.

Cara pulls up the Google search for Edward Morris again, looks at his Wikipedia page, trying to distil guilt or sickness from the photograph displayed. But all she sees is a middle-aged man, with receding grey hair and a thick bushy beard. Starting out in the East End of London, he moved to Hampshire in 1988, to live in the house where his wife grew up. He'd been happily married for over thirty years before he died a month ago, age sixty-one from prostate cancer. She reads the description: began his career as a war photographer, graduated to film soon after that. Called 'the most important documentarian of our time' by *Esquire* magazine in 2003, just before he won his BAFTA. Worked with a few film producers, but always returned to documentaries.

And then comes the interesting stuff. Wikipedia is vague, but a few clicks take Cara to the truth. His father, killed in a workplace accident, when Edward was forty-three. His mother, died by overdose, two years later, closely followed by his daughter in a hit and run. A horrific combination of events, and Cara can see the connection between this grief and a string of convictions on his record. Drunk and disorderly, careless driving and failing to stop at the scene of an accident, finally culminating in a conviction for assault in 2011 and brief jail time. When he got out his career was in ruins, and yet, when he died, he still owned a multi-million-pound house. How had he managed to hold on to that?

Cara flicks back to the shots of the building. It would have been a nice place in its heyday, and a search on the internet reveals a neighbour's property sold for five million last spring. Somehow they'd managed to keep up with the bills, even if the maintenance had eluded them. It was a big house for two people – why had they stayed?

Her phone rings, distracting her from her musing. Jamie. She answers it, settling back in her chair.

'Any luck on the ex-employer?' she asks.

'Not yet,' Jamie replies. 'Couldn't make it past reception. They said they'd get someone to call us back.'

'What? This is murder we're talking about.'

'Exactly. They're worrying we're going to try to pin it on them. Retribution for all the money he stole.' Jamie sighs. 'I don't know. Either way, I said I'd return first thing tomorrow. I heard Griffin and Brody found more films?'

'They did. Another fourteen.' Cara glances up at the clock. Just passed six. 'Head home, Jamie. We're in this for the long haul. Get some rest while you can. Tell Shenton to do the same.'

'Will do, boss.'

'How's he doing?'

'He . . .' There's a pause and a rustle as Jamie moves out of earshot. 'Let's just say, there's a reason he stays at the nick,' he whispers.

'That good, huh?'

'Worse.'

Cara laughs, and Jamie hangs up. Her phone rings again, almost immediately, but this time she almost cancels the call. She rolls her eyes and answers it.

'DCI Ryder, how lovely to hear from you. That didn't take long.' Less than an hour, by Cara's calculation.

A tinkly giggle makes Cara cringe. 'Why waste time?' her colleague says. 'And please, call me Rosie. I don't worry about titles or rank.'

'How modern of you,' Cara replies. 'I assume DCS Halstead has got you up to speed?'

'Gail has, yes.' First name terms, how lovely. 'But tell me more. It sounds fascinating.'

'Fascinating isn't the word I'd use for brutal murder, but okay. And I'm not sure what you can do yet. We're still waiting on the house search, and that could take days.'

'Let us start with the other murders then. We'll take some of the new discs. Our tech team is state of the art.'

Cara bristles on Charlie's behalf. 'Our digital team is already on it. But we'll send you what we have.'

'No need. I'll be in first thing Monday. I'll come and see you after I've finished with Gail.'

And with that, she's gone. The annoying thing about Rosie Ryder – and how old is she, with that name? Thirteen? – is she never actually does anything wrong. She's polite, follows procedure, knows the rules inside and out. Her team solves cases, closes convictions, makes Hampshire Constabulary look good. But she pisses Cara off. Maybe it's the competition – two rival women in senior detective roles, or maybe it's the knowledge that she'll probably be Cara's boss one day. Either way, it's exhausting. Still, she has the rest of the weekend before Ryder swoops in. Maybe they'll solve it all before then.

'That was a big sigh. Long day?' Charlie appears in the doorway of her office, coat on, bag in hand. Her boyfriend usually looks on the messy side of casual, but this evening it's worse: his shirt mussed and untucked on one side of his trousers, his hair ruffled.

'You have no idea,' Cara replies.

'I think I have some. We've started work on those discs. Teams are currently cataloguing methods, victims, subjects, anything they see based on your criteria. Working one hour on, two hours off, because this is some nasty shit we've got here. But we've also been looking at the metadata of when they might have been made.'

'And?'

Charlie drops his bag and collapses into the seat opposite. 'Report's on its way, but upshot is, out of the fifteen, the most recent disc was recorded in October last year. Six months ago. And the oldest is a murder in early 2012, a few years before Terence Gregory. Working on the assumption the date and time was set correctly on the camera, we're looking at crimes being committed over a span of twelve years. Between one and four a year.'

Cara makes a low whistle. 'Shit. Why has nobody flagged this? Surely these victims were reported as mispers?'

'Yes, but doing a shallow dive into a few of the names, it seems that many of the victims were convicted criminals, or at least, suspected of a crime. Utter shitbags, no fixed abode. Easy to snatch off the streets, and nobody misses them.'

'And are the other videos like the first?'

'Mostly. They seem to have refined their methods over the years – in the beginning it was recorded on what I'd guess to be a camcorder on a tripod, evolving to the camera in the corner of the room that we saw for Terence Gregory – but otherwise it's the same. They ask the victim's name, they ask for permission—'

'Permission from whom?'

'No idea. Whoever's watching. And then the carnage begins.'

Charlie presses two fingers against his mouth, composing himself by closing his eyes for a moment. Cara gets up and walks around to the other side of the desk, crouching next to him and placing one hand on his knee.

'Charlie, you shouldn't have to watch this stuff.'

He opens his eyes again. 'I do. This is my job.' He gives her a weak smile, his face tired. 'How would you like it if people told you to stop doing yours?'

'That's all anyone seems to tell me nowadays.'

'And do you listen?' Charlie doesn't wait for Cara's answer, knowing what she'll say. 'So, the other thing I've noticed: the methods of killing. They're varied. From what I've seen and the reports from the team, there's the whole range – knives, guns, baseball bats. It's a devil's playground in there. Everything a psychopath could desire.'

'Isn't that exactly it, though, Charlie?' Cara stands back up and rocks on her heels, thinking. 'We saw it with Terry Gregory. Whatever you've done – that's how you're killed. A revenge, specific to your crime.'

'And they pay someone handsomely to do it?'

'Must have. I need Edward Morris's bank records. I need to know everything about him.'

'You're not going home now, are you?'

'No, sorry. Take the car.' She goes back to her desk, throws him her keys. 'I'll get Griffin to drive me later. But before you go, send me what you have so far. I want to check these match – a suspected offence with the method of killing.'

'Will I see you later? Am I staying at yours?'

'Yes, if that's okay? I haven't got anything with me.'

'It's fine.' Charlie gets up, but pauses in the doorway. 'Cara?'

'Yep?' she says, distracted, already staring at the screen.

'I know this isn't the right time, but I've been thinking. All this driving to and fro. Clothes in the back of my car. I sleep most nights at yours.'

She looks up briefly. Smiles. 'Sorry. I'll stay at yours more often.'

'No, that's not what I meant. Why don't we move in together?'

He has her attention now. 'Me and you? Live together?'

'Yes, why not? My house is big enough for the two of us. You're only renting that place.'

'What about Griffin?'

'He can stay there. Or rent somewhere else. I don't

know – he's a forty-year-old man with a decent job. He'll work it out.'

'And the kids?'

'They can share the spare room.'

'They're too old for that—'

'So we'll buy a bigger place. Cara – I love you. You love me. I think.' He smiles, a bashful grin that makes his eyes crinkle. And she thinks, Yes, I do, you wonderful man. 'This makes sense,' he finishes.

She returns his smile then gets up, joining him in the doorway and pressing her hands gently on both sides of his face. She kisses him. 'It does,' she says, softly. 'And we should. We will.'

'That's a yes?'

'Probably. Let me think about it.' His grin gets bigger and he kisses her back. 'Once this case is over?'

'Of course. Nothing gets in the way of the case.' And with one final snog, he leaves.

She watches him walk out of the office, a spring in his step. And she wonders, Why don't I tell him I love him? It's been over a year, and she's managed to utter *You too* in response to his declarations, but she's never instigated it willingly herself. She should. *I will*, she resolves, turning back to the screen, and immediately she's lost in a world of death and destruction, of money and murder, Charlie the last thing on her mind.

Chapter 9

Day evolves into night, throwing the old house into shadow. Knowing what might be on the discs that have been packaged up and taken away, Griffin can't help but feel unnerved as the gloom turns every figure into silhouette, every corner to an evil devil lurking. The SOCOs become eerie ghosts as they move around in their white suits; Griffin has done the same, donned a coverall, and now sits on the floor of the study, looking through drawers, cupboards, for anything that might be hidden. Zero, so far.

It's thirty years of a life, where nothing has been thrown away. Souvenirs from film shoots, ticket stubs from the cinema. More bloody ducks. Photos from premieres, rendered orange with age. Even the coveted BAFTA is tarnished, the gold dulling to black at the edges.

In the lock room next door, Griffin can hear faint cursing coming from the locksmith employed to break into the floor safe. He's been in there for nearly three hours, the drilling and clattering of tools giving Griffin a headache. He appears in the doorway, his face flushed.

'Any luck?' Griffin asks, pulling himself to his feet, wincing at the familiar ache in his back.

'I'm going to have to try again tomorrow. Speak to a few of the lads, get some reinforcements.'

'Can't you just pick the lock?'

'No, you can't just . . .' His voice tails off as he tuts with disapproval. 'This is a Hydan Platinum floor safe. One of the best you can buy. Five hundred mill steel door, wire mesh preventing access to the door and neck. Continuous welded seams. Key's probably at least three inches long, which means I can't get down to pick the lock even if I wanted to.' Griffin nods in pretend understanding. 'Starting to think the only way will be to dig it out, but I suspect it's concreted in there. Could take days. Do you know what's in it?'

'No. But considering what we found in the lock room, I hate to think.'

The locksmith glances around. Since he first arrived, the house has filled with people – a hive of activity, every resource drafted in. From the flash of the camera, capturing every shelf, every cupboard, every stain on the floor, to the licensed search officers, raking through the garden with their fingertips, everyone has a purpose. Stains on the floorboards are being swabbed; luminol sprayed in the search for blood.

'What happened here?' he hisses to Griffin. 'Murder?'

'Something like that. So – tomorrow? You'll get it open.'

'I'll be back tomorrow. That I can guarantee. Whether I'll get it open?' He sucks breath over his teeth, a mannerism loved by tradesmen all over the world. 'We'll have to see. She's a beaut,' he says with reverence, then grabs his tools and heads home.

Griffin would like to do the same. Work will continue through the night, but shifts will swap out, the teams will change. Griffin's head aches at the thought that every exhibit will need to be checked and analysed. And worse: someone will need to watch those videos.

But not him, thankfully. Charlie's lot in the digital team. Forensic experts, trained to study and catalogue the worst of humanity's depravity. Child pornography, abuse, murder – with counsellors on hand. This won't be the worst they've seen by a long shot, but it scars the brain, every awful human transgression leaving a mark, like bloody fingernails on skin. Each one deeper than the last.

DC Brody started there. The online child sexual exploitation team, before chronic PTSD resulted in her move here. Griffin wonders how this might be affecting her and starts to scour the indistinguishable white suits.

In the end, she finds him. It seems his physique is more obvious among the skinny SOCOs, and she taps him on the shoulder, clutching an Apple laptop in an evidence bag, a rubber duck in the other.

'Quack,' she says, voice muffled through her mask. 'We've bagged up all the ducks.'

'Critical evidence, are they?'

'Probably not. But this is.' She brandishes the laptop in the face of Griffin's scowl. 'Found this. Tucked down the back of one of the bookcases.'

'You're sure it's his?'

'Wife's never seen it before.'

It's the excuse they need; Griffin's had enough of wading through twenty-year-old birthday cards and shop receipts. They can take this back to the nick now. Collect Cara and go home.

Griffin gestures towards the exit, dropping a quick goodbye to the crime scene manager and signing out the laptop. They pull off the crime scene suits and climb into Griffin's Land Rover, breathing a sigh of relief. He starts the engine.

'I'll drop you back at the nick.'

'Unless you want to go somewhere first?' She looks over at him in the half light, raising an eyebrow. 'Truth or dare?'

He should be too tired for Brody's games, but he can't resist. He suspects what's on her mind – her preferred wind-down at the end of the day.

'Alana . . .'

'Nathanial,' she mocks. She rolls her eyes. 'Always so serious. Always with the denial.'

They started out like this. Casual sex, until Griffin called a halt, finding it that little bit too seedy, too transactional. But it's been a year. A year while he's worked, kept sober, spent his evenings watching Netflix on the sofa with his cat, bored out of his skull. And he watches her when she's not looking. Appreciates the curve of her breasts, remembers the softness of her thighs.

'I'm tired,' he protests, weakly.

'What else are you going to do? Sit on the sofa with Frank?' He flushes as she hits the nail on the head. 'Why shouldn't you have a little bit of fun?'

He can't resist her, and she knows it. He feels a little frisson of excitement, not knowing what she has in store. 'Dare,' he says, a small smile forming on his lips.

'Drive. I'll tell you where to go.'

He takes the small country road away from the house, then a left and a right. They don't talk, Brody's silent except for quickly uttered directions, and eventually they arrive in a woodland, the truck's tyres bumping as the gravel track gives way to darkness.

'Stop here.'

He does as he's told, killing the ignition. The woods are quiet, nothing but the tick of the cooling engine and the call from disgruntled birds. She undoes her seat belt and leans over to him, placing one hand on his thigh.

'Brody,' he says. 'Are you sure?'

'Very,' she says, and she grins again. 'Besides, you don't even have to move.'

She leans closer, expertly navigating the gear stick and the handbrake, pushing her body closer to his. Even after a long day at work she smells good – of citrus and cherry shampoo. She looks up at him, eyes questioning. He nods, a small movement, but it's enough. Seeing that all his protestations have come to nothing, Brody slowly undoes the buckle on his belt.

Fucking hell, if only his body wasn't so bloody cooperative. Already he can feel his dick straining against the denim and he lifts his bum, allowing her to manoeuvre his jeans and boxers down his thighs. She looks up with a knowing smile and then her mouth is on him, the warmth, the softness, her tongue and teeth applying just the right amount of pressure.

His head thuds back on the seat, giving into the pleasure. It's been a year. He might as well enjoy it. Because there's no way he's going to last for long.

Chapter 10

Jamie arrives at Adam's to the smell of home-cooked food and the sound of *In the Night Garden* on the television. He replaces his key in his pocket, hangs his coat on the hook and tosses shoes on the pile – more at home here than in his own flat.

He pauses in the doorway to the kitchen, watching Adam cooking. He's singing along tunelessly, but his daughter doesn't seem to care, grinning toothlessly at him from the bouncer on the floor.

Adam spots Jamie and smiles. 'All right, mate?'

'Looking good. Barefoot and in the kitchen suits you.' Jamie bends down and unclips Ivy from her bouncer, tossing her up in the air to gleeful gurgles. 'How's my best girl? Have you been having fun with Daddy?'

'She's just had a bottle, I'd watch . . . Oh, too late,' Adam finishes, as a long line of milky spit is deposited down Jamie's shirt.

'Destined for the wash anyway.' Jamie sits down at the table, resting Ivy on his lap. She bounces up and down on her chubby legs, watching him with bright blue eyes, exactly like her father's.

'Dinner will be in half an hour. Romilly's on her way home.' Adam dries his hands on a tea towel and joins Jamie at the table. 'Tell me about your day. What horrors did Cara Elliott have in store?'

'Snuff film,' Jamie says, and delights in watching Adam's eyes light up. Adam was once his boss, a DCI, the same rank as Cara, before a brutal attack on his last case made him reassess his priorities. The arrival of Ivy turned him into a stay-at-home dad and, while he is out of the limelight, his detective instincts haven't dulled. He leans forward, eagerly.

'And?'

'Cold case, misper from ten years ago. Terence Gregory, do you remember him?'

Adam narrows his eyes, thinking. 'Finance guy, stole millions? Left the country?'

'Didn't go far, apparently. Abducted then murdered in a particularly nasty way.' Adam raises his eyebrows. 'Not fit for little ones. I'll show you after bath time, depending on how good your cooking is.'

'Don't fancy my chances then. Any idea who did it?'

'Griffin and Brody tracked it back to a posh house in a village outside Romsey. Documentary film maker, recently deceased. Left a rather murky legacy to his widow. They're raking through it now, but it looks like he was a bit of an entrepreneur on the side.'

'More videos?'

'Fifteen total.'

Adam gives a low whistle, and Jamie throws him a look. 'You don't miss it?'

'Some days.' Ivy's stopped her bouncing and makes a

disgruntled squeak; Jamie passes her across to her father. 'I miss the chase,' Adam continues, raising his daughter into the air with a whoosh, then resting her on his hip. 'That thrill when a good lead comes in. But the rest of the time, no. I'd rather be here, with this one.'

He looks into his daughter's eyes, and side by side, Jamie is struck by how much daughter looks like dad. Softer, chubbier, but Ivy has the striking blue eyes, the same fold at the tip of her ears, the dark hair and intense expression.

Adam hauls her up into his arms, blowing a wet raspberry on her cheek to rapturous squeals. 'I'm going to do a quick bath, get her sweet smelling. Wouldn't that be nice before Mummy comes home, eh, Ivy?'

Jamie watches him go, the feeling bittersweet. He sees him at least a few times every week, but he misses his best friend. They rose up the ranks together, Adam's ascent steeper than Jamie's, fast reaching the dizzy heights of DCI, while Jamie languished as a sergeant. But Jamie was happy with that. Adam was a whirlwind of arrogance and confidence, and Jamie enjoyed being swept up in his wake. The passenger, the loyal second-in-command. And they had a shared language then. The cases, the lines of enquiry, throwing theories about at the end of the night over a glass of whisky in Adam's messy office.

Jamie looks upwards at the sound of the bath running, the gentle burr of Adam talking to his daughter. This man is calmer, nicer, a good father, a devoted husband – but at what cost? Hampshire Police lost one of its finest minds. And Jamie lost a mentor.

He can smell burning; distracted, Jamie has forgotten dinner and he leaps to his feet, attending to the sauce bubbling on the stove. He gives it a quick stir, peering into the pan. Something with sausage, tomato, wine, maybe? He takes a tentative sip from the end of the wooden spoon and coughs. Vodka. Lots of it. He turns up the heat to burn off the alcohol. There is no cookbook nearby, no sign of what Adam intended.

A key in the front door. Jamie turns and smiles as Romilly arrives home. She shakes the rain out of her long brown hair, shrugs off her coat and kicks her shoes into the pile. She joins Jamie at the stove.

'More of Adam's experimental cooking?' She takes the wooden spoon from him and repeats Jamie's sampling. She tilts her head to and fro, considering. 'This one might be edible, but Michelin chef he ain't.'

'Good day?'

'So so,' she replies. Romilly is a consultant oncologist at Southampton General, keen to return after her daughter was born. But she doesn't like to bring her work home. 'We all deal with enough death,' she's often said. 'We don't need it out of hours too.'

'Is there a bottle open?' she adds. She sticks her head in the fridge, coming out with half of a Chenin Blanc. She pours herself a large glass, offers one to Jamie.

He shakes his head. 'I need to drive back later.'

'Spare room's yours if you change your mind. Bath time?' she says, inclining her head to the upstairs.

'They're waiting for you.'

She grins, squeezes Jamie's shoulder, then heads up.

He stirs idly. Romilly's light tones join Adam's. He hears soft laughter, Ivy's cry, then muffled reassurance. Jamie presses a hand against his chest, massages the ache. Can you miss something you never had?

He senses bath time coming to an end and gets ready for dinner. Boils a kettle, measures out pasta for three, guessing it might go with whatever Adam's made. He lays knives and forks on the table, gives in to his desire and pours two more glasses of white.

Adam comes downstairs, and Jamie hands him one of the glasses.

'What would we do without you, mate?' Adam says, slumping at the table.

'Have a lot more privacy, that's for sure.'

Adam scoffs. 'Come on then, show me. Rom's busy with Ivy, we've got five minutes.'

These things are supposed to be confidential, but Jamie considers Adam as police, on career break or not, and gets out his laptop, loading up the videos. More have been converted into a digital format and loaded to the server; he clicks one he hasn't seen before.

He notices differences straight away. It seems to be a grey concrete pit, cuboid, the sides no more than five feet high. The camera watches from the top, the quality grainy. He notes the time and date stamp. August 2012. Older than Terence Gregory, a shift in location. Interesting, he thinks.

A man sits in the right-hand corner of the hole, dressed only in shorts. His head is bent to his knees, his hands behind him; he jerks up in surprise when a voice speaks.

'Tell me your name.'

The man pulls at his arms, at whatever's attaching him to the wall. Red-faced and sweating, visibly overweight, he stares directly into the camera. 'Let me out of here.'

'Tell me your name.'

'Austin O'Brien. Let me out. I've been here for . . . for days. I've done nothing wrong. You can't do this.'

Jamie notes the name, then types it into Google on his phone as the video continues.

The man struggles for a moment longer, until two large men come into shot. They crouch, then drop into the pit. Balaclavas, black T-shirt, black trousers, black boots.

'Same guys as in the other video,' Jamie mutters to Adam. Adam nods, but his gaze doesn't shift.

The two men approach O'Brien, either side, ready. O'Brien is frantic, squirming and shouting as they get nearer.

Jamie's attention has been drawn by a news item on his phone. July 2012. 'Austin O'Brien,' he reads aloud, 'was released today after a jury at Winchester Crown Court found him not guilty of murder. O'Brien, 26, was charged after his business partner, Nicholas Rice, 27, was found stabbed to death last winter, believed to be related to a deal gone wrong. The victim's mother, Maureen Rice, gave a statement outside the crown court, saying, "Austin O'Brien may have escaped justice today, but we will have retribution. In this life or the next."'

'Strong words,' Adam comments. He points to the screen and the two burly men. 'Neither of these is Maureen.'

'Clearly not.'

There's a tussle on the screen and O'Brien is released from his bindings, but not for long. He's still cuffed behind his back – one man holds him steady, while the other reaches up and loops the rope through something higher, out of shot. He tugs on the rope and O'Brien's arms rise. He screams – the human shoulder is not meant to bend that way and Jamie tenses, but the rope isn't pulled too high. Enough to incapacitate, not enough to maim.

O'Brien stays as still as he is able, begging and crying, to no avail. One of the men reaches out of the pit to get something; Jamie takes a quick breath in when he sees what's in his hand. The resolution of the video is grainy, but there's no doubt what the man is holding. A knife. A really fucking big knife.

'Shit,' Adam mutters, and on the video, O'Brien has the same thought. He struggles harder than ever, screaming at the men.

'You're fucking crazy. I haven't done anything. I didn't kill Nick. They found me not guilty. This wasn't my fault.'

The man takes two steps towards him.

'Okay, okay. Just let me go. Let me go and I'll plead guilty. Is that what you want? Okay, I did it. Lock me up, but please don't . . . please don't—'

The massacre comes quick and fast. Within seconds the man plunges the knife into O'Brien's stomach, again and again, blood spattering across the floor, the walls, soaking into his clothes. The other man waits, a step away, unflinching as the carnage continues. O'Brien's head drops. Silenced.

'Adam, I'm sorry, you shouldn't have—' Jamie begins. If he'd known it was a stabbing, much like the one Adam himself had endured, he wouldn't have let his friend near it.

But Adam silences him with a shake of his head. 'Shush.' He hasn't taken his eyes off the screen.

The man with the knife takes a step back, wiping the blade on his trousers. He looks at his colleague and nods – an action that says more 'job well done' than 'we just committed bloody murder' – then the man without the knife moves towards the camera. The screen goes black.

Jamie turns to face his friend. Adam blinks, then raises his eyebrows.

'Well. Shit,' he says. He sits back, rubbing his palm against the stubble on his chin. 'And they're all like this?'

'As much as I've seen. What do you think?'

'It's nasty, all right. You're assuming revenge, I take it? The specificity of the attack – the knife, the stabbing. Revenge for the crime he was accused of?'

'That's what we thought, too.'

'Now, now, boys,' Romilly interrupts, coming into the room. Jamie closes the laptop with a snap. 'No shop talk over dinner. Jamie – the pasta's boiling over. Adam – grate some cheese. I assume that's what you had in mind for this latest creation?'

'You know me so well.' Adam laughs, giving her a kiss.

The conversation moves on. Adam has a new car, which he hates; Romilly's convinced Ivy's teething and that's why she didn't sleep last night. Jamie half-listens, his head lost in the case.

'Go on then, discuss it,' Romilly says wearily, clearing away the empty plates and sticking her head in the freezer. 'I'll eat ice cream.'

Jamie gives her an apologetic smile. 'I keep on coming back to that same point: if you wanted to take revenge, this is an extreme way of doing it. How would you even know how to get hold of someone who could orchestrate something like this, let alone have the cash to pay for it? Shenton and I met Terence Gregory's wife today. She didn't seem to have money.'

'You're assuming this service cost?'

'Don't you? Why go to the effort of abducting and killing someone in such a specific way if you're not getting paid?'

'Sadism? And where did those millions go?' Adam says. 'The ones Gregory stole? Maybe she has it.'

'If she does, she's doing a good job of hiding it. The house is a mess. And if she has the money, why would she go to all that bother or hand in the evidence? No, the wife doesn't stack up.'

'The boss?'

'Seeing him tomorrow.'

'Ask him how much he knows about the dark web. Watch how he reacts.'

'Will do, guv,' Jamie says with a smile.

Adam winces. 'Old habits die hard.'

Romilly looks up from her ice cream tub, pointing the spoon at them. 'Is that what this is? Revenge for hire?'

'Could be,' Jamie says. 'Everything's available at a price, if you don't care who suffers.'

'Dark world we live in, if this is what it comes down to.' She digs the spoon into the ice cream, taking a large dollop before Adam confiscates it, digging his own spoon inside. 'Just because you can, doesn't mean you should.'

With those words, a long wail begins, starting quietly and evolving in both pitch and volume. They all look up.

'I'll go,' Adam says, handing the ice cream to Jamie. 'And don't eat it all. I want some when I get back.'

'Teething,' Romilly shouts as he runs up the stairs. She looks at Jamie. 'Has he said anything to you? About going back to work?'

'No. Not at all.' He puts a spoonful of ice cream in his mouth before Romilly takes the tub away from him. 'Why?' he says, mouth full.

'I just . . .' She glances to where Adam's gone. 'You heard him. He can't help himself. Putting in his two-pennies' worth.'

'He's happy at home with Ivy.'

'Is he though? I love my daughter, but I'd go crazy cooped up here with her all day long. I just worry . . . I worry that he's staying at home because he thinks it's his only option.'

'He knows he'd have a job back at Hampshire Constabulary in an instant.'

'It's not that.' She stops again.

'Spit it out, Rom.'

'I think he's scared.'

'Adam? Scared?'

'Yes. What happened . . . He had no idea – nor did I – and yet he nearly ended up dead. If it hadn't been for you, working it out in the nick of time.' Her voice chokes and she stops, placing the ice cream tub on the table. Jamie puts his hand on hers; it's cold.

'You know him better than anyone else, Rom. Have you asked him?'

'Yes, and he says he's fine.'

'There you go—'

'But he puts up walls. He says he's changed, and we do talk now – about everything – but being a detective, being a police officer, was such a huge part of his life. I can't accept he can throw it away for nothing.'

'It's not for nothing. He has you now, and Ivy.'

She still looks unhappy. 'I just don't want him to wake up in ten years' time and it be too late for his career. And he hates me.' She chokes a laugh. 'And then what happens? He drops a couple of mill to these people on the dark web and gets me murdered?'

'Romilly,' Jamie says softly. He waits until she looks up at him, her dark brown eyes watery with tears. 'That's not going to happen.' He grins. 'He doesn't have the money, for a start.'

'That's true.' She returns his smile and coughs out a laugh. 'Especially if he keeps buying new cars.'

Later, after Ivy has been soothed back to sleep and the three of them are sitting watching TV, Jamie looks over at his best friends. Romilly is lying on the sofa, her feet in Adam's lap. They look so comfortable together, so sure, he can't imagine anything coming in the way of that again.

But Romilly was right: you never know. Jamie was that person once – happily married, curled up on the sofa with his wife. Until she was murdered by the same serial killer that nearly took Adam.

He feels the pain of that loss every day. First thing in the morning, the empty space beside him in bed. During the day, when he sees something funny she would like, and realising she's no longer there at the other end of the phone. He knows it's not possible to bring her back, but now he considers the next best thing.

If he could get revenge on the person that killed his wife, would he?

And he comes to a new conclusion about their killer. They're providing a service. It may not mend a broken heart, but watching the person you despise more than any other be killed in excruciating pain live on camera?

That he can understand.

Chapter 11

Cara's silent the whole drive home, and Griffin's relieved. He needs time to digest what happened. The blowjob from Brody, him returning the favour. Last year, he swore to himself that it wouldn't happen again – the sex without feelings thing didn't work for him – but over the past year he's found himself enjoying her company. More often than not they'll work together. Either assigned by Cara or just gravitating to each other's side. Asking her for opinions, for advice. Or having a laugh in their lunch breaks. This is the first time the 'dare' has involved sexual favours for a while, but he's sure it won't be the last.

When they get home, Charlie's sitting at the kitchen table, laptop open. Griffin opens the fridge, contemplating dinner, while Cara heads upstairs to get changed and call her kids.

'You need a break,' Griffin says to Charlie.

'I will, there's just something . . .' His voice trails off and Griffin leaves him to it, pulling the pizza delivery menu down from the pinboard and pouring some cat biscuits into a bowl. The noise alerts Frank and he trots into the kitchen, wrapping himself around Griffin's ankles.

Griffin picks him up. The cat pushes his head against Griffin's chin, purring.

'You've had enough of the biscuits, have you?' He carries the cat to the fridge, opening it up.

'Cara will kill you if you give Frank the good salmon again,' Charlie says, not looking away from the laptop.

'But what Cara doesn't know won't hurt her, will it, Frankie?' Griffin pulls off a piece of smoked salmon; the purring increases ten-fold as the cat eats it in a second.

'Are you feeding salmon to that cat again?' Cara says from the other side of the fridge door.

Griffin closes it, dropping Frank to the floor. The cat jumps onto the dining table next to Charlie's laptop, smugly licking its paws.

'Don't know what you mean. How are the kids?'

'Fine,' Cara says, testily. 'Pizza for dinner again?'

The pizzas arrive; Cara and Griffin eat in the living room, leaving Charlie in the kitchen, slices remaining untouched next to him as he types something incomprehensible on the laptop.

Frank begs scraps from the last piece, curling his small, warm body around Griffin's ankles. Griffin picks up the cat and deposits the last slice of meat feast next to him amid purrs of appreciation.

'No wonder he likes you more than me,' Cara mutters. 'You'll make him sick.'

'Does he look sick?' Griffin counters, running a hand down his sleek fur. 'He's like me, an old alley cat. We'll eat anything to survive.'

'He gets premium cat food with line-caught salmon and

Norfolk crab. All organic. That's the best-fed moggy this side of the M4.' But Griffin notices a reluctant smile appear and she bends down and scratches his head. 'Poor deprived Frank.'

'Why were you working late?' Griffin asks.

'I wanted to check something – and we were right. Without exception the way the victims were killed exactly links to the crime they were accused of. Steal money – you get it shoved down your throat. Stab someone – you get massacred. Kill someone by selling them dodgy drugs – expect an overdose coming your way.'

'So it's definitely a revenge thing?' Griffin points to the kitchen where they can hear Charlie talking on the phone. 'Is that what he's working on too?'

'No. Not sure what he's up to. Listen, Nate.' That gets Griffin's attention – the use of his first name. Must be serious. 'Charlie. You like him, right?'

Griffin frowns. 'Yeah. Don't you?'

'No, yes. I do.' She pauses. A light flush works its way across her cheeks. 'He asked me to move in with him.'

'That's great.' Griffin's confused. 'Isn't it?'

'Yes, it's just . . . What about you?'

Griffin laughs. 'What about me? I'll be fine. I've assumed this was on the cards for a while. I'm happy for you both.'

'You are?'

'Of course. Your ex-husband was a dickhead. He cheated on you, multiple times. You deserve to be happy with someone nice.' He pauses, scrutinising his sister. 'Why do I get the feeling you haven't said yes?'

'Because I haven't.'

'But you will?'

Before Cara can answer, Charlie appears in the doorway,

clutching his laptop. His cheeks are flushed, his hair in disarray, as if he's spent the last hour running his fingers through it.

'There's something you need to see,' he says.

Chapter 12

Cara ushers Charlie into the room, sitting him down on the sofa between them. He rests the laptop on his knees, pushing his glasses back up his nose.

'You need to see this.'

She looks over at the screen. He's pulled up a spreadsheet with an almost mind-numbing amount of data.

'You can ignore most of this,' he says. 'The important number to consider is this one—' He points. 'The date when the video was made.'

'Video. Which video?' Griffin asks.

'Sorry, I'm jumping ahead.' Charlie leans back and takes a deep breath in, before turning to Cara. 'My team and I have been working with intel, trying to piece together the timelines of the victims' disappearances with the metadata we've extracted from the videos. As we thought, they contain all sorts of information.'

'A location?'

'Sadly, no. That's been disabled. But they do contain two dates. Firstly, the original time the video was shot. And secondly, the time it was edited and saved into this final version. Are you following me?'

Cara and Griffin nod.

'Good. So, if we look at the dates for Terence Gregory, as we've had the longest time on that one, we know that the video was shot on the seventh of August, 2014, at five fourteen p.m.'

'Two days after he went missing.'

'Yes. Two days. And that's point number one. All the victims were kept for forty-eight hours, almost to the minute, before the video began.'

'He waited two days to kill them?'

'Without exception.'

'Okay,' Cara says. 'What's point number two?'

'Right. Yes. So. Forty-eight hours after disappearance, the victim is killed and the video is made. But, for Terry Gregory, it wasn't edited until a week after that, on the fourteenth of August, when it was spliced into the .mov file we see today downloaded onto the disc.'

'Even your most dedicated bad guy has a holiday, I guess,' Griffin comments.

'Sure, but this is when it gets interesting.' Charlie flips screens to yet more incomprehensible data. 'We managed to break the password into Morris's laptop that you and Brody so kindly dropped off this evening, and here's what the team found. At some point all the videos were stored on here and edited in a programme called Adobe Premiere Pro. Then deleted, but – as you know – nothing's ever deleted unless you go at the hard drive with a hammer, so we were able to pull off all the dates and compare them to those on the videos.

'Every single one of those snuff films was edited by Edward Morris. Some time between a few days and a fortnight after the original film was shot.'

Cara frowns. 'So Edward Morris is our guy.'

'Except . . .' Charlie holds a finger in the air. 'Edward Morris had prostate cancer. And that particular form of cancer meant he was in and out of hospital for operations. For chemotherapy, all sorts of nasty shit.'

Cara's starting to get a bad feeling about this. 'Do we have those dates, by any chance?'

'Yes, we do. Thanks to a particularly efficient medical secretary who sent them across this afternoon. And many of the dates Edward Morris was out of action because he was anaesthetised and under the surgeon's knife at Hampshire's finest, coincide with the dates these videos were shot.'

'Shit,' Griffin mutters, as Cara says, 'You mean . . .'

'Edward Morris may have edited these videos, but there's no way he was there when these people were killed.'

Cara finishes the sentence for him. 'Someone else is behind this. We're looking for another guy.'

Chapter 13

The room is cold. My hands are numb, my feet frozen into blocks of ice. I need to get up and walk around, get some blood moving around my body, but I am motionless. Watching. I don't take my eyes off the screen; this is it. The part I enjoy the most.

All my hard work – it comes down to this. I lean forward, almost pressing my nose against the glass. The video feed from downstairs projects in glorious high-definition technicolour, showing a man sitting in the corner of the room. He is silent, at last.

When he first arrived, he screamed, shouted, cried, until his voice was hoarse. He paced the room, kicked the door, pummelled his fists against the wall. They all do, until they realise their protestations are useless. No one can hear them, except me. No one is coming, except for the men I send inside.

Two days pass. No more, no less. The perfect amount of time. A cooling-off period for the client; to change their mind and unlock the doors. None ever do.

The forty-eight hours has another purpose. Thinking

time for our spineless antagonist. To come to terms with what they have done that led them to me. Any less, and they claim their innocence; any more, and they get weak. Weak humans don't protest, they don't resist, they don't fight.

And our clients like it when they fight.

I pick up the walkie-talkie, press the side button. 'It's time,' I say.

I don't get a response; I don't expect one. I wait and, after a moment, the locks slide open and a man walks into the room. He drops a large black bag at his feet. Trev – the perfect name for this human block of concrete, a solid mass of muscle, including his brain. He gets paid handsomely for what he does, but that's not why he's here. Loyalty. Love. And Trev wants the same as I do – revenge. If we take pride in our work, then all the better.

I never knew what I wanted to do. When the guidance counsellors arrived at school I disappointed them with my prevarication, my thoughtlessness. I was aware of what I liked, what I was good at, but it didn't fit into their boxes.

There is no space on the questionnaire for a compulsive liar. For a thief, a pickpocket, a joyrider. I felt those compulsions – to destroy, to inflict pain. A pressure building, and whoever was closest when the dam burst – well, that was their problem.

So rather than be expelled from school I learned to mask my less sociable traits. I knew my emotional responses were different from those around me, so I studied. How to mimic, how to control. I had a list of rules. Things I could and couldn't do. Hurting someone landed squarely at the top; I shouldn't inflict pain, but now I am older, I have learned.

There are always exceptions.

74

With Trev's arrival, the man wakes up. He gets to his feet, his gaze twitching between the door and Trev. He tries to make a run for it; he fails. Trev grabs him by the arm, pulls it painfully behind his back. I hear the crack, the yelp of pain. Trev lets go and pushes the man back into the room. He falls to the floor, wailing.

Trev takes handcuffs out of his bag and advances on the man, still chattering, random sentences turning even more incoherent as the metal cuff is fastened on his left wrist. The man is as useless as a sack of sand; Trev hauls him across to the metal ring drilled into the wall, clipping the other end of the cuff through. The man is stuck there, his head down, his shoulders heaving. Face to the wall. His broken arm is unsecured, hanging uselessly by his side.

Trev glances up to the camera. He knows me. He knows how much I enjoy this – he will make it last for my benefit as much as the client's.

Trev smiles. He reaches down and takes a large hunting knife out from the sheath on his thigh. It reflects in the overhead light. Clean, sharp. The man glances behind and sees it; his babbling escalates to a garbled scream as Trev reaches forward. And slowly, Trev cuts the clothes from the man's body.

I've been down there. In that room. I know what it smells like. The piss, the stench of sweat as it drips from the man's pores. The leftover reek of blood and pain that no amount of bleach will ever get out from the floorboards.

The man twists and buckles as the knife gets to work, the rip of cloth, the slop of his sweat-soaked wardrobe. Once designer garbs are now reduced to rags, dumped in a pile on the floor. Trev's not careful, nicks appear on the man's skin, blood oozing from the wounds as the man wails in protest, but he should save his energy. This isn't the main event. Not by a long shot.

Trev steps back to admire his handiwork. Naked, the man is quite a sight. An excellent specimen: sculpted abs, muscular thighs, bulging biceps. Worth every one of those millions his club paid for him. If only he could have kept it in his pants.

'I have money, how much do you want?' the man begs, not for the first time. Trev doesn't respond, looks up to the camera.

I lean forward, press the button on the intercom.

'Tell me your name,' I say.

The man flinches, his head snapping around, trying to find the source of the sound. 'Who . . . what? Help me!'

'Tell me your name,' I repeat.

His eyes find the camera, they lock on me, faceless, above him. 'Stephen Allen,' he says. 'Please, please let me go. I haven't done anything. Whatever you think I did . . .'

I remember the photos of the woman, her tear-streaked cheeks. The description, painful minute by minute, of what he did. The bruises and the abrasions. The red, raw scars that remained on her beautiful white skin.

I gave them the warning.

'You will have forty-eight hours to change your mind,' I wrote. 'Once the money is paid, the contract is set in motion. Forty-eight hours. There are no refunds. Make sure you're certain.'

'I'm sure,' they replied. 'Show him. Show him what it was like.'

I look down at the man, pathetic, weak, alone, defenceless, as Trev runs the tip of his hunting knife gently down the man's skin. From his neck, slowly between his shoulder blades, down his sculpted lower back. Trev pauses the tip of the knife above the man's buttocks, just long enough for the man to realise what's coming.

'Oh, no, please, no, I didn't, I swear, she said . . . she wanted . . .'

Trev takes the knife away, then bends to pick something out of his bag. A huge black dildo, anatomically shaped, for her pleasure. Or his.

The man stares. He starts to cry, snot, tears, saliva dribbling down his chin.

The dildo in one hand, the knife in the other, Trev looks up to the camera. He is ready.

'Permission granted,' I say.

The fun begins.

DAY 3

SUNDAY

Chapter 14

Richard Fredricks, of Fredricks and Braverman, didn't want the police coming to the office.

'We get enough bad press as it is, even now,' he says, as Jamie escorts him through to the interview room. 'The last thing we need is coppers showing up and starting it all over again.'

'The business took a hit then?' Jamie asks. 'Tea, coffee?'

'No, thank you. And yes, of course it did. Your star employee takes off with nearly eleven million quid – no wonder nobody trusted us after that. We had to do some real damage control. It's only now the business is taking off, and that's only because all we do now is mortgages.'

Jamie sits down, examining this man. He doesn't know much about suits, but this one is smart, well cut, nice material. No chance this came from Marks and Spencer. Bright blue tie, crisp white shirt. Hair neatly combed; nails short. Cara updated the team first thing, and the news that Edward Morris was only the film-maker, not the killer, sobered them all. Suddenly having an entire team of detectives in Basingstoke doesn't seem so unnecessary.

'What happened back in 2014?' Jamie asks.

'Bloody nightmare, that's what it was. First time we knew something was off was when one of Terry's clients came to the office, shouting and screaming. Said he'd been trying to get hold of Terry for weeks, but he hadn't been answering his calls or emails. Threatened legal action, and rightly so. We had a couple of million of this guy's cash tied up, and he wanted it out.' Richard sighs. 'I thought it would be a simple misunderstanding – Terry said he was worried about this client losing money. There are penalties for withdrawing funds early, in some cases. But I told Terry, the client's always right, and to give the guy his money back, and he did. That was it, I thought.'

'But it wasn't?'

'No. Not by a long shot. Next week, same thing happened. Except this client had gone straight to the lawyers, and we had a threatening letter. That's when I started to get suspicious. I demanded to see all of Terry's records – first thing the next day. But rather than waiting I spent the night digging, and that's when I realised. He'd been stealing from accounts, using funds from other clients to cover it up. A little bit here, a large bit there. All in all, it amounted to just over eleven million.'

Jamie makes a low whistle. 'Did you ever work out where it went?'

'Into some offshore bank account, I assume. Terry knew his stuff, that's why the clients loved him. If you needed money hiding from HMRC – Terry was your man. Next day, I suspended him. A day after that he disappeared.'

'You didn't call the police?'

'Not at that point. I knew how this could wreck the business, so I kept it quiet. But once he disappeared, well, there was no avoiding it.'

'Did it strike you as odd, that Terry would disappear like that? Leave his wife and child behind?'

Richard snorts. 'Unfortunately, no. Terry was a ladies' man. A stereotypical trader – taking his clients to strip clubs, and the best ones. Velvet Oasis, you heard of it?' He doesn't wait for Jamie's reply. 'Down by the docks. A little rough now, but back then only the best girls danced at Velvet Oasis.' He pauses, a wistful look in his eye.

'Mr Fredricks? What else did Terry do for his clients?'

'Oh, you know.' Jamie didn't know – he said as much. Fredricks stuttered a bit and then said, 'Getting them what – or who – they wanted. I didn't like it. I pride myself on not being like those London funds – we're not Wolf of fucking Wall Street – but he was bringing the money in. I could hardly protest if a multi-million-pound client wanted a prostitute brought to his hotel room. I was making money too, it was my company.'

'Did Terry indulge?' Fredricks looks blank. 'In the strippers and prostitutes?'

Fredricks laughs. 'If his expense claims were anything to go by, I bloody hope so. That was a lot of money.'

'Where do you think he went?'

'Cayman? British Virgin Islands? Somewhere like that.' He stops and peers at Jamie. 'You said on the phone that new information had come to light. What's going on?'

Jamie opens the file to the first page. A still from the video lies on the top – Terry taped to the chair before the worst of the horrors began. Jamie turns it around and pushes it across to Richard.

'This video came into our possession on Friday night. We believe that Terry was murdered.'

Richard stares at the photo, then up at Jamie. His mouth drops open.

'Murdered?' He gawps at the photo again. 'This . . .' His finger jabs at the photo. 'This video shows Terry being *murdered*? By who?'

'We don't know that yet. Do you recognise the room in the photograph?'

He looks closer. 'No, not at all. But that's just a white wall, who could tell from that?'

'Do you know anyone who would have wanted Terry dead?'

'Well, yes. All the clients who lost money.'

'Could we have a list of their names?'

'Er . . . okay, yes. I guess so. Since this is *murder*.'

'And you? Mr Fredricks?'

'Me?'

'You lost money, didn't you? You nearly lost your entire company. You must have been angry.'

'Yes, yes, I was angry, but . . . you know? Murder. I wouldn't have killed him. This . . . this wasn't me.'

'What do you know about the dark web?'

'The . . . what? Nothing!'

'Where were you on the seventh of August, 2014?'

'Me? Fucking hell, I don't know. Work or home, probably. That was ten years ago.'

'And Braverman? The other half of your company? Who are they?'

'Oh, my wife. We needed another name. You do, don't you? Two names on the letterhead. She was never involved with the company.' His gaze drifts off to middle distance. 'Murder. Well, I never. I didn't think. You don't, do you?'

Jamie lets Mr Fredricks burble on for a while longer before showing him out, with assurances that the list of names would be sent over as soon as Fredricks got back to the office. Jamie walks up to the incident room, mulling over the last few interviews.

Two stunned reactions from the two people closest to Terence Gregory – his wife and his boss. And two spectacularly different pictures of the dead man. A dedicated husband or a fan of sleezy strip clubs and prostitutes? Neither had alibis. Both had reasons to want him dead.

He's curious to know more about this man and takes a detour down to the digital team.

He's buzzed through by a man with thick bottle-top glasses and an unruly head of blond curls. The man says nothing, but points to the far office, where Charlie is head down, the square of light from the computer in front reflecting on his glasses. He smiles when Jamie knocks.

'Jamie, how are you? How can I help?'

'Terence Gregory's laptop. Have you managed to get in?'

'Yes. But we haven't had a chance to go through it yet. What with all the . . .'

'Death and murder?'

'Yeah, that.'

'Mind if I look?'

'Help yourself. It's all charged up and ready to go.'

Charlie shouts out to one of his team, who brings the laptop over, then gestures to an empty desk in the corner of his office.

'Just clear off the crap,' Charlie says. 'Tea, coffee?'

'Tea, please. Milk.'

Charlie gets up and heads off, leaving Jamie abashed. He could have got it himself, would have done, but for this laptop. He clears the assorted cables and two spare monitors to the floor, then sits down, taking the laptop out of the evidence bag and plugging in the new password, written in black marker on a Post-it on the front.

The screen bursts into life, and Jamie stares at it, annoyed.

It's an old computer, running an ancient version of Windows. Brightly coloured blocks, each one with a logo inside. He hovers his finger over the mousepad, not knowing where to look.

'Start with the email,' Charlie says, placing a mug next to him. 'Back in 2014, anything good would have been in Outlook. See there?'

A turquoise box with a white envelope. Jamie clicks. A window appears, loading excruciatingly slowly.

'It's not connected to the internet so it won't update. What's there is what Terence Gregory saw before he died.'

Charlie goes back to his desk, leaving Jamie with the laptop. He sips his tea, clicks around the inbox. Folders on the left-hand side, some labelled with names, and Jamie clicks on a few, reads emails packed with business jargon Jamie can't understand. Clients, he assumes, although this is a home account, so why was he emailing from here? The reason soon becomes clear – money changing hands, and not for his usual business activities. *Crystal, Candy, Charisma. Full service, bareback, BDSM.* Making sure his clients were happy, as his boss said, but Fredricks had no idea. They talk about cost. They discuss 'add ons', something Jamie quickly realises are drugs. *Blow, brown, bud,* nothing was out of the question for Terry Gregory.

But this is not why Jamie came here. However dodgy Gregory was, it's the job interview he's looking for.

He clicks back to the main inbox. Mostly from Fredricks,

growing increasingly irate as time progressed. No threats though, just inventive name-calling and demands to return his money. He scrolls down.

Terry Gregory had started to apply for new jobs. Confirmation emails from job boards, CV submissions, even a few early declines. And then one that attracts Jamie's attention. Titled *Interview Request*, Jamie opens it and finds a brief email, asking Terry Gregory to come along to Velvet Oasis that night for an informal chat.

'Would you go for a job interview at a strip club?' Jamie asks Charlie.

Charlie snorts. 'Not in my line of work.'

It's odd, and even Terry questions it, receiving the reply. *We want to see what sort of man you are.*

Jamie looks for the email address of the sender, but it's generic. A company called Summit City Financial. He googles it, finds a few similar names but nothing obvious.

He sits back, thinking. How hard would it be to make up a company, lure Terry Gregory out for the evening, with the pretence of offering him a job? And that's twice now the Velvet Oasis has been mentioned.

'Want to go to a strip club?' he asks.

Charlie looks over, his eyebrows raised behind his glasses. 'Now? No. I like to have lunch before I start drinking dirty beer and getting fake tan on my shirt.'

Jamie laughs. 'What sort of strip clubs do you go to?'

'Not many, I have to admit,' Charlie replies with a grin. 'You know who you should take?'

'Griffin,' Jamie replies.

Chapter 15

'You want me to go *where* with you?' Griffin stands on the gravel outside the Morris house. 'A strip club?'

'Purely business,' Jamie says.

'Sure.' He digs into his pocket and pulls out a packet of cigarettes, lighting one as Jamie protests on the other end of the line. 'Okay, okay. When do you want to go? Brody and I are stuck here until that floor safe is open.' Brody looks at him, her eyebrows raised. He listens again. 'No, don't you dare take Cara. Just wait. I'll get an ETA and call you back.'

Griffin hangs up, smoking grumpily, watching the procession of SOCOs filing in and out of the house. Brown cardboard boxes have been stacking up all morning, each one filled to the brim with evidence bags of every shape and size.

'Why does Jamie want you to go to a strip club?' Brody asks. 'And I thought you'd given up the fags.'

'I allow myself one a day. He's got evidence that Terry Gregory went for an interview there. Might be where he was abducted from.'

'Ten years ago?'

'Worth a try,' Griffin says with a grin. 'And before you ask: no, you can't come.'

'That's discrimination. A stripper's more likely to talk to me than you two great oafs. Besides, you're not leaving me here with this mess. Floor safe's our priority, Cara said.'

The original guy arrived with reinforcements this morning. Two more burly men showing extensive butt cracks, armed with drills and tool belts so well stocked it's as if they're going to war. But so far there's just been more swearing and stroking of stubbled chins.

Griffin grumbles under his breath, taking a last drag on his cigarette and crushing it underfoot. He bends to pick up the butt, putting it in his pocket – he doesn't want the new CSM to have a go at him for contaminating crime scenes. Even if he is outside the cordon.

She's standing in the doorway of the house now, looking down at a clipboard. Tall, nearly his height. Slim, black, her hair slicked back into a tight bun, she has distinctive features, and rumour has it she could have been a model but chose this life instead. All Griffin knows is she seems good and her name's Holly something. Watts? White? Griffin can't remember.

She looks up, catches Griffin's eye. Flicks two fingers at him, gesturing for him to come over.

'How are we looking this morning?' he asks her.

'Teams worked through the night,' she says. He can't place her accent. Up north somewhere. Birmingham or Manchester. She looks up from her clipboard, appraising the army of vans and patrol cars parked in the driveway. 'I hope you have the budget for this. You've certainly found a good one.'

Griffin shrugs. Cara's problem, not his. But he knows what she's saying.

Licensed search officers from across the county are raking through belongings in the bedroom; in the garden the victim recovery dogs have arrived and are searching for a trace of blood or cadavers, the spaniels sniffing their sensitive noses over the few acres out the back. This much resource is costly. But it's multiple murder, what else can they do?

'Have you found anything to make it worth our while?' he asks as Brody joins them.

'We've taken samples across the house, so one of those might come up trumps, but apart from the discs you initially found, there's little sign of illegal activity. Wherever those people were killed and buried, it doesn't seem to be here.'

It fits with Charlie's theory that someone else is involved. If Edward Morris was just the film-maker, then nobody was killed here. Which begs the question: where?

The CSM goes back to work and, as Griffin's considering heading inside, he spots Gwen Morris approaching, winding her way up the driveway, her head down. There was no way the wife had been allowed to stay at the house; Griffin wonders who took her in and if they know exactly why she's homeless. She looks up as she approaches, pulls her coat tightly around her. Griffin nods a greeting.

'How are you, Mrs Morris?' Brody asks.

'I'm well, thank you, love.' Her gaze drifts up to the house. 'I'd be better if I knew when I could come home.'

'It might be a while yet, I'm sorry.'

'Mrs Morris,' Griffin says. 'Did either you or Edward own any other properties?'

'Another house, you mean?'

'Or a garage, or a storage unit. Anywhere.'

'No.' She gives a small laugh. 'We barely had the money for this place. Let alone somewhere else.'

'And do you know much about Edward's movements? Where did he used to go, during the day? Did he go out at night?'

'No, never. Especially after he got sick. Edward worked from home most of the days, and if he went out it was with me. To the shops, you know.'

A shout from behind attracts Griffin's attention. He turns – the locksmith waving, a big grin on his face.

'I'm sorry, Mrs Morris. I have to go,' Griffin says, suiting up again and following Brody into the house.

'We think we've got it,' the locksmith says, once they're all crammed into the lock room. 'Tricksy little bugger, but Jonno here managed to get to the drill points.'

Jonno seems to be the weaselly-looking guy next to Griffin, who grins and holds up a substantial drill.

'Then it was just a matter of brute force to get through that steel plate. Some careful manoeuvring, and we were in.'

'Let's see then?'

The team clear out of the way and Griffin crouches down on the floor next to the open safe. There's a smell of burned metal as he gets closer, but sure enough, the door is open. He peers into the gap, wary about what he might find.

'Do you want me to do it, sarge?' Brody says, her blue eyes wrinkling with amusement above her mask.

'I'm fine.' He leans down, propping himself with his other hand on the side, reaching into the safe. It's a long way, his fingers coming into contact with nothing until he hits the bottom. He flinches, until he realises that the inside is covered with velvet, no doubt to protect whatever valuables are placed inside. He gropes around, exploring all four corners.

'Anything?' Brody asks.

Griffin frowns. He searches again, refusing to believe they've gone to all this effort for nothing, when his fingers touch something leaning against the side. It's small, flat, light. He pulls it out, straightening his back with a grimace, then examining his gloved palm.

On it is a small white envelope, the flap unsealed. He opens it and pulls out a stack of photographs. Distinctive white frames, poor quality. Polaroids. The sight of them jars something in his brain. A different time – photos like these stuck on a wall – and he feels instantly hot, his stomach turning over. He passes them to Brody and rushes out of the stifling lock room, out of the back door into the garden, pulling the mask away from his face and taking big gulps of crisp, cool air. He immediately feels better, then reflects on his foolishness. He thought the events of three years ago were behind him, but with one glimpse of a white Polaroid he was back there. In that stale, crowded flat, looking at the souvenirs of a demented serial killer stuck up on the wall in a perfect grid. Back then, one of those photos was of him, bloody and beaten. And one was of his wife, dying. He runs his hands down his face and screws his eyes shut, trying to block out the image.

He feels a gentle touch on his arm; he opens his eyes and Brody is there, holding out a bottle of water. He thanks her, opening it and taking a long gulp.

'What are they of?' he asks.

Brody manages a half smile. 'Dead bodies. Or people dying, one or the other. Must have been taken once the camera had been turned off.'

'For what purpose?'

'Proof of a job well done? Like the videos? Or mementos? We don't know how much Edward Morris was into this. Perhaps he got a kick from it, like any good sadistic killer. Either way, the SOCOs are capturing them now – getting them sent back to the nick so the teams can start matching them to the victims.'

Griffin takes another swig of water. 'Does this mean we can go now?'

'Yes. And I'd say we've earned that trip to the strip club, don't you?'

Now that's something Griffin can look forward to. 'Couldn't agree with you more,' he replies with a grin.

Chapter 16

Cara stares at her computer screen as the photos are uploaded, one by one, to the police server, her mind wandering. She hadn't slept well last night.

Long after Charlie had drifted into his usual gentle snore, she lay awake, staring at the ceiling. A thousand thoughts buzzed in her head, each one more disturbing than the last. The fact that Edward Morris is no more than a hired hand. That there's someone out there killing who has gone unnoticed for at least twelve years. That she has no idea where to start looking.

But they are making progress. A negative on a case is still a result. There are no dead bodies at the Morris house. No sign that's where the victims were killed. And the floor safe is open.

There's a light knock on the door. She looks up – a uniformed PC stands there, a man by his side. She suppresses a wave of irritation.

'Ma'am? This gentleman's here to see you?'

'Thank you. I'll take it from here.'

The PC leaves, relieved; Cara studies the man waiting in the doorway.

Andrew Elliott – known to all as Roo. Her ex-husband. Wearing a light blue sweatshirt, jeans, and a stubborn look of defiance.

'Where are the kids?' she asks. She points to the seat opposite her desk. 'Do you want to sit down?'

He does, crossing one leg over the other and folding his arms across his chest. 'They're with Sarah. I need to talk to you.'

'Couldn't it have waited?'

'No, Cara. Not everything can wait until whatever nutter you're trying to catch is behind bars.'

'Serial killer.'

'What?'

'We're looking for a serial killer.'

He has the audacity to roll his eyes. 'Whatever. It's about Tilly. Has she told you? She's being bullied.'

'Since when? By whom?'

'For ages. Some girls in her class. She and Josh were with you all last week, and she didn't say anything?'

'No . . .' Cara thinks back. To a week's worth of school runs, of rushed dinners, catching up on emails in the evening. How had Tilly been? Quieter than normal, but then it's Josh that's the talkative one. 'She seemed fine.'

'Well, she's not. And Sarah and I are going to speak to her teacher about it.'

Sarah and I. Cara feels the familiar twinge of annoyance. 'When?'

'First thing Monday. Nine a.m.'

'I'll be there.'

'Are you sure? Because I know how busy you are . . .'

His voice takes on a hint of mockery as he says this. It was always a source of hostility between them; Roo could

92

never get the hang of having a wife who worked. And one who earned more than he did.

He doesn't have that problem now. His new girlfriend – fiancée, Cara corrects her internal voice with a frown – works part-time at Josh and Tilly's school. 'Naturally maternal,' Roo had told Cara, leaning hard into all the criticism it inferred. *Sarah* would never hire a nanny to look after her kids. *Sarah* would never work evenings and weekends, missing swimming lessons and parents' evenings and school plays. No, *Sarah* is going to make the perfect mother, when that news inevitably arrives, even if Roo is practically over the hill for new fatherhood at forty-four.

She appraises her ex-husband now. Annoyingly, he seems to have been going to the gym; he's lost the hint of chubby jowls threatening before and now looks toned and strong underneath his sweatshirt. While she will be coming up sadly lacking.

'I'll be there,' Cara repeats through gritted teeth. 'Thank you for letting me know. Was that all?'

Roo stands up. 'Lovely to see you, Cara. As always. Sarah said to tell you hello.'

I bet she bloody did. 'That's nice,' Cara manages. 'You can find your own way out, can't you?' And with that, Roo's gone.

Cara sits back in her seat, seething. Bloody Roo. Didn't waste any time rubbing it in her face as to what a terrible mother she is. Except this time, Cara has to agree. Her heart goes out to Tilly. Bullied, and Cara had no idea. Some mother she is.

She turns back to her screen – and the photographs. She'll get this case sorted. Prove Halstead and Ryder wrong, that her team is more than capable of doing this alone. Then go to the school appointment first thing on Monday, and actually pay attention to her children from now on.

She clicks through the photos, trying to concentrate. They're blurred, messy, poorly lit, but it's possible to make out the focus. The man lying dying on the floor, broken and beaten. Another – clearly Terry Gregory, his jaw broken. And in one: a woman.

She's lying on concrete, her eyes open and glassy. There is a smudge of blood on her cheek, a vivid red gash on her forehead.

Cara leans closer, squinting at the shot. It's clearly out of place. This one's been taken outside, when the others were indoors. And it's a woman.

She picks up her phone, makes a call. Charlie answers on the first ring.

'Out of all the victims,' Cara says. 'Were any female?'

'No. All men.'

'You're sure?'

'Certain.'

She hangs up without saying goodbye. The more she stares, the more she's convinced. This photo doesn't belong. And suddenly she knows. She knows where she's seen it before.

Three years ago, standing next to Griffin in flat 214. The home of a serial killer who also had a penchant for snuff films, who had a whole box of them. VHS tapes, not DVDs like these. But the same content.

Could it be that they were working together?

Cara knows how unreliable eyewitness testimony can be – herself included. How many times have witnesses been convinced, beyond a shadow of a doubt, that a car is red – only for the police to discover it's blue?

She clicks out of this file and into the main folder directory, running a quick search. No matches. Where is it? The case file from back then – the digital archive of the whole investigation. There's nothing.

Frustrated, she gets to her feet and makes her way down to the evidence store. She flashes her ID to the clerk, asks for the shelf and the location. He points, distracted, and she leaves him to it, scanning the rows of identical brown evidence boxes, each one marked with the number and date.

The case is long closed, the killer behind bars, so Cara's hopes rely on the archiving team being slow. Sure enough, when she tracks the case number back, there they are. Boxes of evidence, lined up across the shelf.

Cara hesitates. This was the case that defined her career. Three years ago, a serial killer ran rampant across the country, murdering thirty-one people and destroying the lives of many more. Eleven days of hell that nearly killed her brother and left her divorced, traumatised and distraught.

The Echo Man.

And when it turned out to be someone they all knew, someone they trusted, it broke her into tiny pieces. Noah Deakin: a detective, her partner. Her best friend. Now in prison for life, with no chance of parole.

She stands in front of the rack of shelving, her fingers pressed lightly to her mouth. Only recently has she been able to put herself back together, and the idea of wrecking this fragile peace? It terrifies her.

But worse is the idea of not knowing. She needs to be certain whether this current case links, and she takes the first box down, removing the lid and having a quick flick through. Evidence bags, stacked upon one another. Other boxes: investigator's notebooks, crime scene photos. She flicks through, and finding nothing of interest, moves on. The next: a box of VHS tapes, each one labelled with a six-figure number in black pen. Snuff films – seventeen in total. Plastic tapes in cardboard sleeves. Another connection between the investigations. Then and now. She places the box on the floor. Keeps looking.

Box after box. Until at last, she finds them.

Crime scene photographs from flat 214.

She signs that box out and carries it back to her office. The incident room is quiet as she makes her way through. She's aware Griffin and Jamie have gone to this strip club, following a lead on Terry Gregory, and she's happy to let them go. Let them have their fun. Got to be some moments of joy in this awful case. Not much else otherwise.

She places the cardboard box on the floor and carries the photos back to her desk. Slowly she goes through them. One by one, looking for the Polaroids. The wall of his keepsakes, reminders of his achievements that he must have gone back to, day after day. Revisiting the kills.

She finds it at the back of the pile. First of all, an image taken from a distance, the whole wall visible. And then close-ups, detailing the Polaroids one by one, and here it is. Cara's certain now.

Emily Johnson. A woman killed in the same manner Sutcliffe used, the Yorkshire Ripper. Bludgeoned then stabbed. Her body abandoned where it fell. Except before he left, he took Polaroids. And one has somehow ended up in Edward Morris's floor safe.

This cements it in her mind. Somehow, these cases are linked. And this is *hers*. Sod DCS Halstead, sod DCI Rosie Ryder and her stupid name and ingratiating ways. Cara is the senior investigating officer and nobody will take this away from her.

She's so lost in her thoughts she doesn't notice Shenton come up behind her.

'Anything I can do?' he asks, and she jumps.

'Shit, Toby. I didn't realise you were here. I assumed you were at lunch?'

'Yes, but . . .' He shrugs and she feels bad. She has no idea about Shenton's life. Whether he has friends, or eats his lunch alone in the canteen. He leans down to look at the photographs. 'What have you got there?'

'More Polaroids.'

'From the house?' He gives them a cursory glance, then spots the box on the floor, the case number written on the side. 'From an old investigation?'

She gives him a look; he realises immediately.

'Oh,' he says, peering closer. 'Him?'

'The one and only. Look.' Cara holds the photograph next to the screen. Two shots of the dead woman, side by side. 'Edward Morris had a Polaroid of Emily Johnson in his floor safe. Along with the rest of the latest kills. Their paths must have crossed.'

Shenton considers it for a moment. 'Makes sense,' he says slowly. 'The Echo Man was a sadist. Snuff films would have been catnip to him – a way to fill the gap if he wasn't killing. Maybe Morris made a quick buck on the side – sold a few of these on the dark web.'

'Or maybe our anonymous accomplice did.'

Shenton stares at her – his light blue eyes boring into her soul. He'd been there, three years ago. He lived it; he knew this case as well as she did, maybe better, given he's probably studying it for his PhD.

'The only snag to our theory is that Noah Deakin's been in prison since 2021.'

'But Morris had been involved since 2012. That's an overlap of nine years.'

'You think they knew each other,' Cara says.

'Occam's razor,' Shenton replies, referring to the principle that the simplest explanation is usually the best. 'Someone will have to visit him. In prison. Do a formal interview.'

'He might know something, Toby.'

'So let me go. I can study him. Apply a scientific approach—'

'No,' Cara interrupts. 'I'm the SIO now. I was then. This is my responsibility.'

He stares at her, almost frozen in place. Then, in a millisecond, he snaps out of it. Blinks. Smiles, tense, his lips pressed together. 'Okay,' he says and nods. He points out of the open door, to his desk. 'I'll go . . . Griffin wants me to . . .' He mumbles something about traffic cameras and old ANPR records, and hurries back to his desk.

Cara leans back in her seat and sighs. She didn't mean to snap at Shenton. It was a reasonable suggestion, that their resident expert on serial killers should go and interview the one they know in prison. But Cara doesn't dare take the risk.

'Dammit,' she mutters quietly.

Because the truth is, she's been lying. To Shenton, to Charlie, to Griffin. To her whole team.

And none of them would be happy if they found out.

Chapter 17

Jamie stands outside the strip club and shivers. Above him, *Velvet Oasis* is written in pink, but it's the only colourful aspect of this place. Behind, wind whips across a grim grey patch of concrete bordered by a chain-link fence, no more than ten cars parked up within. Huge container ships cruise by on the water, spewing diesel. As he watches, Griffin's Land Rover comes into view.

Griffin parks up and he and Brody climb out.

'She wanted to come,' Griffin says grumpily as he walks across.

Jamie smiles at her. 'A woman's touch is a good idea. Can't think they're going to want to open up to us.'

'That's what I said,' Brody gloats, batting Griffin on the arm. She looks up at the building. 'Bit grim though. And why's it open on a Sunday lunchtime?'

'The UK's only twenty-four-hour nightclub,' Jamie replies, and Brody pulls a face.

'Grim,' she repeats.

'Are we going in, or not?' Griffin asks.

'After you.'

Jamie follows the pair as they open the double doors, bickering even as they show their IDs to the bouncer.

'Who's in charge here?' Jamie asks.

'Blake. Far side,' the bouncer replies, pointing to a black bar, the edges lit with green neon. It seems to be a theme – the eighties' lighting, the electronic beats of Soft Cell sounding out over the loudspeaker.

There are a number of stages scattered around the huge room, brightly coloured lights rotating across each one as a bored, scantily dressed woman caresses a pole in the centre. The women are dressed in fluorescent headbands and leg warmers – and little all else.

Jamie flushes. He's not naive, he's been to strip clubs before – mainly following Adam after a long night of boozing – but he doesn't think he's ever seen so many women so *naked* before. And why's it so *hot* in here? He pulls his coat off, fanning his face, trying to will the blush away.

Griffin, meanwhile, is having no such problem. He's leaning against the bar, grinning, his attention locked on the gyrating woman in front of him. She is fully nude, except for a brief G-string over her privates, and going through her routine: strut, pout, squat, shove her ass in Griffin's direction, repeat. Brody is equally nonplussed, talking to a man with bright white teeth at the far end of the bar. She taps Griffin's arm, asks him a question. He replies without shifting his gaze; three beers are passed their way.

Jamie shakes his head, dumbfounded at how he's ended up here, drinking, at one p.m. on a Sunday afternoon. He heads over to join Brody.

'Blake Simmonds,' she says, shouting over the noise of the

100

music. He smiles broadly, showing his impressive gnashers again. 'The manager of this place.'

Simmonds holds out his hand; Jamie shakes it as a floodlight colours him green. 'Detective Inspector Jamie Hoxton. Is there somewhere quieter we can talk?'

'Gladly,' he replies, pointing with an exaggerated flourish from the main room to a set of stairs, leading upwards. Brody taps Griffin on the arm, points to Jamie. Griffin replies and she leaves him, joining Jamie halfway up the stairs.

'He says he's going to stay there. Interrogate the strippers,' she adds with a roll of her eyes as they make their way into the office.

Blake Simmonds is pale out of the glow of the club. The pallor of someone used to sleeping by day, partying at night. He closes the door to the office and sits in a squeaky leather chair, an ostentatious dark wooden desk in front of him. A long glass window runs the length of one wall so that the dance floor is in full view, and Jamie peers down at Griffin. Griffin's moved closer to the stage, taking a seat and leaning back, the bottle of beer against his smiling lips. There doesn't seem to be much conversation going on.

'How can I help?'

'Do you recognise this man?' Jamie holds out a photograph; Blake peers at it.

'Can't say that I do. But we get a lot of men through here, as you can imagine.'

'He was a trader. Was suspected of stealing a lot of money.'

'Not that Granger guy?'

'Gregory,' Jamie confirms. 'Terry Gregory.'

'But that was years ago. I remember it on the news.'

'Ten years ago – 2014.'

'I can't help in that case. I wasn't here, and none of our staff were either at that time.'

'Not even the bouncers?'

'Officer . . .'

'Detective Inspector Hoxton.'

'DI Hoxton. Our club prides itself on beauty. And *youth*,' he adds, stressing the word. 'Something I'm sure your colleague down there understands. For someone to be working here at that time and still be employed by us now they would need to have been at least . . .' He squints again.

'Twenty-eight,' Jamie finishes for him.

'Horrendous,' Brody adds, sarcastically.

'Was the club twenty-four hours back then?'

'We've always been twenty-four-seven. Now, if you don't mind – I will invite you to a private booth, so you can finish your drinks, and then I will ask you to be on your way. Our clients don't like police officers hanging around, as I'm sure you can appreciate.'

'I wouldn't want my decaying thirty-something wrinkles to scare the punters,' Brody mutters to Jamie as they're escorted to a small room, on the far side of the dance floor. From here they can see the whole place, including Griffin by the stage, now chatting with one of the strippers.

'I'm not sure what you thought you would gain from coming here,' Brody shouts to him.

He shrugs, his beer up to his mouth. He takes a long swallow, then bellows back, 'Hoped someone would remember Gregory. And wanted to get a feel of the place.'

'Got enough of a feel now?' Brody smirks, clearly enjoying his discomfort. 'Do you think he was abducted from here?'

'I don't see why not.' Jamie points to the series of small booths at the back of the room. 'Get a few beers in him, talk about a fictional job. Offer him a private dance, shut the curtains. Drug him with something, pretend he's a pissed customer, drag him out of the building and away you go.'

'But how do we prove it? No CCTV, and no outside cameras. Traffic cams won't go back that far.'

Griffin appears, throwing himself into the booth next to them. 'Bloody brilliant idea of yours, Jamie. Have we got time for another beer?'

'No. And hurry up with that one, we should be on our way.'

'I used to work in a strip club,' Brody throws in, conversationally.

Jamie blinks in surprise, but Griffin doesn't miss a beat. 'Of course you did.'

'Paid my way through uni. I was good at it too.'

'I'm sure you were. What was your signature move?'

'Be a good boy and I'll show you.'

'I'll hold you to that.'

Jamie watches Griffin and Brody spar, banter flowing naturally between them. He envies Griffin's easy way, knowing he'd be red and stuttering by now, and then wonders whether the two of them are more than colleagues. Griffin's DS to her DC, a relationship between them would be against the rules, but then Griffin's never been one for sticking to procedure.

His musings are interrupted by an older lady. She stands next to their booth, a bright blue tabard over jeans and a large T-shirt, hands on hips. She has silver hair, tied back in a bun, her eyes sparkling as if readying for a fight.

'Are you the coppers?' she says.

Jamie nods and introduces himself. Extends a hand; the woman looks at it dubiously.

'I wouldn't be doing that if I were you. Just had me hand down the lavvies.' She glances back to the stage, where the girl Griffin was talking to is getting ready for another set. 'Roxy said you wanted to chat. Some guy that went missing in 2014?'

Jamie sits up. 'Yes. Terry Gregory. Do you remember him?'

'Yup. Absolutely do. Right prick. Thought the sun shined out of his arse. None of the girls could stand him.'

'You were working here back then?'

'Been here since the millennium. Got a job to cover the big party, never left.' She thinks for a moment. 'Fucking hell. Twenty-four years cleaning up after these arseholes. Would have left years ago except for the girls.' She beams. 'They need me. Right mother hen, I am. Solve all their problems.'

Jamie prays she can solve his. 'Have a seat . . .'

'Patty.'

'Patty. Would you like a drink?'

She sits down next to him. 'No, ta. Not from here. You won't drink a thing once you've seen the state of that storeroom.'

Jamie looks at the dregs of the bottle in his hand. Puts it down unfinished. 'Tell us about Terry Gregory,' he asks. 'How often was he here?'

'He were a regular. Most weekends, a few weeknights, too. Thought the rules didn't apply to him, that he could touch up every girl he fancied. And the bouncers left him be. Money talks. And Terry had plenty. Some of the girls, they were looking for a bit extra on the side, you know what I mean.' Jamie nods. 'And that's their choice. But some of Terry's clients liked it rough. Terry too. That's why I remember him. Even now, after ten years. Because of what he did to Jade.'

Patty glances out of the booth, then leans forward in a conspiratorial whisper. All three coppers do the same, spellbound by what Patty might tell them.

'Poor Jade. She was a sweetheart, but that girl had no idea about boundaries, you know what I mean? Thought if the blokes paid the money, they could do what they liked. I saw her the next day. She didn't turn up for work so I went to her house. And the bruises.' She tuts, sucks air over her teeth. 'Choked her half to death, he did. And that's just what I could see. She wouldn't sit down. Couldn't.' Patty places a battle-aged hand on Jamie's arm, gives it a squeeze. 'I may be old, DI Hoxton, but I'm a traditionalist. I know what God intended to go in and out of the bits down there. And it sure as hell wasn't that.' She nods, certain in her assertion. Jamie's not a hundred per cent sure what she's getting at, but doesn't want to ask.

'What do you think of Blake?'

Patty looks over to the bar, where her boss is talking on the phone. 'Him – he's okay. Been here about five years or so, better than some I've seen. Knows that happy girls are profitable girls.' She cackles. 'He completely forgot about me, didn't he? I'm over fifty, invisible to men like him. That's my superpower. People say all sorts of things in front of the old woman. Think I'm unimportant. They soon learn. I make a lot of money that way.'

Jamie exchanges a glance with Griffin. Griffin shrugs.

'A bit of casual blackmail never hurt anyone,' Griffin says to Patty, and she laughs. She reaches across the table and pats Griffin on the cheek.

'If I were twenty years younger, I'd have some fun.' She catches Brody's eye. 'A pretty woman like you. You should make the most of it. Get as much out of life as you can.'

'I do,' she says with a wink.

'Good,' Patty replies. 'Now if that's all? That puke in the men's bogs ain't going to clean itself.'

And with that, she's off, arse swinging in her faded jeans, seemingly content with her place in the world.

'So Gregory was a bit of a cunt,' Griffin says. 'Not sure how it helps us.'

'Except it provides another motive? Someone else who wanted him dead.'

'With all the people he stole from and abused, I'm surprised he lived as long as he did,' Griffin replies, drily. Then to Brody: 'And you said I couldn't get the girls to talk.'

But before Brody can respond, a scream comes from the side of the club, then a second cry joins it, shouting.

A girl in very little clothing bursts through a side door. She points at Jamie. 'You need to . . . There's . . . Police. Come . . .'

She's out of breath, practically hyperventilating as she starts to cry. Jamie is out of the booth in seconds, breaking into a run to where the girl came from, Griffin and Brody right behind him.

The music is still blaring, the lights flickering, but the dancing has stopped, all eyes on Jamie, Griffin and Brody as they run through the club to the square of daylight at the end. They break out into the sunshine, blinking at the scene.

It's the back of the club, a fenced off area, with a few plastic lawn chairs, bordered by huge green bottle banks. The dancers stand pressed against the fence, cigarettes smoking down to the butt in their hands.

Nobody is talking; everyone stares at the ground.

Because in front of them, lying on the concrete, is a bundle of white plastic sheeting. And in the centre of it, a body.

Chapter 18

At first, the body doesn't look human. A scattering of limbs, loosely articulated to a lump of flesh in the centre. Not a single inch of unsullied skin is visible amongst the blood.

Cara sped there under full blues and twos, and now stands with her detectives, enduring the horrific sight. She directs them inside to interview potential witnesses, then steels herself to talk to the pathologist.

The body has been photographed and transferred to a blue plastic sheet. Dr Greg Ross oversees the mess in a full white suit, hands on narrow hips, staring grimly down. He looks up as Cara approaches.

'Male, although I can't be a hundred per cent certain,' he says.

'Any idea who?'

'Not yet. No clothing, no ID, but I haven't had a chance to fully examine him. We might have tattoos or DNA on file. No use trying for prints.'

He bends down and gently lifts the arm. The hand hangs limp, minus every one of his fingertips.

'Torture or as a means to avoid identification?' Cara says.

'Possibly both. And the majority of this damage occurred perimortem. Extensive bleeding, clotting, and evidence of inflammation around the wound edges would indicate the victim was alive when all this was carried out. I'll have a detailed look when I get him back to the mortuary, but cause of death could be a number of factors. Massive blood loss. Extensive bruising around his neck and throat. And this.'

Ross crouches down and moves the body, shifting the legs apart. Cara has seen some things in her time, but this. This is a level of torture unsurpassed by many.

'The anus and rectum have been completely torn apart. But with blunt force, we're talking ripping and tearing. I'll have to look inside to know for sure, but I'm assuming colorectal perforation, maybe more, which would have resulted in intra-abdominal sepsis, at least. And it looks like a sustained abuse – this would have taken a while.'

Cara swallows her repulsion. 'So, deliberate?'

'This sort of thing doesn't happen by accident.' Ross repositions the body. 'Apart from the missing fingertips, there are other contusions. Extensive damage to the face, broken mandible, shattered maxilla. Jaw and cheekbones,' he explains. 'A midshaft fracture of his right humerus. Neck, as I mentioned before, and bruising on his wrists and ankles.'

'He was restrained.'

'While he was tortured. Whoever killed him knew exactly what they were doing. I doubt this is a sex thing gone wrong. They meant to kill, and in this very specific way.'

Jamie waves from the door and Cara is glad to have an excuse to leave the cramped area behind the strip club.

Inside, the lights have been turned on, the punters departed. The air smells of beer and sweat, but it is an improvement on the mingling of the iron tang of blood and old fags outside. They take a seat at one of the tables, mercifully clean.

'The dancers confirmed that the last time anyone went out there for a smoke was before their shift started at ten a.m.' Jamie's flushed, no doubt from having to interview the women in their various states of undress. 'And Blake confirmed that the back gate is never locked – access for the recycling lorries.'

'Easy to get in, and a three-hour window for someone to dump the body. Why the change?' Cara says. 'Why go from hiding the bodies to dumping this one in a public place?'

'We're assuming this is one of ours?'

'The deliberate abuse and torture would indicate something similar, yes. And if not, we've got two violent killers on our patch. Not a thought I'd like to entertain at this time. Did you speak to Shenton?'

'Yes, he's looking through mispers. Ah, speak of the devil.' Jamie answers the call and puts the phone between them. 'Shenton, you're on speaker. Cara's here. What have you got?'

'I did as you said, and going on our assumption he holds the victim for forty-eight hours before he kills, I narrowed the search to the last few days.' Shenton's voice echoes in the silence of the club. 'Do we know the sex of the victim?'

'Ross said male. How many do we have?'

'On that basis, four. Male, seventy-one, late-stage Alzheimer's patient, reported missing by his care home.'

'Not him. Go younger. This guy was in good shape.'

'Stephen Allen, twenty-eight—'

'Steve Allen?' Jamie interrupts.

110

'Does that name mean something to you?'

'It doesn't to you?' Jamie replies. 'He's missing? Steve Allen is a premier league footballer. How did we not hear about this?'

'The notes on the system are vague, but reading between the lines, the investigating officer has assumed he's out on a bender somewhere, after his not guilty verdict last week. The SIO's kept it hushed up. Put it down as low risk.'

'Sorry, what?' Cara's confused. 'Who is this guy?'

Jamie steps in. 'He played for Southampton until last May when he was suspended after allegations of rape. He got off last week – jury found him not guilty. Said that the woman was a crazed fan and had deliberately targeted him.'

'Complete bollocks,' a female voice says from behind them. Brody and Griffin have returned, Griffin slumping next to them in disappointment.

'We've taken their statements. Sent the strippers home.' He digs into his pocket, pulls out a packet of fags. 'Can I smoke in here?'

'No,' Cara and Brody say in unison.

'You've had your one for today,' Brody adds.

Cara holds out her hand; Griffin reluctantly passes the fags across, watching as Cara puts them in her pocket. 'What's this about Steve Allen?' he asks.

'Might be our victim.' Cara points through the back door. 'Go look again. See what you think.' To Brody, she says, 'What do you know about the case?'

'I've been following it,' Brody replies, pulling up a chair. 'And that crap about it being consensual was bollocks. He tied her up, beat her violently around the face, then choked her half to death, while raping her vaginally and anally. And yet the jury believed him.'

'Why did they find him not guilty?'

'Misogyny,' Brody spits, while Jamie replies, 'She had a previous warning for stalking. Wouldn't leave her ex-boyfriend alone. Defending lawyers claimed it was part of a pattern.'

'The media destroyed her,' Brody continues. 'She forfeited her right to anonymity when the trial began, and the media had a field day. She lost her job, had to pay costs. Luckily, she has a rich family or she would have lost everything.'

Cara notes that last point with interest. 'When did he go missing, Shenton?' she directs to the phone.

'Thursday night, after going drinking with friends. His agent reported it.'

'So he was out on a bender?'

'Yes, but he was supposed to be discussing his return to the club Friday morning. Resurrecting his contract. His agent said he wouldn't miss something as important as that.'

'Thanks, Shenton. We're on our way back to the nick now.'

Griffin comes back in, gives a nod, his expression grim. 'Face is too much of a mess to know for sure, but Ross has found a tattoo on his upper arm which matches our man.'

'So, if we can assume this dead bloke is Steve Allen – he gets off the rape charge scot-free, abducted a week or so later, then two days after that he's restrained, choked and killed, possibly with something large shoved up his arse. Plus, his penis was cut off, did I mention that before?'

Griffin winces. 'Sends quite a message, don't you think?'

Chapter 19

The team gather their belongings and head out to their cars, but Cara hangs back. She has to talk to him – before anyone else does.

'Nate, can I have a word?'

Griffin looks over his shoulder to where Brody has paused by the Land Rover. Holds up his hand to say, *Give me five minutes*.

Cara watches the exchange. Brody could have gone with Jamie, but she's waiting for Griffin. Interesting.

'Is this about the ducks?' Griffin grumbles. 'I told Brody we didn't need to bag them all, but—'

'Ducks?'

'Yeah, the house was full of them. Rubber ducks. Wooden ducks. Ducks with hats on. Brody asked Gwen Morris, the wife – she said that it was their "thing". Her and her daughter's. You know what it's like – express a vague preference once and that's all people buy you from then on. Bet you that now I've got Frank, people will be buying us black cats.'

'It's not about the bloody ducks,' Cara snaps.

'So what's up?'

Cara pulls him over to the side of the building, out of the wind. 'The Polaroids, the ones you found in the floor safe. I went through them this morning. Most of them match to the victims on the DVDs. But one? It was different.'

She pauses, waiting for him to say something. He must have seen it. Must have come to the same conclusion.

'What, Cara?' Griffin pats down his jacket, looking for his fags, his previous verbosity gone. Finding his cigarettes absent, he scowls. 'I didn't look that closely. Handed them over to the CSM.'

'It was one of his victims. The Echo Man.'

Griffin goes completely still. 'Which one?'

'Emily Johnson. One of the early deaths.'

'Sutcliffe. I remember. How did it get into that floor safe?' Griffin's confusion turns to anger. 'Is he involved? That sick fuck.'

'One thing we know for sure is he hasn't been near it for three years. But he could have been – for the early kills. This is a direct link, Griffin. He knows who our accomplice is.'

'Or the only person he met was Edward Morris.' Griffin starts to pace, up and down the bare brick wall. Then he stops. Stares at Cara. 'You want to go and see him, don't you?'

'I think it's worth a conversation, yes.'

'But you can't . . . he . . .' He stops, takes Cara's hands in his. His palms are hot and sweaty. 'Cara, you can't. It's exactly what he wants. He was always obsessed with you—'

'Even more reason for me to go. If he's going to talk to anyone, it'll be me.' She tries to keep her voice level. To convey how important it is for her to go to the prison. 'If he can tell us how Edward Morris got that Polaroid, then that's our first solid lead. You know that.'

114

'And what if he doesn't know? If the sicko network just passes these things around.'

'Then we move on.'

Griffin stares at her for a moment, an array of emotions passing his face. 'Last time I saw that man he shot me in the chest,' he says quietly. 'If you go and see him, this is exactly what he wants. All his Christmases and birthdays will have come at once if you show up at his door. He needs to rot in there. Alone. He killed Mia, Cara.' Griffin's voice breaks, pleading. 'And he damn well nearly killed me. Twice.' Anger pushes through, his words coming out as a growl. 'Leave him. Please. None of us should ever have to see him again.'

'Okay. Okay.' Cara leans forward, pulls him in for a hug. 'I won't go.'

He resists her for a moment, then rests his head on her shoulder. He smells of cigarettes and wet dog and beer and God knows what else, embedded into that old black jacket.

He moves away from her, pulls his shoulders back and clears his throat. He tilts his head towards the Land Rover. 'See you back at the nick?'

'I'll be right behind you.'

She watches him go, an ache forming in her chest. Griffin's going to find out. And when he does, he's not going to forgive her.

Because she's been visiting him. The Echo Man. Noah Deakin. Once every few months, driving up the motorway to HMP Nottingham. And she's told no one.

At first, it was no more than misguided therapy. Facing her fears, the man who haunted her. The killer she missed, right in front of her nose. But, face to face, Noah wasn't the monster she feared. Cowed by prison, he was quiet, restrained, almost gentle. She knows what he did – she was

115

there when he admitted it, hour after hour in that stifling interview room – but something inside her can't make it tally with the man she used to know.

They talk. About her, about work. He asks about the kids, smiles when she tells him what they've been up to, how old they're getting. Sometimes she even finds herself laughing with him, caught in a memory from their time together.

And then it ends as quickly as it began. Every time she leaves that prison she has to remind herself that he's a killer. That he murdered, raped, attacked more than thirty-one people in cold blood. Including her own brother – twice. He killed Griffin's wife, Mia. Raped her, bludgeoned her to death. And each time she tells herself that's it. No more.

Cara had two overwhelming thoughts when she found that Polaroid. Firstly, fear. She's not afraid of him, but terrified that someone will discover what she's been doing. And secondly, a little jump of joy – that she has an excuse to go and see him again.

Because as much as she tries, she can't hate Noah Deakin. She enjoys his company. She values his opinion. She likes to see him smile.

And she despises herself for that.

Chapter 20

Griffin stomps back to the Land Rover, starts the old truck without a word. Next to him, Brody fastens her seat belt and sits back in silence. He can feel her watching him.

'What?' he snaps.

'What did Cara want?'

He shakes his head. He's not ready to talk about it. To have that name on everyone's lips again.

Brody takes the hint. 'Shauna Lloyd will be pleased,' she says after a moment. 'The rape victim? Imagine being a fly on the wall when she's told.'

'Maybe you will be. We'll need to interview her.'

'You can't think she's behind it?'

'Who else? You said yourself she has rich parents. She's the prime suspect, surely.'

'It'll be hard to prove. Something connecting her to the killer. Can't imagine she's left a paper trail.' She smiles, then covers her mouth to hide it, looking out of the window.

'You can't be pleased this happened? Alana – a man was tortured to death.'

'A fate he most likely deserved.' She turns to face him, her eyes hard, mouth turned down. 'We claim we're on the side of the law. That justice will prevail, but what happens when it doesn't? Is Shauna Lloyd supposed to just shrug and move on? Imagine what that woman went through. Raped, beaten, choked – and at the end of it all the whole world laughs at her and calls her a whore. And even if he was sent to prison, is that enough? Wouldn't you—' She stops abruptly.

'Wouldn't I, what?' Griffin has a pretty good idea what she's getting at. 'Wouldn't I want my wife's killer to end up that way, is that what you were going to say?'

'Yes. Noah Deakin is in prison, but what he did to Mia? What he did to you, and all his other victims? It's not enough. An eye for an eye.'

'So we're going biblical now, is that it? You and I both know capital punishment doesn't work.'

'But if the choice was yours, what would you do? If no one would ever know. Truth or dare?'

Griffin falls silent, his eyes on the road ahead.

After the sentencing, Griffin hoped never to hear that man's name again. Now everyone is bringing it up. He said no to Cara visiting Noah, but if they want to find their killer, she's right. He is their best chance. Even if they find who paid for these kills, they're never going to talk.

He can't think about this now. The mental pain of it, the hatred – Brody's right. It flows through his veins, a sickness. He takes the next junction, driving for a few minutes then pulling into an alleyway. Brick walls either side, industrial bins in front – it's hardly the most romantic of places. But nobody's around. Nobody to judge or observe.

He kills the engine, looks over at Brody. She's watching him with interest.

'It's your turn. Truth or dare.'

He knows what she'll go for. A smile catches her lips. 'Dare.'

He undoes his seat belt. She does the same. 'Get in the back,' he says.

She does as he asks, climbing out of the front cab and opening the door. She climbs in; he follows, closing it behind him. The space in the back of his Land Rover is cramped with the seats down the side, but there's more than enough room for what he has in mind as he pushes the toolbox out of the way and pulls the cushion from the seat. He places it on the metal floor.

'Knees on that,' he says. She does as she's told, still clothed, looking back at him with a smile. But she hesitates.

'Are you sure you want this?' she asks.

'I need it,' he replies, his voice thick. 'Do you?'

She nods. 'You know I do.'

She turns away again, undoing her trousers and wriggling everything down, parting her legs as much as she can. No embarrassment, no hesitation; she places her hands on the back of the seats, bending forwards and pushing her perfect arse towards him.

He doesn't hang around. He undoes his belt, his trousers around his ankles; she hands him a condom, he fumbles with it for a moment, then pushes his fingers inside her. She's wet – so damn wet – and she reaches back, grabbing the neck of his shirt, pulling him closer. He can't wait anymore. He enters her, hands gripping her hips. There's no space, his head wedged against the metal roof; he presses his face into the back of her neck, inhaling the smell of her perfume as he thrusts. Hard, fast. Focusing on her and nothing else. Why did he wait so long, why did he stop this? This is what he needs. Distraction. A good solid fuck.

A release.

There's no discussion after. No romance. They re-dress in silence; Griffin disposes of the used condom in a discarded takeaway cup, hurled into the bins. And with a final glance around the alleyway, they're back on the road.

They walk up to the incident room together. Cara throws Griffin a glare, but apart from Brody's flushed face, there's no way of telling what they've been up to.

'Nice of you to join us,' she comments.

'Stopped for coffee,' Griffin mutters. He takes a seat around the table; Brody does the same, opposite.

Cara turns back to the whiteboard where the names of all fifteen victims have been written up, along with the dates they were killed. It sobers him. Reminds him why they're there; the lives at stake while he was pointlessly shagging Brody. He feels a burn of shame; resolves, once again, to be a better man.

'As I was saying,' Cara says pointedly, 'our priority has to lie with Steve Allen. This is the warmest case, our best chance of finding a lead. We have a DNA sample from when he was reported missing so we can confirm ID, and once we have this, the chief super is going to put out a short press release. Allen was high profile, we know the journalists are going to be a pain in the arse, so we need to be thorough. Dr Ross is going to come back to us on the PM as soon as possible, but meanwhile we have plenty to be getting on with.

'Griffin, you and Shenton are in charge of finding who dropped Steve Allen's body off and when. Track down traffic cameras, ANPR, dash cams, whatever you can find. I know it's a deserted area, down by the docks, but there must be something. Jamie, you and Brody are going to reinterview the woman Allen raped.'

'Shauna Lloyd,' Jamie says. 'Do you think she's behind it?'

'It's a possibility we need to explore. She has the strongest motive, don't you agree?' Brody nods reluctantly. 'Caution her, get her in if you can. We need to know who is responsible for these deaths. Someone out there is making money from these people. Killing on demand, and they've made it clear they're not going to stop because their film-maker has died. I'm going to speak to the digital team, see what else they've managed to glean from those videos. There must be something that gives away a location or an ID.'

Griffin looks up at the board, at the map and the photographs that have been put up while he's been out. The strip club has been marked with a red dot, and it makes Griffin wonder.

'Why has he changed his MO?' Griffin asks. 'We haven't found a single body up to now, and today he dumps one in plain sight?'

All eyes turn to Shenton, their resident expert on serial killers.

'Could be that Edward Morris's death has disrupted his routine,' Shenton says. 'The videos offer proof of a job completed for his clients, and without Morris, he needs to find another film-maker. Given the nature of his business, that will take time.'

'Perhaps the client requested the public body dump?' Jamie says. 'Adds a level of humiliation into the mix. Assuming we think Shauna Lloyd is behind this.'

'And it certainly makes her point. "This is the guy who raped me."' Shenton stops for a moment, thinking. 'Would make sense.'

'But why at that strip club?' Griffin adds. 'Did he know we were going to be there?'

'How?' Cara asks. 'Were you being followed?'

'I don't think so,' Griffin replies, looking to Jamie. He shakes his head, his face grave.

'If somehow he knew,' Shenton continues, animated now, his hands fluttering, 'it adds a worrying amount of malevolence into the mix. For years this guy has been quietly going about his business. Killing, hiding bodies. But that's all over. He must have realised that Morris is dead, know we've found the videos and we're on his trail. But he doesn't care. By placing that body under our noses, he's showing off. He's saying, "Look at me. Look what I can do."'

'You think he's going to keep on killing?' Cara asks.

'He's got a job to do. This is a man on a mission – revenge, retribution. It's not easy to find and kill someone specific – if he was in it for the sadism alone he'd go after any old victim. No – he wants these men. He hunts them down, abducts them, then patiently waits forty-eight hours before he kills them. Playing with them, extracting the maximum enjoyment for himself, like a cat does to a mouse. Think of the power he's getting from this! The control. It's any sadist's wet dream. This is an addict. And he's not going to stop until we make him.'

The room is silent, all eyes turn to the whiteboard, to the list of victims, the times they were killed.

'He's speeding up,' Griffin says. 'Look at the dates. It's one or two a year, until we hit 2019. Then it's three. Four last year. He's hitting his stride. Who knows how many more he might have in the pipeline. Someone might be locked in that white room now.' He shakes his head with frustration. 'All this stuff,' he says, gesturing to their lines of enquiry, the list of things to do. 'Nobody who's paid for this is going to talk – they're not going to confess to solicitation of murder unless we have proof and the lab tests, the post-mortem, getting camera footage. That all takes time.'

Griffin looks at Cara. He doesn't like it, but there's no other way. 'You need to go and see him.'

'Nate . . .' Cara's face softens. 'But you said—'

'I don't care. This isn't about me. Edward Morris got that photograph from somewhere, and I'm willing to bet Noah Deakin knows all about it. Those Polaroids were his trophies, his pride and joy. He wouldn't have just handed one over, no questions asked. He would have got something in return.'

The whole room is staring now. And Griffin's certain.

'If we're saying that Edward Morris was our film-maker and that's all he did, then there are three other killers to find. The two heavies that we've seen on tape, time and time again, carrying out the murders, and the mysterious voice. The mastermind.'

He turns to Cara. 'The Echo Man – Noah Deakin – he's serial killer royalty. That photo proves their paths have crossed, and guaranteed, if someone else had been killing at that time, he would have known.'

Griffin looks at the board, taking in the sixteen names. The men murdered and tortured. And Griffin's not going to be the one standing in the way of stopping the killer.

'Do whatever he wants,' he says to his sister. 'Just get him to talk. Before someone else dies.'

Part 2

DAY 4

MONDAY

Chapter 21

Cara knows the route off by heart: up the M3, the A34, the M40, the M1. The service station where she stops for petrol, the best place to park once she gets there.

She pulls her coat tightly around her and strides up the hill to the entrance of HMP Nottingham. A small group linger outside: families and children, waiting to see their loved ones. But Cara doesn't have to queue. This is official police business.

Noah notices the difference the moment he walks in. Normally they meet in one of the old police interview rooms, but this is the state of the art digital suite. Cameras in the corner, microphones on the table.

'Do I need my lawyer?' he asks, straight away. He doesn't have one; he's making a point. 'What's going on?'

'Something's come up. On a case. And I'm hoping you can help.'

Her tone is placatory, gentle. Saying 'I' not 'we'. But he's not stupid.

His previously open manner drops away. As she recites the caution, he wraps his arms around his body, hackles up, instantly hostile. He stays standing as the door is closed behind him.

'I've said all I'm going to say,' he replies.

He's wearing a basic white T-shirt with his usual grey tracksuit trousers. They're baggy, but she can see how skinny he's become – face gaunt, cheekbones jutting. He reminds her of a beaten greyhound: short hair almost shaved to the scalp, showing the scar in his hairline. Skin peppered with marks and scars. His forearms bear the after-effects of his failed suicide attempts, the self-harm – thin white lines running the length of his arms. Today, his knuckles are scabbed and bloody; Cara wonders what – or who – he has hit.

'How are you?' she asks.

'What do you want, Cara?'

He's frosty, and it irritates her. Why shouldn't she come here on police business? It's not as if they're colleagues anymore. Or friends.

She reaches down and takes the photographs out of her bag. She glances up to the cameras – the red light shows that they're recording – and she lays them out, turning them around to face him.

She's starting easy. Shots of the Polaroids, found in the safe. Victims he doesn't know.

'Do you recognise these?'

He leans forward, takes a quick look. 'No.'

'We recovered these yesterday from the floor safe of a man we believe was involved in the murder of sixteen people.'

'So ask him.'

'He's dead.'

He wrinkles his forehead, confused. 'What's this got to do with me?'

She pushes the final one across. 'Emily Johnson. Do you remember?' He ignores her. 'Look at it, Noah.'

He leans forward, a slight tilt of the head. 'What about it?'

'We found Polaroids like this in your flat in 2021. But this one . . .' Cara taps a finger. 'This one was in the floor safe. With the others. How did it get there?'

His eyes meet hers for the first time. Dark, the irises nearly the same colour as the black in the centre. 'I have no idea.'

'Did you know Edward Morris?'

'Never heard of him.'

'So how did he get this Polaroid, Noah? This was a woman you killed. You must have met him.'

'If you say so.'

She decides to change tack. 'Do you like to watch snuff films?'

'Not much of a market for it in here.'

'Because you did. Before. That was another thing we seized from your flat, back then. Another link to Edward Morris. Because he filmed them. And now they're my problem. Fifteen in total – all category five. The worst shit, that you used to buy and watch for your pleasure.'

'If you say so.'

She pauses, trying to read him. He's still cowed, leaning against the wall on the far side. 'How did Edward Morris get that photograph?'

His gaze drops. He stares at his hands, picking at the scabs on his knuckles. 'I don't know.'

'You must. Please. Edward Morris is one of four people involved in this. And they're still killing. Literally dropping bodies at our feet.'

'I can't help you.'

Cara hesitates, then reaches down and pulls the laptop out of her bag. She brought it as a last-ditch attempt, but she needs some leverage. She needs him to see the killer they're dealing with. She opens it and finds the file, turning it around to face him. She waits.

He doesn't move. 'What's that?'

'Something you might like. You're a sadistic killer, right?' His eyes narrow, watching her with suspicion. 'Sit down,' she directs, sternly.

This time he does as she asks, pulling the chair out and sitting a slight distance away. He regards the laptop warily.

She presses play.

The film starts and Noah watches out of the corner of his eye, his head turned to the side. Terry Gregory has paper notes forced into his mouth, his jaw broken. Suffocated, tortured, dying. After five minutes, Noah looks away. He blinks, swallows.

'Why are you showing me this?' he asks. 'I didn't kill that man.'

'I don't think you did. But whoever was involved – they're the same people you gave that Polaroid to. You must know something.'

'I don't.'

'You—'

'I don't,' he interrupts, forceful now. 'I was a different person then. I don't remember. Don't show me something like that again.' He reaches out and closes the lid of the laptop. 'I can't help you.'

His reaction surprises her. Cara expected him to be suspicious, wary, angry even, but what she's seeing now – it's disgust. Horror. When what he did was a thousand times worse.

'I'm sorry.' She finds herself apologising. Going in, she had made a resolution: she would treat him like a suspect. Like the killer he is. But old habits die hard. He behaves like the Noah she knew. Softly spoken. Thoughtful. She opts for a different tactic.

'Can I tell you about the case?'

He leans forward. Curious, despite himself. 'I can't help.' But his tone is less guarded.

'He's killed at least sixteen people, over twelve years. We think he's providing a service. If people want revenge, he'll exact it. Murder, torture. Even rape. Filmed, to prove it's been carried out. Fifteen men disappeared, their bodies never found.'

'So he's careful. Precise. Doesn't show off.'

'Not until yesterday.' Cara meets his gaze; he raises his eyebrows. He doesn't need to say it, she can still read him like a book. He's interested.

'Body turned up at a strip club. Dumped while we were there. Defiled, beaten. A man, who'd just been acquitted for rape.'

'You think the previous victim ordered the hit?'

'That's our theory. We're interviewing her now.'

'Why dump the body? Who was at the strip club?'

'Jamie, Griffin and Brody. We think he did it as proof that the job was done. The guy who used to edit his films is dead. He needed another way.'

'I don't like it, Cara. He could have dumped the body anywhere and he chooses to do it there? Where your guys were?'

'What are you saying?'

'That he wanted you to notice.' He pauses. 'How did he know you were there?'

'We wondered that too. We don't know.'

'And this man – acquitted for rape. How did the killer know where to find him? Where he lived?'

'He stalked him?'

'A lot of work without a starting point. Have all of the victims been acquitted of a crime?'

'What are you saying?'

Noah leans back, thinking. His expression reminds Cara of the man she used to know. The detective, mulling over a case. 'Is someone feeding your killer information?'

'Like what?'

'Names, addresses. Potential targets.'

Cara reels. 'Someone in the police force?'

'Or in the court system. But they'd need to be close to you – to know your team were going to be at the strip club that morning.' As Cara's mind scrambles to catch up, Noah continues: 'But dumping a body right in front of you means you can catch him. He's arrogant. Showing off.'

Cara smiles. 'You're starting to sound like Shenton.'

Noah's head jerks back. 'He's still on the team?'

'Yeah. Old guard now. Shenton, Griffin, Brody, Jamie.'

'These new detectives – you trust them?'

'I think so.'

'And how are you? The kids?'

'I'm fine. The kids are good. Or rather, I thought they were.' She sighs. 'I had an appointment at the school this morning. With Roo and *Sarah*.' She says her name in a funny voice, pulling a face. 'Tilly's being bullied.'

'Shit. Is she okay?'

'Yeah, I think so. We agreed an action plan. As if that's going to stop bitchy nine-year-old girls.'

'Vicious, are they?'

132

'You have no idea.'

They share a smile and for a moment they're not here, in this prison interview room. They're back in the front seat of her car, chatting. The DCI and her DS. She misses those days. Someone who knows her as well as Noah did back then.

'And Roo . . . the arsehole . . . made out that it's my fault. That our daughter's misery is directly linked to my poor mothering. When he's the one who cheated.'

'You're a fantastic mother, Cara. Don't believe his shit.'

'Am I though?'

He smiles, but it's tight and pinched. 'Look after yourself.'

She senses the conversation coming to an end. 'I put some money on your spends account. And I got you these from the tea bar downstairs.' She reaches into her pocket and pulls out two tubes of Polo mints. He takes them with a half-smile.

'Thank you.'

'Are you seeing someone? In here?'

He frowns, confused. 'A therapist, you mean? No.'

'Who's helping you?'

'Helping me?' he scoffs. His fingers go to the packet of mints, opening the end and putting one in his mouth. He offers them to her, she declines. 'The only person who helps me is you.'

'So why won't you tell me where the Polaroids came from?'

He gets up then, putting the mints in his pocket and backing away from her, as though she's going to hurt him.

'I can't. I don't know where that photograph came from.' He bangs on the door, trying to attract the attention of the guard. 'Thank you for the spends,' he says softly.

The door opens and the guard appears, ready to escort him back to his cell. And Cara gets a sudden rush. A sense of desperation. Loss. That he's going to walk away and she won't see him again.

'Wait,' she calls. The guard stops. Noah turns.

'Noah?' she says. 'Please. Be careful in here.'

He smiles, but it's wistful. 'It's too late for that,' he says, and he's gone, the light tread of his trainers almost lost in the heavy footsteps of the guard.

She sits for a moment longer, gathering the photos, putting her laptop in her bag, trying to hold back the tears. The connection she feels with him, the friendship, it's still there, and it weighs in her gut, conflicting with the knowledge of what he's done, the people he killed.

He confessed to it all. Yet he won't help her today. It doesn't make sense.

She walks quickly out of the prison, collecting her belongings, signing out. And it's not until she gets to the car that she realises what's been bugging her.

The way he said it. *I can't. I don't know where that photograph came from.*

I can't.

What's stopping him? Or – more importantly – who?

Chapter 22

Jamie and Brody agree: Brody will lead the interview with Shauna Lloyd. Her previous work in the sexual exploitation team at the Met holds her in good stead for interviewing traumatised victims. Plus, and Jamie doesn't want to say it, she has the feminine touch. Gentle, delicate; Jamie can't imagine Shauna will want a man anywhere near.

Her guard is up the moment Jamie and Brody arrive at her house. A huge Victorian place – white framed bay windows, ivy creeping up the walls. An expansive brick driveway leads to a slick red front door, daffodils starting to make an appearance around the edges. A shiny Tesla and a Range Rover Evoke are parked next to an 08 plate Nissan Micra.

A young woman opens the door, painfully thin, dressed in a blue hoody and tracksuit bottoms that hang off her hips. Ugg boots on her feet, scraggily blonde hair tied back in a messy bun.

'Shauna Lloyd?' Brody asks. The woman nods. 'DC Alana Brody and DI Jamie Hoxton. We spoke on the phone.'

They're ushered into a living room with exposed dark

wooden beams, where an older man and woman wait. They introduce themselves: Bill and Jane, mum and dad, and the surroundings start to make sense.

'I moved back here . . . after,' Shauna says.

The mother takes her hand in hers. 'Shauna needed support. To be with people who loved her.'

'That's nice,' Brody says, taking the mug of tea from the dad with an appreciative smile. 'And how are you doing, Shauna?'

'I'm okay,' she says quietly, pulling the sleeves of her hoodie over her hands.

Brody begins the interview, her tone soft, talking about a connection to a recent case.

'Another rape?' Shauna asks, nervously. 'Has he done it again?'

'I knew this would happen!' the mother explodes. 'You should have never let him go. This is the police's fault—'

'No, Mrs Lloyd,' Brody interrupts. 'It's nothing like that.' She pauses, looking across to Jamie. He gives her a small nod. 'Mr Allen is the victim this time. He was murdered. We found the body yesterday.'

'Murdered! By who?' the mum says. 'Deserves it, that bastard, I hope he suffered.'

'We're in the early stages of our investigation. But it seems he was targeted and abducted.'

'Targeted? Why?'

'Mum, please,' Shauna says, patting her mother's hand. She looks back to Brody. 'I don't understand why you're talking to me. I was here all weekend.'

'She was,' the mother chips in with a confident nod. 'Both Bill and I can confirm it.'

'That's helpful, thank you,' Brody says. 'But we believe

he was killed as a retaliation for what he did to you. His injuries were . . . similar.'

'Similar?'

'He was beaten. And raped.'

Shauna gapes. 'Raped, but how? Oh,' she realises, her hands going to her mouth.

'We're sorry to have to ask you this. But were there any details about your attack that you may have left out? Anything you didn't mention at the time?'

The reaction is immediate. Shauna starts to cry, her hands shaking. She curls herself up into a ball, her knees tucking to her chest, her arms wrapping around.

Her mother glares. 'How dare you come here? Bringing all of this up again. Hasn't she been through enough?' She turns to Jamie. 'You're in charge. Put a stop to this.'

'We're sorry to ask,' Jamie says. 'But it's important. The attack was so . . . specific. The details are important.'

'Did he do something to you, Shauna?' Brody pushes. 'Something you haven't told the police before?' And with that Shauna runs out of the room.

'Look what you've done,' the mother snaps. 'Bill,' she directs to the father. 'Go after her. Check she's okay.'

Bill does as he's told and the mother turns back to Jamie. 'She said this was the worst,' she hisses. 'She didn't want to talk about it then, I won't make her now.'

'But you know?' Jamie says.

The mother glances to the staircase, then back. 'This goes no further. But he made her do . . . that.' She points to her mouth.

'Oral?' Brody says.

'She said he grabbed her hair and pushed his . . . you know what . . . into her mouth. He called her a slut. He . . .'

Her voice lowers to a whisper. 'You know. In her mouth. She could barely tell me. There was no way she could report it to the police. But what does this have to do with us? I'm glad he's dead,' she spits. 'You saw Shauna – she doesn't leave the house, barely eats. I'm glad he suffered. But there's no way we killed him. We were here, all weekend.'

'We believe you. But we have a theory that whoever killed him paid someone else to do it. So we can rule you out of our enquiries, could we get access to your bank accounts?'

The shouting started soon after that. Jamie and Brody leave quickly, the mother hurling accusations after them, threatening to put a complaint in to the IOPC.

'That went as well as could be expected,' Brody says drily once they're back in the car. 'Did you believe Shauna's reaction?'

'What? You think she was faking it?' To Jamie, the ingrained trauma seemed real, the lasting effect it had on her. 'No, she seemed genuinely surprised when she found out he was dead. But the mother?'

'Too much?'

'Like she was over-acting.'

'But if that was the case,' Jamie counters, 'why did she tell us about the oral rape? Wouldn't it have been best for her to keep that to herself? And the stuff about her being glad he suffered? No. She would have kept quiet.'

'True.'

They drive in silence for a few miles, until something occurs to Jamie.

'But the dad?' he comments. 'Did you see?'

'I barely noticed him.'

'Exactly. He blended into the background, didn't say a word. Didn't even blink when you said Allen was dead. And if the mother knew the full story, what's the chance she told him?'

'A hundred per cent. Do you think it's enough to get a warrant for bank records?'

'Only one way to find out,' Jamie replies. 'But what I don't get is why didn't Shauna tell the police about the oral at the time. After all she went through, why was she so ashamed about that?'

Brody shrugs. 'Sex means different things to different people. You saw how the mother was – she couldn't even say the word – maybe her upbringing had been sheltered. You see it with rape cases all the time. Some acts bring particular shame to the victim. To Shauna it was that.' She sighs. 'Poor girl. We shouldn't have asked.'

'We should have. I'm sorry we put her through it, but it might give us an indication. We find signs that Steve Allen had forced oral, what does that tell us?'

'That someone in the household ordered the hit.'

'Exactly,' Jamie says with a smile.

Chapter 23

Laid out on the table, washed clean, the body of Stephen Allen hasn't improved. His face is unrecognisable under the contusions and bruising; his hands, the fingertips bloody and bare, rest by his side. Mercifully, the body lies on its back, so the rest of the trauma is hidden.

Staring at CCTV isn't Griffin's forte, and having spent the last few hours wading through endless footage, he was desperate to get out of the nick. So when Dr Ross called, Griffin volunteered.

He's seen his fair share of dead bodies in his time, but this has to be one of the worst. Suited up, he joins Dr Ross at the table, standing at his side as he appraises the body with a clinical eye.

'DNA has come back a match: your victim was definitely Stephen Allen. And he was in good physical shape,' Ross comments. 'Twenty-eight, six foot one, roughly eighty kilograms. He wouldn't have gone down without a struggle.'

'He was out drinking the night he disappeared,' Griffin replies. 'He could have been pissed.'

'Or someone could have slipped something in his drink.

'Too late to find out for sure, unfortunately, but my findings back up your theory he was held for forty-eight hours before death, so whatever was in his bloodstream is long gone. Stomach was empty, body was mildly dehydrated.'

'Was he restrained for that time?' Griffin asks, pointing to the blue and purple contusions on his wrists and ankles.

'No, I think that happened closer to death. The bruising is fairly new, consistent with the marks on his face and throat. And I was right about that. Broken mandible, broken nose, broken maxilla on the left-hand side. He was beaten, severely. And whoever did it had some heft. But that didn't come first – your colleagues were right.'

Jamie and Brody called Griffin from the road, explained about the oral rape, which Griffin had passed on to Ross.

'He was forced to give someone a blowjob?' Griffin says, with disbelief. 'How can you tell?'

'I swabbed his mouth and lips.' Ross's eyes wrinkle with satisfaction behind the protective glasses. 'Presence of semen.'

'You're kidding.'

'Sent to the lab. We should have a full profile of your killer within hours.'

'Fucking hell.'

'My theory is that happened first. Knife at the throat, see the surface cuts, here and here on the left-hand side.'

'So, blowjob complete, he kicks the shit out of him?'

'I'd agree with that assessment. But that wasn't his biggest problem.' Ross gestures to his pathology technician and together they roll the body on to his front. Ross parts the legs, displaying the extent of the damage. Griffin can't help but shudder.

'As I said at the scene, blunt force trauma to the perineum, completely destroying the rectum and perforating the colon.

Something large, and I mean, *large*, Griffin, was forced repeatedly into this man, over a brief period of time. But death wouldn't happen quickly from this, something I think your killer realised.'

'It wasn't COD?'

'No, the victim was still alive after this torture. Bleeding profusely, in a huge amount of pain, but this is what killed him.' Griffin's relieved as they turn the body again, covering up the worst of the trauma. Ross diverts Griffin's attention to the neck. 'Broken hyoid, multiple fingertip bruises. Prolonged pressure resulting in cyanosis, oedema and petechiae in the eyes and face. Cause of death was manual strangulation.'

'Bloody hell, poor bloke,' Griffin mutters. 'I mean, what he did to that woman was hideous, but this is overkill.'

'Someone certainly wanted to be noticed,' Ross agrees. 'Do you want time of death?'

'Please.'

'Body was warm and stiff, ambient temp was about ten degrees, so we're looking at no more than eight hours before he was found.'

'Early hours of Sunday morning?'

'That would be my assessment. Between three and six a.m.'

'Driven straight to the dump site from where he was killed,' Griffin mutters to himself.

'And despite the plastic sheeting he was wrapped in, he would have made quite a mess. No way this body didn't leave blood behind.'

'The sheeting has gone to the lab?'

'Being processed as we speak.' Ross pauses. 'I heard about the case. You think this is a vigilante killing?'

'Yes, and not the only one. You know about the videos?' Ross nods. 'Fifteen in total.'

'That's going to keep me busy when you find the bodies,' Ross says, darkly. 'Have you got any leads?'

'Cara's gone to see Noah Deakin.'

Griffin blurts it out, more anger than he expected. Ross raises his eyebrows, questioning. 'We found Polaroids – and one matches an early victim. Emily Johnson. Cara thinks he knows the killer, and that he'll tell her.'

The two men walk away from the body, pulling off the protective suits. 'And you don't?'

'I think we're playing into his hands. He'll love seeing Cara. You know what the two of them were like when they worked together. Noah was a lovesick puppy.'

'So if anyone can get him to talk . . .'

'I know, but it pisses me off, that's all. It'll make his day.'

'Did she want to go?' Ross asks.

'It was her idea.' They're outside the mortuary now, and Ross pauses in the corridor, watching Griffin closely. Dr Ross was there at the time, the pathologist on call, attending to the bodies as they came in. He watched it unfold. Knew Noah Deakin well.

'What?' Griffin asks.

'I'm just surprised she hasn't been before. As you say, those two were close. If I were her, and my partner did what Noah confessed to, I'd have questions, that's all.' He points at the sign for the restaurant above his head. 'Lunchtime. I'll call when the lab comes back.'

'How can you eat after that?'

'Practice,' Ross laughs, and he heads off. Griffin watches him go, his head churning the doctor's last words. Three years. It's been three years since they arrested the Echo Man, plenty of opportunity for Cara to visit her former partner. But she hasn't, until today.

If that had been him, would he have stayed away? Back then, the whole station knew that DCI Cara Elliott and DS Noah Deakin were close. It was a source of antagonism between the siblings – as colleagues, there was no love lost between Griffin and Noah, and he never understood why Cara had partnered with the man, sometimes wondering whether their relationship went deeper than just friends. But she was married back then. And he was a loner. A strange man, even before they knew.

Everyone missed it. Even Griffin. Until that fateful night in the forest. The team at the time reeled, shocked as Noah spent hours confessing, detailing every murder, including the death of Griffin's wife and the attack on him, leaving him for dead.

Griffin shakes his head, trying to drive away the memories. He strides from the hospital and, when he gets outside, he pats down his pockets looking for his cigarettes. Nothing. Dammit. He takes out his phone, calls his sister. She answers on the second ring.

'I'm on my way back now,' she says. 'Be another few hours.' There's a pause, and he hears an inhale, the crack of a lighter.

'Are you smoking my fags?'

'Don't know what you mean.' A long exhale.

'Cara!'

'What are you going to do? Tell a teacher?' she mocks. Another pause: the noise intensifies his craving. 'I needed it.'

'How did it go?'

'Fucking awful. I . . . I don't know, Griffin. Seeing him. It's not . . . I don't know.'

144

'The first time was always going to be the worst.' He deliberately leaves a gap, waits for her to contradict him. 'Cara?'

'I'll be back in a few hours,' she repeats. 'We'll talk then.'

She hangs up, leaving him staring at his phone, desperate for a fag.

He'll never forgive Noah Deakin for what he did. And he can understand why someone paid to have Stephen Allen killed.

He'd do the same. If he got the chance.

Chapter 24

With Cara on the M1, Jamie's in charge. This is what he wanted when he applied for promotion – a chance to prove himself, to run a murder investigation. But it strikes him that it's only at times like this – when Cara is out and Griffin is who knows where – that he can. Cara is too hands-on, and Griffin? Well, Griffin does what he likes, despite the fact that Jamie now outranks him.

Still. There is work to be done.

Shenton has been slaving away on the traffic cameras all morning and now Jamie joins him, pulling up a chair.

'Show me what you've got,' Jamie says.

Shenton switches screens, showing grainy black and white footage that Jamie recognises as the M271, the stretch of motorway running out of Southampton and the most likely exit route for the killer.

'I've been going through all the available recordings for the hours when our killer must have dropped the body off and . . .' He flips screens, showing another shot. 'Well,' he says, blush making its way up his neck. 'We have nothing.'

'Nothing at all?'

'Velvet Oasis is situated down on the West Quay Industrial Estate, where there are two roads in and out. This is one of them.' He points to the empty grey tarmac. 'And the other . . .'

'Let me guess. Doesn't have cameras?'

Shenton nods. 'A few cars and vans pass on the first road, but I have tracked them back and they go nowhere near the strip club. It's likely our killer knew what he was doing and took the other route.'

'Any witnesses?'

'Response and Patrol are still making enquiries, but nobody in the strip club saw anything, and there are few other properties nearby. The closest industrial units were empty yesterday – it was a Sunday after all – and any security camera footage is too narrow and coming up blank.'

Jamie scowls. 'So what do we have?'

'Not a lot. But!' Shenton grins. 'While I was waiting for the CCTV to come in I went through the Polaroids found in the floor safe. And, with the exception of the shot of Emily Johnson and one other, it's a perfect correlation – one photo for each victim.'

'So why did he have them?'

'Perhaps it was his own way of keeping a log of who he'd killed. Maybe he was a killer who liked souvenirs – it wouldn't be unusual.' He shuffles the photographs of the Polaroids on his desk. 'But look at this. The other exception.'

Shenton finds what he's looking for and hands it to Jamie. Jamie looks at it, intrigued.

It's different. Where the victims in the other photographs are obviously in the same white room or the concrete pit, as seen in the videos, this one is darker and seems to be outside. A body lies half on rough concrete and half on a grassy verge, his eyes open and staring skywards, a smudge of blood visible on his cheek.

'Cara didn't mention this,' Jamie comments.

'It was stuck to one of the others. The photo only came through this morning.'

'Do we know who this is?'

'No idea, but I'll get straight on it.'

'Thank you. This is excellent work, Toby.' Shenton beams. 'Have you heard from—'

But before Jamie gets a chance to finish, a cheerful female voice calls out.

'Coo-ey! Detectives! Reinforcements have arrived.'

Jamie turns to the door, already on edge. DCI Rosie Ryder approaches him in a flood of floral perfume and optimism, a smile so saccharine it makes his teeth ache.

She holds out her hand. 'Rosie Ryder. And you are?'

'DI Jamie Hoxton. We've met before.'

He stands up to his full height, towering over her.

'Well, aren't you a big boy.' She taps him on his protruding stomach. 'Cara around?'

'Cara's following up a lead. She'll be back shortly.'

'I'll wait in her office.' She leaves Jamie without another word, heading inside and pulling up a chair.

'So that's DCI Ryder,' a gruff voice says. Behind Jamie, Griffin's discarding his coat, staring into Cara's office. 'Ambition personified.'

'I'm sure she's just here to collaborate,' Jamie replies, but his gaze shifts back to the office, where Ryder's now sitting behind Cara's desk, idly thumbing through paperwork.

'Keep an eye on her,' Griffin mutters, and wanders off to the kitchen where Brody is making coffee. Jamie watches the two of them for a moment, noticing the way Griffin's hand lingers on her waist, how she smiles when he's talking. Someone else crossing a line, he thinks, but he doesn't have time for office politics and turns his back, refocusing on the job at hand.

For the next hour, Jamie busies himself with parts of the investigation where he can make a difference: updating the board with the results from the post-mortem, following up with the duty skipper on the house-to-house, requesting a warrant to access the bank records for both the Lloyd family and Richard Fredricks and his wife, looking for a possible killer for Terry Gregory and Stephen Allen.

Before he knows it, Cara is back. She takes one look at Ryder in her office, raises her eyebrows at Jamie, then heads in after her. He watches with interest as she turns on the charm. Smiles, laughter, hands are shaken and hair is tossed, before Cara emerges, Ryder following behind.

'DCI Ryder is going to join us,' Cara says loudly. 'Update us all on what her team have been up to. Have we all met?'

Introductions are made, and Jamie enjoys the fake smiles and displays of deference – especially from Shenton – as a coffee is fetched and an extra chair dragged in.

'Take your seats, everyone,' Cara says, obviously fed up with the love-in. 'And best behaviour, please.' She throws a quick glare to Griffin. 'We have a guest.'

'Oh, treat me like one of the team,' Ryder replies, and Jamie catches a grimace from his own DCI, noting it with interest.

'DCI – sorry, Rosie. Would you like to begin?'

'Would love to.' Ryder gets up and stands in front of the group. 'As you all know, my team up in the 'stoke' – another face contortion from Cara – 'have been working through the victims named in the videos, and I'm pleased to

149

say, with the help of our colleagues on Response and Patrol, we have now notified all relatives of the final fate of their loved ones.'

'Fuck me, that's quick,' Griffin whispers to Jamie. 'What did they do, get them to form an orderly queue?'

Jamie snorts in return, receiving a glare from Cara.

'Cara doesn't like her,' Griffin continues, immune to the dirty looks. 'Ryder. My sister needs to work on her poker face.'

'Your sister needs to get a move on or Ryder'll take it out from under her,' Jamie whispers back.

Griffin sits to attention. 'You think?'

'They've got a full team up in Basingstoke. Analysts, civilian admin, DCs and DSs, and more being transferred in by the day.' Jamie pauses, as Cara looks their way. Then mutters, 'If I didn't know better, I'd say DCS Halstead was getting ready to move the whole operation up there.'

'Nice cost saving – why run two Major Crime investigation teams when you can have one?'

'Exactly.'

The thought plunges them into silence. Nobody likes the idea of budget cuts, especially when it might not just be Cara who loses her job.

Ryder's still talking: 'We've now started reinterviewing the most likely suspects for ordering the hits,' she says. 'With the exception of the two victims your team are working on, Cara. And although it's early days, we are optimistic we will unearth something to help with the investigation.'

'You're reinterviewing every single one?' Cara asks, disbelief creeping into her voice. 'We're finding it more useful to concentrate on one at a time. Focus our resources.'

'We're a bigger team. We don't have the same limitations as you do down here. And doesn't everyone deserve justice?'

'You can't possibly think that we can try every case in court? Even with killers like Shipman and Bellfield they focused on one or two of the murders to get a conviction.'

The phone starts ringing in Cara's office. Cara glances towards it, annoyed.

'Scant reassurance for the relatives of his other victims. Yes, it's ambitious, but that's me,' Ryder says, with a sickly smile. 'At least I'm not wasting time driving up to Nottingham. What role did Noah Deakin have to play in these deaths?' she adds. 'Did he mastermind it from his jail cell?'

Cara's eyes narrow. 'There is a significant crossover between these cases. One I thought it vital not to ignore—' She stops abruptly, glaring at the phone in her office, which has stopped and started again. 'Toby, would you answer that?' Shenton gets up and does as he's told. 'There's a likelihood,' Cara continues, after taking a deep calming breath, 'that he can offer a lead as to how that Polaroid ended up in the floor safe, taking us directly to our killer.'

'Well, if you say so. But—'

'Boss?' Shenton interrupts from the doorway of Cara's office. 'You need to take this.'

'Can't they leave a message?'

'I tried that, but . . .' He hesitates. 'It's the governor of Notts prison. He says Noah Deakin was attacked this afternoon. He's in hospital. And it's bad.'

The whole room stops, staring at Cara. She's paled, looking at Shenton.

'How bad?' she asks.

'He might not have long.'

Chapter 25

'What do you mean, he was attacked?' Cara bellows down the phone. 'He's supposed to be in the VP wing!'

'There are still other prisoners in the VP wing,' the governor says, trying to defend himself. 'Vulnerable doesn't mean alone. And he was in his cell. There are no cameras in there – we can only see who was going in and out, no way to prove what happened—'

'You should have been watching him.'

'We intervened as soon as we saw—'

'He was beaten up. Stabbed four times!'

There's a long pause. 'I agree it's unfortunate, DCI Elliott. But budget cuts have hit the prison service hard. We have fewer trained officers, less time, fewer resources. Something I'm sure you can understand.'

'How did someone have a knife in there anyway?'

'We believe it was a shank. Prisoners can fashion anything, these days, if they want to. Look, DCI Elliott. I will investigate. And I will update you on Mr Deakin's condition when I know more.'

'I want him moved. Today. Get him transferred to the Royal South Hants Hospital, and then to HMP Winchester. He's the potential witness in a multiple murder investigation. We need him here.'

'You want him moved for police production?'

'Yes.'

A long sigh. 'I'll speak to the governor at Winchester. Get that arranged. I'll let you know.'

The governor hangs up and Cara leans back in her seat, running her hands down her face. The door to her office is closed but it's not soundproofed; she's certain the whole team heard her lose her shit. And in front of Ryder, too. Not her best look.

There's a gentle knock on the door and Jamie sticks his head around.

'Everything okay?'

Cara beckons him inside; he closes the door after him, sitting in the chair opposite.

'How much of that did you hear?'

'All of it. He's in a bad way?'

'Yeah. Four stab wounds to his abdomen, plus a good kicking once he was down. Doctors are operating now.' She sighs loudly. 'What was he thinking? He knows he's a target, he needs to keep his head down.'

'Perhaps—' Jamie stops abruptly.

'Perhaps what?'

'Perhaps he was asking for it. I mean . . . he's had multiple suicide attempts in the past. Perhaps this was him having another go.'

'Oh, shit,' Cara mutters. 'Something I said must have set him off. Something about this case. So why didn't he talk to me?'

Jamie shrugs, his face sympathetic. 'How can I help?'

'Get rid of Ryder. I can't stand having that woman around.'

'No problem, boss.'

Jamie heads back out, directing the team and quickly getting Ryder on the road. He's good, her DI. Not for the first time does she appreciate his calm nature, the way he puts everyone at ease. They need someone like him, especially when she's not exactly working at peak. She's concerned about Tilly, about the bullying her daughter's been suffering. And now there's Noah to worry about.

Her attention drifts to her desk. To the photographs lying to one side, the shot of Emily Johnson – the link to the Echo Man – on the top. She picks it up now, wonders about Ryder and whether she saw it. What else did she rifle through while Cara was out? Getting up to speed, or looking for ammunition? How long before Ryder tries for a land grab? Attempts to have Cara removed as SIO?

It's no secret that the Echo Man conviction was one close to Cara's heart. And now, with the connection between the cases, she's jeopardising the impartiality of the investigation. But she's damned if she's going to let it go, and they need more resource on this case. Having Ryder's team working alongside them is vital.

No, they'll keep it professional, and they'll find their killer. Follow process and procedure, break no rules, and there'll be no need for Halstead to pass it over. No one can argue if they're getting results.

And on that thought, her gaze shifts to Griffin. He's talking to Brody at the whiteboard; she glances up at him and laughs; he smiles back. And fucking hell, she recognises that look. The half-closed eyes, the predatory grin. When it comes to Griffin, nothing good comes of that look.

The day passes, little progress is made.

They nag the lab for the results on the semen found on Stephen Allen and the trace on the plastic wrapping, but the answer is the same. *We're doing our best.* Not good enough, Cara thinks. The same could apply to her.

At seven p.m. Charlie swings by the office and persuades her to leave. She tells the team to do the same. Shenton is still working on the traffic cameras and ANPR, but coming up a blank; Griffin and Brody are reading witness statements, where little actual witnessing seems to be involved.

'I'll see you at home,' Cara says as she passes Griffin. He looks up and nods. He's been avoiding her all day, most likely because of her obvious concern about Noah.

'Have you heard from the hospital?' Charlie asks as they head back to hers, Charlie driving her Audi.

'Out of surgery but sedated. They'll give me an update in the morning.'

Charlie nods, but stays quiet.

'What?'

'Why did the governor phone you?' he asks, eyes forward. 'Of all people.'

'Because I'd just been visiting him, I assume.'

That nod again. Then: 'So you're not his emergency contact?'

'Why would I be his emergency contact?'

'You tell me.'

He glances away from the road, for a moment. Enough

155

to meet her gaze and read the guilty expression on her face. She holds the silence, determined not to give in to his lazy interrogation tactic. He pulls into her driveway and turns off the engine. Undoes his seat belt but doesn't get out of the car.

The radio is playing some awful pop song. It annoys her and she turns it off.

'I've been to see him before. Noah.'

Charlie doesn't say anything; she turns to look at him.

'How many times?' he asks quietly.

'Four, plus today.'

'Four,' he repeats under his breath. 'When?'

'First one was last January. And then, I don't know. Every few months.'

There's a long pause. A lorry passes on the road behind them, making the car shake.

'Does Griffin know?'

'No.'

'You should tell him. You should have told me.' Charlie looks at her for the first time since they've arrived back, the hurt clear on his face. 'Those times you said you were visiting a friend in Nottingham. That was to see him, wasn't it?'

'Yes. I'm sorry.'

'Why couldn't you tell me? I would have understood.'

'I just . . . I don't know. I felt ashamed. That even after everything he's done, I still want to see him. My logical brain says he should disgust me and I should hate him. But he was my best friend for three years. It doesn't just go away.'

'I get that, Cara. But don't lie to me.'

'Okay. I'm sorry.'

He nods, and she thinks that's it, conversation over, but he pauses, hand on the door.

'What?'

There's clearly more he wants to ask, but he doesn't, just nods one last time, and gets out of the car. Cara follows, lets them both into the house and watches as he takes his shoes off and goes into the kitchen. Head down, deep in thought. She should have told Charlie where she was going, and now she wonders why she didn't. Charlie has never given her reason to doubt him. He's always been supportive, understanding of the demands of her job, of why she's sometimes quiet and doesn't want to talk. Why she sometimes has nightmares, waking with a cry and a jolt. He would have understood her need to face her fears, to come to terms with what Noah had done.

But was that all it was?

When the governor had phoned her and told her the news, the panic in her chest had been real. Worry that he might not survive; anger that the people supposed to protect him were doing such a terrible job. Is that the reaction of a DCI concerned about her witness?

As if reading her mind, her phone rings: the hospital. She pauses. If he's dead, how will she feel? Relief? Closure? Upset?

And if he's alive? What then?

She takes a deep breath. And answers the phone.

157

Chapter 26

Griffin spends all evening at the nick, long after everyone's gone home. Disparate thoughts churn his brain, but work's not the distraction he needs.

His thoughts turn to Brody, and what they did this afternoon in the back of his Land Rover. In work hours, too. None of it good.

He enjoyed it, yes, at the time. But now. Now he's back to feeling shitty. She's worth so much more. Twenty-year-old Griffin would have loved an arrangement like this with Brody, but forty-year-old Griffin? Not so much.

He's had it the other way. He's experienced what sex can be like with someone you love, someone you would give your life for. Mia, even his ex-girlfriend Jess, before that fell apart.

This will too, a little voice in his head tells him, and he gives in to the self-doubt, allowing himself to wallow. He doesn't deserve anything good. He doesn't deserve her.

By the time he gets home, the house is quiet. Cara and Charlie are already in bed, it's past midnight, but there's no way he can sleep.

He watches television in a darkened room, Frank purring next to him, happy to have nocturnal company in the quiet of the night. But Griffin can't focus, flicks programmes mindlessly until he gives up and switches it off.

He sits in darkness.

In the past he would have turned to alcohol to silence his mind. A nice tumbler of whisky or a few beers, but he knows what path that leads him down and he doesn't like it. Instead, he tries to rationalise his thoughts.

Noah Deakin.

When that call came through his first thought was, Good, he's dead. Out of their lives, at last. But the truth is that even dead, he would still haunt him. What Noah did to him, how Mia died. In Griffin's darker moments he thinks about her last minutes on earth. He hears her cries, her screams of pain, calling his name, again and again, and him, hog-tied and defenceless, unable to do anything. He didn't go to Noah's sentencing, was still too ill after being shot, but he's often wondered about visiting him in prison. What would he say? What *could* he say that would help?

The truth is: nothing. So he stayed away. And now he wonders what Cara discussed with him today. How that conversation went.

Griffin's twitchy. And if he can't have alcohol then nicotine will do. He checks his usual places for half-smoked packets and, finding nothing, spots Cara's keys hanging on the hook. He picks them up and heads out to the driveway, opening Cara's car and throwing himself into the passenger seat. He opens the glove box: a packet of cigarettes stare back. Success.

He takes one out, puts it between his lips and lights it, relishing the relief and not giving a shit about smoking in

Cara's car. She did herself, earlier today, so sod it – if it stinks of fags, it's not his fault. He's blowing smoke out of the open door into the cold night air when Dr Ross's words from earlier echo in his mind. *I'm surprised she hasn't gone before.*

He stares at the centre console of her Audi. At the button for the built-in satnav. He presses it, and the map springs into life, showing his current location in the middle of Southampton.

The button calls to him. *NAV.* He presses it, searches under recent locations. The first one that comes up is Nottingham prison, left in there from today, and he runs his finger down the touch screen, scrolling past random postcodes, most with the SO prefix. Places she's visited for work, or in the evening or weekends with Charlie. So far, so boring.

But there. A month ago. There it is. *HMP Nottingham.* He keeps scrolling. Again and again, it pops up. Four in total, until the memory won't go back any further.

Cara had been to visit Noah before. She'd made out today was the first time. She lied, and Griffin doesn't like it.

He grabs the cigarettes and gets out of the car, slamming the door and locking it, lights flashing. He looks up to Cara's bedroom window, where she's sleeping with Charlie. Does he know? Are they conspiring against him, laughing behind his back?

The thought makes his blood boil and he stomps through the side gate into the back garden. He slumps onto the garden bench, smoking furiously. He wants to shout, scream, punch. Maybe even fuck.

But no. Time for change.

He pulls his phone out of his pocket. And before he can give it too much thought he sends a message.

Truth or dare?

Brody will be up; she's a night owl, like him. Sure enough, three little dots start to rotate at the bottom of the screen.

Dare, it says, as he knew it would.

Go on a date with me, he replies.

The two ticks turn blue before he can change his mind and delete it. She starts typing, stops.

Tomorrow night, he writes as a follow-up. *Just me and you. A few drinks. Dinner.* And then because he knows it's not her style. *Nothing fancy.*

He waits. Nothing.

'Bugger,' he hisses under his breath. Now it's going to be awkward tomorrow at the nick and he'll be reduced to partnering with bloody Shenton.

He puts his phone on the bench, face down, while he lights another cigarette.

'You all right, mate?'

Griffin turns and Charlie is standing on the back doorstep, hair askew, feet bare. He squints through his glasses.

'Yeah. Couldn't sleep. You?'

'Nope.'

'Want one?' Griffin holds out the packet and Charlie smiles.

'No, thank you.' He pulls a jumper over his head, then carefully walks out to the bench. He holds up the mug in his hand. 'Camomile tea. Rock and roll.'

'Did you know Cara was visiting Noah Deakin?' Griffin asks. Charlie gives him a cautious look. 'Before today, I mean.'

'Not before tonight, no. She told me earlier.'

Griffin grunts, annoyed. The fact that Charlie didn't know either makes him feel worse, for some reason.

'She was only trying to protect you, Nate.'

'But why does she have to go at all? After what that man did?'

'She has some things to work through. Noah betrayed her. The lies. What he did. It's a lot to get your head around.'

'It's simple to me. He's a serial killer. Let him rot.'

Charlie stays quiet, sipping his tea. Griffin regards his sister's boyfriend in the half-light. Charlie Mills is nothing like Roo, Cara's now ex-husband. Roo was flashy, with his red Mercedes. Once named one of 'Britain's best' by a national newspaper, Roo was ambitious, working all hours as head chef in his restaurant, while Charlie? He seems happy with his lot. He's head of the digital team but it's a job with a ceiling. Nowhere to go beyond that. Not that Charlie seems to mind. He's thoughtful and calming, and Griffin has liked having him around this past year. He's good for Cara. Good for him, too.

'What's keeping you up?' Griffin asks.

'This case. The videos. I watched a few of them, and . . .' His voice trails off. 'I can't get them out of my head. Why do we do this to ourselves? Day in, day out. We must all be crazy.'

'Perhaps we are.'

Charlie smiles. 'I'd feel better if this guy was off the street. Behind bars where he deserves to be, but he's so elusive. There's little to no digital trace on the videos, and whatever there is just leads us back to Morris. And he's a dead end.'

'Literally,' Griffin says with a grin.

Charlie laughs, a quick exhale. 'There was one thing I noticed, from watching the videos. But you probably know this . . .'

'Go on?'

'There are two distinct locations.'

'Two?'

'Yeah. Have a look tomorrow, but . . .' Charlie leans back on the bench, thinking. 'Most are in that boring white room, but the early tapes are somewhere completely different.'

'The concrete pit.'

'Exactly. The white room has a wooden floor, white painted brick walls, while the pit is all grey concrete. Both have a metal ring drilled into the wall – but it's more important in the pit, where there's no doors or windows, nothing else keeping them restrained.'

'Did you look at the dates? Does the killer move partway through?'

'Absolutely. Terry Gregory was the first in that white room, so 2014 onwards. Before that, it's the concrete pit. The tech looks better too. Shot from the corner of the room, rather than on a wobbly tripod next to them.'

'You think they upgraded? Got some cash. Got serious?'

'I guess so.'

'Fucking hell.' Griffin lights a new cigarette from the old.

'Do you think he's going to keep killing?' Charlie asks.

'I think it's likely. Why would he stop?'

'Conscience. Fear of getting caught?'

'A killer like this? No chance.'

'So what does that mean, Griffin? He could be looking at his next target now. Maybe he's got someone already.'

'Maybe,' Griffin says, darkly.

Charlie slumps back on the bench. The two of them sit in contemplative quiet for a moment, listening to the screech of an owl, the lone car on the road. Until their silence is disturbed by the beep of Griffin's phone.

Griffin looks at the message.

Okay, Brody says. And that's it.

He smiles, despite himself.

'What's that?' Charlie asks.

'I asked Brody out on a date.'

'Alana Brody? And I assume she said yes. Look at your face, mate. Grinning ear to ear.'

'I know.' Griffin tries to stop smiling, but can't. 'We've been . . . you know . . . hooking up a few times. And I thought I'd try something a little more conventional.'

'Good for you.' Charlie knocks him on the arm, spilling a bit of his camomile tea. 'Who'd have thought it. Nate Griffin. Asking women out on dates rather than no-commitment sex.'

'I know. Maybe I am a grown-up, after all.' Charlie's still smiling at him. 'Stop that. It's getting creepy.'

Charlie laughs, getting to his feet. He throws the remainder of his tea out onto the lawn, watching Griffin as he smokes his cigarette down to the butt and mashes it into a plant pot, leaving the end crumpled and dirty.

'That's going to piss off your sister,' Charlie comments.

'I know. Isn't it great?'

Charlie snorts, waiting for Griffin to go back into the house, closing and locking the back door behind him. 'Maybe not so mature, after all,' Charlie whispers in the silence of the house, and Griffin smiles.

He heads up to bed, trailing the smell of cigarettes. When it comes to annoying your sister, there is no expiration date.

Chapter 27

Do you know how long a human body can survive without food? I do. Forty-two days, six hours. And counting.

It's a fascinating process. Without food, fatigue sets in. Irritability, anger, lack of concentration, but that soon fades. Within hours, the body will start to eat itself, consuming energy stores within – carbohydrates, fats, even the protein part of tissue.

Metabolism slows, the body can't regulate its temperature, and the immune system weakens, until there is nothing left for the body to consume except muscle. And when that happens, things are bad.

For the heart is a muscle – and that shit will kill you. Assuming the electrolyte imbalance doesn't finish you off first.

I lean forward, squint at the screen. I've been watching this guy for over a month. Locked in this tiny room, with only the clothes on his back and a bottle of water every few days. Dehydration will kill you quicker – three days at most. And we can't have that.

At first, he paced. Shouted. Pummelled his fists against

the door. As they all do for the first forty-eight. But this guy was different. Nobody came. And he got quieter, and weaker, and thinner, wasting away to this bag of bones I am watching today.

Trev and Ty have a sweepstake. A bet on when he'll die. But not me. No, I am gripped. The shivering, the stomach pain, the diarrhoea and the vomiting. We've left it all in there; the smell is repulsive, but I doubt he notices. He doesn't notice much, anymore.

He's not moved in hours, his eyes closed, his body still. I make a call, and after a few moments, the door is opened and Trev steps inside, his hand over his mouth. Trev retches, body convulsing, then quickly walks across to the bundle of rags in the corner, nudges it with his foot.

The man opens his eyes. Looks up with the slightest move of his head. He opens his mouth, stretching his chapped lips. A plea. Desperation.

Trev looks up to the camera, knowing I'm watching. He holds up a fist; he's asking, should I? One hard punch and this guy would be toast.

I lean forward, press the button on the intercom.

'Leave him,' I say.

Trev drops the bottle of water at his feet and walks out.

The man makes no attempt to escape, I doubt he even can. He just looks up to the camera. No more than skin and bone, his hair thinned, body covered in sores. A pathetic sight.

'Please,' he mouths.

'Tell me your name,' I ask. But he doesn't reply.

I look down, turning my attention to the paperwork. To the photographs, the police report, the acquittal. The reason this man is here.

166

I saw this one on the books, and I felt the tug. The moment when I imagine doing the forbidden act. Wouldn't it be fun?

The brief was specific – this man must starve. Slowly, painfully.

Exactly as he did to her.

DAY 5

TUESDAY

Chapter 28

That night, Cara dreams. Of flat 213; the heat, the flies. A fridge containing a severed head. A bedroom with a bloodstained mattress and a blue plastic drum in the corner.

A serial killer copying Dahmer.

She wakes with a jolt and a gasp, her T-shirt soaked with sweat. It's still early, and she lies in the semi-darkness, in that strange state between nightmare and wakening. It's been months since she dreamed of that; it doesn't take a psychotherapist to tell her why. Because she's welcomed him back into her life, befriended him even, and her psyche is telling her no.

She's fully awake now, and shifts in the bed, moving closer to Charlie, taking comfort in his warmth. He's on his side, facing towards her; she can just make him out. The mess of his hair, needing a cut, dark curls falling over his forehead. The flicker of his eyelashes, the relaxed gape of his mouth.

This, him, their relationship – it amazes her. How she's managed to make it last – more than a year now. She was working on their anniversary, a familiar tale, but he didn't complain. Her favourite takeaway when she got home, the house lit with candles, Griffin banished for the night. Small things pepper their everyday: a quick kiss passing in the corridor at work, the touch of his hand in hers as they watch television. He never pressures her, never questions. A steady presence, day after day, letting her know how much she's loved.

And she loves him. She knows she does. At the beginning it was that buzz of excitement, the flush when she saw him. Wanting to talk to him, talk *about* him all the time. But now, that love has matured into something more steadfast. A gentle anchor, a reassurance. That whatever she does, he has her back.

She leans into him now and he mutters in his sleep, rolling over to his back. She snuggles up into his chest, his arm going around her automatically. A fumbled kiss on her forehead before he's even opened his eyes.

'Charlie,' she whispers. She smiles in anticipation of what she's going to say. 'Do you still want me to move in?'

'Hmm?'

'Wake up.' His eyes open a fraction, still asleep, lost in his dreams. 'I want to move in with you.' They open fully now, a slight furrow on his forehead.

A mumble. 'What?'

'I love you. I want to live with you.'

At last, he seems to be awake. He lifts his head, runs his hand through his hair. 'Are you serious?'

'Yes, a hundred per cent. I don't know why we haven't done this sooner. Do you still want to?'

'Yes. I mean, definitely yes. I can't think of anything I want to do more.'

She reaches up and kisses him. Even his morning breath is inoffensive as the kiss turns into a full-blown snog, as his hands roam under her T-shirt, tugging it over her head. As her knickers come off, his boxers, as she straddles him, his hands on her hips as they move, she thinks, there are worse ways to start a day.

With him, here, together.

They spend too long, lost in each other, to the point she doesn't have time for breakfast. They rush – showers, getting dressed, a hastily drunk mug of coffee – and out to the car, Cara noting with interest that Griffin has already up and left.

She makes a call as Charlie drives; the governor confirmed last night that approval had come through for Noah's transfer and he now adds that the move is complete. Noah Deakin now resides in the Burrell Ward of the Royal South Hants Hospital, under the care of HMP Winchester, at her request. His tone is arctic, but she doesn't care: she needs Noah here, close.

His condition is described as serious, but stable. He has regained consciousness overnight, but he's not out of the woods. The stab wounds were nasty, but fortunately shallow, hitting his left flank and spleen, with a superficial injury to his lower bowel. His spleen had to be removed. Along with a fractured cheekbone and broken ribs, he has a long way to go.

'Not fit for police interview,' the governor confirms. 'And not receiving visitors, he's still an inmate,' he finishes bluntly, and hangs up.

'Arsehole,' Cara mutters. Charlie glances across, questioning. 'The governor. Won't let me see him.'

Charlie grunts but doesn't reply.

The team is all assembled by the time Cara arrives. Waiting, for her.

'Give me an update,' she says. 'And for God's sake, some-one get me a coffee.'

Shenton scurries off, always the obedient, while Jamie shuffles his papers. Griffin refuses to meet her eye.

'Please tell me we have something?' Cara almost begs, thanking Shenton as he places a steaming hot mug of coffee in front of her.

'We're no further forward than we were last night,' Jamie confirms. 'Still waiting on the lab for results on both the semen sample and the trace on the sheeting. Traffic cams have come up blank,' he adds, receiving a confirmatory nod from Shenton. 'Whoever he is, he knew where the black spots were.'

'And how did he know where we were?' Cara asks. The team falls quiet, glancing between them. 'It's odd, don't you agree? He happens to dump a body at the exact same time and place that we're there? That can't be a coincidence?' The team is still silent. 'Who knew we were going?'

'You can't possibly be insinuating that one of us is involved?' Griffin says.

'No, Griffin,' she says sarcastically. 'But someone knew. Jamie – you were driving a pool car, right? And that had a tracker on it. Who has access to that?'

'I'll find out.'

'Plus this person knew that Stephen Allen had got off the rape charge. Released last week, goes out on the piss Thursday night, and bam, he's abducted. That's fast work.'

'Everyone knew he'd got off,' Griffin retaliates. She's frustrated by the lack of progress, but he's getting on her nerves.

171

'Who was *first* to know?'

'Journalists, anyone who works at Winchester Crown Court, his lawyers, the prosecution.'

'The police.'

'Boss . . .' Jamie says tentatively.

'All his victims were either cleared of their crimes or about to be investigated. How did he know that? How does he find them so quickly?'

She looks out at the baffled expressions of her team. 'Look,' she says, softening. 'I'm not saying it's definitely a cop. I just think we should consider that it might be. We took our eye off the ball once. Let's not do it again.

'Thank you, everyone. Crack on. You know what you're doing, shout when we have a lead.' She glances at her brother. 'Griffin, my office. Please.'

She notices him widen his eyes at Brody, pissing her off even more.

'Now,' she barks.

Chapter 29

'What?' Griffin snaps as he closes the door behind him. He can barely look at her, he's so angry. 'There's no need to be pissy.'

'You're one to talk,' Cara says, sitting down behind the desk. 'Your behaviour this morning is unprofessional. All you've done is swipe at me.'

'Unprofessional?' Griffin crosses his arms over his chest, pulling himself up to his full height. 'You – a DCI – have been visiting Noah Deakin regularly over the past year. You're telling me that was on official police business?'

Cara goes red. 'That is none of your concern.'

'How? How can you say that? That man killed my wife. He tied me up, beat me, left me for dead. And you say that has nothing to do with me?' Griffin's aware he's shouting, but he's furious, he can't stop. 'You're my sister. You're supposed to be on my side.'

'I am—'

'How can you say that when you've been willingly sitting in a room with the man for the past year? What did you talk about? Did you laugh with him? Joke? *Flirt*?'

'Nothing *ever* happened between Noah and I—'

'But you wanted it to, didn't you?'

She looks at him, hatred in her eyes. 'Fuck you, Nate. You think this is all about you? Well, here's some news – it's not. You weren't the only one damaged by that man. I lost something too. My best friend. My partner.'

'If you were so close to him, why didn't you know?'

'You think I don't ask myself that? Every night, before I go to sleep? I was the SIO, and I didn't see it. I didn't see what he was doing.' Griffin watches with horror as she starts to cry, but she carries on shouting, her voice breaking with every word. 'That's why I went to see him. After he was put away, I built him up in my head to be this master manipulator. This evil demon.'

'He is—'

'He isn't. He's just a man. A fucked-up, broken mess of a man who did a series of horrible things. We caught him. We locked him up. And he's spent the last three years being beaten, isolated and destroyed, and now it's possible he might die. Can't you at least have some compassion for that? A tiny bit, deep inside you.'

Griffin shakes his head. In disbelief, in refusal of what his sister is asking.

'We were lucky, Nate,' she says, her voice softer. 'We had a mother and a father who loved us. Noah – fuck knows what happened to him, but I know he ended up in a children's home. Can you imagine what that was like?'

'We didn't have it so easy either, Cara,' Griffin replies. 'Our dad killed himself when I was sixteen. You were eighteen, but you didn't see us slash women open, hang them from trees.' She flinches. 'You're being selective in what you choose to remember.' Griffin punches a finger to his chest. 'I'm not. I can't. Every day I wake up and my wife is dead. Because of him.'

'I know—'

'She was raped, by him.'

'I know—'

'I was beaten, by him. And still you go to see him. I should report you. Get you suspended. Anything, to keep you away from him.'

'Don't you fucking dare.'

'Why shouldn't I?'

'You're one to talk.' Her eyes flash and she points out to the incident room. 'Don't think I don't know.'

His stomach drops into free fall. 'About what?'

'About you and Brody. Fucking. And in police time, as well.'

Griffin feels his face growing hot. 'Leave Alana out of this.'

'She's your DC. An officer under your command. Do you know how many rules you're breaking? You could be fired. Charged with misconduct in a public office. And you talk about reporting me?' She scoffs. 'How long has it been going on? Is it just in your Land Rover, or in the office, too? I hope she was a good shag, because that's your whole fucking career.'

'Shut your fucking mouth, Cara.'

'You come at me, all holier than thou, and that's what you're up to? You've got a fucking nerve—'

She stops, interrupted by a knock on the door. Neither of them moves, glaring at each other across the desk.

The knock comes again.

'What?' Cara shouts.

Jamie opens the door, stepping inside. 'First of all,' he says. 'The whole team can hear you.'

Griffin glances behind him through the door. Everyone's paused, staring.

'And secondly,' Jamie continues. 'The lab called. The semen on Stephen Allen has come back. We've got a match.'

Chapter 30

The raid is fast, the arrest swift. It takes three burly officers twenty minutes to get this guy in cuffs, he's so big.

Jamie watches as they escort Trevor Brown to the police van. He's huge – taller than Jamie's six-two, and nearly twice as wide. Muscles on his muscles, head perched directly on his shoulders, no neck at all. He's wearing a black T-shirt, black jeans, black trainers. Nearly the same outfit as the guy in the video, minus the balaclava. Jamie would put money on it being him.

Jamie waits for the police van to leave, then gets out of his car, heading towards the house. It's in a nice part of Southampton, a new build with lush green lawns and small leafy trees, still encased in their protective plastic tubes. Clearly making some money from his endeavours. Jamie dons shoe covers and gloves and goes inside.

Money can buy a nice house, but it can't change the man – the place is disgusting. Sparsely furnished, the living room is little more than a reclining easy chair and a massive, wide-screen TV on the wall, an overflowing ashtray and empty beer bottles on a wooden box he's using as a coffee table. A line of dirt shows a pathway on the plush cream carpet walking from the living room to the kitchen, where piles of takeaway containers spill out of the bin.

The place smells foul – a mixture of curry and day-old sweat, the latter intensifying as Jamie opens the door to the back room to discover a home gym. He steps inside for a moment, breathing through his mouth. Weights that no human should be able to lift are arranged around a dumb-bell. Jamie couldn't tell you the names of most of this equipment, but it's clear where the man makes his muscles.

His mobile rings, he answers it.

'What have you got there?' Griffin says. 'The incredible hulk has just been booked into custody. In a shitter of a mood.'

'Not much yet,' Jamie replies, going back into the kitchen. He opens the cupboard doors, finding them empty except for beer. 'Oh, here's something.' He picks up the boxes of pills. 'Testovis, Stanozolol, Trenbolone. That mean anything to you?'

'Wait a sec, I'll google. Spell that?' Jamie does. 'Okay, so you've got testosterone and anabolic steroids. That's not going to help with his anger issues. Have you been upstairs yet?'

'Griffin, this house is repulsive.'

'I'm going to be trapped in a room with this guy, least you can do is check his bedroom.'

'Ugh.' He's got a point, and Jamie trudges upwards. 'You okay? That was a hell of a barney you and Cara were having.'

'Yeah. Brother and sister stuff.'

'It sounded a little more than that,' Jamie says, not wanting to repeat that he and the whole of the team heard every bitter word, Brody turning red for the last part. 'You might want to speak to Alana.'

A pause. 'I will,' Griffin says quietly.

But Jamie's too distracted to interrogate his friend properly. His eyes stop on a photograph next to the bed. It's in an elegant silver frame, and seems out of place in such insalubrious surroundings.

'Does Trevor Brown have a wife?' Jamie asks Griffin, picking up the photo and peering at it. It's a younger Trevor, more hair, skinny, his arm around a pretty brunette.

'Only family is the brother, as far as we know.'

Jamie considers the photo, then puts it in an evidence bag, placing it next to the door to take with them. Might be useful.

'How are we going with the brother?' Jamie asks. Tyler Brown, two years older than Trevor. Likely the second man on the video. Registered address: the house next door. Empty.

'Still in the wind. But we know his number plate, we'll find him.'

'Keep me updated. Oh, here's something dodgy.'

Jamie crouches next to the unmade, crumpled bed, looking at the row of DVDs next to a television. He picks up a few, studying the spines. 'Porn. And lots of it.'

'You're sure?'

Jamie opens a few of the cases – the matching discs stare back. 'Yeah, looks that way. But it's hardcore. Bondage, whips and chains, not your average Friday night.'

'Not yours maybe.' Griffin chuckles. 'Keep looking. Call me back.'

'Will do.'

Jamie pushes his phone in his pocket, reflecting on their

friendship. Griffin isn't someone he would have chosen to call a mate, but fate had thrown them together and, since getting to know him, he's found Nate Griffin to be a mass of contradictions. Kind, but brash. Quick-thinking, but impulsive. Honest to a fault, but never gives much away. Jamie's come to like him. Even if he does have an annoying habit of telling Jamie what to do.

He flicks through the rest of the DVDs. Threesomes, ball gags, one of the boxes declares 'girl on girl action', but nothing illegal. They have the snuff films; they can pin him on that and hope that he'll talk, but Jamie wants to find something here that'll take them right to the killer's lair.

There's no way the murders have been carried out in this house. Sound carries in a small housing estate like this one and Jamie's sure his neighbours wouldn't hesitate to call the police at the slightest infraction. He checks the wardrobe – clothes balled up at the bottom, a few shirts dangling pathetically on wire hangers at the top. He opens the first drawer, a mass of monochrome underwear, but then, at the back – a wooden box. Little baggies of white powder inside.

'Nice,' Jamie mutters, putting the lot into an evidence bag, and heading back into the hallway. He checks the next few doors – two more bedrooms, both completely empty, and a filthy bathroom, a pair of soiled white boxers pride of place in the middle of the floor. Jamie wrinkles his nose and closes the door firmly behind him.

He stands in the hallway, surveying the scene. There's nothing here. It feels like this house was bought on a whim, barely lived in by a man with little to his name. There's no laptop, no phone. None of the crap and paper and detritus that people need to wade through life. This guy is a ghost.

Jamie frowns and looks to his left. On the other side

of this wall is a garage. Jamie starts walking, back to the kitchen, looking for the door that leads through. Sure enough, there it is. He'd been distracted before, but he turns the key and steps into the darkness. He gropes around for a switch, flicking it on and blinking in the light of a thousand LEDs.

'Well, hello,' he whispers. To the brand new, sparkling white BMW 8 Series.

Chapter 31

It's definitely him, no doubt about it. The man in the videos. Griffin gets a chill seeing him up close. Griffin's a big guy, but this bloke? Different league.

He sits down opposite, Shenton by his side. He asked Brody to join him, but she wouldn't meet his eye, muttering a solitary 'no'. Griffin wonders how much of the row with Cara she heard. How much apologising he's going to have to do and whether that promise of a date is now off the table. He feels the familiar drag of failure, internally cursing himself for letting his sister get to him in that way. They've argued before – of course they have – but never at work. And never about something that matters so much to both of them. He can't understand Cara's empathy towards that psychopath. Never will.

But there's no time to worry about that now. Not with a suspect to interview.

'DS Griffin, DC Shenton,' Griffin begins after the usual caution. 'For the benefit of the video, please state your names.'

'Thomas Sutton,' the solicitor stutters.

'Trevor Brown.' Their suspect speaks in a deep baritone. He watches them, as motionless as a rock, eyes interested.

They bide their time, take it easy. Place the bulky folder on the table, but don't open it. The solicitor stares at it, sweating. He looks more nervous than the suspect, twitching and glancing at his client.

Griffin opens the folder to the first page. It's a photograph from the crime scene on Sunday, Stephen Allen's body laid out on the concrete.

The solicitor recoils. Brown doesn't move; doesn't even blink.

'This is Stephen Allen,' Griffin begins. 'You've been arrested for his murder.' He turns the photograph around. 'Do you recognise him?'

'Hard to tell from that,' Brown says. And then he smirks.

Griffin's unperturbed. Smirk all you like, big guy, he thinks. Just you wait.

'Mr Brown, do you know how we found you?'

Brown stares.

'You used to be a police officer. Back in 2008. Short-lived career, lasted less than a year, but enough for us to have your biologicals on file. And your DNA was a match. To semen we found in Stephen Allen's mouth.' Griffin pauses. Lets that sink in. 'Were you and Mr Allen in a relationship?'

That gets a reaction. 'I'm no fag,' he says, placing two meaty hands on the table with a thump.

'So how did your semen get in his mouth?'

Brown stares at them.

'Would you like to know what we think happened? We think you were paid to force Mr Allen to . . . what's the best way of putting this?'

'Suck your cock,' Shenton says.

'Yes, thank you, DC Shenton. Suck your cock. And after you came in his mouth, you beat him, so severely that you broke his jaw and his cheekbone. Before shoving something large into his anus so many times you ruptured his rectum. Is that what happened, Mr Brown?'

'No comment,' Brown says.

'Then you strangled him, wrapped him in plastic, and dumped him out the back of the Velvet Oasis strip club. Is that right? If you can provide another explanation, we'd love to hear it.'

'No comment.'

'Bit of an oversight though. Leaving something as obvious as your own semen in his mouth. As an ex-cop you must have known that would be a giveaway. Were you trying to get caught?' A thought occurs to Griffin. 'Or did you assume Stephen Allen would be disposed of like the rest of them? That his body would never see the light of day?'

'No comment.'

But the corner of Trevor Brown's eye twitches. A tell. Griffin knows he's hit paydirt. 'Did someone else dump the body without your knowledge? Your brother, Tyler, maybe?'

The tic again. 'No comment.'

'Are you angry about that? Angry enough to tell us where your brother is?'

'Go fuck yourself.'

More of a reaction. Griffin smiles. 'Moving on. Could you tell us what you do for a living, Mr Brown?'

'I'm a bouncer.'

'Yes, you are. Does being a bouncer pay well?'

'A bit.'

'Does it pay so well you have forty-seven thousand pounds in your bank account?'

He takes out a piece of paper and pushes it across the table. Brown stares at it. 'We got hold of your bank records. Isn't that nice? Some banks can be uncooperative, but HSBC, why – they handed those right over. Murder is a serious business, it tends to make financial institutions twitchy. All the better for us. Can you explain this money, Mr Brown? Because we can't. We can see your salary as a bouncer come in, see that? Right there? But the rest, it seems to have arrived via cash payments. Regularly, a couple of thousand a month. And that's not mentioning the top of the range BMW in your garage. That's eighty grand, easy. How have you got so much cash?'

'Tips,' he replies.

'Tips? You must be good at your job.'

'I am.'

'Good for you. Because it wouldn't be anything to do with this, would it?'

Griffin pulls up a laptop and places it on the table. He loads the video, presses play and turns it around.

Brown's eye goes into overdrive as he watches. The solicitor does the same, but his expression is different, his eyes frantically blinking, his mouth open with horror.

'This is a man called Gareth Stokes. He went missing a little over a year ago, after being accused of some pretty nasty crimes involving illegal dog fighting.' Griffin can't see the screen but he's watched this one before. And the sound of the dog's barking tells him exactly the point they've got to. The begging escalates, followed by muffled growling and the sound of flesh being torn from bones. The solicitor has gone white; he looks away from the screen, his hand over his mouth.

'But what's really interesting in this video, is this tattoo,

185

here.' Griffin takes a photograph out of the file, a shot of the attacker holding the dog, blown up to twice the size. 'Distinctive, don't you agree? And identical to the one that you yourself have in the exact same position on your right arm?'

'Lots of people have those tattoos.'

'Sure. But not a lot of people look like you. You may have been wearing a balaclava, Mr Brown, but you're distinctive. And this isn't the only shot.' Griffin takes out photographs, and one after the other he places them in front of Mr Brown and his solicitor.

'This is Terence Gregory, he suffocated, his jaw broken. This is James Harvey, Jimmy to his friends. Nasty little drug dealer. Had his leg broken, then injected with something that looks to me like an overdose of some sort of morphine. Whatever it was, he didn't last long. This is Keith Thompson, Roger Harris – the list goes on. And each time – there you are. Sometimes with someone else – your older brother, Tyler, maybe? – but always you. Do you agree, Mr Brown?'

He pulls the photos closer, looking at them with a smile. 'No comment.'

'Where's Tyler, Mr Brown?'

'No comment.'

'Because we've been to his house and he's not there. We've put an all-units alert out on him and his car, but it would save us some time if you could tell us.' Griffin slaps down photo after photo, stills from the videos, this time another man with Trevor. Killing, stabbing, torture.

The solicitor retches, then runs out of the room with his hand over his mouth. Brown watches him go, then turns to Griffin with a smile.

'Some people don't have the stomach for it.'

186

'And you do?'

Brown sits back, crosses his arms over his massive chest. 'I need my solicitor present to answer any more questions.'

'Then let me do the talking. Trevor Brown, you are further arrested for the murder of Gareth Stokes, Terence Gregory, Keith Thompson, Roger Harris and James Harvey. And don't get comfortable – those are just the names I remember now. There will be more when we've double-checked those tapes. You do not have to say anything but it may harm your defence if you do not mention when questioned, something you later rely on in court. Everything you do say may be given in evidence. And there will be more where those came from. Do you understand?' Griffin leans across the table. 'Do you understand that you will be charged with these murders and we have more than enough to try and then convict you? You will never see the light of day again.'

'Whatever you say, matey.'

Griffin leans back, appraising their suspect.

'But I don't think for a moment that you're the mastermind behind this operation. Look at you. Any brain cells you once had will have rotted away from all those steroids you've been taking. You've never had an original thought in your life. No, someone else is behind this. Give us their name. Give us a location.'

Brown stares. 'No comment.'

There's a light tap on the door. Griffin looks away from Brown, expecting to see the solicitor return, but instead Jamie appears.

'We've got it,' Jamie says. 'Be ready.' And he leaves again.

Griffin grins, gathering the photos back into the folder. 'We don't need you to talk. Because you know that stupid car of yours? That brand-new BMW with the alloy wheels

187

and the leather seats and the top of the range satnav? Well, that car is continuously monitoring everything about itself. What systems are working, tyre pressures, speed, engine temp. And exactly where you are.' Brown's eye twitches. 'We've downloaded everything. We know where you've been going every day.' Griffin gets to his feet. 'And we're going there now. Interview concluded fifteen twenty-four. Thank you, Mr Brown. For your help.'

And with that, Griffin and Shenton leave the room.

Chapter 32

'Trevor Brown doesn't go anywhere else in that car,' Charlie is explaining on the phone as Cara races out of her office. 'The telemetry has him driving to work, his house, and this other location. And he goes there a lot.'

'How often?'

'Every day over the past week. Sometimes he stays there for half an hour, sometimes all day. I've sent the coordinates to Frost, he's with the team now.'

Cara thanks Charlie and hangs up as she arrives in the briefing room, sneaking in the back and leaning against the wall. Sergeant Frost is at the front, talking to a full house of burly coppers in black, the air thick with aftershave and testosterone.

'We're in the dark as to the layout of the building,' Frost is saying. Like his team, he's of sturdy build, biceps bulging out of a black T-shirt, an impressive sprout of chest hair poking out of the top. 'Five thousand square foot spread over three floors, in varying states of repair. Multiple entry and exit points.'

There's a collective groan from the team.

'On the plus side,' Frost continues, 'the area is empty, so we have zero risk to unsuspecting members of the public. We can surround the building easily, ensure no one's going far. But they will see us coming, so we'll need to go in hard and fast.'

Intel have done as much research as they can. The building in question is an abandoned pub, once owned by a company called FQC Brewers, going bust in the nineties and left to rot. The only director recorded on Companies House is dead – the paper trail ends there.

'DCI Elliott,' Frost concludes, 'is there anything you'd like to add?'

All eyes turn. She stands up straight and clears her throat. 'First of all, thank you for responding so quickly. Sergeant Frost has gone over the basics, but the reality is we don't know what you're going to face in there. From the intel we have gleaned from the videos, we're looking at a building with multiple small, locked rooms, all with CCTV. We don't believe there will be many suspects in the building, possibly only the brother Tyler Brown, but we know you'll be facing a number of weapons. From baseball bats to knives to tasers. We haven't seen evidence that they have firearms on the property, but be prepared for the worst.' She pauses, taking in the army of fidgety men, all desperate for the off. 'Good luck.'

'You know your positions,' Frost says. 'We depart in ten.'

The room explodes into action; Frost makes his way to Cara.

'I assume you'll be in the control room?'

'Yes, but my team will be down there, standing by. Once you give the all-clear, they'll go in. See exactly what we're working with before we call the SOCOs.'

Frost nods his approval. 'I've heard about the videos. It'll be an honour to catch this guy.'

'We can only hope,' Cara replies, and he leaves. She makes her way to the front of the now empty room, looking at the outside shots of the old pub. It would have been glorious in its day – red brick walls, a few gold letters from the Wagon & Horses sign remaining, high windows and traces of bright blue paint across the front. Cara imagines a large pub garden instead of the scrubland, a dry-stone wall where now there are only rocks.

Every window is covered with brown chipboard, the glass smashed. It's hard to see this as anything other than an abandoned pub, and initial reports from the OP – the hastily set up observation post – say there is no sign of movement at the scene.

Frost is one of the best, the team is armed and ready to use deadly force, but Cara can't help unease settling in her stomach. This guy has killed for over twelve years, unnoticed. Fifteen people, dead, with no sign of their bodies.

It can't be this easy.

It can't be.

Chapter 33

Jamie and Griffin follow the armed response team down to the patch of wasteland and the abandoned pub. They keep their distance, Jamie driving in silence, worried about what they might find. The wasteland is surrounded by a high chain-link fence, rusted barbed wire around the top. The main gates are locked shut with a chain and a padlock, but it's quickly and quietly breached, the AFOs heading inside.

Jamie pulls up on the outskirts, radio in hand. He winds down the window to silence, the only sound the growl of cars on the main road some distance away. It's an isolated spot, perfect for what any would-be killer might have in mind.

He looks across to his colleague: Griffin's brow is furrowed as he reaches into his pocket, pulling out a packet of cigarettes. He opens the car door and gets out, a dark figure against the impending night, his face lit as he bends down to light the cigarette. He takes a long inhale then rests against the car bonnet, staring at the old building, lurking in the dusk.

Jamie climbs out of the car. The radio is still silent and he imagines the rumble of heavy boots, the AFOs crouching behind their rifles, helmets on, ninjas shrouded in the darkness.

'Twenty quid we don't get him,' Griffin mutters.

Jamie shakes his head. 'I'm not going to take those odds.'

With a crackle the radio bursts into life. The authorisation is given; shouts echo in the cool night air, bouncing between the buildings. Incomprehensible, multiple calls of 'Armed Police!' battle as the team splits, searching every corner, taking down every door in search of their quarry. Shouts, crashing as locks break, as the raid is carried out with utmost precision.

Until the quiet. A voice on the radio: Cara back in the control room.

'Update, Bravo Whisky One?'

'Area is clear. All in order.'

'State nine?'

'Negative.'

No arrests. There's no one there. Until the voice speaks again.

'One male, unconscious, not breathing. Suspected G28.'

A dead body. Griffin drops his cigarette on the concrete, stubs it under foot and strides towards the pub. Jamie follows.

When they get there, it's hard to tell what of the destruction was caused by the team, and what was already there. Doors are off their hinges, detritus lies across the floor – wood, plasterboard, glass, all under foot. In the main saloon, the ceiling has fallen in showing bare rafters overhead, but the once-varnished wooden bar remains, a poignant reminder of how lovely this place could have been.

Jamie takes his torch out of his tac vest and switches it on; behind him Griffin does the same.

The torch does nothing to dispel the butterflies in Jamie's stomach. It lights his way with an eerie glow, catching the AFOs as they leave, guns down, dispirited. He hears a shout from a distant part of the building and follows the sound, towards an old wooden staircase, down to the basement. The shadows dance. Every nerve in Jamie's body tells him to stay away, get out. Get out now.

When he reaches the basement, everything changes. The corridors are narrow, the ceilings low, Jamie has to stoop to walk through. The walls are all painted white, and the floorboards are clear. Someone has gone to some effort to make this area serviceable. And clean – there's a strong smell of bleach throughout.

Frost greets him at the start of the corridor. 'Upstairs is clear, and a health and safety nightmare, don't go up. But I suspect this is what you're looking for.' He moves out of the way, shining his torch down a long corridor, doors lining the side.

'You've got four rooms here. We suspect they were once storage for the pub, but they've obviously been modified. Heavy locks on the doors, full security system.' He shines his torch up, showing Jamie the camera in the corner of the ceiling. 'And what's more – electricity.'

Frost leans over and clicks a switch; instantly the corridor is awash with bright light. Jamie blinks.

'Probably siphoned from the power line behind.'

'Resourceful,' Jamie says, as if they didn't know that already about their killer. 'Where's the G28?'

'Last room. Enjoy that one. It's not pretty.'

Griffin starts to walk down the corridor, while Jamie hesitates, taking a step into the nearest room.

Seeing it in person does nothing to dispel the horror they've observed in the videos. The ceiling is higher, Jamie no longer has to stoop, but the walls close in as he sees the metal ring concreted into the brick wall. The overhead strip highlights the stains on the floorboards: dark brown, dark red. Blood. Some fresh, some not. It reeks of bleach, making Jamie's head spin.

He hears his name called, echoing down the corridor. He needs no further encouragement to leave this godforsaken cell and follows the sound into the room at the end.

As he gets closer, the reek of bleach fades away, replaced by something else. A smell of death, of decay, getting stronger the closer he gets. He gags as he steps into the room, pressing the back of his hand against his mouth and nose, swallowing it down.

The room is the same as the others, claustrophobic and close, made worse by the pervading smell. It sticks in his mouth, his nose; every part of him screams to leave. That to look will cause him irreparable harm.

'Hoxton!' Griffin barks, his voice hoarse. Jamie takes a step closer, seeing the horror at last.

It's a man, although it's hard to recognise the body as human. He's scrunched up in the corner of the room, knees tucked to his chest, head back, mouth open, leaning against the wall. His hair is straggly. The body is covered in filthy rags, once clothes, now destroyed. It's not hard to make out cause of death.

The body is little more than a skeleton. Bones protrude, covered in paper-thin skin, angry and jutting. Jamie wants to puke. He wants to cry, scream with rage, punch something. He turns away, taking in the rest of the room, the cause of the smell becoming clear. The only sanitation is a single bucket in the opposite corner, full and overflowing with the most disgusting stench Jamie has ever experienced. Next to it lies a pile of plastic bottles. Must be more than forty, fifty even.

'I can't stand this,' Griffin says, his voice thick, and he leaves, quick footsteps echoing down the corridor. Alone, the strip light flickering overhead, Jamie tries to imagine what this man's last days would have been like. Starving to death, in this filth. No way out. Only his thoughts to keep him company, day in, day out. What did he do? What was his crime? There is nothing that could excuse this, surely?

Jamie needs to get out of there. But an impossible curiosity threatens. He's studied the misper reports. Maybe he knows this guy. Maybe he can put a name to the face, give them a head start on who this actually is.

He steps closer. Pinching his nose, he crouches down, his face level with the man's, desperately searching for recognition in the gaunt cheekbones, the scraggly hair. A fly buzzes around Jamie's head; he swipes it away, wobbling slightly, resting his hand on the wall behind to regain his balance.

And in that moment, Jamie's face next to the victim's, the worst possible thing happens. The man opens his eyes.

Chapter 34

Griffin freezes when he hears the screaming. Then Jamie's voice, shouting down the radio.

'State zero, emergency assistance NOW! Victim is alive, repeat, alive. Ambulance towards. NOW!'

Griffin turns, sprinting back to the room, stopping horrified in the doorway. It looks like dawn of the dead, a skeleton come to life, the mouth opening and closing wordlessly, eyes gaping. Jamie is standing in the middle of the room, the radio against his ear, his spare hand raking his hair.

He turns and looks at Griffin. 'How?' he screams, his voice breaking. 'How is he still alive?'

The ambulances arrive, adding to the number of ashen faces vomiting outside the old pub. After some debate, the hardier of the paramedics carry the stretcher inside, and emerge with the man wrapped under a blanket. Two older women who look like they've seen it all.

One of them turns to Griffin as she leaves.

'Don't hold your breath,' she says, slamming the back door after herself, the blue lights hooning off into the night.

Griffin takes a long breath in. He lets it out slowly with a long, 'Fuuuuck.'

'You're telling me,' Jamie says, next to him. 'When he opened his eyes – fucking hell. I thought I was going to have a heart attack.'

'All I heard was the screaming,' Griffin says. 'You big wuss.'

Jamie laughs, slightly hysterically. 'You weren't there, you fucker. It was *The Walking Dead*. All that shit and piss and vomit. Oh, fuck.' He bends, resting his hands on his knees, head down. His whole body sways.

'Here. Mate, sit down. Before you fall.'

Griffin helps Jamie to the ground, then sits next to him on the rough concrete of the car park. Jamie remains still, his head between his knees, taking deep breaths.

'You going to be sick?'

'Thought I might pass out.' Jamie lifts his head, looks at him. 'Who does that to a person? How long does that take? To starve someone to death. Weeks? Months?'

Griffin shrugs.

'Did he know we were coming?' Jamie says.

'Maybe. If he realised we'd taken Trevor Brown into custody?'

'Who was the victim anyway?'

'I have some idea,' Griffin mutters, taking his phone out of his pocket and typing in a name.

Like the rest of the team, Griffin's done his fair share of looking through missing persons, trying to match names with the unfortunate souls on the videos. And this guy was someone that particularly caught Griffin's eye.

'"Newly released footage shown here,"' he reads, '"shows the accused, David Foden, 31, leaving Winchester Crown Court yesterday morning, while his wife, Melinda Foden received a guilty verdict for the murder of their two-year-old girl, Emma. Emma was found dead by social workers in April 2022. She suffered cardiac arrest after being starved, beaten and burned at the hands of her mother."'

'Oh, Christ. I remember this,' Jamie says. 'The father got off because he claimed his wife had kicked him out and he had no idea what was going on.'

Griffin nods, grimly. 'The kid was found in a playpen surrounded by piss and shit. Absolutely hideous case. The wife got life. Husband walked out a free man.' He looks over at the building. 'Somebody obviously disagreed.'

'You think that man was David Foden?'

'Don't you? Starved, beaten. Locked in a room with his own piss and shit? Couldn't have happened to a nicer bloke.'

'But that? Fuck, I don't know, Griffin, I really don't.'

The two men fall into silence, sitting together in the darkness. As Griffin watches, white vans arrive, unloading their cargo of floodlights, foot plates and cameras, everything the SOCOs need to start their analysis of this old, abandoned pub.

They're going to find fingerprints, blood, saliva, footwear marks and more. But untangling the mess left by the AFOs is going to take weeks. Months even. Assuming they even find something left by the killer. Griffin remembers the smell of bleach when he walked in. Someone knew they were coming – what's the bet they had the sense to clean up after themselves as well?

Thinking about going back into that pub makes Griffin

shiver. But a memory niggles – something seemed out of place. Something he can't put his finger on now.

'Come on,' Griffin says, hauling himself to his feet, waiting as Jamie does the same. 'You can take me back to the nick. We're not going to solve anything sitting here.'

They wearily walk back to Jamie's car. Griffin remembers the nerves and the optimism on the drive over – that they were going to catch this guy. Instead, all they have is more death.

Jamie's phone rings as they set off; he hands it to Griffin.

'Jamie's driving,' Griffin says, noting that Cara has called Jamie and not him. 'I assume you've heard?'

'I'm heading to the hospital now,' Cara says. 'See if this guy will talk.'

Griffin remembers the state of the man. 'I wouldn't put money on it. And you need to look up David Foden.'

A quick intake of breath. Cara remembers the case too. 'You think this is him? Shit. That would make sense. I'll update you later.' She pauses. 'Will you be back for dinner?'

'I'm going out.'

'Okay.'

Another hesitation. The first conversation since their argument, Cara's voice tense and short. 'I'll see you later then, Griffin. Tell Jamie to go home.'

'Will do.' But she's already hung up.

'Was that Cara?' Jamie asks.

'She says go home. She's going to the hospital.'

'I hate to ask again, but everything okay between the two of you?'

'Same old shit.'

'Was it though?' Jamie looks away from the road for a

200

moment, catching Griffin's eye. 'That was some argument earlier. You've never done that before. At least, not at work.'

Griffin grunts in reply.

'It was about Noah Deakin, right?' Griffin stays silent, but Jamie ignores the hint. 'It must be tough. For both of you. A situation like this.'

'Look, I know you like to talk and you're this modern-age man, Jamie. But I don't. Okay?'

Jamie flushes, then nods. 'Okay.'

They drive the rest of the way in silence.

Chapter 35

They may not have made an arrest, but they have the next best thing: a witness. Someone who could have seen their killer.

Cara shows ID and is escorted to the Intensive Care Unit. But she makes it no further than the door. A doctor meets her outside, his face grave.

'David Foden is in a serious condition, DCI Elliott,' he says. 'Just because he's alive now, doesn't mean he's going to stay that way. His heart could give out at any moment, and that's the least of his problems.'

Cara tries to peer through the small window in the door. 'But . . . he's just hungry, right? You can . . . give him a feeding tube?'

The doctor blinks at her. 'This man has been starved for over a month. He went missing on the twenty-ninth of January?' Cara nods. 'Then I would estimate all he's had since then is water. His body has literally eaten itself from the inside out. His skin is starting to fall off, like . . . like wet tissue paper in the rain. He's suffering from acute malnutrition. Giving him normal food will result in refeeding syndrome, leading to vomiting, stomach pain and diarrhoea, so we have to introduce sustenance slowly. Everything in his body is out of whack – electrolytes, fluids, levels of fats and proteins. And that's assuming no long-term damage has been done – which in this case, it almost certainly has. If he makes it through the night, it'll be a miracle.'

'In that case, Dr . . .' Cara glances at his ID, 'Gibson. I need to speak to him now. We're chasing someone who has killed sixteen people – seventeen if he doesn't make it – and I have no doubt he will continue to kill if we don't catch him. Please. Let me speak to him.'

'Even if he was physically well enough, I don't think he can help you. On the few occasions he has regained consciousness he's been so agitated we've had to sedate him. He's severely traumatised, and talking about what happened is only going to make matters worse. My priority has to lie with my patient. I'm sorry, detective. I'll call you as soon as he's well enough.'

Dr Gibson pushes through the doors into the ICU and is gone.

'Shit,' Cara mutters. Their only witness, and chances are he's going to die overnight. Cara consoles herself with the thought that he's probably only seen Trevor Brown. He's the only consistent figure in the videos. The creator of this nightmare is a disembodied voice, commanding from a distance. Chances are he can't help at all.

Cara turns and starts to walk away from the ICU. It's been a long stressful day, and a large glass of white is calling her. But before she leaves, a sign catches her eye. Burrell Ward. She takes a left and walks swiftly along the corridor before she can change her mind.

A woman is sitting behind reception when she arrives. She shows her ID.

'DCI Elliott, to see Noah Deakin.'

The woman hesitates. 'That's the—'

'Yes,' Cara confirms, decisively.

'Well, let's see if you're on the list of approved visitors.'

To Cara's relief, her name is present, and the woman directs her to the left. 'Last room at the end. You'll know you're in the right place because of the prison guard,' she adds pointedly.

Cara thanks her with a sarcastic smile and starts the walk down the long corridor. Sure enough, outside, a man sits on a chair, reading a paper. He looks up with interest as Cara approaches.

She offers her ID. The man checks it, looking at Cara's face then at the ID again. 'Fifteen minutes,' he says, and waves her through.

Inside, another guard sits by the far side of the bed, the cuff on his wrist connected to an identical one on Noah's with something that looks like a bike chain. An escort cable, ensuring there's no chance of Noah getting out of there unaccompanied. But otherwise, it's like any other hospital room. Even the guard seems unbothered. He looks up as Cara enters, his head bobbing, and she realises he's wearing headphones, dancing to an inaudible beat. Not exactly procedure, but she allows him some amusement to get through the day.

Noah himself is silent. He seems to be sleeping, a blanket pulled up to his chest. The sight of his face makes her breath catch.

It's a mess of black and blue and red. A line of dark stitches bisects a cut across his forehead, his nose and mouth blown out of proportion with the swelling. She can hardly recognise him.

Machines blink at his side. There is a white clip on his middle finger, a cannula in his arm.

She doesn't want to wake him. He needs his recovery time, but something about how vulnerable he looks makes her reach out and touch his hand. Just two fingers, gently, on his upturned palm. His fingers curl in to meet hers and she pulls away quickly.

He opens his eyes.

'Cara?' His voice is husky, mumbled. She glances across to the guard; he hasn't even looked their way.

'Hi Noah. How are you feeling?'

'Not good.' He turns his head to look at her.

'I can't believe what happened. Have you told the governor who did this? I've moved you now, this won't happen again, they should have looked after you, they should—'

'Cara. Stop.' He closes his eyes, looks away. 'You need to go.'

'No. No, I won't. What happened? Tell me.'

She leans forward, and takes his hand in hers. She notices how it doesn't have a mark on it, as if he didn't fight back.

'Noah,' she whispers. She remembers Jamie's words from yesterday. 'What did you do?'

'They hate me,' he mumbles through his broken mouth. 'It was only what they've wanted to do for years.'

'You goaded them, didn't you? Noah, look at me? Please?' After a moment, he turns, his dark brown eyes the only undamaged part of his face. 'Why?'

'It's better this way.' A tear runs down his cheek.

'Better for who? No – you don't get to check out. You . . . you can't.'

'Why not?' He meets her gaze and for a split second she can still see him. Her friend. Behind the bruises and the blood. 'I confessed. I'm never getting out of prison. You're . . .' He stops. 'Don't come and see me anymore, Cara. Please. It's not . . . You're not . . .' He screws his face up in pain, then turns away. He pulls his hand from hers. 'Go.'

She stands, a lump in her throat. The guard glances up, and she turns away, walking quickly out of the room. There's nothing more to say. Nothing will make this better.

She's been a fool – her brother was right. Noah Deakin is a killer, currently serving a whole life tariff for the sadistic murder of thirty-one people. That's not to mention the rape and the beatings served on those who survived – including her own brother. She hurries from the hospital room, past the apathetic guard, down long corridors and into the cool night air. She stands outside the main entrance, gulping down oxygen, feeling as though she can't breathe.

Cara knows he did all those things. Her brain – the logical part of her – knows it; she saw it with her own eyes. He's a cold, sadistic killer. So why, at the sure and certain thought that she will never see him again, is she crying?

Chapter 36

Dates have never been Griffin's forte. Everything about them – from the starched atmosphere to the fact he might have to use an iron – makes him uncomfortable.

And he suspects Brody feels the same way.

Nothing about the two of them has ever been conventional. They were shagging before they were even friends. They bond over beer and a mutual love of catching bad guys. And – as Cara pointed out – he's her senior officer.

After his apparently public argument with Cara this morning, Griffin wasn't sure whether Brody would still be up for going out, but at half five she messages: *What time are you picking me up? And where are we going??*

He replies – brief and to the point, *7.30* – but leaves the second question unanswered. Mainly because six p.m. rolls around and he still doesn't have a clue. But once Jamie has dropped him at the nick, he looks up and sees the stars sprinkled across a jet black sky. And he knows where they should go.

Now he's on his way to pick her up, he worries that he's

misjudged this. Will they have anything to talk about outside of work? Do they have the slightest thing in common? If this goes wrong, Cara will be pissed at him, and work will be awkward as hell. But if it goes right, the voice in his head says, surely it will be worth it?

Griffin arrives at Brody's house at seven thirty on the dot, showered, in a clean, ironed shirt over a black T-shirt, and a pair of non-ripped jeans. He rings the doorbell and hears the patter of feet, his stomach jolting with nerves even though he's picked her up a hundred times before. She answers with a scowl.

'I need more information,' she says, self-consciously smoothing down her dress. It's black with small red flowers, with a low neckline that shows the top of a lacy bra. It makes Griffin want to pull it off to see what's underneath. 'Where are we going? Is this too smart? Not smart enough?'

'You look beautiful.'

'Seriously, Griffin.'

Griffin smiles. She likes to be in control and he's cheered by her awkwardness. That makes two of them.

'Bring a coat.' He points to her heavy black boots. 'Wear those.'

'Where the fuck are we going,' she mutters as she pulls them on. She plucks a black ski jacket from the hook, shoves a beanie over her hair.

'You'll see,' he says.

Maybe this evening will be fun, after all. He plays the part, holding the door open for her with a flourish. She frowns, but climbs in.

The roads are clear, but even so the drive takes the best part of an hour, rattling through the blackened countryside, around Lyndhurst and through the New Forest.

208

Brody peers out of the window, puzzled for the majority of the drive.

'Truth or dare,' she asks after half an hour has passed.

'I'm not going to tell you. You'll have to wait.'

'Will there be other people there?'

'Yes.'

'Is it outside?'

'Alana, this isn't twenty questions. You'll have to wait.'

She humphs and sits back in her seat, arms folded across her chest.

'Truth or dare?' Griffin asks.

She scowls at him. 'Dare.'

'We can only go for truth this evening.'

'That's cheating.'

Griffin shrugs, looking at her with a smile.

'Truth then,' she says.

'Does this make you uncomfortable?'

'Yes.'

'Why?'

She sighs. 'Because I like to know what's going on. I like to be able to prepare.'

'Don't you trust me?'

'I do. But.'

'But?'

'It's me I don't trust. How I'm going to react to something. I'm not good at hiding my emotions. What if I hate it?'

'Then you'll tell me you hate it and we'll go somewhere else. Okay?'

She stares at him for a moment. 'Okay.'

They fall back into silence, but it's companiable this time. Brody seems to relax and even Griffin starts to enjoy himself. The roads turn residential, and Griffin follows the

209

signs. Brody must know where they're going now, as she sits up in her seat, looking out of the window.

Griffin pulls into a deserted car park and cuts the engine.

'We're at the beach,' Brody says. 'In the dark. In winter.'

'Best time,' Griffin replies. 'None of the crowds.'

'There's a reason for that.'

'You don't like it. Shall we go—' Griffin is about to turn the key when Brody stops him, her hand on his arm.

'No. Don't.' He can see her smiling in the half-light. 'But I am starving. I hope you've thought about food.'

Griffin points out of the windscreen to the bright lights of a restaurant on the other side of the car park. A low building, on the sea front.

'I've made a reservation. Or we could get takeaway?'

'Let's eat in.' Brody pops the door and gets out into the cold. She wraps her arms around herself and shivers, pulling the beanie further down on her head. 'We're definitely eating in,' she adds with a smile. Griffin offers an arm and the two of them walk to the restaurant.

Inside, it's warm and friendly, with a low burble of conversation as they're shown to their table next to the window. Simple silver cutlery sits on single white napkins, soft pink water glasses by each setting. A small lamp provides low lighting as they're handed their menus. Griffin casts his eye down, his stomach rumbling at the thought of lobster linguini or haddock and chips.

He looks up at Brody; she's staring out of the window, her face in reflection as she peers at the pitch black sky, the waves lapping at the sand.

'Good choice?' he asks.

She looks back, her eyes shining. 'Perfect. How did you know about this place?'

'Cara and I used to come to this beach when we were kids. The restaurant was different then – more like a shack selling fish and chips – but I loved it. It would always be freezing cold, but we'd paddle in the sea, and Mum would be ready with a hard scratchy towel, and then we'd go home and get sand in the house and Mum would complain, but it was the best day, mainly because . . .' He pauses, lost in the memory, wondering how much he should share.

'Truth?' Brody says quietly.

'Because my dad wasn't there.' He shrugs. 'Mum was always happier out of the house, away from him. Like we were on holiday even though it was barely an hour down the road. Something about being next to the sea.'

'It's calming.'

'It is.'

The waiter comes over and takes their order – tiger prawns, fish and chips, a bottle of beer for Brody, a Coke for Griffin.

'Anyway, enough about my dead parents,' Griffin says with a weak smile. 'Tell me about your family? I'm hoping for some dysfunction here, Alana,' he adds. 'Please don't say they're normal and living in Surrey.'

'Kent, but yes. Sorry,' she adds with a wince. 'Even down to the Labrador. They have two.'

'No.' Griffin mimes being shocked. 'That's horrible.'

'I know. One yellow, one black. All very dull. They were supportive of my choice to join the police, my mum ignored me for a week when I got my eyebrow piercing, but after that she didn't complain. I try to visit them as much as I can.'

'Eyebrow piercing?'

She leans forward, showing him the slight scar on her right brow. 'It was 2005, all the rage. I was cool.'

'I'm sure. Siblings?'

'Four brothers.'

'Four?' he says, almost horrified.

She nods with a grin. 'Two younger, two older. Typical middle child. Always the peacekeeper, great mediator, used to compromise. Independent.'

'And I'm the wilful, risk-taking, fun-loving youngest child?'

'You forgot charming,' Brody adds. 'As opposed to Cara – the goal-orientated, perfectionist, rule-following oldest.'

'Makes sense. Do you get on with them all?'

'Mostly. Don't see them as much as I'd like. Get together for birthdays, Christmas, you know.'

'So it was the job that fucked you up?'

'A hundred per cent,' she says with a chuckle.

'Do you regret it?'

Her face turns serious. 'Do I . . .? No, I don't think so. Everything I've seen, the people I've met – it all made me who I am today. And I certainly don't regret locking those fuckers up. Without me, maybe that wouldn't have happened. Although . . .'

She picks up her beer, takes a long gulp. She looks at Griffin over the top of her glass. 'He's getting out soon. That man. The one where I . . .'

'Drove a biro through his hand?' She grimaces. 'But how? Production and distribution of indecent photographs of a child, that's, what? Ten years, surely. How's he getting out now?'

Her face darkens. 'They couldn't prove he was involved in the production of the photos, and claimed that any admission of guilt was compromised because of the – and I

quote – "threatening behaviour of the interviewing officer".
He pleaded guilty to possession, got three years.'

'Still. That's—'

'That's the reality. I got off lightly – they wanted to arrest
me for GBH. My DI argued PTSD, that the guy was taunting
me, but it was his word against mine. The CPS accepted a
lower charge to make it go away.'

Brody pauses and takes another gulp of her beer. She's
feigning nonchalance, but her face is flushed, she looks close
to tears. This case still affects her far more than she'd like
to admit.

Griffin lets it go. 'At least this way you transferred to
Hampshire. And you got to work with me.'

'Christ, no. A fate worse than death. Should have stabbed
the guy.' She laughs, little more than a cackle, but the mirth,
however forced, releases the mood.

The food helps too. Steaming hot baskets of chips arrive,
the outsides golden, the inners white and fluffy. Crispy
batter-coated fish, tiger prawns smelling of garlic and lime.
Brody coats the chips in tomato ketchup, a move Griffin
approves of.

The conversation moves on to easier things: Brody's love
of running; Frank, and the cat's continued dislike of Cara;
Griffin's terrible Land Rover and the fact it's about to fail
its MOT, again.

'Can't you get a new one?' Brody argues. 'A decent car,
I mean. You don't need to be driving around in a massive
truck all the time. Think of the environment.'

'This is for the environment – I'm preserving my classic
car.'

'Classic just means old. And you can probably flog

it to some farmer somewhere. Buy yourself a nice Ford Focus.'

'Fuck no. Besides, you can't screw in the back of a Ford Focus,' he adds with a grin.

'Does that happen often?'

'Only when you're around.'

'Good to know.' She takes a bite of a chip, giving him a cheeky grin. 'Truth or dare?'

'You know we're only doing truth.'

'Okay then, what did you think of me when we first met?'

Griffin pulls off a piece of fish and batter and pops it in his mouth. He chews, thinking. 'I thought you were hot, obviously—'

'Obviously.'

'And that you were more interesting than the average DC. I couldn't work out why you wanted to be there. And you didn't like me much.'

'I did!'

'You barely spoke to me for the first few days.'

'You were the boss's little brother. I was pissed off that you just swanned in and did your own thing.'

'So what changed?'

'Luckily you were so fuckable I couldn't resist.'

He raises an eyebrow. 'Truth?'

'Go on then.'

'Are you seeing anyone else?'

Brody appraises him cautiously. 'What do you think?'

'I think you probably are.'

'Does that bother you?'

Griffin replaces his knife and fork on the plate, pushing

it away. He considers her question. 'If it's just sex, then no, I guess not. You're free to do what you want. But . . .'

'But?'

'But this.' He points to her, then at himself. 'This could be something. And if it is, then yes, it would bother me.'

She pauses. Reaches across and takes a stray chip from his discarded plate. 'Okay.'

'Okay?'

'Okay, I won't sleep with anyone else. I'll give this a chance. Me and you.'

'Are we done here?' The waiter comes over, interrupting them. 'All good?'

Griffin looks over at Brody. She meets his gaze, and smiles. 'Yes, we're all good, thank you.'

Chapter 37

Cara spends too long at the office, burying herself in paperwork and reports and ignoring the phone, so by the time Charlie swings by her office, coat in hand, it's late.

'You have to go home some time, love,' he says. 'You have to sleep. Eat.'

'Not now. There's too much . . .' She cranes forward to look at an email and the words swim. She feels dizzy. When was the last time she ate? 'Maybe I will come back with you,' she says, admitting defeat. She can always log on once she's home.

She walks with Charlie to the car park and he's quiet, unusually so. She senses there's something on his mind, but she doesn't have the energy for an argument. Not now.

They get back; she leaves Charlie in the hallway while she goes up to change. She notices the door to Griffin's room is open, two shirts lying on the bed next to a ball of sleeping black fur. So he's been home and gone out. She wonders where.

She strips off her work trousers and shirt, puts on tracksuit bottoms and a hoodie. Ties her hair into a rough ponytail and goes back downstairs to where Charlie is peering into the fridge.

'Someone needs to do a Tesco order,' he comments, and it annoys her. She's not the only one living in this house. Griffin could go to a supermarket once in a while, even Charlie could. He backs up, holding eggs and bread. 'Scrambled eggs?' he says. 'Best we can do.'

She nods and slumps into the nearest chair. Charlie places a glass of water in front of her. 'Drink that.'

She does as she's told, suddenly thirsty.

'I heard you and Griffin got into it this morning,' he says. He's cracking eggs into a bowl, his voice light. 'What was that about?'

Cara looks at him, her eyes narrowed. 'How did you find out?'

'My whole team knew. And for it to have got down to the basement?' He pauses, putting bread in the toaster. 'One slice or two?'

'One. And it was nothing. He was being a twat, I called him on it. He didn't like it.'

'So it was nothing to do with you visiting Noah Deakin?'

'What did you say to him?'

'Nothing! I spoke to him last night, after you'd gone to bed, and he knew already. I told you he'd find out. He's not stupid.'

There's a long pause while Cara grinds her teeth, suppressing her anger. Next to Charlie, the toast pops. They both ignore it.

'I assume Griffin was upset,' Charlie says, breaking the silence.

'Yeah. Happy now?'

'No, why would I be happy?'

'Because you don't want me visiting him either. You'd rather I stay away, leave him to rot.'

'I don't—'

'Well, you'll be glad to know, that's it,' Cara continues. 'He tried to kill himself yesterday, riled some thug up and got himself stabbed. If you're lucky, he'll do it again once he's back inside. Then you won't need to worry about him at all.'

Charlie stares at her, mouth open.

'I don't want the man dead, Cara,' he says quietly.

'Yeah, well . . .' But her throat closes up and her nose aches, and to her annoyance she starts to cry. 'He might,' she whispers.

She fixes her gaze on the tabletop as she sniffs, dabbing at her eyes with the sleeve of her hoodie. Charlie pulls out a chair and sits at the table, but he doesn't reach for her or offer any comfort like he would normally do.

'Answer me one question,' he says after a moment.

'What?'

'Did anything ever happen between the two of you?'

Cara's surprised. Her head snaps up and she looks at her boyfriend. He's staring at her, hurt clear in his eyes, and it makes her wonder how long Charlie's wanted to ask the question.

'Between me and Noah? I was married, Charlie.'

'Your husband was cheating on you.'

'So, what? You thought I was shacking up with officers in my team?'

'Don't be ridiculous. I only asked about Noah. Because there were rumours, Cara. At the time, that you and Noah—'

'Were what? Fucking? You need to stop listening to the gossip-mill, Charlie. I thought you were on my side.'

'This isn't about sides. This is a straightforward question. And one which you haven't answered—'

'No! No, I wasn't screwing Noah Deakin. Happy now?'

'Was he in love with you?'

'Fuck off.'

'Was he? Did you love him? Because I've been thinking about this, since yesterday, and that's the only conclusion I can come to. Why you've been visiting him for the best part of a year and you didn't tell me.'

'I'm sorry I didn't tell you. I've said this already. And we were *friends*! That's all! I went to visit him because finding out your partner is a serial killer is a hell of a mind fuck, and I thought it might help.'

'Did it? Did it help?'

'No. Okay? No! No, it hasn't fucking helped. I'm more confused than ever, especially now I've found out that my boyfriend puts more faith in the gossip from the nerds in his team, than he does in me.' She points to the door, a defiant stab. 'Get out, if you don't believe me. Fuck off and never come back.'

Charlie stares at her, then gets up from the table and strides out of the room. After a moment she hears the front door slam and the engine of his car start and rattle off down the road. She stares at his empty chair for a moment, then drops her head on the table. She knocks her forehead against the wood, once, twice, the dull ache better than the pain in her soul mocking her for the mistake she's made.

'Shit,' she whispers, resting her cheek on the cold wood. 'Shit.'

Chapter 38

Griffin pays and they leave the restaurant, the cold wind hitting their faces the moment they step outside.

But Brody walks in the opposite direction to the car.

'I could do with a stroll,' she shouts, the wind snatching her words. 'Come on,' she adds, when Griffin looks at her dubiously. 'A nice brisk walk. Do you the world of good.' She holds out her hand.

'Bloody runners,' Griffin mutters, but he follows, taking her hand in his. They walk down the promenade, moving away from the bright light of the restaurant into the inky darkness. Beach huts line up to their left, the pastel blues and pinks rendered grey in the murk. To their right, the sea rushes in over the sand, and Griffin enjoys the silence. He relishes her warm hand in his, the way they fall into step, their strides matching perfectly, and he looks down at her. Her black hair tufts out of the side of her beanie, her cheeks are pink, and for the first time in years he thinks, this could be it.

Since his wife was killed, it's been hard to imagine himself with someone else. Not sex – he's done that a thousand times – but in the way that matters. He came close with Jess Ambrose – uprooting his life to be with her. But that soon went wrong, and he's barely dared to consider it since. Sharing your life, your innermost thoughts. The part of himself he keeps hidden with the fear other people might find it pathetic or laughable.

As if reading his mind, Brody says, 'Do you want kids?' She looks up at him, meeting his gaze. 'Or is that too much for a first date?'

'I . . . No, it's fine. And yes, I always assumed I would. But then Mia died and . . .'

She squeezes his hand in understanding. 'Cara has two, right?'

'Tilly and Josh. Tilly's nine, Josh is . . . oh, I don't know. Ten? Eleven?' He laughs. 'I'm a terrible uncle. I only remember to buy them birthday presents because Cara sends me a link to whatever they want on Amazon.'

'You'd be a wonderful father.'

'Oh, I doubt it. What example do I have? My own dad was barely there. I'm an alcoholic with a painkiller addiction, and work all hours in an unsociable and dangerous job. I can barely look after my cat.'

'Frank's still alive, isn't he?'

'Pretty sure that's the minimum requirement.'

Brody stops, making him do the same. She takes his other hand in hers and turns him around so he's facing her.

'You'd be a wonderful father,' she repeats. 'Okay?'

'Okay.'

She nods with satisfaction, then bends down and starts unbuckling her boots.

'What are you doing?'

'Paddling. Come on.' She leans over and tugs at his

221

laces. 'You didn't bring me to the beach and expect to leave without going in the sea.'

'Okay, but I'm not swimming. Fucking lunatic,' he adds, watching her pull off her tights, shove them into her boots, then run down to the shore. He does the same, almost toppling over standing on one leg, rolling his jeans up as far as they'll go.

He follows Brody's excited yelps as she runs headlong into the sea, showing no regard for the cold. He takes his time, tentatively dipping a toe into the swirling surf.

And it is bloody freezing. His toes go numb instantly, but he steps forward, enjoying the sand under his feet, the noise of the waves. Brody stops her leaping and waits until he's next to her; she wraps her arms around his waist, pressing herself against him. He scowls down.

'See? Told you this would be fun.'

She reaches up and kisses him, her lips salty. 'Now can we go and warm up somewhere?' She raises an eyebrow, making it perfectly clear what she's referring to.

'Nope, no way. It's our first date. First base only.'

She stares at him. 'What? No sex?'

'No sex.' He nods, resolutely. 'We're getting to know each other, Alana,' he adds, laughing at her disgruntled face. 'This is what normal people do.'

'This sucks. Normal people are idiots.' Her hand reaches under his coat, easily finding skin beneath all the layers. He jumps at her cold hands as she pushes them down the back of his jeans, grabbing his bum.

'You only said no sex,' she says, her lips back against his. 'You didn't say anything about groping.'

*

They kiss until Griffin fears frostbite, then they walk to shore, massaging blood back into their frozen feet, replacing socks and boots, Brody balling up her tights and stuffing them in her pocket.

They walk to the Land Rover in silence, hand in hand, Griffin opening the door for her with a smile, then walking around to the driver's side. The truck starts first time and they head home.

The radio plays as the cabin slowly fills with hot fuggy air, Brody rubbing her hands under the vents with a sigh.

'Next time, we go somewhere warm,' she says.

He feels a glow at her words, cosier than any in-car heating can provide. *Next time.* This could go somewhere. But there's the problem of work to deal with.

'Tell me about the crime scene,' she says. 'Was it as bad as it sounds?'

'Worse. And the smell. Never known anything like it.'

'Maybe it's a good thing I stayed at the nick. Do you think we'll get anything from it?'

'I don't know. I hope so, but it stank of bleach.' Griffin's thoughts go back to that strange niggle, the nagging doubt he had standing in the corridor – that something had been missed.

'Maybe they knew we were coming,' Brody says, interrupting his thoughts.

'Huh?'

'Maybe someone on the inside is talking. As Cara said. Someone in the police.'

He glances at her, curled up in the passenger seat, rubbing her bare legs and thinks, What a strange job we do. First date with a beautiful woman and they're back to talking about murder. And in this case, dodgy cops.

'If that's the case, then we really are fucked,' he says.

Half an hour later, Griffin pulls up outside her house. She opens the car door, then looks back. 'Do you want to come in? Coffee? I promise I won't try to seduce you.'

'You wouldn't have to try very hard. Believe me, you have no idea. But I need to go home and sort things out with Cara.'

'She's pissed at us?'

'She's pissed at me. But don't worry, I'll fix it.' He leans over and gives her a quick kiss. 'See you in the morning.'

She smiles and closes the door.

He watches until she's safely inside, then taps his fingers on the steering wheel, thinking. It's late – past midnight – and chances are Cara will be in bed already. But there's one place that will still be open at this time of night: the crime scene.

The conversation with Brody comes back to haunt him. There was something odd about that place, and not just because of the state of the victim they found there. He'll take one quick look. To settle his mind. And then he'll go home.

The truck is toasty warm now, and as he drives he thinks about his evening with Brody. The food was delicious, the location perfect. And Brody – she was wonderful. For once, it's nothing to do with sex – no post-coital glow – but how he feels when he's with her. The wariness when he first met her has gone. That sense of being wrong-footed. Either he understands her better now, or she trusts him enough not to play games. Either way, he likes it. And he likes her.

This could be something.

He pulls up outside the crime scene feeling lighter than he has for weeks. Should he go in? Surely seeing that awful place will only ruin his good mood. But he's unsettled. One quick look, and he'll go home.

The place is bustling with people. Three white vans are parked up outside, SOCOs with the unfortunate short straw of a night shift walking to and fro, an eerie sight in their white suits.

He signs in with the scene guard, then suits up and heads inside. Once again, he's hit by the scale of the work needed from the scene of crimes team. So much evidence to be collected, so much crap that needs to be sorted and tested, that might lead to their killer. Might – there are no guarantees. The work has only just begun.

The majority of the activity is focused on the cell where they found their unfortunate victim. With no wish to see that mess again, he heads to the other end of the corridor – two more rooms, both empty when they arrived.

They had been cleared at the time by the armed teams, but since that point, someone has closed the doors. Griffin looks through the small window into the first, then presses the handle down.

The room is completely empty. White painted brick walls, white ceiling, wooden floorboards. One fluorescent light in the middle – turned off, with no obvious switch. The whole rooms stinks of bleach, but there's something else that differentiates it from the first cell – it's cold. The room where they found the starving man was strangely warm – a result of being insulated from the outside by layers of building and brick – but this one is freezing. He holds his hands out in front, gauging the air around him like a clairvoyant commanding ghosts. And yes, there it is. There's a breeze, a definite gust where there should be nothing.

Lights shine through from the corridor, but it's not

enough. He steps inside the cell, looking for a switch, but the walls are clear. And that's when he notices it. A small red light in the corner of the room.

He walks another few steps, squinting through the darkness. It's a camera. Same as in the other rooms, except this one is on. The red light looks back at him. It turns off for a second. Then on.

And Griffin realises.

There's somebody there. And they're watching.

DAY 6

WEDNESDAY

Chapter 39

Cara drives to work in a stinking mood. She's knackered, having spent the evening sitting on the sofa, waiting. Firstly, for Charlie, who never returned. And then for Griffin. Even Frank looked at her with pity from his spot next to the radiator as she went to bed at one a.m.

She drops her coat and bag in her office, then gathers the team with a clap of her hands.

'Give me some good news, please,' she says, resting her arse on the side of a desk, managing a thankful smile as Shenton hands her a coffee. 'Jamie? Has that bloody sheet been processed by the lab yet? The one the rapist footballer was wrapped in?'

He scowls at her choice of words, but answers the question. 'Yes – and no. They've taken samples from the whole sheet. No prints, and the only DNA came back to Stephen Allen.'

'Bugger. Any news from the crime scene?'

'SOCOs have been working all hours, but the CSM suspects they'll get very little. The whole place has been hosed down with bleach. Zero prints, zero blood spatter. Except for the cell, of course.'

'And what of our victim? Any news from the hospital?'

Brody leans forward. 'No change since your trip yesterday, boss. Out of it, but still alive. They'll call us when they know more.'

'CCTV, ANPR, witnesses, house to house? You can't tell me in this day and age that there's no sign of anyone going to or from that building? If they killed people there, how did they get the bodies out?'

Silence from the team. 'Any news on the brother?' Cara pushes. 'Tyler Brown?'

'His photo has been circulated to Response and Patrol, but they're coming up blank. He has no previous record, no known associates. They'll keep looking.'

'And have digital come back about tracing the webcams?'

The room goes silent. They all shuffle their feet until Jamie says, 'We thought you would . . .'

'You thought I'd speak to Charlie, is that right?' Nods all around. 'Well, I would thank you to keep my private life out of the workplace. We're not snogging in the corridors, we're all adults, you know. Something I'd thank a few of you to remember.' She glares at Brody, who has gone a bright shade of red. 'Where is Griffin?'

'He—'

'Phone him. Tell him to get his butt in, now, or I'll suspend his ass. I'll go down to Charlie, since that's what you think I'm doing with my time anyway. Well, go on then,' she snaps at her shell-shocked team. 'Get a move on.'

She gets up and charges into her office, collapsing behind the desk. Jamie follows in behind, every step tentative.

'Er, boss,' he begins. 'That was a bit . . . dramatic.'

She slumps deeper in her chair. 'Fucking hell, I'm sorry. I'll buy cakes later to apologise.'

'Everything okay?' He closes the door behind him and sits in the chair in front of her desk, leaning forward, elbows on his knees.

'The usual. Serial killer nobody can find. Brother going AWOL. Boyfriend . . . well. Who knows if Charlie is even my boyfriend anymore.'

'You had a fight?'

'A big one.'

'Want to talk about it?'

She shakes her head. 'No. Because if I say it out loud I'll realise how ridiculous I was being and how he's right and then that's someone else I have to apologise to.' She drags her hands down her face, screwing her eyes shut. 'Do me a favour, Jamie? Run this investigation. For today?'

'Of course. No problem.'

She heaves herself to her feet. 'I'll go and see Charlie. Kill two birds with one stone: apologise and find out about the webcams.'

He nods and she squeezes his shoulder as she passes. She walks through the incident room without comment, heading down the five flights of stairs to the digital department and pressing the doorbell. An echoing buzz announces the door release – they're used to her now – and she pushes through, traversing the usual assault course of cords and cables and disused keyboards.

Charlie's in his office on the phone, but he spots her through the window and waves her inside. She sits down silently and waits.

It's clear he's speaking to someone in authority. His tone is polite but friendly, the technical terminology simple. But also – Cara realises with shock – it's a woman. He's *flirting*.

She watches with interest. She didn't realise Charlie could be this charming. Maybe early days in their relationship. First dates, when they were trying to impress, but she was so wrapped up in her own self-consciousness she didn't notice what Charlie was doing. It's like watching an endangered species in the wild. He's smiling, laughing. Saying phrases like, 'You're in charge for a reason,' and 'You don't need me to tell you that.' She feels . . . jealous.

He meets her eye and mimes *Sorry*, then holds out his hand, fingers splayed. *Five minutes*. She nods, gives him a thumbs-up. Checks her email on her mobile, but keeps one eye on her boyfriend, taking in the conciliatory tone of his voice, the way he gives a small chuckle to the woman on the other end of the phone.

And she realises how much she's missed this. Missed him. Work – and the distraction of Noah and the Echo Man – has taken her away from just enjoying the beautiful things in life. Like flirting with Charlie and having him laugh with her. Not this nameless harlot at the other end of the line.

His tone is changing, coming to the end of the call, and with a final goodbye and thank you, he hangs up and turns to Cara.

'I was coming to see you,' he says. 'But you've beaten me to it.'

'I was hoping you'd made some headway on those cameras.' His face falls. 'But also,' she continues quickly, 'I want to apologise. I shouldn't have been so defensive when you mentioned Noah. You were only asking the question a thousand people wanted to know. And you deserve an honest answer.'

Charlie waits, his head tilted to one side.

'The truth is that yes, I often thought that there might have been something between us. Griffin always said Noah thought of me as more than just a friend. But no. Nothing ever happened. And nothing ever will.'

'Was he in love with you?'

Cara pauses. 'Maybe,' she confesses quietly.

'Were you in love with him?'

'I think I could have been,' she whispers. Something she's never admitted before, not even to herself. 'Maybe I could have fallen in love with the man I thought he was. But I never knew him. Not really. He was . . .'

'A killer.'

'Yes.'

Charlie nods, digesting her answer. 'Are you still going to see him?'

'I did. Yesterday. To check he was okay.'

'And was he?'

'No. But that's the point, isn't it? He never will be. After what he did. And I need to get used to that fact. Stop trying to save him.'

Silence falls in Charlie's office, punctuated only by the tapping and clicking from the digital team next door. Charlie leans across his desk, reaching out to grab her hand.

'I'm sorry I walked out. I needed some space.'

'That's okay.'

'Do you still want to move in?'

Cara smiles. 'Yes. Please. When this case is over.'

'Okay. Now, what did you want to know? Those cameras?'

231

'Who was it on the phone?'

'DCI Ryder.'

'Really? You were flirting with her.'

'I was not.' Cara gives him a look. 'Okay, maybe a bit,' he admits. 'But technical genius can only get me so far. Sometimes I need to turn on the charm to get what I want.'

'Which was?'

'The hard copy of the DVDs. They're still with the lab, being processed for biologicals, and I wanted her to apply some influence, get them to release one at least. There's more data on there, I know there is. We just need the originals.'

'I could help. I'm a DCI, too.'

'I know.' He gives her an apologetic smile. 'But you have enough on your plate. And yes, the cameras.

'All the cameras in that building were connected to the internet via Wi-Fi, but that's where the good news ends.' Cara's optimism fades. 'As much as we can tell, that Wi-Fi was a hot spot, probably created by a SIM card in a burner. The lab hasn't found a mobile phone?' Cara shakes her head. 'So from there it's anyone's guess. My theory is they have a laptop somewhere, again, probably linked to a nameless hot spot, which connects to the camera. If they're using a VPN on the laptop – a virtual private network?' he adds when Cara looks blank. 'Essentially a VPN is a tool that redirects your internet through an additional location and encrypts the data. So even if we could trace the laptop, it would give us the IP address of the VPN company.'

'Who could give us their client?'

'Assuming the client used their actual details. Which, as they don't seem to be stupid, they probably haven't. They could be in Russia. They could be in Romsey. We can't tell. All they would need to do would be to get close enough with the first burner, create the hot spot, connect to the camera, and away they go.'

A knock interrupts them. John, Charlie's chief consultant, sticks his head around the door. 'DCI Elliott, DC Brody is here to see you. She says it's urgent.'

'So let her in.'

'I wasn't sure whether you could be interrupted.'

'Fuck's sake.' Cara cranes her head around as Brody comes flying in. 'What is it, Alana?'

'It's Griffin.' She comes to a stop in the doorway, getting her breath back. 'He's not answering his phone.'

'So what? He's probably out following a lead somewhere. What time did he leave you last night? And I know about you two, so let's get over that for now, shall we?'

'No, that's just it, boss. He didn't stay with me last night. He dropped me home just after midnight and he said he was going to talk to you. But you said—'

'He didn't come home,' Cara says quietly. She looks at Charlie. 'Can you trace his mobile number?'

Charlie's already on his feet, shouting through the doorway. 'John, put a trace on . . .' He looks at Cara. She shouts Griffin's number out of the door to the techie waiting by his computer. He types it in and the three of them rush to stand behind him. It hangs for what feels like an interminable amount of time, until a little blue dot comes to rest on a map, sandwiched between a patch of grey and white.

'West of the Southwood estate,' Charlie reads. 'Isn't that—'

Her vision blurs, her mind woozy. 'Where the crime scene is, yes. What time was this?'

'About half midnight. Then the signal was lost. Look,

Cara. This means nothing. His phone's run out of battery, that's all. That place is crawling with SOCOs. There's no way something has happened to him. Call the CSM.'

'Yes, you're right. I'm sure you're right.' Cara takes her phone out of her pocket and places a call. It rings out, cuts to voicemail. 'Holly, this is DCI Elliott. Call me back. It's urgent.' She hangs up and glances at Brody; she's gone white. 'Alana, let's head back to the incident room. We can wait for a call from there.' She smiles at Charlie, but her cheeks feel tight.

She follows Brody up the stairs, then stops her in the corridor. 'Tell me exactly what Griffin said last night. Where was he going?'

'I told you. He dropped me back at mine, said he was going home to speak to you. I sent him a text later, at about one a.m., but he didn't reply. I assumed he'd gone to bed. But this morning . . .' Her chin wobbles, she presses her lips together, looking as though she's about to cry.

Cara touches her gently on her arm. 'Charlie's right, we're getting ahead of ourselves. You know Griffin, always doing his own thing.' Her phone rings, *Holly CSM* on the screen. She shows it to Brody. 'This is her now. Holly'll tell us exactly what's going on.' She answers the call on speaker and starts walking again. 'Holly, thank you for calling me back.' She listens while the CSM talks. 'No, I know you don't have anything yet, I wasn't calling about that. It's about DS Griffin. Can you get him to call me, urgently, his phone's dead.'

'Griffin? Wait a sec, I'll ask the scene guard.' There's muffled conversation, then Holly speaks again. 'Yeah, he signed in at half midnight last night. And his Land Rover's here. But I haven't seen him.'

'Sorry to be a pain,' Cara continues. She arrives back in the incident room; the team look up expectantly. 'But could you go and find him? He's easy to spot, even in a crime scene suit.'

'Yes, sure.'

There are footsteps, an echo as the CSM goes inside. Cara looks at the team, the phone clamped to her ear. Everyone has stopped, worried eyes meeting hers.

The CSM comes back on the line. 'I'm sorry, I don't know what to say. He's not here, and Griffin's a hard guy to miss. He must have left already, forgotten to sign out.'

'Without his truck?' Silence at the other end. 'Stay where you are. Don't let anyone leave – we're coming to you.'

She meets the eyes of her team. The block of lead that's been hanging, ready, drops in her stomach. She starts to shake, but she knows what she has to do.

'Everyone, listen up. We have an abduction in progress. DS Griffin was last seen at zero-zero thirty last night, when he disappeared.' She looks back to the board, to the photos of the other victims, their bodies beaten and battered. To the timeline of their abductions.

'You know what we have to do,' she says. Her voice shakes, but she will not cry. She will find her brother. 'From this point, every minute matters.' She pauses, knowing what's at stake.

'We have forty-eight hours.'

Chapter 40

Look at you. Perfect, in your T-shirt and jeans. Bare feet, bare arms. Muscles bulging as you strain against your cuffs, as you shout and scream like the caged animal you are.

Fuck, you were angry when you woke up. You must have realised instantly what had happened, how you ended up here. And I must admit, it was a surprise to me too. Serendipitous, one might say, you going back in that way.

I was watching you then, as I watch you now. You had no idea what was coming – there is a fine trickle of blood running down the back of your neck, but otherwise Ty didn't do too much harm. And thank goodness for Ty. Because there was no way I would have got you back here by myself.

But here you are. You beautiful specimen of a man. Almost a pity to do this to you, but orders are orders. The money has been paid; the contract signed. Now all we have to do is wait.

Forty-eight hours.

My mouth is dry with anticipation. I won't sleep tonight, knowing what I have in store. I don't usually like to get down and dirty. But my time is coming to an end, and it's not enough to sit and watch. I want to feel the splinters under my skin, taste your blood in my mouth. Smell your sweat and spit. See the fear on your face when you realise what is coming. How much pain you will have to endure.

Forty-eight hours, until you are mine.

How wonderful it's going to be.

Chapter 41

Jamie watches as his team dissolves into chaos. Brody starts shaking, her face drained of blood; Cara oscillates between barking orders and staring into space; Shenton opens and closes his mouth like a goldfish.

Jamie freezes. All he can think about are the men on the videos. How they spent their last moments. And the question pops into his brain – why?

'Why Nate?' he says. Then louder: 'Why are they going after Griffin?'

The team stops and looks at him. Jamie gestures to the board. 'These men, all our previous victims – they've done something awful. They've raped, they've killed – and most of all, they got away with it. What's Griffin done?'

Cara looks at the board, then flinches. A tiny recoil, but enough. 'What, Cara?'

'Nothing,' she snaps. 'He's done nothing. But we all know how close to the line Griffin can get. He's arrested countless shitbags, but he's also done some things that weren't strictly speaking by the book. Maybe someone wants revenge for that?'

'Someone with money? With the means to order a hit like this?' Jamie turns to Shenton. 'Toby, get on this. Speak to intel – get them to run a report of every single arrest Griffin has made. We're looking for someone out of the ordinary – a big value criminal who stood to have more to lose than your average street rat. Maybe a conviction that didn't stick, or a reputation ruined. Brody – you and I are heading down to the old pub. I want to see where Griffin went missing – and work out how on earth they abducted a six-foot guy from a busy crime scene.

'Cara?' He stops, aware he's telling his boss what to do. But she nods. 'Stay here, speak to DCS Halstead. Get as much resource as you can. Even involve Ryder if needs be. Our top priority is finding Griffin. But all these cases are connected. We get one route in – we might be able to work out where they're holding him.' He walks across to the board and writes *00:30* in neat digits. 'This is his last known sighting – we must assume that the countdown starts from then. We've lost nine hours already. Get to work.'

He lets the remaining breath out with a whoosh, forces himself to lower his shoulders. Brody appears by his side, coat on.

'You okay?' he asks.

She nods, tight and quick. 'Let's go.'

They take an unmarked car, driving through rush-hour streets with the blue lights flashing. They don't talk, don't make eye contact. They know what they're facing.

Griffin's Land Rover is waiting in the car park, surrounded by Scientific Services vans. Holly gets out of the front seat of the closest when they arrive.

'He's definitely missing?' she says. 'I just can't understand how he left here and we didn't notice.'

Jamie places a reassuring hand on her arm. 'You were busy. Anything?' he directs to Brody, who's been peering into the Land Rover through the driver's side window.

'All looks normal.' She tries the handle – it opens. 'He left it unlocked, but that's not unusual.' She gets into the driver's seat and holds up an iPhone. 'His mobile's here. No battery.' She cradles it in her lap, lost in thought. 'He has to come back,' she mumbles.

'We'll find him,' Jamie says. He strides decisively towards the building, stopping only to sign in and look at Griffin's signature a few lines above. It's definitely his – that nearly indecipherable scrawl. 'Did anyone talk to him? Make conversation?'

'No, I've asked around,' Holly replies. 'A few people noticed him arrive, but everyone was busy. He suited up and headed down to the cells.'

They start walking into the building, Brody following, donning all the usual white suits and shoe covers. The smell of bleach still lingers; a few marks adorn the walls – circles in yellow chalk where samples have been taken. Jamie notices there's precious few – in a crime scene normally the place would be coated in yellow – small, numbered triangles marking each spatter or exhibit. But here there's barely anything.

They cleaned up. They left no trace.

Jamie walks along to the cells. The final one, at the end, still stinking of shit and puke, being processed by an army of SOCOs. Then to the second. The third, and the fourth.

The empty white rooms look the same: clean, painted

and pristine. Nothing to distinguish one from the other – except the fourth is cold. Almost the same temperature as outdoors, despite the brickwork all around him.

'Has anyone been in here?' he throws backwards to Holly.

'We took some samples early on, but there was little of interest.'

He scuffs his feet along the floor. Had Griffin been in here? What was going through his mind to come back at midnight? Was it something to do with the case?

He studies all four walls, each as unremarkable as the last, then up to the camera. The eye watches him, dark, unblinking. The things that must have happened in this room. The torture, the murder. But that's all over now – the police are here.

It's scant reassurance, and he continues his tour of the small room, head down, looking at the floor. He frowns at the sight of two small droplets. Calls back to Holly.

'Was this originally here?'

The CSM bends to take a closer look. 'No. We would have noticed blood spatter like this.'

'You think that's what it is?'

Holly takes a fresh evidence tube out of her pocket, opens it and dabs the sterile cotton bud on the dot. She shows it to Jamie. It's red.

'Get that to the lab, put a rush on it,' Jamie says. 'I want that confirmed as Griffin's asap. And what the hell?'

He reaches down and pokes at a line of rusted brown metal, flush to the floorboards. Nearly impossible to see. It's supposed to be there, a part of the design, almost as if . . .

He stands up again, takes a step back. Some of the

boards are split into two, along a line. And there are four of the metal pieces.

'It's a fucking trapdoor,' he exclaims. Brody enters at the sound of his voice, Jamie points to the floor. 'Here, and here. This is a trapdoor. It's concealed, but it's definitely there.' He jumps a few times, his heavy tread echoing around the room. 'What's under here? Holly!' he shouts back to the CSM, who reappears in the doorway. 'What's beneath this room?'

'Nothing. Just the cellar.'

'There's a fucking cellar? Show me.'

Holly leads the way – outside, then around the back. They walk down a set of concrete steps to the side of the building, hitting a lower level, buried in the side of the hill, stopping in front of a set of double doors. They're wide open, showing a large empty space.

'See?' Holly says. 'We haven't even started on this area yet.'

Jamie walks inside, stooping to avoid the low ceiling. He looks up at the wooden boards above him, then comes to a stop. Sure enough, it's a trapdoor. Not huge – no more than a three- or four-foot square – a large metal arm securing it shut. He pulls, wincing, expecting a grind of old rust, but it opens smoothly. He dodges out of the way as the two doors fall open.

'It makes sense in an old pub like this,' Holly says. 'A trapdoor from a storage room to the cellar would have been in place for the barrels – to lower empty ones into a waiting truck or haul up new.' She stops. 'You don't think . . .'

'This is how they got Griffin out. Someone was waiting under here.' Jamie points to the room above. 'Knock him over the head, open the trapdoor, and away you go. Shit.' He rushes out to the pathway. It leads to a small track. Narrow, but more than possible to get a car down. He stares down it, hands on his head. 'That's why you didn't see anything. They could have been wearing a coverall – blended in. And you were so concerned with the crime scene up there, nobody stopped to consider there might be another way in. And out,' he adds with a grimace. 'They must have been following him. Tracking him until he was alone, until they could abduct him. Did you see anyone last night?' he directs to Brody. 'Notice anything strange?'

She shakes her head, her face pale. 'No one,' she replies. 'But then we weren't exactly looking. This is my—'

'No, it's not,' Jamie says, cutting her off. 'This is nobody's fault. But Brody – start looking for cameras, CCTV, anything that might be on this road. Fuckers,' he growls to himself.

He steps back into the cellar, but as he does so his attention is caught by fragments of what looks like grey stone on the grass outside. He bends down and picks up a lump, rubs it. It breaks into rough grains between his fingers. Concrete. He looks back to the cellar – the whole of the floor is lined with the same. Grey, rough concrete.

Jamie steps back, squinting at it for a moment. An old pub like this, there's little need for a new floor.

He looks up again, to where the cells are, then back down. All these victims, none found. The killers must have been disposing of the bodies somehow – and where better than right under their feet.

'Get on to the dog unit,' he directs to Holly. 'We need VRDs. Now. And contact the Met or the army – whoever can give us the equipment we need to see into concrete.'

The colour drains from Holly's face. She stares at the slab

under their feet with fear in her eyes. 'You don't think . . .
But how many . . .?'

'They could have dug down. Who knows how deep.'

'Layer upon layer . . .' Holly says, her voice faint.

Jamie nods. 'Dead bodies,' he concludes, his face dark.
'We could be standing on the bodies.'

Chapter 42

Cara's been to see Halstead, but her boss provided little relief. Halstead merely repeated she should go home and let Ryder be in charge, but she's damned if she is going to sit around and wait for her brother to be killed. No – she's going to be here on the front line, doing everything she can. If only she could work out what that was.

Jamie has taken over – driving out to the crime scene and not only discovering how Griffin was abducted, but also the possible burial site of the bodies. Teams are flooding there now – pathology, more SOCOs, forensic anthropologists, victim recovery dogs. No doubt standing over that slab of concrete and puzzling how to get to the horrific depths within. Through the door of her office, she can see Shenton at his desk, head close to the screen, examining CCTV footage and traffic cameras, but she doesn't hold out much hope. They already know there is nothing useful out there: this killer is smart. They'd been using that old pub for ten years without being noticed, there is no chance of them making a mistake now.

She opens her email and starts reading reports, but

the text dances in front of her eyes. She can't think, can't concentrate. There's a light knock on her door – Charlie's standing there, his face stricken.

'So it's true? Griffin's missing?'

Cara nods, and Charlie is by her side in a moment, kneeling next to her and encasing her in a tight hug. She leans into his shoulder, taking comfort for one brief moment before pulling away.

'You should go home,' he says. 'You shouldn't work on your brother's case.'

'I can't.'

'Halstead will understand.'

'Halstead said the same as you.' She frowns and looks back to her computer. 'I need to be here.'

'You're too close. You'll compromise the case, if nothing else.'

'I won't go near Griffin's investigation – I'll look into the other victims.'

'They're related—'

'It's *fine*, Charlie,' she snaps, and instantly regrets her tone. 'I'm sorry. You're trying to help. But I'll go mad sitting at home. I need to be here. I need to do *something*.'

Charlie hesitates. 'Should I stay with you?'

'No. Go back to work.' She looks at him, desperately. 'Please. We need to find who's behind this – and you're as important in that as anyone.'

'Okay. But call me. If . . . If anything happens.'

'I will.'

Charlie leaves, and she heaves a sigh of relief. She was short with him; all he wants to do is be there for her, but once again she's hurting the people she loves. She turns back to her computer and opens the report that's come through from intel: every case Griffin has worked on since he joined the police. That's twenty-two years of arrests and convictions and sending bad guys to prison. She scrolls the spreadsheet; there are hundreds here. A million officers raking through, and it'll still take them months. They don't have that sort of time.

The phone rings by her elbow and she answers it.

'DCI Elliott? This is Dr Gibson, from the ICU. The starvation victim – David Foden? He's woken up.'

'Thank you,' she replies. She grabs her coat and heads out.

The doctor meets her at the door of the ward.

'He's conscious,' he says. 'But asleep now, and only awake for short periods of time. He's still in a critical condition.'

'I'm aware of that,' Cara replies, trying her best to keep her voice steady. 'I wouldn't ask if this wasn't important, but it's essential we speak to him soon. We have lives on the line.'

The doctor looks back, reluctantly. 'Okay. Give me half an hour. If he's not back awake by that time, I'll try to rouse him.'

Thirty minutes. Cara paces the corridor, receiving annoyed glances from the nurses. She looks at her watch – barely five minutes have passed. She'll get coffee, she resolves, and starts to walk, but after a few moments realises she's going in the opposite direction. Towards Noah.

She hesitates. In the past he was the first person she would speak to when things got tough, and that instinct is still there, buried. She takes another few steps, remembering his words – *don't come and see me anymore, go* – but something pulls.

She walks the corridors quickly, as if any hesitation will change her mind, showing her credentials to the guard and walking in. Head high, shoulders back.

There's only one guard now; the room is empty, but for her and Noah. He doesn't look up.

'I told you—' he begins, directing it to the wall.

'I don't give a shit what you told me,' Cara replies. 'And I don't want to listen to your woe-is-me bullshit. I need your help.'

'I can't—'

'Griffin is missing.'

That gets his attention. He turns, his forehead furrowed. 'When? How?'

'Last night. He went to the crime scene. Jamie thinks they were following him, abducted him via a trapdoor to the lower levels. Knocked him down. Drove him out. The place was crawling with SOCOs, yet nobody saw a thing. We didn't even know the trapdoor was there.'

Cara's aware her voice is getting hysterical, and slumps down in the seat next to the bed. Noah's silent, studying her.

In the twenty-four hours that have passed, the swelling has subsided on his face. He looks more like the man she used to know.

He opens his mouth, closes it again.

'What?'

'Why Griffin?'

'Someone he's pissed off. That wouldn't be so unusual.'

'But why now? Why him? There must be a thousand coppers that have made arrests. More hardened criminals

248

than this killer. There are gangs out there, drug cartels, and Griffin is the one abducted?'

'You think he's sending a message?'

'I think you have to assume it's closer to home than you think. He's not a small bloke, he wouldn't have gone down without a fight. They obviously realise you're getting closer – the sensible thing would be to hide. Go quiet and wait for your investigation to stall. But instead, they're abducting people right under your nose.'

'You didn't stop.'

He looks at her, unblinking.

'You knew we were onto you. And yet you kept killing.'

'That's different.'

'How?'

'Don't you remember Shenton's profile?' He wrinkles his nose with disdain. 'The Echo Man had to kill. A sexual sadist, remember? That was a compulsion. He couldn't sit back and wait – something drove him to behave that way. Fucking miracle you haven't still got bodies dropping at your feet.'

'Because we caught you. Because you're in here.'

He stares at her. Expressionless. 'I let you catch me. I showed you what you needed to see. So you'd believe me. Your new killer is the same – they're showing you something. You need to work out what.'

Cara's phone buzzes, but she doesn't look at the message, just stares at Noah.

'Why did you come here, Cara? Why do you continue to come here?'

'I don't know,' she says, honestly, and turns on her heel. The half an hour is up. She needs to go and see their victim, but as she walks, Noah's words rattle in her head.

I showed you what you needed to see. So you'd believe me.

She's always doubted that Noah was the Echo Man. She put that down to a reluctance to let go of her friend, to accept that her professional radar was so piss-poor that he had been killing right next to her and she'd never realised. The Noah she'd known had been calm, kind, trusting. Not a psychopathic sexual sadist, as the papers said.

But as she strides away, a niggle of doubt starts up in her head. A little voice – a new one – asking a different question.

What if her instincts were correct? What if Noah Deakin wasn't the Echo Man, and never had been?

What then?

Chapter 43

The skeleton now has eyes, bloodshot and yellowed, that look at Cara from within his shrunken face.

'Who are you?' he croaks.

Cara repeats her introduction. He says nothing as a reptilian tongue pushes out of his mouth and licks his cracked lips.

'Can I . . .?' Cara asks, picking up the plastic beaker of water. He nods and she guides the straw into his mouth, slowly taking a sip, a trickle spilling onto his chin. Cara pushes down her revulsion, wipes it gently away with a tissue.

'Police?' he says. 'Why didn't you find me?' A chuckle, little more than a wheeze from wet lungs. 'First time in my life I pray for the police.'

'We didn't know you'd been abducted. I'm sorry.'

'They said it was about Emma.'

'Your daughter?'

He nods, wincing, every movement painful. 'Since the moment that bitch pushed her out into the world, everything was about Emma. Why would this be any different?'

Cara swallows her disgust, for this man who let his daughter starve. 'Can you tell me anything about the people who took you?'

He closes his eyes for so long Cara wonders whether he's fallen back asleep. But then he speaks.

'There was one. Big man. He gave me water, blankets. I begged him for food, for anything, but he didn't care.'

'He was the only person you saw? What about a voice? Did anyone talk to you? Over the speaker?'

'Not often. Once at the beginning – to ask my name. But I knew I was being watched. That little red light. Always on. How long was I there?' he asks. 'I tried to keep track in the beginning, but there was no day or night. I lost count. How long?'

'Forty-three days.'

'No food for forty-three days. Who does that? Leave me in that room, like an animal.' He reaches out an arm, no more than bone, grabs at Cara's with dry scratchy fingers, a skeleton risen from the grave. She resists the urge to recoil. 'Am I going to die?' he asks. 'Tell me.'

'The doctors say it's likely, yes.'

He sags back into the bed. 'A gun to the head. That's what they should have done. If they wanted me dead.'

'Did you hear any other prisoners?'

'I heard one. A man. Just shouting, annoyed at first. Then later – the screaming.' He looks at Cara. 'What did they do to him?'

'You don't want to know,' she replies, remembering Stephen Allen, the blood, the tearing. 'Is there anything? Anything else you remember? Something he might have asked you over the speaker? Noises, smells?'

'He ate lunch in front of me, once. Can you believe that?

Walked in and stood there, eating a meatball sub. I could smell it. Fuck, that smell. Hot meatballs, dripping fat. Some of it hit the floor – I crawled across and licked it once he'd gone. If I could have one of those now.' He sighs. 'But the doctor says my innards can't take it. Too fucked.'

Cara stands, unable to bear this man any longer. This is a waste of time; he knows nothing that will help them. She gets to her feet, walking across to the door. Disappointed, she turns back one last time. 'If you remember anything else, the nurses have my number.'

The man opens his eyes, stares at her across the room. 'You're wrong, you know.'

Cara pauses. 'Wrong? About what?'

'About the voice. The person behind the camera.'

Two quick steps bring her back to his bedside. 'What do you mean?'

'You said "he". "Did he speak to you?"'

'And?'

'The person that came into the room – he was a man all right. But the voice on the speaker? That was a woman.'

Chapter 44

'He definitely said it was a woman?' Jamie says. He's arrived back in the incident room with Brody, to find Cara frantically scrolling videos in her office.

'He was certain,' she replies. 'But I've been going through these, and it's a man's voice. There's no doubt about it.'

She points to her screen and he watches over her shoulder as Terence Gregory, the man who started this whole thing off, meets his horrific end. And she's right. It's a deep, masculine voice.

'Some sort of distorter?'

'Doesn't sound like that to me. What if . . .' Cara sits back in her chair. 'What if it was a man at the beginning? Say Edward Morris – our film-maker, but once he died someone else took over? All of these videos are at least a few years old.'

'David Foden had been locked in that room for a month and a half.'

'When Morris was too ill to get his hands dirty?'

'It's a possibility. Toby?' Jamie shouts out to the incident room. Shenton looks up with interest. 'Come in here for a sec.'

He does as he's told, sitting opposite Cara. Jamie does the same, the three of them in a triangle.

'Cara's discovered something interesting: we think there's a woman involved.'

'Really?' He frowns, but looks interested.

'What do your studies have to say about female serial killers?'

'I could do some research—'

'No, now, Shenton,' Cara interrupts. 'You know this stuff. Give us your initial thoughts.'

'Well.' He stops, thinking. 'It's generally thought that female serial killers are so rare they are an impossibility. Aileen Wuornus – an American who shot and killed seven men in 1990 – was considered an anomaly, and in the UK, almost, without exception, British serial killers are white men. There are only four women in the last century: Rose West, Myra Hindley, Beverley Allitt, and most recently, Lucy Letby.'

'Joanna Dennehy?' Jamie says.

'Dennehy killed three men and attempted to kill two others in 2013 in a ten-day spree, therefore wasn't a serial killer.'

'Semantics,' Jamie says. 'But go on.'

Shenton casts Jamie a disgruntled look, but continues: 'So female serial killers do exist – they just operate in a different way. Allitt and Letby, as we know, were so-called "Angels of Death" – caregivers working out of hospitals. West and Hindley both operated with a dominant male. Do we think that's what's happening here?'

Jamie glances at Cara. 'If the dominant male was Edward Morris or Trevor Brown, one's dead and one's in custody. Yet the killings are still going on.' He shies at his choice of words. 'Sorry,' he directs to Cara. 'I didn't mean Griffin.'

Cara waves it away. 'Unless the dominant male is the brother – Tyler. Who we still haven't found.' Jamie nods. 'Carry on, Shenton.'

'Assuming it's not Tyler Brown calling the shots – motive is an important consideration. Women are often described as "quiet killers" – they tend not to butcher or torture. They prefer poison or asphyxiation, and are generally location specific, they kill at home or at work. Men – like Bundy or Dahmer or Gacy – kill for power and control, while the motive for women, overwhelmingly, some research has found, is money. In modern history, there is no case of female sadism without a man.'

'But our killer is definitely sadistic,' Cara says. 'Look at how these people are dying.'

'As revenge. Retribution. She – if we're assuming it's a woman – is on a mission. Ridding the world of those she sees as bad guys, one at a time. She's getting a thrill out of it, just in a different way.'

'How so?'

'There is a massive lack of research into women serial killers, but it's widely believed that women go directly to murder. Males express power and control through sexual sadism, while women get their gratification from the actual death of their victim. By killing, they feel strong. They become someone who matters, when in their real life they are considered weak or frail.'

'And is the cause the same?' Jamie asks. 'Childhood abuse?'

Shenton glances to him briefly. 'Most likely. Emotional, physical, sexual or all of the above. But again, women differ in the way they respond to this. Men from abusive backgrounds often come out of the experience hostile

256

and abusive to others, women from similar backgrounds tend to direct the rage and abusiveness inward and punish themselves rather than others. While a man might kill, hurt or rape others as a way of dealing with his rage, a woman is more likely to channel it into something that would hurt primarily herself, such as alcohol or drug abuse, prostitution or suicide attempts. That's almost a direct quote from John Douglas,' he adds, somewhat smugly. 'The grandfather of criminal profiling. It is more socially acceptable for a woman to self-destruct than be outwardly aggressive.'

'Yet we know it does happen,' Jamie says, thinking about the terrible events from a few years ago. 'Women kill. We've experienced it first-hand.'

'And you're right, they do,' Shenton says. 'In your case, your wife was killed by someone operating in conjunction with a dominant male, but there are cases, now and throughout history, where women have been involved in hideous crimes. In genocide, in so-called honour killings, in human trafficking and terrorism. Women do kill, and more research needs to be done into why sociologically, we're so conditioned to believe that women are nurturers, carers and therefore when women murder, we find it hard to believe. As if they're going against their own biology.' He snorts with mirth, obviously getting into his stride. 'Here,' he continues, 'we know our killer is making money, substantial amounts from the enterprise, but where they could be killing swiftly, they're taking their time. Enjoying the experience – breaking all the norms of their gender, if the witness is to be believed and the killer we're searching for is, indeed, a woman.'

'So how does it help us catch them?' Jamie asks.

'It doesn't. It just gives us a new perspective. A woman this way inclined will either be an outcast, with few friends or family, or a social chameleon. A sociopath, able to adapt to fit society's norms, possibly even a mother. She may have carefully crafted a persona, playing a conventional role. Blending in.

'But with this killer, as with men, the same principles apply. Abducting their victims, locking them away in a different location, torturing them, carefully disposing of their bodies – this takes time and perseverance. And this fits with what we know about female killers – they're rarely disorganised. An organised offender like this one probably has their own car, but given the demands of these abductions I doubt they have a job, or at least, not one full time. They're meticulous, planned, smart and personable, with knowledge of computer systems and the dark web. Plus, she's probably older. Female serial killers are more likely to start killing later in life, and well into middle age. Males rarely murder beyond forty, but it seems menopause galvanises women into action.'

'Something to look forward to,' Cara mutters darkly.

Jamie gives her a small smile, then asks, 'How does Trevor Brown fit into this?'

'From what I've seen of him, I doubt he's the dominant male. He's the hired hand, the muscle, and he's not talking, which makes me think he's connected to the mission in some way. Because, as I said before, that's what this is – a mission killer. I have no doubt both Trevor Brown and our killer are getting something out of this – so a sadistic streak is likely – but more than anything, they believe in their cause. People are paying them to take revenge on the nasties out there, and they're doing it willingly. Even making art out of it.'

'Art?'

'The videos. Yes, sure, they're probably used as proof of a

job complete, but they're edited well. They could have done it themselves on a laptop, but instead they get a BAFTA-winning film-maker to do it. That's no coincidence.'

'Morris's daughter was killed by a drunk driver,' Cara says. 'In 2009. That fits our timeline.'

'And Morris's inciting incident, no doubt. Why he's involved. What we need is what started it for Trevor and our offender. But she's getting more brazen. She dumped Allen's body for us to find. She abducted Griffin from under our noses. She knows she's a hair's breadth from getting caught, and doesn't care. That makes her the most dangerous of all. She's got nothing left to lose.'

The room is silent. Jamie glances across to Cara; she looks moments away from tears.

'What does this mean for Griffin?' she asks quietly.

Shenton frowns. 'Nothing good.'

Chapter 45

Griffin's situation is grim. He tells himself to stay calm, to keep a clear head, but after who knows how many hours sitting here with a raging headache, freezing cold, chained to a fucking wall, he's more than aware things aren't looking good.

When he woke up, he knew exactly where he was. The first location – the concrete pit with the blinding floodlight. It smells of diesel and oil, of sweat and something awful. People have died here. It may have been a while ago, but the stench lingers.

His hands are cuffed behind his back, then attached to a metal ring, drilled into the wall. His wrists and shoulders are aching from his efforts to get away; his head pulses from the hit – whatever they did to knock him out and get him down here. They've taken his socks and boots, his shirt. He's bloody freezing.

He glares up at the camera; a small handheld thing, attached to a tripod, peering over the lip of the hole. Nobody's been in to see him, but they're watching. He doesn't know how long he's been here; there is no daylight, no light or dark. Just the single blinding floodlight, blasting down.

Above him sits a metal rig. Simple parallel bars, attached to hydraulic struts. He remembers what it was used for when Austin O'Brien was killed. Hands tied, hauling him up. He tries not to think about that. Tries to forget the screaming.

He's thirsty, stomach empty. He needs the toilet, but there's nowhere here, and it'll be a last resort going on the floor. His date with Brody feels like a different world, another time, and once again he berates himself for being so stupid. For letting himself end up here.

But there were SOCOs at that pub. Police all around. Someone will have seen where he went, surely?

He tries to conserve energy, but all he can do is shiver. He hasn't slept. He won't. He can't.

He jerks awake, a noise in the darkness. A door opening, heavy footsteps on concrete. A man stands on the edge of the pit, then drops down the few feet so he's standing inside. He's huge, muscles bulging from a tight black T-shirt. Balaclava on.

'Let me go, Tyler,' Griffin says.

The man recoils. 'How do you know my name?'

'I'm a police officer. A detective. Let me go. My whole team will be looking for me. You don't want to do this.'

The man chuckles. He pulls his hand out from behind his back, something small and black in his palm. He clicks a button and a bright purple light crackles from the top. 'Let's see about that, shall we?'

Griffin pushes away from him, struggles as much as he

can, but he's stuck. He has no defence as the man advances, pressing the taser to his neck.

A bolt of pain. He jerks, collapses. Out cold.

When Griffin wakes he realises that things are worse. Far worse.

He's now upright, hanging from his cuffed hands, stretched above his head, secured with rope to the rig above. He plants his feet on the cold concrete, tugs; there's little give, and he turns a full 360, recoiling when he sees the man's still in the pit with him, leaning nonchalantly against the wall on the far side.

'Why am I here?' Griffin asks. 'Give me that at least.'

The man says nothing, but looks up to the camera. A voice speaks.

'Tell me your name.'

Her voice echoes off the walls – she's there. She's in the room. He turns, frantically looking, but he can't see anyone, only the glare from the floodlight, creating flares of white in his vision.

'Tell me your name,' she repeats.

Griffin tilts his head, glaring upwards towards the sound. 'Fuck you,' he spits.

The punch breaks a rib; he hears the crack, then a searing pain flares in his chest. Griffin chokes, gasps, tries to breathe, his contracting lungs inflicting more agony as the man backs away, cracking his knuckles.

'Tell me your name,' the voice says again.

'Who are you?' he gasps.

The second punch on his kidneys makes him buck, then vomit on the floor. His legs buckle and he hangs for a moment, cuffs cutting into his wrists, panting, spitting puke onto the concrete.

'Tell me your name.'

Griffin blinks at his bare feet, tears obscuring his vision. 'Nathanial Mark Griffin,' he says, barely more than a whisper.

The man steps forward. Griffin flinches, but he just taps Griffin gently on the cheek.

'See? That wasn't so hard,' the man says, and then he's gone. Pulling himself up out of the pit, heavy footsteps fading away.

Griffin listens to a door opening and closing, the grind of a key in a lock. He finds his feet again, taking some of the pressure from his now bleeding wrists. Two thoughts bubble and pop in his head.

I'm fucked.

And, I'm not getting out of here alive.

Chapter 46

Cara sits at her desk, Jamie opposite. The door is closed, shut as Shenton left.

'What's the plan of action?' Cara asks Jamie.

He stays quiet, giving her a look.

'You think I shouldn't be working this case.'

'I *know* you shouldn't be working this case. You can't be impartial – it's your brother that's missing.'

'What would you do?' she asks. He stays silent. 'What's your take?'

He regards her, warily. Then sits back, crossing one leg over the other. 'I'm willing to assume this killer is female. But whoever they are, they're coming to the end of their story. They've killed in silence for nearly fifteen years. Never wanting any recognition for what they've done, never asking for praise for all the arseholes they've taken off the streets. But we've found their ground zero. If I'm right, we have their burial ground. And Trevor Brown, their muscle man, locked up in a cell. This is it. Their end game.'

'So what would you do? I need to find my brother, Jamie.'

Cara glances up at the clock – twelve hours have passed. 'Before they kill him.'

'*We* need to find your brother. And we will. But you should be with your family.'

'Griffin is my family.'

'Your kids?'

'They're at school. And it's their week with my ex. Griffin's all I have.'

Jamie sighs. 'Fine. Stay here. But we need to decide on a way forward that doesn't involve you heading up the investigation. Before DCI Ryder comes along and makes that decision for us.'

Cara's silent for a moment, mulling it over. As much as she doesn't want to relinquish control, the last thing she wants is Rosie-fucking-Ryder in charge. She trusts Jamie. Plus, she has something else on her mind.

'Jamie – if I tell you something, do you promise it won't leave this room?'

He blinks; he's intrigued, but says, 'You have my word.'

Cara takes a deep breath. This is it. The moment of truth. 'I don't believe Noah Deakin is the Echo Man. I don't think he killed all those people.'

Jamie stares at her in surprise. He's silent while he digests her words.

Then: 'What makes you think that?' he asks, slowly, carefully.

'I went to speak to him about the snuff films. About the Polaroid and where it came from. I showed him one of the videos. And his response – it was disgust, hatred. Any self-respecting sexual sadist would have loved seeing that, but he couldn't stand it.'

'He's putting on an act, Cara.'

'He won't help us with the Polaroid, won't tell me where it came from—'

'More games.'

'But I don't think it is that. I don't think he *knows*. Yes, I'm biased – I'm aware,' she repeats, seeing Jamie's face. 'But there's something about the way he is now. He doesn't fit Shenton's profile, never has, and he seems worn down, beaten. He's not the master manipulator that the press made him out to be. Never has been. He's depressed, suicidal—'

'Because he's living the rest of his life in prison. Look, Cara,' Jamie says, cutting her off before she can start again. 'He's presenting the image of himself you want to see. You want him to be contrite, remorseful, because that fits in with the Noah Deakin you knew. He's playing a part. And he's doing it well. He confessed, Cara. To everything.'

'Someone put him up to it.'

'Who?'

Cara can't answer that. There were never any other suspects, no one else in the frame. Except . . .

'There was a second DNA sample. One we couldn't match – the whole flat was covered in it. We found nothing in his house after he was arrested – no blood, no guns, no weapons—'

'Because he killed them somewhere else—'

'Where? Nobody found a second location. And the handwriting in the diaries was nothing like Noah's. Explain that.'

'I can't, Cara—'

'That's for starters, there'll be more, I know it.'

Jamie looks at her with the expression she's come to know so well. Sympathy, understanding. But also condescension.

Like she's a five-year-old and needs a pat on the head. It makes her mad.

'That case is closed,' he says gently. 'Noah Deakin has been charged and sentenced. This isn't what we should be focusing on right now.'

'So take it – be the SIO of the investigation. Find Griffin. Find the killer. And I'll . . . I'll look into this.'

Jamie pauses for a moment. 'Fine. Just don't do anything stupid. And I know nothing, right?'

'Right. Please, Jamie. Find my brother.'

'I will,' he says, and he leaves her in her office, alone.

She watches him go, calling the team around him, getting ready for a briefing. Jamie Hoxton is a good detective – the best there is. And knowing Jamie, he'll get Ryder's team working on it too, under his command.

There's nothing she can do. But this – The Echo Man case – this is hers.

She looks away from her computer to the storage box on her floor, considering the others in the archive, the information contained within. Those days were a blur, she can't trust herself to remember the detail accurately, the little things that build and make a case. She'll get them brought up, but, in the meantime, she pulls the solitary box over, removes the lid.

She'll start here.

Chapter 47

To Jamie's surprise, the added responsibility doesn't come with fear, or trepidation, or the stress he thought it would – it's determination that floods his veins. And anger.

Jamie's always prided himself on being an even-tempered man, but with Griffin's abduction, all he feels is hot-blooded rage. Not the out-of-control kind, but a steely focus, a tensing of his muscles that makes him feel strong. He will find his friend. And he will take them down.

The team recognise his iron will and crack on with their allotted tasks. Brody looks washed out, but is on the phone to the CSM, back at the old pub, requesting an update on what – or who – might be underneath that concrete floor. Shenton's studying the traffic cameras and ANPR for any roads leading away from the pub. And Jamie's called Ryder in Basingstoke, receiving surprisingly little resistance, galvanising the team there.

Both intel and the boots on the ground are searching for Tyler Brown, but the man has vanished. Charlie and the digital team are desperately trying to break into the security surrounding the cameras, and the lab has nothing.

Jamie fidgets, unhappy with their progress. But what else can they do? He empathises with Cara's frustration from earlier today, and glances back to her office. She's sitting quietly at her desk, flicking through crime scene photos, her head down. He wonders at her words earlier: wishful thinking, that her friend and past colleague is innocent, or something more sinister? A sign she's losing the plot; too many years of traumatic detective work, finally taking its toll. PTSD, or worse? Either way, he can't worry for long, as Brody waves in his direction.

'Holly needs us at the old pub. They've found something.'

They drive together, Brody silent in the passenger seat. Another detective who shouldn't be working this case, assuming her romantic ties with Griffin are more than just gossip.

'Are you okay?' Jamie asks. All he seems to ask nowadays. He manages a quick glance across to her; she's staring blankly out of the windscreen.

'Yes, boss, everything's fine.'

'You can talk to me, you know. I'm aware you and Griffin were . . . close,' he concludes, not sure how to describe their relationship. She stares at him for a moment, clearly debating whether to confide in him. 'I won't say anything to Cara.'

'You're still my DI.'

'For the next ten minutes I'm not. I'm worried about you, Alana. I hope you'd call me a friend?'

'Yes.' There's more hesitation, and Jamie chances another look away from the road. She's staring at her hands, laced together in her lap, then looks up and sniffs. 'I find it hard to trust people – men, particularly. Before I . . .'

She trails off again.

'Sleep with them?' Jamie tries, and Brody lets out a short laugh.

'No. Not that. No problems there. Before I, you know. Fall in love.'

She says it with slight disdain. As if it's something only idiots would do.

'I can understand that,' Jamie replies. 'Are you and Griffin . . .?'

'In love? No. But we could be, you know. If I gave it a chance. You know we went out last night – but it was a date. A real one. Did he tell you?'

'No, he didn't.'

'It was . . . nice. He's the first person I could imagine being with . . . properly.' She sniffs again, and Jamie realises she's crying. 'And now he's been abducted by a crazed murderer and he could die. You won't take me off the case, will you, boss? I'll go mad, sitting at home, waiting.'

'No. No, I won't. We need detectives, for one thing. But, if you want space, if it's all getting too much, you'll tell me?'

Jamie pulls up outside the pub and looks over at Brody. She's blowing her nose, dabbing under her eyes with a tissue. 'Please?' he adds.

'Yes. I will.'

Holly has walked across the car park to meet them, and now waits outside the car, her breath blowing frozen gusts in the cold. Jamie climbs out and greets her with a serious nod.

'You've found something?' he asks.

'Someone,' Holly confirms, and walks quickly back to the crime scene.

They sign in, suit up, and Holly leads the way down to the loading area, where Jamie had stood that morning. But what was once a solid block of grey now has lines of red chalk marked across it, dividing it into a grid. A figure in a white crime scene suit is bent over on their knees in the centre of the floor, meticulously working at something with a small trowel.

Holly guides them to the side. 'The dogs gave a positive indication across this whole area,' she says, 'but couldn't pinpoint to just one spot, probably because of the depth the bodies are buried. Next step was to run the GPR across it – Ground Penetrating Radar,' she clarifies, and Jamie nods. 'See if an area has been disturbed. Different mixes of concrete will look different under the radar, as will things like drains or pipes. But here. You can see the picture of what we're facing is fairly clear.'

She points away from the concrete slab, to where a laptop has been set up on a folding table. On the screen is a colourful image – a background of black, with a mixture of red, yellow and green splotches, lined up down the screen like a spine from a dinosaur. And among those are white and grey blobs.

Holly points to one. 'This is a cross section into the concrete, from grid D4 over there. And those,' she points to the grey, 'those are dead bodies.'

'But there's . . .'

Holly nods. 'A lot. An assumption at this stage, based on what you've told us. Could be animals, could be something with the same density as bone. So, to be sure, the forensic anthropologists started a test pit, looking for the target we believed to be closest to the surface. And this is what they found.'

She steps over to the middle of the floor, where the hunched figure pulls himself up with a stretch, letting them see what's underneath. Jamie crouches down and looks into the hole.

The concrete has been carefully chipped away, all scrapings deposited in a separate bucket, revealing a scrap of blue cloth just below the surface. And that's not all – a small patch of light brown, no more than three centimetres in diameter.

'We know a bit about how bodies decompose in concrete,' Holly says, dispassionately. 'Protected from the ambient environment, and because of the alkaline nature of the concrete, putrefaction is typically slowed. What you're looking at here is the formation of adipocere – a chemical change in the body fat that we believe corresponds with the six-month point of decomposition within concrete.'

'So this victim was killed six months ago?' Jamie nods to Brody, who's already looking through the case files on her phone.

'Approximately,' Holly confirms.

'How long until you can get them all out?'

Holly frowns, looking out across the grey slab. 'Weeks. Months. Who knows. We're going to need a structural engineer before we go much further, to confirm that the whole building's not going to come down once we dig out the foundations. Ideally, we'd prefer to take the whole slab out and run it through a CT or fluoroscope to see exactly what we're looking at, but that's just not possible. Too many bodies, all overlapping. Take one out whole and we risk disturbing another.'

'James Harvey,' Brody says, looking up from her phone. 'Jimmy – the drug dealer. Killed last October.'

'That would tally,' Holly replies. 'We also found this. Thrown in with the concrete.'

She bends down to a nearby box and pulls out an evidence bag. Inside is a ring, grey with dust, a few patches cleaned to show the gold underneath. She passes it to Jamie; he holds it up to the light.

Engraved on the ring are the initials JH.

'That's him. Jimmy Harvey,' Jamie says. 'We saw him in the video. We watched him die.'

'And now we know where he is buried,' Holly finishes.

Chapter 48

Between the mind-numbing, soul-dragging worry about Griffin, Cara thinks about Noah. About those fateful few weeks on the Echo Man case.

The bodies, the death, the murders – Noah by her side every step of the way. He was withdrawn, stressed, not sleeping – but then none of them were. It was the worst time in her life; never once did she suspect him.

Raiding flat 214 and finding box after box of mementos and artefacts. Newspaper clippings, sex toys, the worst kind of porn. His diaries, scrawled, frantic words dominating the page. Handwriting that didn't look like Noah's, fingerprints that didn't match.

And the DNA. She keeps coming back to that. The DNA found in the flat wasn't Noah's and didn't match to anyone on the system. It was another nameless, shapeless person. One who'd never been found.

Noah hadn't admitted to an accomplice, but she'd always wondered. How had Noah had the time to kill all those people? He worked with her, a DS in a busy Major Crimes team. And yet he'd managed to commit thirty-one murders, without her knowing. How?

And then there's the confession. Hours in an interview room, reciting facts about the victims, the murders, details only the killer would have known. That the police then had to corroborate by reaching out to the families. There was no arguing with that.

She arrives home, tired and weary, to an empty house. Frank greets her with a meow, winding his smooth furry body around her ankles. She reaches down to pick him up, but he dodges, elegantly leaping up to the kitchen table where he stares, his amber eyes level with her own. Questioning. Frank doesn't want her, the cat wants Griffin, and doesn't understand why his favourite person has left.

'It's not my fault,' Cara mutters to the cat, then goes to the cupboard and pours a bowl of Frank's biscuits. The cat ignores her, stalking away to the living room, tail in the air in disgust.

'It's not, you know,' Charlie says from behind her. She turns, surprised.

'You said you weren't coming back tonight?'

'I changed my mind.' He takes his coat off, standing in the doorway. 'It's not your fault,' he repeats.

'Who else's is it, then? I'm the SIO on the case, he was an officer in my team. And he's my baby brother.' Her voice cracks. It seems ridiculous saying it, her six-foot, built-like-a-shithouse brother, but she's all he has. 'I should have been looking after him, and instead all I could do was shout. I pushed him away.'

Charlie's next to her in moments, wrapping his arms around her. She rejects his comfort and pulls away, swiping angrily at her eyes. 'I should be out there, looking for him, and instead I've been sidelined.'

'They took you off the case? So what have you been doing at the nick all day?'

'Just . . .' She can't tell him. Shouldn't. But she doesn't want to lie again. 'Reading case notes,' she says, warily.

'What case?' Charlie takes a step back, realising. 'You're not . . .'

'I'm just reviewing it.'

'But why?'

'Because I don't think he did it, okay?'

Charlie stares at her for a moment, his mouth open. 'He—'

'Yes, I know. Thank you. But . . . but . . . Fuck's sake, it doesn't matter, I knew you wouldn't understand.'

'Don't attack me, Cara. Try and see this from my point of view. First you tell me you've been lying to me, visiting him, for the last year. And now you say you don't think he did it?'

Cara glares. 'What are you saying?'

'I'm saying . . . Fuck, I don't know.'

'What? Tell me, Charlie.'

'I'm saying that maybe whatever feelings you had for Noah Deakin are still very much there. And you can't reconcile that with the truth that he's a murderer, so instead of leaving the whole fucking mess alone, you're making it worse. Trying to get him off. Trying to prove he didn't do all those terrible things.'

'Fuck off.'

'You're in love with a serial killer—'

'I'm not in love with him. I never was. But there's something off about the case. We found foreign DNA. His handwriting didn't match—'

276

'He fucking confessed, Cara!'

Cara stops, stunned. Charlie never raises his voice, never shouts. Yet here he is screaming at her across her kitchen. As if shocked by his own response, he turns and leaves, his quick footsteps echoing out into the hallway and up the stairs to the bedroom. She hears a door slam.

She stands in the middle of the kitchen, frozen. Blood races in her veins; a droplet of sweat trickles down her spine. What is she doing? Ruining the one good relationship in her life, with a man who loves her, who wants to move in with her. And for what? For whom?

Slowly, she makes her way out of the kitchen, up the stairs. She looks at the closed bedroom door for a moment, then opens it with a shaking hand.

Charlie is lying on the bed in the dark. Staring at the ceiling, his shoes kicked off. She takes a few steps, but he doesn't shift his gaze, not even as she climbs on to the bed, shuffling towards him.

It's dark in the room, the only light from the open door, but she can see the expression on his face. Annoyance, anger, but also hurt. She has done this to him. This is her fault.

'Charlie, I'm sorry.' She lies down by his side, her face level with his. He still doesn't turn.

'You're going to drop this?' he directs to the ceiling.

'I can't . . . I need—'

'What about what I need?' He's not shouting this time – his voice so full of disappointment it's almost a whisper.

'Charlie, I'm not in love with him. This is about justice.'

He shakes his head, turns away.

She runs her fingers through his hair, then reaches out and touches his chin, trying to get him to look at her. He shakes his head, refuses, so she shifts her body, straddling him, bringing her face close to his.

His eyes are screwed shut.

'Charlie, please.' It's almost a beg, and he opens his eyes, meeting her gaze. In the darkness, his pupils are black. So full of animosity she almost recoils; she's never seen him look at her in this way. So she's shocked when he reaches up and kisses her.

There's nothing loving about this kiss. It's a clashing of mouths, his hands on the back of her head, pulling her against him. It's anger, frustration. A turn-on.

She finds herself responding, kissing him harder, pushing her body against his. His hands move, exploring inside her clothes, pushing, grabbing, almost ripping the garments off her. They flip, her underneath, and she does the same, fumbling over his belt, pushing his trousers, his boxers down, tugging his shirt over his head.

They've had frantic sex before, but nothing like this. This is a want, a desperation, craving the closeness, but eager for a release. She grabs at him, wraps her legs around his; licks, sucks, almost bites at his neck as his fingers find her, rough. Almost too rough, but she likes it, this side of him.

As if reading her mind, he moves away, grabs her hips and flips her over, pushing her onto her knees. Her hands grip the bed head; she hears him reach into the bedside table, rip open a condom and then he's inside her, one hand on her hip, the other grabbing at her neck, pulling her hair. It's hard, forceful, but this, this is what she needs. She's not thinking about work, not even thinking about Charlie, not really. This is just sex. Just fucking.

This is about him. Noah.

And then he's in her head.

She can't stop it: the thoughts race, intrusive, all-consuming. She reaches one hand between her legs and, while Charlie fucks her, she thinks of him. Noah behind her. Noah's hands on her hips. Noah's cock— And she comes, with an exclamation, a cry of relief, Charlie behind her, doing the same.

They collapse on the bed, Charlie on top, still inside her, his breath hot on her back. After a moment, he moves damp strands of her hair and kisses her softly on the nape of her neck, then pulls away and walks off.

She doesn't move, her body throbbing from the orgasm, the images of him, of Noah, still seared into her brain. She hears the chain flush and Charlie return, the bed moving from his weight as he gets under the duvet. He reaches out an arm, but she moves away, getting up and going into the bathroom.

She stands in front of the mirror, naked. She doesn't put the light on, but in the glow from the street light outside she can see herself. The flushed cheeks, the damp, sex-ruffled hair. The bags under her eyes, the lines on her forty-something-year-old face.

And she thinks, What are you doing?

What – the fuck – are you doing?

Chapter 49

You haven't moved in a while. I watch you through the video feed as you battle sleep, standing upright, your eyes closed, your body sagging. We have offered you water; you refused. But you need your strength. It is not time. Not yet.

It is getting late, but there is still work to be done and I turn my attention to the laptop by my side, to the video I am editing on the screen. I am no expert; this will have to do.

I scroll to the beginning of the film and watch it again. Amateur footage, a lonely road, a car losing control, tyres skidding. It twists, turns, then leaves the tarmac, tyres bounce on grass, then it's rolling, crumpling metal. And the people inside, tossed around, dolls in a washing machine. I imagine bones breaking, skulls cracking, until the car comes to rest with a hiss and a creak.

I stop the video, eject the disc. I carefully place it in a plastic case, then into a white envelope. Ready to go.

I pick up a pen, and on the front, in black block capitals, I write:

On the screen, you have woken up. You shift position, your once-handsome face contorted with pain. I check the clock.

Save your strength, Nate Griffin. There is still time.

DAY 7

THURSDAY

Chapter 50

Cara wakes before Charlie and leaves for work without him. She has two priorities – she addresses the most important first: finding her brother.

She calls Jamie on hands-free while she drives. He answers on the first ring, his voice gruff.

'And a good morning to you, boss. Are you aware it's half six?'

She glances at the clock. 'Did I wake you?'

A sigh. 'No. I'm up.'

'I'm on my way into the nick now. I want an update first thing.'

A pause. 'Am I still the SIO?'

'Yes, yes. But I need to know what's going on. Please?'

'I'll be there in the next hour.'

She hangs up, satisfied, and pulls into the car park. Grabbing a coffee from the kitchen on the way through, she arrives in her office, surprised to find a large brown envelope on her desk, a Post-it note attached.

You owe me one! it says.

She tugs her coat off and sits at her desk, opening it and

pulling out the thick file within. It's a worn, buff folder, *Northbrooke Children's Home* stamped in thick black capitals across the top. And below it, the name.

Deakin, Noah. DOB 05/02/84.

Coffee forgotten, she opens to the first page with shaking hands.

She spends the next hour absorbed in the information within. She reads reports written by psychologists, men with little sympathy for the child in their care. Annual summaries of Noah's progress, or the lack of. Social services reviews, carefully detailing the parental abuse that led to Noah ending up in the home. And the photographs. The horror of these. She can't look at them at first, unable to digest the small, skinny boy with the scared saucer eyes, but forces herself to analyse them as a critical detective rather than a mother of two.

Footsteps at the back of the office divert her attention, and she glances up as Jamie arrives. She shouts to him and he heads over.

'Close the door,' she says, and he does so. 'Look at this.' He sits down and she pushes the file across to him. 'Noah Deakin's file from the children's home where he grew up.'

'What? How did you get this?'

'We requested it after he confessed. But after the sentencing, no one gave a shit. I called in a favour last night from a former colleague down in the archives. But look, Jamie. It's all here.'

'What's all here?' He flicks through the endless pages with disbelief, then sits back in his seat, crossing his arms over his chest. 'Give me the summary.'

His scepticism is no more than she expects. But she can convince him. 'Noah Deakin arrived at the children's home in 1994, after his mother died from a drug overdose,' she says, finding the photos and pushing them across to Jamie. 'He was ten but weighed the same as a six-year-old. Chronically underweight, filthy, covered in cigarette burns. Signs of sexual abuse. Father unknown. Reports from that time describe him as withdrawn, almost completely mute, until another child arrives in 1996.' She stabs at the file with her finger. 'This child, described only as RDK, becomes his best friend. To the point that the psychologist describes it as an unhealthy attachment. They're inseparable, until Noah leaves in 2002. That child is the key.'

Jamie still looks doubtful. 'Your theory is that child is the real Echo Man?'

'Yes! Who else could it be? We just need to work out who RDK is, and we have our answer.'

'He left in 2002 – Noah would have been eighteen? Who knows who else he met after that? When did he join the police?'

'Straight after.'

'Where he spent time undercover and in the drug squad. I know his background too, Cara. What's more likely is his history of sexual and emotional abuse puts him squarely within the ranks of all the other serial killers out there.'

'But look, here. The psychologist, Dr Mark Singleton,' she reads, 'describes him as "easily influenced", "forming an unhealthily close attachment to anyone who shows interest". We need to find this man. Speak to him.'

A knock on the door disturbs them, and Cara scrabbles around, hiding the file before Shenton pokes his head around the door.

'Everyone's here,' he says. 'Do you need us, boss?'

A shock as Cara realises he's talking to Jamie. He's in charge now. Jamie nods and gets up, looking back at Cara. He pauses in the doorway.

'You're looking for something that isn't there,' he says, quietly. 'I know you're frustrated because you can't help search for Griffin, but this isn't the answer. Come and listen to the morning briefing. You might notice something we don't.'

Cara forces a smile. 'Okay. Give me five minutes.'

Jamie leaves her; she watches the team gather in the incident room, Jamie standing at the front. She puts the photographs and notes back in the file and puts it in the drawer of her desk, but before she gets up, she hesitates. She looks down at her computer screen, then opens a window in Google.

Dr Mark Singleton clinical psychologist, she types.

A few entries emerge. Mainly scientific papers, but also a listing at a university in the north of England. With an email address.

She selects it and drafts a quick note with her name and contact details, requesting he call her immediately. *Help on an urgent case.*

She clicks send without a second thought.

Jamie might be right. But if he isn't, this man holds the key.

Chapter 51

Jamie faces the team – and is struck by how few of them there are. Brody and Shenton, now joined by Ryder to update them on the army of faceless detectives and civilian investigators working in Basingstoke. How are they expected to find Griffin like this? So much evidence, so few leads.

He spent last night in his empty flat. Alone, laptop on, reading emails, updates, reports, getting nowhere. The burden of the investigation weighs heavily on his shoulders. They're into the thirty-third hour, and Jamie is inexperienced; a newly promoted detective inspector, who's never run a multiple-murder investigation before. He's seen Adam do it, he watched Cara last year, but here he is, alone. When making the wrong call could mean life or death for one of his closest friends.

Jamie can't help but imagine what Griffin is going through. He's seen the videos. The victims and their final moments. What might be Griffin's fate? What 'crime' is he being held for?

'Shenton,' he says now, forcing confidence into his

voice. 'Where are we with the back catalogue of Griffin's convictions and arrests?'

Shenton frowns, glancing back to his computer screen. 'I've been going through them, but there are so many it's impossible to know where to start.'

'Nobody jumping out?'

'Not at this point. I've been looking for someone with money who might have cause to go for Griffin now – someone who's just got out of prison, someone who's just gone in – but any of these shitbags could hold a grudge.'

'Good job my team is working hard,' Ryder says, stepping forward. She's been fidgeting since she got here, barely looking at him, disconcerted by not being the one in charge. 'Do you mind?' she says, shirtily. For someone who claims she's unbothered by rank, this clearly pisses her off.

'No, please, update us,' Jamie replies, forcing politeness.

Ryder moves to the front and starts talking, going through the progress the other team has made. Contacting family members of the victims, reinterviewing witnesses from the abductions, warrants, social media, CCTV. She's smooth, commanding the room with confidence, and Jamie can see why she's got where she has. How easily she could take over. He glances back to Cara – she's watching Ryder, her chin cupped in her hand, her eyebrows low. Is she doubting her decision to make Jamie SIO?

'Jamie?' Ryder pulls him back into the here and now. 'DI Hoxton?'

'Sorry, yes. What?'

Ryder smiles, the grin of a crocodile. 'Shenton was just saying that the bank came back with the statements from the Lloyd family. The rape victim?' she adds when Jamie looks blank.

'Yes, thank you. And?' he directs to Shenton.

'And the family has money. A lot of money,' Shenton stresses, as Jamie pushes his self-doubt to the side. 'But nothing out of the ordinary until Monday the fourth of March, four days after Stephen Allen was released, when there was one large payment to a company called CryptoStreamline. They buy and sell Bitcoin.'

'Paying the killers?'

'That's my theory. But there's no way of proving that unless the good people at CryptoStreamline respond to our messages or we get a warrant. Neither are forthcoming.'

'Keep trying. How far did you get with the CCTV and traffic cams to and from the old pub?'

'The closest one is on the M27. Ten miles away from the location.'

'And Tyler Brown. Have we found him yet?'

Brody takes over. 'No luck,' she says. 'He's gone to ground. Intel are still looking for possible connections and acquaintances, they've been going through his ex-employers . . .'

Her voice trails off as her gaze shifts to the whiteboard – to the screenshots of the two locations in the videos.

'Brody?' Jamie says, and her attention snaps back to him. 'What are you thinking?'

'Just . . . location one. The concrete hole where the first victims were killed. Does that look like a mechanic's pit to you?'

'A what?'

'The hole in the floor of a garage. My brother has one – you park the car over the top so you can easily work on the underside. Tyler Brown is a mechanic. Have we searched his previous places of work?'

'No – get on it. Good thinking.'

Jamie's getting into his stride when a PC sticks his head around the door and the conversation stops.

'DCI Elliott?' he says. Cara looks up. 'I'm sorry to interrupt, but this was dropped off at the front desk last night. They said it wasn't urgent, but they were insistent that it should come to you.'

He holds a small white envelope in an evidence bag. Everyone stares. Nobody moves.

'What's in it?' Cara snaps.

'A DVD of some kind? I'd guess . . .' the PC says, unsure, sensing the chill in the room.

'And who dropped it off?'

'They didn't get a name. I mean . . . I can check CCTV . . .'

'Yes, do that. Urgently.'

He holds it out; nobody wants to take it, least of all Cara. She looks at it, scared.

'I can't,' she stutters. 'It might be . . .'

It might be Griffin on that disc. Jamie takes it from the PC, turns it around in his hands. It feels hot, as if it's charged.

There's nothing good on here.

'Boss?' Shenton speaks, and Jamie stares at him, stunned before he realises what Shenton's getting at. The stand-alone computer is on, the disc drawer open, ready. Shenton hands Jamie a pair of blue gloves; he puts them on before taking the package out of the evidence bag, unwrapping it as carefully as he can. Sure enough, it's a DVD in a plastic box. Blank, unmarked. He opens the box and places the disc in the computer. The drawer slides in with an ominous clunk and a whirr.

After a few tense seconds, it plays, showing nothing but

black. Jamie glances up at the clock – it's nine a.m. They have fifteen hours left. That can't be what this is?

The whole team watches in silence, Cara included. She's standing a few paces back, half turned away, and Jamie doesn't want her to watch this – fuck, *he* doesn't want to watch this – but before he can usher her away, the screen comes to life.

It's not what they were expecting.

There is no small white room. No concrete pit. It's a country road – a hedge on one side, a grass verge on the other. Shot from inside a car, a view from the back seat. It's too dark to make out who's driving except for the curve of an arm, the collar of a jacket. The radio plays quietly, there's no conversation. It's night, the road pitch black except for the headlights, cutting through the gloom. *13/03/24, 23:26* the time stamp proclaims. Last night.

Jamie's confused. This isn't the killer's normal MO.

And then it all becomes clear.

The car jerks, as if the driver has braked suddenly, a shout, then a sharp turn to the left. The whole vehicle shakes; the image through the windscreen blurs as the car flips, rolls, over and over. Smashing, grinding, a cry of pain, a scream. A terrifying crash and the car stops, rocking on its broken wheels. There is no sound. The video ends.

Nobody moves. Jamie glances to Ryder, who's staring at the screen, mouth open, then back to Cara. She leans forward and rewinds the video; they all watch it again, but this time Jamie's looking for a road sign, an identifying mark. Something, anything that will help them find these victims.

'It's a Mercedes,' Brody says next to them. 'The logo on the steering wheel. A nice one too – see that dashboard?

Top of the range. I know my cars,' she adds, in response to Jamie's questioning look. 'Four brothers.'

'And it's red,' Shenton adds. 'Look at the trim.'

Cara utters a quick gasp, then grabs for her mobile, making a call. It rings out; she tries again and again, ever more frantic.

'Cara?'

She starts crying, small sobs as the number refuses to connect.

'Cara,' Jamie asks again. 'What's going on?'

She doesn't reply until he stands in front of her, stopping her by placing his hands gently on her upper arms. She stills, looking up at him.

'Roo,' she says. 'I can't get hold of Roo.' She points to the screen. 'My ex-husband,' she repeats. 'He drives a red Mercedes, an expensive one.' Cara meets his gaze, her panic barely contained, and for the first time, Jamie understands. A chill prickles down his spine.

'He has the kids,' she continues, her voice shaking with fear. 'He's looking after my fucking kids. What if my children were in that car?'

Chapter 52

Cara's mind descends into free fall. The panic is overwhelming – she can't focus on what needs to be done, how they can find her family. She's aware of Jamie leading her back to her office, plonking her in her chair, then a flurry of activity, barked instructions, calls being made.

She watches Jamie speak to Brody, their concern evident as they glance back to her, then they part and the chaos continues. All she can do is keep pressing the green button on her phone, dialling Roo again and again.

Hello, this is Andrew Elliott. I can't get to the phone right now, but if you would like to leave a message hello this is Andrew Elliott this is Andrew Elliott this is Andrew Elliott . . .

The two figures in the front seat, could that have been Roo and Sarah? Because if Sarah is with him, then surely the kids were there, too? They wouldn't have left Tilly and Josh at home alone. She tries to remember when she last spoke to her children, but her brain is scrambled. Monday evening, definitely. But last night she was distracted, and if they were in that car then . . . then . . . then . . .

But why hasn't anyone called her? She's no longer Roo's next of kin, but Roo's parents would have been contacted. Unless Roo's dead, and the kids are dead, and they're so lost in their grief that they've assumed she's been notified, and . . . and . . .

'Cara?' Jamie comes into her office, grabs a chair and pulls it up next to her.

'Just tell me.'

'The kids are fine. They were with Roo's parents. They had them overnight, dropped them at school this morning. They have no idea anything's wrong.'

'Tilly and Josh are fine?' She starts sobbing with relief. 'They're at school?'

Jamie smiles, hands her a tissue. 'Safe and well. But Cara . . .' His face falls. 'We phoned all the hospitals: they had no record of either Roo or Sarah, so we put a call out to R and P to search for the car. And they've found it. Just outside Sparsholt. It's a quiet spot, small country road, but the teams are out there now. The air ambulance is on its way, fire and rescue. We should know more soon.'

Cara clamps her hands over her mouth in shock. 'Who did this? Why go after Roo? It must be the same woman, the same killer?'

Jamie looks at her, sternly. 'I'm sorry, Cara. But Griffin's abduction, and now this attempt on Roo. I think we were mistaken.'

'Mistaken, how?' Cara's brain is in overload; she can't think, can't process what she's hearing.

'We've been looking for someone with a reason to target Griffin, but we've had the focus all wrong. They're not looking to punish him. It's about you.'

Chapter 53

Why me? The thought races around Cara's head, followed by another: Why not? She's been a police officer longer than anyone on this team, for over twenty years. The horrors she's put away – the wife beaters, the drug dealers. The stabbers, the punchers, the killers – any one of those might have come into money and be out for revenge. But she's never done anything wrong. She was only doing her job.

The team are busy doing what they do best – studying their computer screens, talking on the phone – and she feels redundant, helpless in the face of an oncoming avalanche. She wants to speak to her kids, but she doesn't want to pull them out of school until she has something definite to tell them. Whether their father is dead or alive.

Her mobile rings, making her jump. She looks at the number – doesn't recognise it – and tentatively answers.

'DCI Elliott? This is Dr Mark Singleton. You left a message for me. I hope this is a convenient time?'

The relief. It's the psychologist. Something she can look into; something to distract. 'Yes, thank you,' she says. She pulls her notes towards her. 'It's about your time at Northbrooke Children's Home. I have some questions about a child you saw there.'

There's a long pause. 'As I'm sure you know,' he says, eventually, 'this is covered by doctor–patient confidentiality.'

'Yes, but I'm talking about a situation with a risk of death or serious harm.'

'Go on,' he says, tentatively.

'Noah Deakin.'

A sharp intake of breath. 'I was wondering when someone would talk to me about him. What's happened?'

'You're aware he's in prison for multiple counts of murder?'

'The Echo Man, yes.'

'Can you tell me about him? When he was in the children's home. What was your view?'

'I'm assuming you've read his file?'

'I have.'

'Then it'll come as no surprise to learn that Noah was an incredibly traumatised child. He came to us when his mother had been found dead from a drug overdose. He'd been alone with her body for two weeks when the police found him.'

Cara gasps. 'He didn't call the police himself?'

'No. It seems his mother had drilled into him that they were the enemy. For obvious reasons – she was a dealer, a prostitute, God knows what else. So when she died, he didn't know what to do. He was malnourished, selectively mute. He didn't speak for months. From his behaviour and the intel we received from the police, we believe he'd also been sexually abused by male clients of his mother's, although he never admitted as much.'

'What was your professional opinion?'

'PTSD, primarily, with a secondary diagnosis of depression, anxiety, and a high risk of suicide and self-harm. But he responded well to therapy, and the structure the children's home offered was a great relief to him. He liked to know where he should be, and how to behave. Unlike many children at the home, he liked rules and regulations.' He pauses. 'He went into the police force, didn't he?'

'Yes,' Cara says, with sadness. 'He was an excellent officer.'

'That doesn't surprise me. He was incredibly empathetic. He always knew how to defuse a situation.' Another long pause. 'DCI Elliott, may I be candid with you?'

'Yes. Please.'

'I know you were involved with the investigation and Noah's conviction, but . . .' He stops.

'Dr Singleton?'

'I read a lot about the case. I saw Noah's name in the newspaper coverage, and my first reaction was surprise. So much so, that I wrote to you at the time.'

'You did? I didn't receive anything.' But Cara had been signed off work, shocked by the events. It's no surprise the letter didn't get to her. 'What did you say?'

'I didn't think Noah Deakin had done it.'

Cara's skin prickles. She feels nauseous. 'What made you think that?' she manages to ask.

'The papers described a sick man, a sexual sadist who planned his kills in minute detail, murdering a number of people over a long period. Is that right?'

'Yes.'

'That wasn't the Noah Deakin I knew. As I said, Noah was kind. He was the sort of kid to give up his turn on the swing, to offer the last toy in the box. He cared about people, even when they didn't give a shit about him. Yes, he was traumatised, and I was worried for his mental health when he left the children's home, but only because I thought he might do something to himself. I had no worries that he was a danger to others. What do you know about attachment theory, DCI Elliott?'

'Not much.'

'I'll give you the basics. Attachment between a child and usually its mother evolves from a need for the child to maximise its prospects of survival. In the beginning, that's food, safety. Later, it's a secure base from which to explore the wider environment. It's a learned behaviour developed within the first eight months of life. Simply put, DCI Elliott, an abused or neglected child like Noah doesn't develop that secure attachment.'

'What does that mean as an adult?'

'A range of problems. Depression and anxiety, as I mentioned before, but also low self-esteem, low self-confidence. Noah desired that closeness, but it was the thing that scared him the most, so in the majority of cases, he pushed it away.'

'The majority of cases? You mean there were times when he didn't?'

The psychologist pauses, sucking air over his teeth. 'For a select few, and I mean, very few, Noah welcomed that close contact. And he'd forgive those people anything. The bond with his mother, for example, even though she must have subjected him to horrific ill-treatment. He kept in touch with the first copper on the scene, the woman who found him. He even used to write to me, every now and again. My biggest hope for him was that he'd find someone – a good influence – who could guide him. And for a while, I suspect that person was you.'

'Me?'

'Didn't the two of you work closely together?'

Cara swallows. 'Yes. For years.'

'Then I'd be prepared to bet he would consider those the best years of his life. Which is why it makes no sense to me that he'd be out there, killing.'

'Is it likely he was under another person's influence at that time?'

'It's possible.'

'Someone driving him to kill?'

'Maybe . . .' he says warily.

'Do the initials RDK mean anything to you?'

Singleton takes a sharp breath in. 'I can't . . .'

'Please. Lives are on the line.'

For a moment, there's a pause, and Cara thinks she won't get any further. But then he speaks.

'Robert Daniel Keane.'

Cara's heart thumps hard in her chest. For the first time they know what the initials stand for. With a shaking voice, she asks, 'Who was he?'

'Robert was at the home at the same time as Noah. A couple of years younger – they were close while Noah was there, but Noah left and I assumed he hadn't spoken to him since. Why do you ask?'

'The initials were in the file. Your report. You described it as an unhealthy attachment.'

'It was. Noah would do anything for Robert. But Robbie left two years after Noah. I can't imagine they got back in touch.'

While Dr Singleton's been talking, Cara has typed his name into the police databases.

'He doesn't have a record,' she says. 'There's no trace of him on the system.'

298

'He wouldn't have. Not now. When he left his name was legally changed. There was a court order in place to protect him.'

Cara's baffled. 'Why?'

Singleton sighs. 'It was a recommendation I made – me and the other medical staff at the home. We concluded that Robert wouldn't have a chance of a normal life without it. You must have seen the case at the time? Mid to late nineties. Robert came to the children's home because he killed his uncle and his father.'

'What?'

'Marcus and Gary Keane, that was it. Christ, I still remember their names now. They'd been sexually abusing him, sustained violence for his entire life, and then one night Robbie got up and stabbed them both. Chopped off his father's penis while he was still alive.'

'Fucking hell.'

'Quite. And Robert had issues – he ran the whole gamut of mental health problems. PTSD, depression, OCD, generalised anxiety disorder – all ones you'd expect given his history. But he was smart, studied hard. We thought he'd be okay.'

'Was he happy at the children's home?'

'Yes, as I said, he settled in well. Northbrooke wasn't as you might imagine – a workhouse or orphanage from the movies. It was a friendly place, with a real emphasis on rehabilitation. Qualifications, training, some vocational stuff too. A lot of the kids learned trades and got good jobs afterwards.' Singleton pauses. 'Are you telling me you think Keane was working with Noah?'

'Do you think that's possible?'

'Shit. It could have been.'

'How can we find this man?'

'You can't. That's the point. His name was legally changed, protected by law. All his medical records and any biological samples linked with the crime were destroyed. He was given a fresh start.'

'So he could be anywhere?'

'I'm sorry, DCI Elliott. But yes.'

Cara's still digesting his words, when Jamie appears in the doorway. She slowly moves her phone away from her ear.

'He's at the hospital,' Jamie says. 'Roo. They're saying you should go now.'

Chapter 54

Cara's driven by a patrol car, sirens blaring. Jamie offered to go with her – to get Charlie to go – but she needs everybody working on the case. Griffin is still missing. They can't forget that.

She arrives at the hospital in double quick time, the patrol car dropping her outside the emergency department. She runs in, straight up to the reception desk where she presents her ID.

'DCI Cara Elliott. I'm here for Andrew Elliott?'

'Cara?' A voice behind her makes her turn, and there's Sarah. Her ex-husband's twenty-eight-year-old fiancée, with a large bruise on her forehead and blood in her blonde hair. When she sees Cara she falls into her arms, sobbing.

Cara stands, stiff, while the young woman cries. She's never liked this girl, feels awkward now, comforting her, when the only reason she's there is for the father of her children. She encourages her out of her arms, almost propping her back on her feet.

'Where's Roo?'

'Oh, Cara.' Sarah almost starts crying again, but sees the

stern look on Cara's face and holds it in. 'He's in surgery,' she says. 'The doctors said he's got a bleed on the brain, fractured skull – it's awful. He might not regain consciousness.'

'What happened?' And then, as an afterthought: 'How are you?'

Cara guides her towards some chairs in a corner of the waiting room. Sarah sits down with a thump.

'I'm okay.' Her hand goes up to the egg on her forehead; her fingers explore it gingerly. 'I hit my head on the window, lost consciousness. Came round to the sound of sirens and the paramedics. They said they need to do a CT scan if I get any other symptoms but I'm okay. Just a bit of a headache. I'm so worried about Roo. He . . . he . . .'

'Who was driving?'

'I was. We'd been out for dinner. I didn't want to drink. I can't . . . I . . .' Her hand drops to her lower stomach, and Cara realises. For fuck's sake.

'How far along are you?' Cara says, as evenly as she can.

'Not much. Ten weeks or so. We were going to tell you. After the scan.'

'And the baby's okay?'

'Yes, fine. I heard the heartbeat, Cara.'

'Yes, yes, magical moment,' Cara snaps. 'What happened?'

'I really don't know. There was a car behind us. Driving fast, right up my bumper. We were on our way back from the Stag.' Cara knows the pub. Posh. Somewhere to go if you're celebrating. 'The road's fast, but it's full of blind corners. I didn't want to rush, but—'

'What colour was it? What make?'

'I'm not sure. I'm not good with cars. Roo would know, but he . . . And the car – it bumped into us. A little knock at first, and then a bigger one. A huge crash, I lost control. I tried to . . . I turned the wheel, but it . . . it . . .'

'The car flipped.'

'Oh, God.' Sarah buries her head in her hands. 'They said his airbag didn't go off.' She looks at Cara, tears streaming. 'Why would that happen? Did someone deliberately make us crash?'

'I don't know. Stay here.' Cara gives her hand an ineffectual pat, then gets up and makes a call. Jamie answers on the first ring.

'How's Roo?'

'Not good. Look – Sarah says someone tried to run them off the road and that Roo's airbag didn't deploy. Can you contact the SCIU – see what's going on? They need to properly investigate the crash. Get onto Sergeant Danny Cohen if needs be – he used to partner with Griffin, he'd be happy to help. And tell them about the camera in the car – something recorded that video. Any progress at your end?'

'We might have a lead on Tyler Brown. A garage where he used to work.'

Cara notices a doctor purposefully walking down the corridor towards Sarah. Dressed in blue scrubs.

'I've got to go,' she says. 'Call me when you know more.'

'I will. Look after yourself, Cara.'

She hangs up and joins the doctor as he speaks to Sarah. She introduces herself quickly and he nods a hello.

'As I was saying to Ms Wright, I am the neurosurgeon that's been operating on Andrew. He sustained a depressed skull fracture in the accident which led to a subdural haematoma, putting pressure on the brain. We've relieved that pressure via a burr hole for now, but what we don't know is how much damage was done while he was out there overnight. The next twelve hours are going to be critical.'

'Is he going to wake up?' Sarah asks.

'We don't know. We have him intubated and sedated at the moment. We'll watch overnight, keep a close eye on what's going on in there with CT scans, and see what the ICU doctors have to say in the morning. We'll know more then.'

'Can we see him?'

'Yes, but not for long. One at a time.'

Cara lets Sarah go on ahead, walking with her and the surgeon to the ICU, taking a seat in the waiting room outside. She holds her phone tightly in her hands, so when it rings, she jumps.

She looks at the screen, expecting Jamie. Wishing for a call to tell her they've found Griffin, that he's safe – so when she sees Charlie's name, she's disappointed.

She answers it.

'Cara? Are you okay? Why didn't you tell me Roo was in an accident?'

'I . . . I forgot, I'm sorry.'

'What's going on?'

'He's been in surgery. He's now in the ICU.' She swallows, pushing the emotion down. 'It's not looking good.'

'I'm so sorry. I'm on my way—'

'No, Charlie, don't. They need you at the nick. I'm fine.'

'You're not fine. I can be with you—'

'I need you to stay there. You have to find Griffin. I don't want you here.'

There's a long pause. Cara screws her face up, realising what she's said, how it might sound.

'I didn't mean—' she begins, but Charlie interrupts, his voice full of sorrow.

'It's fine. I get it. Give me a call if that ever changes.'

And he hangs up. She looks at the phone, regretting her words, but the truth is that however much she'd like a hug from Charlie right now, that's not what's important. She's not important.

Sarah emerges from the double doors to the ICU, her eyes red with tears.

'They said that even if he wakes up, he might not be the same. He might have brain damage. What do I do then?' She slumps on the chair next to Cara, putting her head in her hands. 'I can't do that,' she says to the floor.

Cara studies her for a second, remembering what she was like at twenty-eight. All that optimism, not a care in the world. And here's Sarah – a baby on the way and a fiancé with the possible scenario of needing around the clock care. There's nothing she can say that'll make this better.

Cara gets to her feet, blinking tears away, and pushes the door open to the ICU. Nurses point her to the bed in the corner, where Roo lies still and silent. Machines beep; a ventilator connected to the tube in his mouth keeps a steady rhythm.

Cara sits by his side, tentatively taking his hand in hers. It's reassuringly warm, blood still circulating, the physical body ticking over, but she wonders how much of the mental side there is left. A white bandage covers his whole head, a few strands of grey and brown hair poking out of the sides. His face looks banged up, peppered with small red cuts, no doubt from the glass shattering, but otherwise he looks like the same man she married all those years ago.

The early days – Roo working all hours as a sous chef in the restaurant, Cara making her way up the ranks. Night shifts, late turns – sometimes the two of them would only connect as she climbed wearily into bed, an intertwining of limbs before he got up to start his day.

Cara lets tears fall, remembering how much they were in love. How much she adored him. She could watch him do anything and find it a turn-on, but especially when he was in the kitchen. Chop vegetables, sauté onions, even the most run-of-the-mill recipes turned into magic in his hands. Late at night he'd experiment, offering spoonfuls of red wine jus, of chocolate sauce laced with brandy. Spicy sriracha sauce that made him laugh when her eyes watered.

They grew up together, became adults with mortgages and responsibilities. And children. Oh, God, what will she say to Tilly and Josh? How can she tell them? They'll be home from school by now, Roo's parents making them dinner, putting them to bed. She needs to take over, let his mum and dad come here. See their only son.

She sniffs, wiping her eyes with a tissue, dabbing at her cheeks. There is no time for this. Not now. While she's been here, night has closed in, reducing the world to shadows. She can't wallow; she must stay strong.

She stands up, leaning over the bed, placing a gentle kiss on Roo's forehead. Hot tears threaten, but she blinks them away.

'You'll be okay,' she whispers, her voice choked. 'You are so loved.'

She straightens up, pulls her shoulders back and leaves the ICU. She looks towards the waiting room where Sarah is still sitting, her head in her hands. Then up to the sign above her head.

Burrell Ward. Left.

She starts to walk.

Chapter 55

Darkness falls, and Jamie watches the police officers trudge away from the building. An old second-hand car garage where Tyler Brown once worked – theoretically perfect, but in reality, empty, bare, discarded. Nobody's been here in years; no signs of foul play, let alone a murder.

On the far side, Brody sits on the kerb, her head in her hands. Jamie can't bear it. The crashing disappointment, the drag of failure that they've been wrong, yet again. Time has been cycling through; the thought that their friend is out there, about to be killed, while they're here, useless, is excruciating. He walks back to his car, sits in the front seat and thinks through everything they know.

'What are we missing?' he mutters. 'Where are you?'

The systematic targeting of these victims. Money changing hands – aggrieved relative to contract killer. How are they communicating? Jamie's aware it's probably via the dark web, a world of shady marketplaces where anything and anyone is traded. But how would someone know to go there in the first place? Your average Joe wouldn't consider a transaction like this; someone like Shauna Lloyd wouldn't have a clue where to start. No, they must have been poked and prodded, encouraged in the right direction.

His phone rings. He answers it.

'Do you have something, Holly?' he asks, eagerly. Hope blossoms.

At the other end, the CSM sighs. 'No. And I'm sorry to have to ask this, but do you have any of the videos?'

'Which ones? The snuff films?'

'Yes. One's missing. The original disc. Austin O'Brien, the guy that was stabbed. No sign out in the exhibits log. Nowhere to be seen.'

'It's not just misfiled?'

'I've got them scouring the lab. What a bloody nightmare. If we can't track it down soon it's useless from hereon in. The chain of evidence is buggered.'

'We have the copy, right?'

'Yes, but we need the original. Last thing we need is a defence lawyer using it to argue incompetence.'

Which you are, Jamie thinks, but stays quiet. Losing evidence is dangerous territory, but he can see how it has happened. Everyone working around the clock, operating on little sleep. All Jamie would like to do is go to bed and not emerge for days, but he can't. Not while Griffin is still out there.

'Look, it's not your fault. Go home. Get some shut-eye and check again in the morning. Someone's just forgotten to sign it out – it'll turn up having never left the lab.'

'I hope so.'

Jamie says his goodbyes and hangs up. He gets out of his car and walks across to Brody, placing a hand on her shoulder.

'We need to go.'

She looks around the car park, blinking as if the rest of the coppers have vanished into thin air.

'Go where?'

'Back to the nick. Regroup. Take another look.'

'I can't, Jamie. It's too much. This.' She gestures around the empty lot. 'We're just waiting for him to die.'

Jamie knows how she feels. The helplessness, the fatigue. Everyone close to collapse. But how can they stop?

'We'll find him,' he says, and he holds out his hand, pulling Brody to her feet. She stands, her head bowed.

'I know we'll find him. They'll make sure of that.' She looks at him with bloodshot eyes, on the edge of tears. 'I just think he'll be dead when we do.'

Chapter 56

Cara strides down the corridors, mind focused, determined. She's fed up with the lies, of feeling like a victim. She wants answers, and she's not leaving until she gets them.

'Who's Robert Daniel Keane?' she asks the moment she gets into the room.

'What?'

Noah shuffles up in his bed, surprised. He's looking better than he was – colour in his cheeks, bruises fading – but the way Cara's feeling right now she's prepared to make fresh ones if he won't talk.

'You heard me. Robert Daniel Keane. Who is he?'

Noah pales, reminiscent of that scared kid in the photographs in the file.

'You were in the children's home with him. I spoke to your psychologist, Dr Singleton? He told me a lot about you.'

'That's . . . that's . . . confidential.'

'Not after what you've done, Noah. Or what you say you've done. Who's Robert Keane?'

'He was a friend when I was growing up. That's all.'

'What's his name now?'

'I don't know what you're talking about.'

'You do. Robert Daniel Keane. Killed his father and his uncle when he was nine. Went to Northbrooke Children's Home instead of being sent to some juvenile detention centre. Thought he was worth saving. But he wasn't, was he, Noah?'

'I . . . I don't know.'

'You bloody well do. Don't lie to me. Not now. He got out – changed his name. He was working with you, wasn't he? He was the one who killed, who planned this whole thing. He's the DNA sample, the person who wrote the diaries, who owned that flat. That's why you can't tell me where the Polaroid came from – because you damn well don't know.

'Do you know where I've just been?' Noah shakes his head. 'The ICU. Car accident. Roo was run off the road. He could die. And instead of being with him, I'm here. Because I've had enough.' Her voice breaks. 'Please, Noah.'

She collapses into the chair next to his bed, her vision blurring with tears. 'Please. Tell me. You don't have to protect him anymore.'

'I . . . I can't. Why are you doing this? Leave me alone. Leave things the way they are. I confessed. Isn't that good enough?'

'No. Because he's still out there. And you're . . . you're in here. You could be helping me. Finding whoever has Griffin, whoever tried to kill Roo—'

'Are the kids okay?' he interrupts.

'The kids are fine. They weren't in the car. But I have to go to them after this. Tell them about their father. That he might not make it. Please. Let me help you. Tell me who he is.'

'You have to let this go—'

'It wasn't you.' Cara almost shouts it, pulling herself back at the last minute, remembering the guard outside. 'You didn't kill all those people,' she hisses.

'I did enough to deserve this. I need you to be safe.'

'It's too late,' Cara says, and Noah looks up sharply. 'Someone's after me already. Griffin. Roo. Who's to say that I won't be next? I worked it out – why they're targeting me. Because I started looking into you.'

Noah stares at her. 'No . . .'

'On Sunday, when we found that Polaroid, I went down into the archives and I took the files for the Echo Man case. Not all of them – some had already been archived – but that's when I started to wonder. All those loose ends – the DNA we never managed to match, the cypher, the handwriting – none of it was you.'

'Please, Cara. You have to stop.' He reaches forward and grabs at her hand, squeezing it tightly. 'I'm begging you. Whatever you're doing, stop now.'

'No fucking way.' She stands up, pulling away from his grasp. 'Tell me how to find Robert Keane.'

'I can't. Please, Cara.' He's pleading, almost crying.

'Tell me.'

He shakes his head, one last time, and she turns. Out of the room, past the confused guard, heading out of the hospital. She doesn't care anymore. Her brother is missing. Her ex-husband is in the ICU. She's going to find the person behind this. She's going to find Robert Keane. And she knows how she's going to do it. She won't rest until she's locked them up and thrown away the key.

She calls Jamie as she walks. 'Give me some good news.'

'I'm sorry, Cara. He wasn't there. It was a dead end.'

'So go back to the nick. Start again. Find Griffin. Find my brother.'

There's a long pause at the other end of the phone. 'But Cara, the time.'

She glances at the clock on her phone, and, as if a switch has been flipped, all the energy drains from her body.

It's midnight.

'It's been forty-eight hours, Cara. Time's up.'

Chapter 57

Time has no meaning here. There is no sun, no moon. No day, no night. Only the floodlight, buzzing from the edge of the pit. And the pain. The constant burning pain.

Griffin drifts in and out. The exhaustion is all-encompassing, he exists in a half-consciousness. Desperate to sleep but unable to rest. Every part of him aching, every breath sending a bolt of agony from his broken ribs. His hands are numb, all blood drained south from being raised above his head for so long. Too long. He can't see how he'll survive.

At first, once the man left, he pulled against his bindings. Put all his weight on the cuffs, on the rope tied high above his head, hoping that something would give. But the rope stuck fast, and all he succeeded in doing was digging the metal into his wrists, blood trickling down his arms.

He hasn't eaten since he's been here, feels dizzy, confused. Wants water, anything, but knows there's no point.

His time will come.

The grating of the lock confirms his worst suspicions. Griffin raises his head and watches as the man stands at the lip of the pit. The same guy from earlier. Broad, strong – but no balaclava. It doesn't bode well that he's letting Griffin see his face.

'You look like your brother, Tyler,' Griffin says. His voice is croaky, throat sore.

The man doesn't reply, just folds his arms across his substantial chest.

A disembodied voice speaks. The woman. 'Tell me your name.'

Griffin's tired of this shit. 'Fuck you,' he mutters.

The man takes a step forward and drops down into the pit, landing with a thump, next to Griffin. He balls his hands into fists.

'You're going to kill me whether I carry out this little performance or not, so you might as well get on with it.'

'It depends how you want to go, Nate Griffin,' the woman says. 'Fast or slow.'

Tyler smiles.

Griffin assesses the situation. He can't see any weapons. No chair, no baseball bat, no dogs.

'Why am I here?' he asks. 'Give me that, at least. Which one of the wankers I put away paid for this?'

She chuckles. 'So self-obsessed. Why does everything have to be about you?'

'But . . . who?' A few possibilities pass through Griffin's head. An ex-boyfriend of Brody's. Some stalker wanting him out of the way. Or . . . or Cara?

'Your sister's been digging where she shouldn't. Somebody wants her to stop.'

'So . . . what—'

But Griffin doesn't have a chance to ask any more – a blow catches him by surprise, a fist, connecting with his stomach, knocking him off his feet and winding him. He chokes for a moment, snatches a strangled breath as he hangs, his shoulders screaming as they take his entire weight. Then the second, a strike to his jaw. He tastes blood.

Time out. He breathes, retches, then tries again. Spits a glob of blood to the floor, watching it through blurry eyes as his feet trail on the concrete.

His ears ring, a voice sounds through the mist in his head. *Permission granted.* And it starts again.

No time to breathe, no respite. The blows come thick and fast, the man using Griffin as a punching bag. A left hook to his kidneys, an uppercut to his jaw before his nose is flattened. Blood pours down the back of his throat; he gags, mumbles through shattered bones. His ribs crack, muscles scream. He does nothing to stop it; can't, too helpless, too weak.

And through his pain, through the beating, Griffin accepts – this is his time. People have tried to kill him before and failed. Fights on the job, being cornered in a rough area by a gang of scrotes. He got out of that unscathed. And then when his wife was killed. Tied up and beaten as Mia was raped in the room next door. He wanted to die then, but someone pulled him back.

He's been shot, beaten, poisoned, and survived. He's made it through addiction – but enough is enough. He's exhausted. Broken.

The punches slow; the man tires. He feels a handful of his hair grabbed, his head lifted, an assessment of his battered face. Griffin forces a swollen eye open, peers out through the gap.

'Had enough?' the man says.

Griffin closes his eye. He works his tongue around in

his mouth, tasting blood, saliva, a wobbling tooth, then spits a gob of it right into the man's face. It lands true, an exclamation of disgust, and the beating begins again.

Faster, heavier blows, fuelled by anger rather than obligation. A crunch of bone, blood spattering on concrete with the spit, the sweat, the sorrow. Agony everywhere now, the constant burning pain. His consciousness drifts.

He's never believed in heaven or hell, but in these, his final moments, Griffin wishes there was. He would like to see Mia. For one last time.

Oblivion is coming.

Part 3

Chapter 58

It's way past midnight, most of the staff in the police station have gone home. But the Major Crimes team remains. What's left of them.

So few. So bloody few, Jamie thinks as he stands next to the whiteboard. DC Alana Brody, pale-faced but determined; DC Toby Shenton, ever-present, clutching his folder of notes and scientific papers. To their left, DCI Rosie Ryder. For once, she's quiet, letting someone else take the reins.

DCI Cara Elliott stands at the back of the room. Her arms are folded – a defiant gesture. It's her brother who's missing, who might be dead. Her ex-husband, targeted and lying unconscious in hospital. Cara shouldn't be here, but Jamie's not going to be the one to tell her.

Next to her, the head of digital, Charlie Mills. Her boyfriend, but from the way they're standing, you couldn't tell. They're at work, so Jamie would expect them to be professional, but still. There's a good metre between them. They don't look at each other, not even a glance.

But Jamie doesn't have time to worry about broken

relationships. He's the SIO, the man in charge. And he has an investigation to run.

'We know why we're all here,' Jamie begins. 'Primary objective – to find Nate Griffin. Secondary – catch the bastard who's been doing this. We have zero suspects, and after the events this afternoon, zero lines of enquiry. We're back to square one, and I know how you're feeling. Frustrated. Angry. You want your pound of flesh, and so do I, but that time will come. For now, we need to be focused.

'Brody, have we got our hands on the CCTV from when the latest disc was dropped at the front desk?'

'No, we . . .'

'Got distracted. I get that, but let's find it now, please? DCI Ryder – what has your team been doing in Basingstoke?'

Ryder stands up, but Jamie can detect hesitancy in her stance. Defeat.

'The team have been working hard, reinterviewing everyone connected to the disappearances of our victims. Every suspect, every alibi checked.'

'And?'

'And there's nothing.'

'Bank accounts?'

She looks sheepish. 'We're still waiting on the warrants.'

'Get them.' Then he remembers her rank and adds, 'Please, ma'am. Shenton?'

'We've had the reports through for Richard Fredricks,' Shenton says. 'Terence Gregory's boss. That Bitcoin payment is there – the same one we saw on the Lloyd family's statement.'

'And why haven't we traced these payments?' Jamie directs to Charlie.

Charlie shakes his head. 'You can't. It's not like a normal

bank – that's why Bitcoin is perfect for transactions like these.'

'Why?' Jamie pushes. 'Explain it to me like I'm a child.'

'So . . . anyone can buy Bitcoin, legally, through a cryptocurrency exchange site.'

'CryptoStreamline, in our case?'

'Yes. That company transfers your Bitcoin into a virtual wallet. Now, transactions between these wallets are held on opensource ledgers. You can see them happening and the exchange of coin, but what you can't tell is who owns the receiving wallet.'

'Why? Can't we get the relevant company to tell us?'

'Yes, sure. If you can find out which one. But each wallet is identified by a hexadecimal code. And that's completely untraceable.' There's a long pause while the team digests the information. Charlie continues: 'We know the code name of the receiving wallet. And we know how much, or at least can guess, based on exchange rates at that time. But we can't find who owns it.'

'Do we know for sure if Richard Fredricks and the Lloyds sent their payment to the same wallet?'

'Yes, and yes, they did. For a similar amount.'

'Isn't that enough to arrest them?' Brody says.

'It's weak, but it's suspicion—'

'Where does that get us?' Cara says from the back of the room. 'Even if they confess and tell us everything they know, it doesn't take us any closer to whoever's holding Griffin. If this person's smart enough to use Bitcoin, I'd put money on them not meeting with the killer. They probably message through the dark web – agree everything that way.'

'But what if we don't need them to?' Everybody turns towards Brody. 'What if we can find that out for ourselves?'

'Go on . . .' Jamie says.

'We arrest Fredricks. We arrest the father, Bill Lloyd. And we get them to talk, reduced charge, whatever, if they'll tell us how they got in contact with the killer. And then we do the same ourselves.'

'You mean . . .' Jamie says slowly.

'We pose as someone looking for revenge. We contact them, asking for their services. And then somehow, we pull them out into the open. We offer them more money, we ask to meet face to face. Something.'

'How long does it take to set up an op like that?' Jamie says.

'I don't know. But it's worth a try. Isn't it?'

The whole room is silent, pondering the plan. It's better than anything they've come up with so far. Except there's one snag.

'Who would the victim be? Because we're putting whoever it is into the firing line – and remember, it has to be plausible. Some utter shit the world would be better without.'

Brody smiles. 'That's the easy part. I know just the man.'

Chapter 59

Good cop, bad cop – the old ones are the best. Cara missed this – working with Jamie.

They sit together in the interview room. On the opposite side of the table – Bill Lloyd. They got him out of bed, woke up the whole street, much to Cara's delight as she whacked the cuffs on his wrists, recited the caution. She's missed the hands-on side of policing. Hanging out in her office all day has made her soft.

Now, the man glares. The solicitor is also grumpy, another hauled from their slumber at two a.m. 'A man's life is on the line,' Jamie had said down the phone. 'Abduction in progress.' And nobody had been able to argue about that.

'Once again, we're sorry to carry out this interview now,' Jamie says. His tone is soft, his manner gentle. 'And to remind you, you're still under caution.'

'Say what you want to say,' Lloyd growls. 'And then we can clear this whole matter up and go home.'

'Let's hope we can do that,' Jamie replies. Cara pushes the file across to him and Jamie opens it with a smile. 'Let's see what we have here.'

Cara almost laughs at Jamie's manner. Part primary school teacher, part patient politician, this is what Jamie does best. The mild manner, the gentle encouragement, lulling the suspect into a false sense of security. Cara sits back, letting Jamie do the work.

'Now,' Jamie begins, pushing a piece of paper across the table. 'Let's start here. Bank statement for you and your family. The usual stuff we'd expect – Sainsburys, Amazon, and someone has a real fondness for expensive mail order pick-n-mix from a company called CrunchyMunchies.'

'That's my wife,' Lloyd mutters. 'She says they're for Shauna, but they're not.'

'Well, that's up to her. But I was wondering – could you explain this?'

Jamie pushes the statement across the table – two lines highlighted. Lloyd peers at it.

He colours quickly, his whole face turning puce. 'No comment,' he says.

'CryptoStreamline are a company that buys and sells Bitcoin. Why are you using them?'

'No comment.'

'You paid twenty-five grand to these people, twice. Once on the fourth of March, a few days after Stephen Allen was released from remand, and once on Saturday, in the early hours of the morning. Moments before he was killed. Seems a strange coincidence to me.'

'Don't mention that man's name around me,' Lloyd says quietly.

'Who? Stephen Allen?'

'Yes.'

'And why is that?' Jamie asks sweetly. Lloyd glares. 'You hate him, don't you?'

'Wouldn't you? After what he did to my daughter.'

'And you wanted revenge?' Jamie says it softly, slipping it into the conversation like a knife down silk.

'Yes. I mean – no! Not like that. I didn't want him dead.'

'But you wanted him punished.'

Lloyd glances to his solicitor. 'No comment,' he says.

'Stop bullshitting us, Mr Lloyd.' Cara leans forward, her voice loud, bouncing off the walls of the interview room. Lloyd sits to attention, his gaze locked on Cara. 'I'm not going to lie – things aren't looking good for you right now. We have the Bitcoin payments made to CryptoStreamline, and I'm sure, once we've finished searching your house and going through your laptop we'll have even more evidence linking you to the murder of Stephen Allen. And do you know what's going on in the interview room next door? We have another suspect in there. A man who wanted someone dead. Someone else who sent Bitcoin to that same company. And if he talks first, we're not going to need you. You're going to prison, and what would your little girl do then? She's struggling, she needs her father.'

'Leave Shauna out of this,' Lloyd growls, and Cara knows she's hit gold.

'Or,' Cara continues, 'here's a thought – how about we get Shauna in here? What if we arrest her? She lives with you. Getting hold of your bank account details wouldn't be a huge stretch. Maybe it was her? We could hold her here, twenty-four hours, drag her through those awful days, all over again. Make her relive—'

'Stop!'

Lloyd shouts it, his eyes bulging, a prime candidate for a heart attack, leaning across so his face is almost next to Cara's. 'You leave her out of this. Hasn't she been through enough?'

'Why should we? We're trying to stop a murder—'

'I'll tell you what you need to know—'

'Mr Lloyd, as your solicitor, I should advise you—'

'Shut up. Shut up all of you.' Lloyd slumps in his seat. 'Look, it was me, okay? Shauna had nothing to do with it. Not even my wife is aware. But I had to do something.' He looks from Jamie to Cara, pleading. 'Can't you understand that? He got away with it. He was going to play football again, no doubt on some multi-million-pound contract. Yes, I wanted him to suffer. But I didn't know they were going to kill him.'

'How did you get in contact with the killer, Mr Lloyd?'

'I didn't. They contacted me. A message on WhatsApp. All encrypted, all secure. They said they could understand how I was feeling. That they could help.'

'Do you have that message?'

'No. I deleted it, as they told me to. And the number's no good anyway – I tried calling it after you guys arrived on Saturday and it was cut off. But . . .' He hesitates.

'But what?'

He clamps up, pushing his lips together in a thin line.

This isn't enough. Cara was bullshitting earlier. They do have Richard Fredricks next door, but he's useless. Lawyered up with the most expensive criminal defence in town, repeating no comment in a monotone to everything Brody and Ryder ask. They need to know how to find these killers.

She leans forward, waiting until he looks up, meeting her gaze.

'Your wife told us what he did to Shauna,' she says slowly. 'How she didn't tell the police about the oral rape.' She takes photograph after photograph out of the file,

328

lines them up in front of Bill Lloyd. Shots from the post-mortem. He glances down, quickly at first, then studying them – the abrasions across Allen's face, the bruising on his neck. 'That's how we know it was you. We found semen in Stephen Allen's mouth. They forced him to do the same.'

'He deserved it,' Lloyd whispers. 'After what he did to my little girl.'

'You hired them to kill him.'

'I never said kill. I didn't. I just wanted him . . .' Lloyd pauses, his cheeks flush. 'Hurt. In the same way he hurt Shauna.'

'Did you ever contact them any other way?'

'Yes. I . . . I found them on the dark web. I looked up how to do it – download that browser. They'd given me a link – how to find them. They asked for details. Exactly what I wanted.'

Cara forces herself to stay calm. This could be it. 'Do you still have that link?'

'Yes. Yes, I think so.'

Cara closes her eyes for a moment. Says a silent thank you.

Jamie takes over. 'And did you say anything else?'

'No, just who and how. And they gave me a price and a Bitcoin code thing – somewhere to send the money. They said they'd send me proof of job complete, and that would be it. I guess they did that, didn't they?'

Cara takes a photo out of the file – one of Stephen Allen lying dead on the concrete outside the strip club, covered in blood, his body torn to shreds, his face unrecognisable. She pushes it across to Lloyd.

'Yes,' she says. 'I guess they did.'

Chapter 60

'Absolutely no way,' Ryder is saying when they get back to the incident room. 'We're not pissing about on the dark web, soliciting murder.'

Brody stands in front of her, face pink, hands in fists by her side.

'But we'd stop it before it got that far. We'd ensure Darren Gladwell was safe—'

'Do you know how long it takes to plan an operation like this? Days. Weeks even. And you're talking about doing it in a matter of hours.'

'We don't have days! Griffin might be dead now!'

'What's going on?' Cara says, interrupting them both.

'She won't let us do it,' Brody cries, close to tears. 'We finally have a way in, and she won't let us near.'

'DCI Ryder?' Cara says. 'A word?'

Cara gestures to Jamie, and the three of them go into Cara's office. Once the door is shut, she turns to Ryder.

'You know this is our only chance.'

But Ryder shakes her head. 'Look, I know this is personal to you all. And that is exactly why I'm stepping in. None of you are making rational decisions. Putting a man in harm's way? It's insane. I won't do it.'

'Darren Gladwell is a paedophile and should never have been released from prison.'

'It's still *murder*, however much we don't like the man.'

'You didn't raise an objection earlier.'

'Because I thought we'd get something else out of the interviews. A location, a description. Something we could follow in line with procedure and policy.' She pauses, her face hard. 'Don't force this. Either of you.' She turns to Jamie. 'You've just been promoted. You have a promising career ahead of you. I will go to Halstead in the morning. To the chief constable if I need to. And get you both removed from this case. This insanity has gone on too long. Neither of you are objective enough to be SIO.'

And with that, she opens the door and marches out of the room.

Brody watches her go, then storms into Cara's office.

'Please don't say you listened to her?' she says. She looks from Cara to Jamie and back again. 'You know this is our best chance. Our *only* chance.'

'We can't, Alana,' Cara replies. She's exhausted, broken, but even she can recognise that their plan holds too many risks. 'Nobody's going to authorise this.'

'Then Griffin's dead. You know that!'

'Look at the clock. He might be dead already.'

She slumps into her chair as Brody rushes out. The door to the incident room slams behind her.

Cara puts her face in her hands and squeezes her eyes shut.

'It's the right call,' Jamie says. She feels him gently touch her shoulder, then move away. 'I'm sorry, Cara.'

Soft footsteps as Jamie leaves her office. She looks up, watching him talk to Shenton, sending him home. There's nothing more they can do tonight; Ryder was right, the plan was deeply flawed, but what else do they have?

Sixteen murders and not one shred of evidence. An address on the dark web, untraceable by design. And a Polaroid. A link to The Echo Man.

The idea she had before, back in the hospital, germinates and multiplies in her mind, growing stronger by the minute. Find the Echo Man, find their killer. And where better to start?

First thing tomorrow, she'll share her theory with everyone here. She needs a team she can trust, detectives she's known for years, who worked alongside Noah at the time. Who were as surprised and shocked by his confession as she was.

But first, elimination.

She makes a call. The CSM is awake, answers the phone on the first ring.

'Holly, if I get samples to the lab now, will you push them through?'

'Of course. What do you need?'

'DNA,' Cara says. 'Compare them to one we have on file. The one we found at the flat, in January 2021. For the Echo Man.'

Chapter 61

Fuck, he's missed this. The death, the torture, the agony. Naked, he sits in front of the screen as the murder plays out. Rewinds and watches the man die, over and over. The blade piercing his stomach, the blood, the begging. The cries, the rasping screams. But it's not enough, he wants to be there. Make it last, extract the most pain, the most suffering.

Because these guys are amateurs. They know nothing. They haven't perfected the craft, as he has. Haven't abducted someone off the street, dragged them into the kitchen. Kept them bound for days, safe in the knowledge that nobody knows. Nobody can find him.

He watches the video again, but he's barely getting hard. It's not enough. Not once you've had the real thing.

He stands up and walks the few steps into the kitchen. There, a woman is tied up – hands and feet bound, secured to the ring drilled into the wall. He stands over her; imagines what he could do, giving his dick a quick tug. It feels good and he nudges her with his foot. She makes a noise through her gag. A pathetic whimper.

She's been here for a week now, this hooker. Joyce Hunter,

assumed dead from the amount of blood he used to douse the homeless man, but no, here she is. Alive, when someone else has been charged with her murder. She's not the first, she won't be the last, but these nameless nobodies from the street, they're like drinking a box white, when all he wants is 2005 Bordeaux. He needs the thrill of the chase, a quality kill. Someone like Nate Griffin. He's jealous of them, having him chained up in their pit. If he had his way . . . Fuck! Think what he could do.

The woman on the floor moans quietly. She's annoying him, with her defeat, her pathos. He reaches over and takes a knife out of the sink. Bloodied and dull from overuse, but it'll do the job.

He stands behind her. She tries to turn, but he grabs a handful of her hair, holds her still as he runs the blade across her throat. The blood is instant and gratifying; he releases her and she slumps, her eyes rolling back as life is extinguished.

The blood spreads across the floor, glutinous and beautiful, and he bends down, slowly placing his hands, palms down in the pool. It's slippery and warm and when he lifts them, perfectly round droplets fall, spattering the lino.

This is what he needs.

He walks upstairs to the bathroom, trailing spatter, and when he gets there, he looks in the mirror, placing one finger in his mouth, then two, sucking like a baby from its mother's tit. The blood coats his tongue; he tastes pennies and he closes his eyes, gripping himself tightly. As he masturbates, he runs his left hand across his bare chest, covering himself with the gore, and he likes it. The way it makes him feel. Strong. In charge.

But he won't let himself come. Not yet.

He reaches down, opens a drawer. And there it is – a Glock 17 9mm handgun. Black, semi-automatic, capable of holding seventeen rounds. Bought for a song off the dark web, used, but he likes that about it.

It's got pedigree, like a trained Pitbull. Just the tool for the job.

He looks at himself in the mirror. Holds the gun in one hand, his finger on the trigger. Puts the barrel in his mouth. Watches himself as he wanks, finally coming with a guttural scream, pulling the trigger, hearing it click, empty, again and again.

The rush. To be close to death. Knowing the end is coming. Soon.

He stares at himself. Then takes two fingers and draws parallel stripes on his cheeks. In blood. In cum.

He sees the discussions. The talking, whispered conversations behind closed doors.

But he's ready. Ready to go to war.

DAY 8

FRIDAY

Chapter 62

The incident room is quiet this morning, the energy low.

Cara sits in her office, cradling her mug of coffee – her third of the day and it's not even nine a.m. She didn't sleep last night. Couldn't. Her brain rattles, she struggles to maintain focus, and she's thankful to Jamie, sitting straight in the middle of the incident room, talking to Shenton, exuding a quiet calm.

Cara had left the office when she could last night, driving half an hour out of town. A trip she had done many times in her marriage, stopping outside a thatched cottage, with white painted window frames and vines up the outside. She'd knocked quietly on the front door of Roo's parents' house, her heart beating hard; Roo's father answered.

'Have you caught the bastards?' he said, showing her in.

'We're working on it, Barry. I'm sorry it's so late.'

'It's fine,' he said, when the worry lines etched on his face told a different story. 'As we said on the phone, we want you to do everything you can to catch who's responsible.'

She crouched to unzip her boots, walked into the living room in socks.

'Is there any change from the hospital?' she asked.

'None. Karen is still there, with Sarah.'

'Good. And the kids?'

'We explained as best we could. But they need you.' He pointed skywards. 'They're upstairs. In our bedroom. They didn't want to be alone.'

'I'll go up now. Thank you.'

He nodded once, and she took the stairs two at a time, hurrying to the main bedroom. Her children were two small lumps under the duvet, huddled together on one side, a slight compression where Barry had obviously been lying. She got in next to them and Tilly snuggled up into her armpit, her cuddly owl clutched in her other hand.

Josh was slower to forgive. 'Where have you been?' he asked.

'At work. At the police station.'

'Is Dad going to die?'

Cara swallowed her tears. 'I don't know. He's in a bad way. The accident – he banged his head hard. He might not wake up.'

She looked from her daughter to her son. They were pale, black smudges under their eyes. Tilly was sucking her thumb, a habit from her toddler years, one Cara thought she'd left behind.

'Where will we live if Dad dies?'

'With me, of course.'

'And Uncle Nate?'

'Yes,' Cara said, without hesitation. Because yes, Griffin will come home. Time has run out, but Cara refuses to believe he's dead. They'll find him, and they'll save him. The alternative is unthinkable.

Tilly removed her thumb from her mouth. 'And Frank?'

'Yes, and Frank. Now get some sleep, both of you.'

'Will you stay here?'

'I'm not going anywhere.'

Her children cosied up to her, closed their eyes, quickly asleep. Cara looked at them both – perfect skin, soft hair. Tilly with Roo's dark brown eyes and light hair, Josh more Cara's colouring. It struck her for the first time how much her son resembled her brother now he's getting older. The same long limbs Griffin had at his age, the permanent frown, as if neither can understand the injustices of the world.

In the darkness, bookended by her children, Cara closed her eyes. But she couldn't sleep. She thought about Griffin – alone out there, in pain. Maybe even dead. And if so, how all of this is for nothing.

And of Charlie. Her boyfriend who messaged earlier on that evening. *I'm going home tonight. I'll see you tomorrow.* Something and nothing; a distance between them she hates, something they've never had before.

She hasn't seen him that morning; he's down in the basement, with his team, trying to get a grip on the link from the dark web, trying to trace the owner of the Bitcoin wallet. Something, anything, when they all know it's a dead end.

Jamie knocks gently on the door; she gestures him in.

'You want to talk to me?'

'I do. Close the door.'

He does as he's told, sitting down in front of her desk. The look on his face tells her he knows what this is about.

'You've got something? On the Echo Man?'

She shakes her head. 'But I'm making progress.' She pauses, knowing he's not going to like what's coming next. 'Last night, I took samples from everyone here. The whole team.'

'Samples? How?'

338

'Coffee mugs, mainly. Shenton's water bottle. Chewing gum from the bin. Charlie's was the easiest – I swabbed his toothbrush at home.'

'Even Brody? She wasn't around at that time.'

'But she arrived out of nowhere last year. Even you must be able to see that was suspicious?'

'Fine, but there's one big flaw in your theory,' he counters. 'All coppers give elimination samples when they join the police. And you ran that DNA against that database at the time – no match.'

'Swabs can be swapped, profiles changed.'

'Fucking hell, are we in that deep?'

'I don't trust anyone. Not anymore.'

'So why are you telling me this?'

'Yours came back this morning. And mine. No match, not even a partial. So I know that Griffin's in the clear too.'

'What's your plan?'

'I get everybody else's back. And then we bring in the team. We find that match.' Jamie shakes his head in disbelief. 'Okay?' she asks him.

'Okay,' he replies.

She can see he wants to ask more, but a flurry of activity in the incident room distracts him. A PC has arrived – the one who brought the disc to them yesterday morning – and he sits down at Shenton's desk, taking control of the mouse. Cara gets up, Jamie following.

'What's going on?' Cara asks, watching as the PC pulls a video file from the server.

'It's the CCTV from Wednesday night,' Shenton replies.

Cara leans forward as it starts to play. A man walks in, tall, broad, arms like overstuffed sausages. He's wearing a black hoodie, but they don't need to see his face.

'It's Tyler Brown,' Jamie explodes. 'Our prime suspect – the man everyone is supposed to be finding – walks into this very nick and nobody realises?' He's shouting now; Cara's never seen him so angry. 'And what do we do?' He jabs at the screen. 'We let him walk straight out again?'

Somehow Cara keeps her calm. 'Shenton, follow up on this. We know his licence plate – check ANPR. How did he get here? Where did he go?'

'On it, boss.'

'Brody?' She's quiet, her face deathly white, and Cara realises she hasn't said a word all morning. 'Get on to the duty sergeant in Response and Patrol. Remind them of who we're looking for and why it's important. Jamie?' He's still pacing, running his hands through his hair in exasperation. 'Take a moment. Get a cup of coffee. Get one for me.' He stares at her for a moment, then nods.

Cara turns her back, returning to her office, closing the door behind her with a quiet click. She stands behind the doorway, in a corner that can't be seen from outside. And only then does she allow herself to cry.

Chapter 63

Jamie doesn't like the subterfuge, but he can see the logic in Cara's plan. Noah Deakin apparently committed serial murder under all their noses. If they're going to involve the team, they need to be sure. Their prime suspect, Robert Keane, could be anyone, and that thought makes a shiver run up his back.

He takes a seat next to Shenton, watching him work, deftly checking ANPR systems, running Tyler Brown's car number plate against the traffic cameras and CCTV he's already managed to get his hands on from Wednesday night.

'Anything?' he asks.

Shenton gives him a look. 'Give me time.'

There's a knock, and a man appears in the doorway. Tall, in full uniform, with a mop of unruly black curls and a bushy beard. He looks around the incident room, searching for someone.

'Can I help you?'

'Sergeant Danny Cohen. Serious Collision Investigation Unit. I'm here about Andrew Elliott's car crash?'

'DI Jamie Hoxton. We spoke on the phone.' Cohen nods a greeting. 'Cara's through here.'

Jamie knocks on the door of Cara's office, then goes in. She smiles as soon as she sees who Jamie's with.

'Danny,' she says, getting up and greeting him with a kiss on the cheek. 'Please come in.'

'I'm so sorry about Griffin. Do you have any news?'

'No, nothing. Not yet.' They come inside and take a seat in front of Cara's desk. 'You have an update on the car? Sorry – tea, coffee?'

'No, thank you. And yes, but this stays between us for now. Nothing's been confirmed, but I thought you'd like to know my initial assessment. How is your ex-husband?'

'Still in a critical condition. What can you tell us?'

Cohen pulls a notepad out of his pocket, then sits back. His face is grave. 'Honestly, it's hard to say for sure at this stage. The Mercedes was found at the bottom of a steep incline, so it must have rolled more than a few times to get there. There are skid marks on the road, and matching damage on the tyres, so the driver clearly tried to stop. But why, I don't know.'

'No cameras?'

'Not out there. And no dashcam. We're appealing for witnesses, but given the car wasn't found until you raised the alert yesterday morning, we have to assume that nobody's going to come forward. Sarah Wright's blood alcohol was zero when it was taken at the hospital, Andrew's was over the legal limit, but as he wasn't driving, that's irrelevant. The Mercedes is a fairly new model, and we've sent the driver monitoring system away – the car's equivalent of a black box recorder – so we won't have a full picture until later.

But one thing they have told us is that the car was going around fifty-five miles an hour when it crashed.'

'That's fast on a road like that,' Jamie comments.

'It is. Within the speed limit, but it would have meant that if something bumped them from behind, as Sarah says it did, she would have had little time to react.'

'Do you agree with her statement?' Cara asks. 'Did you have a chance to watch the video sent to us?'

'I did. And we found the camera in the car – it's with your digital team now, although Charlie said to tell you something about VPNs and hot spots?'

'He means it's basically useless,' Cara mutters.

'And as for Sarah's statement.' Danny frowns. 'She maintains that something drove right behind and then bumped her. She lost control, the car went off the road, then rolled until it came to rest at the bottom of the hill. That *could* be what happened. There's significant damage to the rear of that car – no way of knowing if that's from a collision or from rolling down a hill.' He squints at Cara. 'What are you thinking? That's she's lying?'

'I don't know. I really don't. I just find it odd that Sarah walked out of there, but Roo was critically injured? And why didn't she call an ambulance straight away?'

'Doctor says she banged her head,' Jamie says.

'Yes, but she and Roo were there for nearly six hours. And she's fine? How could that be possible?' she directs to Danny.

'Sometimes I look at a car and nobody should have got out alive, yet there they all are, chatting by the side of the road. Other times, the victim should have been unhurt, yet one is dead and one's in hospital. As for Sarah and Roo . . .'

He glances at his notepad then back at them. Jamie can tell he's holding something back.

As can Cara. 'Danny, please,' she says. 'For Griffin.'

He sighs. 'Look, I shouldn't be telling you this until we've done some further tests, but yes, I have my concerns. The passenger side airbag didn't deploy, it was switched off manually.'

'The airbags didn't go off?'

'Most of them did. The ones in the pillar, in the footwell, and all of the driver's side ones deployed. But the one in front of Roo – it was turned off.'

The whole room is quiet.

'So, if I'm getting this right,' Jamie says. 'Sarah was going fast down a single-track country road. She says a car came up behind and bumped them, causing her to lose control. The car rolled down the bank. She had the full protection of the airbags, but Roo didn't?'

Danny nods slowly. 'That's the upshot of it all, yes. That car would have been like a washing machine – Roo would have been thrown all over the place. Even with his seat belt on.'

Cara looks at him. 'In your opinion, could Sarah have done this deliberately?'

Jamie turns sharply. 'Cara—'

'We're looking for a woman, aren't we? Why are we ruling her out? Danny?'

'I mean, she *could* have done it deliberately. But it was a big risk to take. Rolling a car down the hill. Car accidents are incredibly unpredictable.'

'We should arrest her.'

'Cara, we're not arresting your ex-husband's pregnant fiancée,' Jamie replies.

'Why not?'

'We have no proof, for starters.'

'Isn't this reasonable belief? Someone disabled the airbag and planted a camera. Someone who must have had access to the car.'

But before Jamie can counter, Shenton sticks his head around the door.

'Er . . . boss,' he says, looking between Cara and Jamie. 'We have a problem. A fucking big one.'

Chapter 64

Jamie drives Cara and Brody out to the body. A blood-spattered corpse laid out for all the world to see, in the middle of a disused car park, in the middle of the day.

Dr Ross walks over to meet them – approaching Cara first.

'It's not him,' Ross says, articulating the base fear that's been running through her head since Shenton walked into her office. 'It's not Griffin. It was the first thing I asked when I got here. You needed to know.'

'Thank you,' she says. 'I mean that, Greg. Thank you.' He gives her a brief nod. 'So who is it?'

'Still waiting on ID. But I'm assuming it's one of yours. Given the violence.' A SOCO approaches them, handing out the white coveralls. They put them on, then follow Jamie across to the body.

Cara glances behind to where Brody is hesitating by the car.

'Are you coming?' she asks. Brody suits up and joins them, pulling the mask over her mouth. Cara gives her a long look, puzzled. It's not her first body, by any stretch. Why the hesitation?

The man is naked. Stripped of all clothing, he lies at an odd angle, his limbs seemingly disjointed, his head tilted back showing a rich red line on his neck. He's thin, jutting ribs covered in purple bruises, more of the same marking the lines of the restraints around his wrists and ankles. But it's his face that draws Cara's attention. The mouth, open with a silent scream. And two bloodied holes – his eyes have been removed.

'Perimortem,' Dr Ross says, appraising the gaping voids with a gloved hand. 'And some time before death, maybe an hour or so, judging from the clotting and margins of the wounds. Removed with something blunt. I'm guessing a spoon or similar.'

'Fucking hell,' Jamie says, thickly, next to Cara. 'Cause of death?'

'Strangulation, with a narrow ligature. From behind, by the looks of things. Yes,' he says, as a technician helps him turn the body. 'Shoe mark here. She – and I'm assuming it's a woman from the size – placed her foot on the small of his back, pulling with the ligature. Looks like he didn't have it in him to struggle.'

'Brody?' Cara turns, looking for her DC. She's a few feet back, half-turned away. 'I need you to get on to missing persons straight away. Work out who this man is.' Brody takes a few steps closer, then retches. Her hand over her mouth she runs to the other side of the car, taking leave of her breakfast.

Cara throws Jamie a puzzled look then walks slowly across to her.

'Are you okay?' she asks Brody, still bent in two, heaving. 'You've seen worse than this?'

Brody straightens up, wiping her hand across her mouth. And the look on her face tells Cara all she needs to know.

'Oh, fuck,' Cara says, warily. 'What did you do?'

Darren Gladwell. Paedophile. Registered sex offender. Just released from prison for procurement of prohibited images of children. And now dead in a concrete car park.

Cara sits next to Brody in the back seat of Jamie's car, just the two of them. She watches Jamie through the windscreen, discussing something with Ross.

'Talk,' Cara says. 'And make it quick. Before Jamie comes back.'

'I thought . . . I didn't think . . .' Brody sniffs. 'I didn't think they'd kill him. Like that. I assumed they'd reply. And I could have a back and forth with them, try to get a face-to-face meet.'

'You messaged them on the dark web?'

'Yeah. On the link Bill Lloyd gave us. I just gave the name. Didn't even say why or what he'd done.'

'I think they worked that out for themselves,' Cara says, drily.

'And now he's dead. They killed him. No payment, nothing. Why?' Brody starts to cry again. 'What's going to happen? Are you going to arrest me? Oh, God,' she slurs through her tears. 'I'm going to prison, aren't I? I did this. He's dead because of me.'

Cara puts a stiff arm around her, taking a long breath in, thinking.

'I should tell Jamie now. Tell Halstead. I should—'

'You will do no such thing,' Cara snaps. 'Look at me.' Brody does, tears still streaming. 'Who knows about this?'

'Only you.'

'What laptop did you use to message them?'

'My personal one. It's here, in my bag.'

'Get rid of it. I don't care what's on it,' Cara adds, seeing Brody about to protest. 'Go home. Take it apart. Smash the hard drive.'

'But . . . but why?'

'Because . . . oh, I don't know. Because that man deserved more than three years in prison and a biro through the hand. Because I won't let this killer take anyone else from me. Not Griffin. Not Roo. And certainly not you. Go home. Go to bed, whatever.'

'But as soon as his ID comes back they're going to know. They're going to know it was me.'

'We'll—'

Cara stops abruptly as Jamie opens the driver's side door, throwing himself inside and turning back to face them.

'You okay, Brody? Don't worry about it – the dead bodies get to us all at some point. This one's worse than most. Ross says he hasn't been dead for long. Less than three hours. He'll do a proper temp shortly, but the body's warm. Rigor hasn't kicked in. Any idea who it is?'

'Darren Gladwell,' Cara says.

'Oh.' Jamie's face turns grave. He looks from Brody to Cara and back again. 'Well, this confirms it,' he says slowly. 'They have someone from the force feeding them information. How they knew we were at the strip club. And now this.'

Nobody speaks. Jamie's not stupid; he knows.

'Brody's going to go home, Jamie,' Cara says. 'She's not

feeling well. And then can you drop me at the hospital? To check on Roo?'

He stares at them a moment longer. Then he turns around and puts his seat belt on.

'Okay,' he says, and that's all.

Chapter 65

Jamie drops Brody home and takes Cara to the hospital. He stops her as she's getting out of the car, one hand on her arm.

'Are we doing the right thing?' he asks. 'A man died.'

She sighs. 'I'm not even sure what side I'm on, right now. That man was a shit, pure and simple. And yes, by allowing this to happen, we're accomplices. But Jamie, you were right before. Brody gave them Darren Gladwell's name, but they must have known who she was. They didn't ask for money, didn't engage in conversation. They just killed him. Someone in the force is in on it. And we're going to find out who.'

She gets out, closing the door behind her and marching towards the entrance of the hospital without a glance back. Jamie envies her determination, her unerring confidence in her decisions. When he's just getting through the day, hour by hour.

He arrives back at the nick to find the incident room empty. That's it now. There's no team here – the whole investigation has been moved to Basingstoke, exactly as Ryder wanted.

He stands next to the whiteboard, pondering Cara's words. Is she right? Or has three years of serial killers gone

351

to her head, making her paranoid? He works through what they know – the real evidence. The Polaroid from the floor safe, showing a victim from the Echo Man case. How the old pub was deserted and sanitised before they got there. How the killer knew they were at the strip club at the exact time Stephen Allen's body was dumped. And what's more – how did the killer find their victims?

The slow realisation that Cara might be right creeps its way up his spine, so when his phone rings, he jumps, then laughs at his foolishness.

He sees the name and answers it. 'Holly?' he says to the CSM. 'What have you got for me?'

'Still nothing from the old pub – the only DNA found at that place comes back to David Foden. But Jamie, there's something else.' She clears her throat, awkwardly. 'DCI Elliott said I could speak to you and she's not answering her phone. I've left a voicemail, but . . .'

'She's at the hospital. Probably has it turned off. What is it?'

'Those samples she gave me. One's come back. And it's a match.'

She gives Jamie a name. He frowns. 'Are you sure? I mean . . .'

'Yes, I'm sure. That particular sample that DCI Elliott gave us matches to unknown DNA from the Echo Man case.'

But Jamie doesn't have a chance to reply. He hears a click behind him – a sound he's never heard in real life, but one that makes the blood freeze in his veins. The slide of a gun being racked. A round in the chamber.

And a voice.

'Don't fucking move.'

Chapter 66

Roo's status is unchanged. The doctor speaks to the three of them in the corridor outside the ICU – Cara, Sarah and Roo's mother, Karen. In a monotone he tells them that Roo has stabilised, but that he remains unresponsive despite being off sedation.

'What does that mean?' Cara asks.

'It means we're still keeping a close eye on him.' He pauses, seeing their stricken faces. 'But we have reasons to be optimistic. He is making respiratory effort, even though he isn't fully waking, and there have been no signs of any seizure activity. We just need to give him a little more time.'

'How long . . .' Sarah begins. Her hands drop protectively to her still-flat stomach. 'How much time?'

'A few days.' The doctor gives them all a sympathetic smile and Cara hates him for it. She wants this man to fix Roo, bring him back to life. And instead, all they're getting are platitudes and tired clichés.

She feels a tensing in her muscles, frustration building, and she excuses herself, walking quickly away from the ICU. She wants to scream at the top of her voice, shout, punch something, but instead she pushes into the women's toilets so hard the door bangs against the wall on the other side.

She goes to the sink and takes a handful of cold water, splashing it over her face, not caring if it smudges her mascara. It helps, a bit, and as she dabs her skin dry with a hand towel she looks at herself in the mirror. She feels dizzy, not sure which way to turn. Everything demands her attention: Griffin, still missing. Roo, in the hospital. Noah, and the truth in his confession.

And the investigation. A killer for hire. A nameless, faceless woman on a mission who defeats them at every turn.

Her phone beeps in her pocket, finding reception for the first time since she left the ICU. She takes it out and looks at it – a voicemail from the CSM. But before she can listen, it rings. Unknown number.

Cara stares at it for a moment. Then presses the green button.

'I'll give you that one for free,' a voice says. A woman. It's her. 'Next time, you'll have to pay.'

'You took his eyes out,' Cara replies. Her voice comes out strangled. She clears her throat, tries again. 'Was it you who killed the others?'

A pause, and Cara thinks she's hung up. Then: 'No. But I was there. I watched them die. No more than they deserved, DCI Elliott. I did you a favour.'

'Please. Please give my brother back.'

'I provide a service. Same as you. We're ridding the world of vermin, one after another.'

'Griffin's never done anything wrong. He's a cop—'

'He's your brother. Andrew Elliott was your husband.

354

Get the hint – someone wants you distracted. A paying customer. A loyal customer. Who am I to argue? I do what I'm told. Unlike some.'

'What do you want me to do?'

'It's not personal, Cara. This is business.'

'But it's not just business, is it? You're not just doing it for the money. It's retribution.'

A pause. 'Correct.'

'So what have I done?'

'You've been digging. Sticking your nose where it's not wanted.'

'The Echo Man case.'

'Correct again. You're on a roll. Leave Noah Deakin to rot in jail. Stop looking. Do that, and we'll return your brother. But do it fast. I don't think he has long.'

And with that, the phone goes dead.

Cara looks at it, disbelieving. She was speaking to her. The woman responsible for killing and torturing and inflicting pain on twenty people, talking to her on the phone as if this was a negotiation. As if Cara would walk away.

No fucking chance.

Cara's indecision has crystallised into a steely determination. She will find this woman. She will track down Robert Daniel Keane. And with that thought, she returns the call to Holly.

'You have something for me?' she asks, immediately.

'Yes, as I was telling DI Hoxton . . .' She pauses, her voice changes, coming out as a whisper. 'Oh, God. He was at the police station. I told Jamie, and the line went dead. The man . . . the match to the Echo Man sample. He must have been there.'

'Who? Who is it?' Cara shouts.

And as Holly tells her, it all makes sense.

Cara hangs up, redials 999. 'Come on, come on,' she mutters as the call is answered. 'This is DCI Cara Elliott. I need all units to the Major Crimes incident room at Southampton Central police station, immediately. 10-10. Officer in need of emergency assistance. Search the whole damn place. Arrest on sight.'

The man Cara never suspected. Quiet, unassuming. A member of the team from the beginning. Since their first serial killer. Robert Daniel Keane – the Echo Man.

'Our offender . . .' she says, her voice shaking. 'The man you're looking for, is DC Toby Shenton.'

Chapter 67

All Jamie can see is the muzzle of the gun. Stark, black metal. Pointed right at him. And the man holding it – Toby Shenton.

'What are you doing, Toby?' Jamie says. His voice is strained, his mouth sticky, dry. 'You don't want to do this.'

'I don't?' Shenton takes a step closer, closing the door behind him with a mule-kick back. 'Seems clear to me. What did Holly say on the phone?'

'She said . . .' Jamie pauses, swallows. 'She said that one of the DNA samples Cara took came back as a match – to you. That you're the Echo Man.'

Shenton nods, slowly, a smile forming on his lips. 'Well, fuck. And it was going so beautifully. Three years since Noah Deakin went to prison. Three years he's kept his mouth shut. And then Cara Elliott wades in and everything goes to shit.'

'It was you. You paid to have Griffin abducted. To run Roo off the road.'

'I thought it would distract her. Get her far away from the investigation. But no, she just doubled down. Fucking

357

forensics. Fifty years ago, a man could kill and get away with it. Now it's all DNA, and CCTV monitoring everywhere you go. Isn't a man allowed a hobby?'

Keep him talking, Jamie thinks, his gaze locked on the unwavering gun. We're in the middle of a busy police station, someone's bound to notice.

'You killed all those people,' he says. 'But why?'

'Because I enjoyed it. Fuck, why is this so difficult for people to understand? My brain isn't like yours. I grew up with a father and uncle who beat the shit out of me, day and night. And when they weren't doing that, they had their little mates around and I became their personal plaything. They did things to me that you can't even imagine, Jamie. That's why I turned out like this. That's why I kill. And why I will continue to do so, day in, day out.'

'And what do you think is going to happen now? You'll just walk out of a police station? I won't let you do that. And you can't shoot me.'

'Why not?' Jamie watches as Shenton moves his finger from the guard, resting it on the trigger.

'The whole station will come running.'

Shenton laughs, a brief cackle. 'And what? This isn't America – they don't know what to do if a gun goes off. In the chaos, I'll walk out of here.'

Jamie pauses. He's right. The armed response team are trained for this sort of thing, but not your average copper. This whole situation is surreal. Who knows how anyone will react.

Jamie's shaking, adrenaline charging around his body, his chest rising and falling rapidly. Hyperventilating. He tries to keep calm, to keep his breathing constant.

'Shenton, you won't get away with this. Too many people

know what's going on. The lab have the results. Holly will phone Cara. They'll catch you.' He takes one step towards Shenton, his hand outstretched. 'Give me the gun.'

Shenton frowns, backs away. 'You know, that might be true. But I'm going to have a fucking great time in the meantime.' He pauses, thinking. 'Fuck. I like you, Jamie. I always have. You're honest, hardworking. You give a shit. But that doesn't mean I won't shoot you.'

And in that moment, there's no time to react. Jamie sees Shenton's eyes narrow, the muscles, the tendons in his arm tense, and all Jamie can think is, *Pippa*.

Images flash before his eyes. His wife, laughing in their old kitchen, dabbing a blob of cake mix on his nose. Sleeping, her blonde hair a halo on the pillow. The look in her eyes when she walked down the aisle on their wedding day.

He hears the bang, ear-shattering in the small room; he watches as a tiny plume of grey emerges from the barrel. And then his legs drop out from under him.

Shenton rushes out of the room. Jamie wants to go after him, tries, but something's not working. His brain won't connect, his body won't move. He stares up at the ceiling.

Faces appear in his eyeline. Concerned people making calls, phoning 999, even though they're in a police station, they're surrounded by cops, and Jamie tries to laugh. But then the pain starts. Waves of agony, a red-hot poker in his middle, creeping up until his whole body is consumed by it.

'What . . .' he manages, but nothing else will come out. His mouth is ferrous, the taste of blood on his lips. He can't think, can't move. Struggles to take a breath, something heavy sitting on his chest.

'Don't move. Help is coming. Stay calm,' somebody says, and Jamie wants to reply, *I am. I am calm.*

Because all he feels now is peace. Reassurance, as if he's lying under a weighted blanket. He senses a small hand grip his. Warm fingers, comforting against the cold.

Pippa. Pippa.

Jamie's sinking. Faster now, through the floor, down, down. The voices dwindle and die. The pain fades.

His eyes close.

He's with her again. And he's happy.

Chapter 68

Shenton knows he should run. Get as far away from here as he can, but arrogance has always been his problem. Everything will catch up with him soon, so why not have some fun. And fuck, what fun he has in mind.

Nobody stops him as he sprints away from the incident room, the gun still hot in his hand. He tucks it out of sight as he runs, into his pocket. Down to the car park and into his car, throwing it into reverse and getting out of there, not caring about the vehicles he clips on his way out. But at the junction he pauses. To the motorway, or up Hill Lane to the hospital? And he can't resist.

Nobody's expecting him to come here. It's the stupid move, and Hampshire Police will be thrown into chaos, struggling to make sense of the mess he's left behind. He parks up quickly, hurrying to the ward, then slowing to a walk as he approaches. The guard appraises him with boredom as he shows his police ID.

'Quite the popular one, isn't he?' he mutters, with an apathetic wave. 'Go on then.'

Shenton thanks him with his best smile and pushes the

door open. Inside, he closes it behind him, then stands at the end of the bed, appraising Noah as he sleeps. He looks almost peaceful, the pathetic little bitch. Shenton could kill him now – just lean forward, place two hands around his neck. Squeeze until his eyeballs haemorrhage, until his face turns puce. But no. There is still work to be done.

He takes the gun from his waistband then taps it, twice, on the end of the bed. A *clink clink*, metal on metal, and the noise wakes Noah. His eyes open, then widen when he sees Shenton, pushing himself up in the bed. But there is no distance to be gained, not while Noah's chained to the side.

'Fuck off,' Noah says, the tremble in his voice giving him away. 'I'll shout for help.'

'Yes, but then another innocent will be dead, and you don't want to be responsible for that, do you?'

'What do you want?'

'To see you, of course. And chat.' He takes a seat by the side of the bed, leans in towards Noah. 'We had a deal.'

Noah shakes his head, but his whole body vibrates, making his handcuff rattle. 'I haven't said anything. I've done as we agreed.'

'But you're still here. Despite your best efforts.' He points to the scars on Noah's wrists, the bruises on his face. 'You remember the deal. You confess, I keep Cara safe. You weren't supposed to start flirting. Putting doubts in her tiny little head.'

'Leave her alone.' His face is steely, his eyes determined. 'She's done nothing to you.'

'I haven't touched her. Yet.' Shenton raises the gun, pointing the barrel towards him, then away. He makes a noise – '*pew pew*' – then smiles at Noah. 'But who knows what we could get up to if she doesn't behave.' He taps the gun on the bed rail with a clink. 'Hold this against her pretty head, tie her up, fuck her raw. Do things you only dream of.'

'You fucking psycho,' Noah spits.

Shenton grins at Noah's reaction. The hatred, the helplessness. 'And what are you going to do about it? You're a self-confessed serial killer. Nobody will listen to you.' Shenton leans forward. Reaches out with the gun and places it against Noah's temple. Noah freezes. 'You have no idea what the last few years have been like for me. Having to keep quiet. Sneak around in the dead of night. Abduct the hookers, the homeless. Hear them scream and know there is so much more I could do. You remember what I said, don't you? It won't just be your precious Cara who suffers. I'll get to her kids. There's enough people out there who would welcome a young child.'

'You sick fuck.'

'And you're not? Remember what you did, Noah. Remember who you are. The son of a drug-dealing whore.' He presses the gun hard against Noah's head, grinds it against his skull until a trickle of blood runs down his face. But Noah doesn't flinch. His eyes open; they lock on Shenton.

'If you're going to kill me, get on with it.'

'Me? Kill you?' Shenton cackles, removing the gun and putting it in the waistband of his trousers, pulling his shirt over the top. He takes a step backwards. 'Hell, no. This is your fault – I'm going to show you exactly what happens when you don't do what I say. I'm going to kill Nate Griffin – get the job I paid for finished – and then I'm coming after her. Your precious Cara. And you have no idea – no fucking idea – how bad things are going to get.'

Noah's face is pale. He glances at the closed door, then back at Shenton.

'Go on,' Shenton says. 'Try me. And you can spend the rest of your life knowing that Cara Elliott's last moments were spent in excruciating agony. That beautiful body violated in the worst possible ways.' Images play out in Shenton's head. Things he's only let himself dream about for the last few years, and he stops for a moment, savouring the thought of the fun he's going to have, the fucking, the cutting, the feeling of her flesh as he fillets her skin.

'Oh, Noah,' he says with a smile. 'I'm going to do them all.'

At that thought, Noah unfreezes. He starts to scream, shouting incoherently, pulling at his cuff, kicking off the bedclothes, making the whole bed rock.

The door opens in a flash. The guard looks between Shenton and the hysterical, frantic Noah.

'What happened?' he barks.

Shenton shrugs coolly. 'Just went crazy. You know what these men are like. I'd get a doctor if I were you – get something in him, tranquillised nice and heavy. You don't want anyone innocent in this nice hospital getting hurt.'

The guard thumps the red button at the end of the bed and sirens go off. Shenton backs away, satisfied, as Noah kicks and screams. As the guard tries to subdue him. As doctors barrel into the room, bellowing for assistance, for lorazepam, for restraints.

Calmly, Shenton leaves. Planning his first move.

Who's going to suffer next.

Chapter 69

Cara paces the corridors of the hospital, waiting, begging for her mobile to ring. She phones Jamie, over and over, his number ringing out.

Unable to stand it any longer she strides out of the hospital, then runs, sprints, towards the car park. She'll head to the nick, find out first-hand what's going on, and she starts her engine, trying Jamie one last time. And it's answered.

'Jamie, thank fuck, what's—' But a female voice interrupts.

'Cara, it's Gail Halstead.'

'Guv, what's going on?' But her introduction is strange, her boss's tone flat. Cara stops, dreading what's coming next.

'It's Jamie, he . . .' Cara hears a sob, her voice cracking with pain. 'I'm sorry, Cara. He's been shot.'

'Shot?' Cara struggles to catch up. 'By whom? And Jamie – he'll be okay, right?'

'No. He's dead.'

The world stills, quietens. Blood rushes in her ears. Her vision blurs, and for a moment she thinks she's going to pass out and grips the steering wheel, dropping the phone to the passenger seat. She can hear Halstead talking, a tinny voice, asking if she's still there, telling her to come into the nick, but Cara stares at it, confused.

Jamie. Dead. Shot. How?

Shenton.

He's Robert Daniel Keane. And the Echo Man. A cold sadistic killer – Noah Deakin's best friend as a child, who came back into his life as an adult and forced him to take the blame. But why? That, Cara doesn't understand, but she knows she needs to stop him.

Toby Shenton is the reason Roo is lying in hospital. Responsible for Griffin's abduction. She doesn't know how that Polaroid got into Edward Morris's floor safe, but she knows that without a doubt, he's involved with the snuff film murders. A sadist of his calibre, able to stay away from death and torture and pain? Not a chance.

And the world comes into bright, stark focus.

She picks up her phone again, ending the call to Halstead and dialling one last number, praying he answers.

'Dr Singleton speaking?'

'DCI Cara Elliott. You told me on the phone that Robert Keane was happy at the children's home. That he liked it there?'

'Yes. He was sad when he had to leave.'

'You said the kids would get qualifications. Train for future jobs. Dr Singleton, this is important – did it have somewhere they could work on cars? A mechanic's pit – something like that?'

'Yes, it had a fully functioning garage. Why—'

But Cara doesn't have time to explain. She hangs up, then types in the address. Northbrooke Children's Home. Closed since 2011. A perfect place to kill.

Chapter 70

Cara drives, battling her emotions. The ache in her chest, sorrow for Jamie, threatening to grow into a grief that'll derail her. Shame, embarrassment – that once again she had a killer in her team going unnoticed for years. She trusted Shenton; how could she have been so stupid? So fucking blinkered.

She nurtures those feelings. Turns them into pure, unmitigated anger. There is no time for pity or self-recrimination – she has to save Griffin. The woman on the phone said he was alive, and she clings to that thought. Because if he's dead, she will never forgive herself.

She follows directions on her phone, taking her out of the city and into the suburbs as houses grow shabby and the scenery turns industrial. Run-down estates, shuttered shops. Graffiti on walls; glass on pavements. At last, she pulls up outside a disused building on a waste ground, surrounded by a high wire fence. The other buildings have been demolished – this is the only one standing, lonely and abandoned, a miserable-looking place.

Cara can't imagine children growing up here. But the sign on the front is clear: Northbrooke.

This was where Noah had been sent, aged ten. And where Shenton followed a few years later, after killing his uncle and his father. Cara's read the file. That boy endured horrific abuse, and yet she finds it hard to reconcile Robert Keane with what she knows about DC Toby Shenton. He'd been quiet, yes. Strange, even. But a serial killer?

She opens the rusty gate and walks slowly towards the building. Her feet crunch on broken glass; the ground is uneven with bricks and cement debris, small silver nitrous oxide canisters scattered among the cigarette butts and litter. There are two cars parked outside: an old Ford Fiesta and an expensive BMW, an exact copy of the white 8 series now impounded in the garage at the nick. Tyler Brown – he's here. She peers through the window, but there's no sign of life.

Cara stops. In the silence, she realises how foolish she has been to come here. In her addled haze she hadn't thought about how she was going to do this – only that she had to, and now, when she looks at her mobile she realises there's patchy reception. One bar, fading in and out.

She's alone, with only her pepper spray and ASP – the retractable, police issue baton. Something, although they feel pathetic, knowing what she might be facing inside. Even if she could call it in, backup is ages away. But Griffin is here. She's not walking away now.

The huge front door is bolted with a chain and padlock, so she circles the house, looking for a way in. She eventually finds a back door, locked but the glass in the top window is shattered. She carefully reaches through and opens the latch, pushing the door open with a subdued creak. She hesitates, listens. And for the first time she can hear something. Voices, male. Coming from her left. She glances at her phone – one bar. Enough, and she phones 999, requesting backup in a hushed whisper. They confirm – half an hour.

She should wait. But then she hears it – a cry of pain, echoing through the empty corridors of the house.

Without thinking, she follows the sound – the voice, the screams – down corridor after corridor. Wallpaper peeling, carpets wet with mould. Windows shaking in their frames as gusts of wind break through. Down to the garage, smelling of diesel and oil. And something else. Something cloying and dark, that sticks in her nose. That tells her to leave, get the fuck out. Because something bad is happening here.

The body confirms it. Lying on its back, stomach slit open, eyes staring glassily to the ceiling. Black jeans and wife-beater vest. Tyler Brown. The other muscle man on the videos, now little more than a pile of guts and gore. Who did this? But she knows the answer.

Him.

She needs to get out of here. Now. But how can she leave?

She grips her baton, fingers the pepper spray in her pocket. She takes out her phone, wishing for an update. No signal. Fuck. *Fuck*. She should turn back, wait for the armed teams to get here, and is about to retrace her steps when a scream echoes throughout the house. Almost inhuman, animal, but it comes again and she knows – *knows* – it's Griffin.

She's shaking now. So scared she thinks she's going to pass out or wet herself or both. She stands, her back against the wall, the open doorway to her left. She recognises Shenton's voice, and a croak, no more than a whisper, coming from her brother.

There's no way she can walk away. Griffin yells again, and she wants to cry with frustration and fear. What can she do? Shenton's slight, but he's tall. Could she stop him?

She grits her teeth, racks her baton, and walks towards the sound.

Chapter 71

There is no pain anymore, only her. Griffin's mind fractures, snippets of memory punctuating the black.

. . . *their wedding day. Mia, beautiful in her white dress. Him, uncomfortable in a jacket and tie, wondering how he got so lucky . . .*

. . . *day he met her, inexplicably making her laugh. Her smile. Her beautiful green eyes . . .*

. . . *tied up on the floor of his bedroom, listening to her scream in the room next . . .*

. . . *heavy leather boots coming into contact with his stomach, his back, his face. Fractured bone, spattered blood . . .*

. . . *ketchup. Fish and chips. Brody, bare legs, bare feet, her yelps as the cold sea rushed over her . . .*

. . . *softness of her skin. The touch of her lips on his. How she says his name, that hint of mockery. Truth or Dare, and the way her smile curves, wickedly, knowing which he'll . . .*

His consciousness stutters; the regrets pour in. He should have done more to help Mia. Should have stopped that man when he could. Should have killed him. Should have said yes to Brody after their date. Enjoyed her while he could.

He lets his mind drift, disassociates away from this pit. Ready to go, until something pulls him back. A new pain, biting. Red hot and sharp in his side.

And a voice. Jarring his consciousness, a memory from deep, deep inside. Buried, until now. Someone he thought he'd never hear again. Sing-song, jeering. Right next to his ear.

'Nathanial Griffin. Wake up. It's not your time to die.'

All those years ago, lying hog-tied on the floor. Blood in his mouth, heart thumping in his ears. This is what he heard. This man.

His eyes open. Blurry. Can't see.

'There you are.' That voice again. He blinks. 'Don't die yet. I haven't had my fun.'

Slowly his vision clears. Still hazy around the edges, but enough so he can make it out. A knife. Sharp, silver. Shining right in front of his eyes, the tip stained red. And a man.

Shenton.

'Toby?' he mumbles through a shattered mouth, his eyes closing again. 'What . . .'

'Oh, Griffin. Put it together. I know you're stupid, but you're not this dense.' He holds up the blade again. 'What's this?'

'A knife.'

'Not just any knife. The knife I used to kill your wife. To cut her beautiful face. I held it to her neck while I raped her.'

Griffin's eyes snap open; a flush of adrenaline as the realisation hits. All this time. And he'd been wrong.

'You killed her. You're . . . him.'

Shenton gives a slow patronising clap, the knife shining in the darkness. 'I thought about telling you, so many times. Just so I could see this look on your face. And it's so worth it. What would you like to do to me now? Kill me? Reduce me to a bloody pulp? But look at you. Fucked.'

Griffin forces strength into his legs, pushing himself upright. He lifts his head and the world swims.

A gun joins the knife, Shenton holding them in front of Griffin's face.

'Take your pick,' he says. 'Choose your poison.'

'Shoot me in the head, you think I give a shit?' Griffin says, his voice rasping, his throat sore. 'You've taken everything from me. Mia. My future. Everything I hoped for.'

'Fuck you and your future. Why should you be happy? No.' He lowers the gun. Pushes it in the back of his trousers. 'You're like a cat with nine lives, Griffin. Well, this time you've run out.'

He smiles, a look that chills Griffin to the bone. Pure evil. As he pushes the knife into Griffin's side.

This time the pain is worse. Slow, creeping, turning his insides red hot, an all-encompassing burn of agony. Griffin screams as Shenton smiles, twisting the knife, pushing it deeper.

He sees colours, darkness, black, white, flashing. He hears the drip of his blood as it splashes to the floor, tastes the salt of his tears as they catch on his lips.

'Do you know the secret to keeping victims alive, Griffin? Take it easy. Nice and slow.' Another twist – a moment of black – then the knife is removed. Shenton pats him gently on the cheek with a bloodied hand.

'Avoid anything necessary for life. The heart, the brain, the lungs. It's incredible how much the human body can take. Look at you. Three days you've been here. And you're still breathing.' He raises the knife again, holding it close to Griffin's eye. So close a droplet of blood gathers and falls, catching on the tears on Griffin's eyelashes. 'Push this into your brain, and you're gone. But take out an eye. Take out two, and you'll survive. I could cut you into tiny pieces, right here, and, as long as your body still has blood for your heart to pump around, you'll be alive. In excruciating pain, yes, wishing you were dead. But alive.'

He holds the knife horizontal, the tip almost touching the eyeball. Griffin throws his head back, but Shenton catches him by the hair. Pushes, closer, and he screws his eyes shut, twisting, turning, not caring as clumps of hair are pulled from his scalp.

And then the pressure releases. He hears Shenton take a step back and he opens his eyes again, wincing, afraid. But Shenton is watching him, appraising, his chin cupped in his hand.

The respite doesn't last for long. Shenton takes a step forward and jabs, a sabreur, once, twice, hitting bone. Every muscle in Griffin's body tenses with pain; he loses his footing, cries out as Shenton drives the blade into his flesh.

'You can scream all you like. Nobody's coming.'

'Please,' Griffin says. 'Please.'

And for the first time in his life, Griffin prays. To a God he doesn't believe in, for a world he doesn't think exists. Let there be something more. Let him see her.

His vision blurs, the room fades. And as everything trickles away, he hears a voice.

'Stop. Put your hands above your head.'

And his last thought before he passes out: the same as all those years ago.

No. Not Cara. Please.

Chapter 72

'Stop. Put your hands above your head.'

The scene is worse than Cara ever imagined. The grey concrete mechanic's pit, and in it, her brother, practically suspended from the rig, almost unrecognisable under the bruises, the scabbed lacerations. Head bent, hair falling over his face, wearing a black T-shirt, jeans. Bare arms, every inch of skin covered with blood. Some dried, brown, almost black. Other fresh, bright red, spattered and smeared under his bare feet. And in front of him – Shenton. Wearing a look she's never seen before, his face thrown into harsh shadows – a ghoul. A night walker.

At her words, Shenton wheels around to face her, the knife raised in his hand, dripping blood to the floor. He laughs – and she hates him more than she thought it possible.

'Boss, hello. How nice of you to join us. You're just in time for the end of the show.'

'Shenton, you're surrounded by armed officers. You have one last chance to turn yourself in.'

'Fuck off, I'm not. Do you think I'm stupid? I've been a police officer for fifteen years, do you think I don't know how it works? If armed officers were anywhere near this place I'd have red dots on my chest and my face pressed into the floor by now. What are they waiting for? Come on in, boys.' He opens his arms wide, looking around. 'What? Nothing. Guess you're fucked then.'

He takes a step towards her. This man, this confident arsehole – he looks like Toby Shenton, but he's nothing like the shy DC she's worked alongside for five years.

'Who are you, Shenton?' Cara exclaims. 'Really? Or should I call you Robert?'

That gets his attention. His lip curls. 'I'm whoever I want to be. Whatever I decide that day. It's easier to get through life being nice, being *weak*.' He spits the word. 'Especially when I know I can go home and be who I like. Kill who I like. I paid for this' – he points the knife at Griffin – 'this was my doing. Once I realised you didn't believe Noah, I had to distract you. A few thousand quid, and you, Cara, can barely dress yourself in the morning.' He laughs. 'Of course, I should have asked for a freebie, given it was all my idea in the first place.'

'What was?' Cara asks, but she knows. The Polaroid found in the floor safe, the link to Edward Morris, the film-maker. Only one person could come up with an idea as depraved as that.

'His daughter was killed, hit and run. Siobhan, her name was. Eighteen years old, and the bastard didn't even stop to see if she was okay. Turned out she might have been, if he'd called an ambulance. I'd just joined the force. I was the one who had to notify the parents, saw the look on his face. Edward wanted revenge. So I helped him achieve exactly that. Slipped him a name, once we knew. Said I could do them a favour. And before you can say wham-bang-thank-you-ma'am, Ethan Davis is mashed under the wheels of Edward's four-by-four. Poetic, if you ask me.'

'You killed him?'

'One of my first,' he says proudly.

'But what about the others? Terence Gregory. Jimmy Harvey. Stephen Allen.'

'That was all them. Edward Morris, Trevor Brown and his brother. Trev was Siobhan's boyfriend at the time – they were going to get married, did you know that?' Cara's shocked expression must give her away because he continues, 'Nah, I guess not. You don't kill and torture that many people without being that way inclined. Trev and Tyler. Muscles for brains, but they sure know how to deliver the goods. I saw it in Trevor when I first met him. Sat on the sofa next to Edward as I told them that Ethan was dead. More of a skinny little runt then, but I saw the signs. Dead behind the eyes, bruises on his face. Abused kids, poor sods. I looked up their father when I got back to the station. GBH, drunk and disorderly, domestic violence. Aggression starts in the home, but it's ingrained in the bones. Passed down through generations. They found their calling – they saw their father in the eyes of every one of those men they killed. May he rest in peace.'

'You killed him. Tyler.'

'Didn't even see it coming. Knife in his guts, boom. Game over. Just me and her, now. And she – well, she's something else. The driving force.'

'Who is she?'

Shenton laughs, long and loud. 'Cara Elliott,' he giggles, pointing the knife at her. 'I'm not going to make it easy for you.' He stops abruptly. 'Not that you're getting out of here alive.'

He takes a step towards Cara; she recoils.

'You don't want to do this, Robert.'

The use of his childhood name stops him in his tracks. 'Don't call me that.'

'I know what you did,' Cara continues. 'What was done to you when you were a boy. Nine years old, and nobody helped you. Not your teachers, your neighbours, your father's friends. Nobody was on your side.'

He blinks at her. Those light blue eyes. 'I didn't need them,' he says. 'I got myself out.'

'Yes, you did. And you made a nice life for yourself. A career. Studying for a PhD. Or at least, you were. What now, Robert?'

She glances to Griffin, but he's still head down. Not moving. Her chest aches with fear and sorrow, but she can't let him win.

Shenton points the knife at Griffin. 'I'm going to finish what I started. Stick my knife in Griffin's stomach, gut him like a fish. And then I'm going to kill you.'

It all happens in a split second – Cara doesn't have a chance to act, let alone think. Shenton turns back to Griffin, but before he can raise the knife, Griffin's eyes open, his head lifts. And he brings his forehead down hard onto Shenton's nose in a perfect Glasgow kiss. Cara hears the crunch of hard bone against cartilage as Shenton's nose explodes in a shower of blood and snot; he backs away, falling and landing heavily, the knife clattering to the floor.

And in doing so, something else skitters away. Across the concrete. Towards Cara.

A gun.

There's no time for hesitation – Cara picks it up,

appreciates the weight, the feel of the cold metal against her skin. She points it right at Shenton.

He shakes his head, laughing. 'What are you going to do?' he says, his voice wet, choked from the blood from his busted nose. 'Do you even know how to use a gun? You've never shot one, have you? It's not like the movies. You're no John McClane.'

The weapon gives her confidence. A conduit for her anger, her hatred.

'How hard can it be?' she says. Her arm is eerily steady, the gun an extension of her hand. She closes one eye, looks down the barrel at Shenton's bloody face, the scorn in his eyes. 'This is a semi-automatic, right? Don't you just point and shoot?'

'But you're a good guy, Cara. You're—'

The gunshot explodes in the silence, bounces off the walls, sending a high-pitched squeal direct to Cara's brain. Shenton's head explodes like a watermelon, the bullet entering just above his eyes and bursting out of the back of his skull, spattering blood and brains on the wall behind him. He looks at her, his eyes registering that last moment of surprise, before his body collapses.

Cara takes a sudden breath. A gasp of oxygen, turning her muscles to jelly, her resolve to water. She's killed him. She's killed a man.

But there's no time to take it in. The room is suddenly full of AFOs in black, muscly men bellowing in her face, and she holds up the gun, letting them take it out of her hand. Attention is diverted to Griffin as they cut the rope, gently lie him down as paramedics rush in, applying an oxygen mask, talking about securing his airway and wide bore access and major trauma centres.

Cara stands, frozen. Stunned. The words rotate in her head. She's killed a man. She's going to be arrested for murder.

Murder.

She takes a step back. Griffin is in good hands. Nobody is watching her.

And she runs.

Chapter 73

Cara gets in her car, starts the engine and drives without a thought of where she's going.

Street lights pass in a blur, streaks of white in her vision until a horn jolts her out of her daze. She slams on the brakes, receiving a blast of bad language and a few hand gestures for good measure.

She pulls over at the side of the road, letting the traffic pass. She's gripping the steering wheel so tightly her knuckles have blanched, and she pulls her fingers away, looking at her shaking hands.

She's the last detective in her team. Jamie dead. Griffin about to go to hospital. Brody at home, unfit for work. Shenton – dead.

She's killed a man.

She could claim self-defence, but whatever the justification, she's going to be arrested for murder. Suspended from her job. Locked up.

And this case is far from over.

Tyler Brown may be dead, and Trevor Brown in remand, but the woman, the disembodied voice at the end of the phone – she's still out there. And that thought hardens her resolve.

On the passenger seat, her phone rings. She glances to the screen – Charlie. He'll be desperate with worry, but he can also trace her phone. And she's not done yet.

She rejects the call, but before she turns her phone off she dials one last number. Brody answers on the first ring.

'Cara? The news is reporting a shoot-out. What's going on? Where's Griffin?'

'He's being taken to hospital. He's in a bad way. You need to go, be with him. Please?'

'Of course—'

'And I need you to do something for me. Can you look up Shenton's address?'

'Yes, but why?'

'He was behind it all. He's the Echo Man.'

'What?'

'He's dead. I shot him.'

'*What?*'

'Alana. Focus. Where does he live?'

'Yes, right. Er . . .' There's a pause as she logs onto the system. 'Here it is.' She recites an address; Cara knows the location. An awful place, and she realises she knows nothing about the man who's worked in her team for five years. Nothing about his personal life, what he did outside of work. She never asked; he never told her.

'Go and be with Griffin. I'll be in touch.'

She ends the call and turns her phone off. She's desperate for information about her brother, and her nose stings, a lump forms in her throat. But she swallows it down, screws her eyes tightly shut. She doesn't have time for theatrics now – she needs to get to Shenton's house

383

before the police do. Look for something that will lead her to their killer.

She has no idea what she's going to do next, but she can start there.

The house is a small mid-terrace in a bad part of town. Dark dirty windows, rough broken brick. The neighbouring houses look empty, boarded up, weeds swathe the tiny front gardens. As Cara walks through the darkness to the peeling front door, a rat runs out in front of her, scampering into the bushes on the other side.

She shudders. Dread eats at her insides as she peers through the closest window. Dark, nothing but a shabby sofa and a small coffee table. She knocks, once, and it echoes around the estate. There's nobody here.

She places her palm on the door and gives it a push. Locked. But that's no obstacle – she turns around and gives it a swift backward kick with her heel. It splinters, and a further whack pushes it inwards.

She steps carefully over the threshold.

Inside it's cold, the air stale. Gone-off food, and something distinctive she's only smelt at crime scenes. Rotting flesh.

She reaches forward, her fingers locating a light switch. A bare bulb illuminates the hallway as she steps further into the house.

She should be calling the SOCOs. She should leave this to DCI Ryder, but this is *her* case. She'll see it through to the end. There's no prosecution to worry about – Shenton's dead, he won't have his day in court – but if she can find something, anything, that leads her to the final killer, then it will have been worth it.

On her left, a door leads to a squalid living room. The grubby sofa she saw through the window, an old TV, and a coffee table. Nothing else. She continues walking, coming to a kitchen at the far end. Her feet stick to the lino as she flicks the light switch; a fluorescent bulb flickers, casting a yellow light over a horrific scene.

On the left-hand side are a few old kitchen cabinets, the doors wooden, handles broken. A cooker, coated with mould and dried-on stains. A sink, empty. But it's the rest of the room that draws her eye. The source of the smell.

A woman is slumped against the wall, her throat slit, a bib of dark red down her front. Her face is grey, but Cara recognises her from the photographs. From the case they were working a week ago. Joyce Hunter, the missing sex worker.

Bile rises in her throat. She was here all along – in Shenton's kitchen, while he was working the case. Mocking her, laughing.

Shenton never stopped killing. A man like that – he was driven by something deeper, a compulsion he couldn't suppress. All they did when they arrested Noah was drive him underground.

She looks out to the garden, to the patch of churned-up mud, imagining the bodies they'll find out there. Later. That's not what she's here for.

She leaves the kitchen, forcing herself to take one step after another. Up the stairs to where the air smells sweeter. Of soap and disinfectant. Shower gel and aftershave. Shenton couldn't raise suspicion – he had to make sure he was clean and fit for work. This is where he did it.

The bathroom is insignificant. Clean white sink and toilet. Shower over the bath. Then two bedrooms. The first is the master and what Cara would expect from any normal single guy. A double bed, the duvet pulled up, the pillows straight. A wardrobe, and Cara opens it, finding a row of ironed shirts, suits from Marks and Spencer. The facade of normality he hid behind. Fooling them all.

On to the second bedroom. And this is where Shenton shows his true colours.

It's small, plush blue carpet on the floor, curtains drawn across the window. Cara flicks the light on and the extent of Shenton's depravity becomes clear.

Polaroid photos line every inch of the back wall. Trophies of his kills. Faces streaked with blood, contorted with pain. Eyes pleading. Mouths open, begging for their lives. Men, women, of every age and colour. The only similarity is the pain he put them through. The lives he ended.

Some she recognises: the victims from the snuff films. Photos taken of their prostrate bodies, passed on to fuel his addiction. She looks at the shots more closely, searching for unfamiliar surroundings, different faces.

And then she spots one. It's a country lane, similar to where Roo and Sarah were run off the road. A young man lies on the gravel, limbs bent at odd angles, face bloody. A car's headlights shine in the background.

And Cara knows exactly who their killer is.

Chapter 74

I sit in my living room. The clock ticks on the wall, but otherwise it's quiet. I'm wearing my favourite dress, the one with the pink flowers, a woollen cardy over the top. And I wait.

I know it's only a matter of time. That detective – she's clever when she's focused. And right now, she's laser sharp.

The loss of a loved one can do that to you.

Footsteps on the gravel, a knock on the door. I stay put, and sure enough, she turns the handle, tentatively stepping into the hallway. She calls out, and I reply.

'In here.'

As if she's a friend, arriving for a cup of tea and a chat. Or my daughter, coming to visit.

Siobhan had been walking home from the pub when she was killed. Her broken body was found by the side of a quiet country road by an early morning dog walker, the police told us. She had broken ribs, a punctured lung, a comminuted fracture to the right femur, and a fractured skull. Despite all this, the pathologist later said, she would have been alive for hours after the accident. She could have lived.

She was eighteen.

She'd spent the evening with her boyfriend, Trevor, and his older brother, Tyler, celebrating their A level results. It was a warm summer night, and Trev offered to walk her home. She said she'd be fine. She wasn't.

The police woke us at eight a.m. A slim young man with blond hair and light blue eyes, smart in his crisp new uniform. Caring, concerned, we thought at the time. How wrong we were.

The police called it a hit and run. They opened an investigation, but there were no witnesses, nobody came forward. They had suspects, including eighteen-year-old Ethan Davis, out at the pub for the first time after passing his driving test. But he said he only had one pint, and by the time the police breathalysed him the next morning he came up sober. His car was fine. Signs of a new bumper on his freshly washed Astra, but they ran it for tests and there was no trace of blood. He was innocent. Wasn't he?

We disagreed. The papers argued that justice needed to be served, but there was no evidence, nothing the police could do.

But they have laws. Rules and regulations they have to follow. They're not supposed to follow Ethan Davis in the dead of night. Wait until he's alone and then mount the pavement, mowing him down. Enjoy the thud as he bounces over the bonnet. Put the car into reverse and relish the bumps as he's run over, time and time again, leaving him little more than a pulped mess on tarmac.

The police interviewed us, sure. But we had an alibi – we were at a party that night, making sure everyone saw us. But that copper wasn't. That sweet young police officer who revealed he had a dark side, a taste for blood, for revenge.

Trusting him was our only mistake.

That murder started it all. We saw the pain in the face of others. The bereaved relatives, the widowed wives as the law failed them. And we wanted to help.

I've always felt a little different. I never wanted to be this way, but I don't have the same emotions, that same empathy, as other people do. As a child I controlled this with small acts of deviance – I played truant from school, picked locks, broke into houses. Stalked lone men, seeing how far I could go before they turned around, before they saw me. And stranger's funerals – they were catnip. Those heightened emotions – I studied them, a student of the craft.

Viciously bullied at school, I ached to get my own back. But I was small, insignificant, and any acts of retaliation always ended up with me in trouble. I had no friends. I was lonely.

I worried about having a real relationship. A baby. Could I love? I slept around, I enjoyed sex. Multiple men, sometimes more than one in a day. Until I met Edward. He understood. He was away with work for months at a time, and when he was home I enjoyed his company. And Siobhan? My child. She was the love of my life; I needn't have worried. From the moment she was born, I knew I would do anything for her. Protect her. Nurture her. Even kill for her.

So I didn't mind the murders. And Edward wanted revenge. But we couldn't do it alone.

I first met Trev when he was thirteen. Siobhan brought him home, this quiet wee boy, covered in bruises. Fighting, he said, but I knew the violence was one way. Their father had a reputation, I'd heard the rumours. How he liked young girls. Young boys, too, it turned out. Those poor kids. We provided a refuge, where food was always on the table

389

and nothing bad would happen. They came to depend on us; all they needed was a bit of love. Love – and motivation. Revenge for Siobhan, each and every one.

Trevor was always my favourite. When Ty dropped that body off at the strip club, I knew the police would come for him. But I wanted him out of the way. I knew the end was coming.

Because Robbie – how he liked to be known – I saw how he enjoyed it. The torture, the deaths, the bloodier the better. He suggested the first location, at the old children's home, and had access to names, addresses, crimes. He helped us find the victims, hunt them down, rolling their names around in his mouth like a gourmand savouring a meal. All in return for a souvenir. A Polaroid, to add to his collection.

I'm scared of Robbie, I'm not ashamed to admit that. The look he gets, as if you're a mouse and you're the next part of his fun. I don't regret what I've done, but I don't want to end up like them. Tortured, murdered, strung up. A photograph on his wall.

Siobhan was the catalyst, Ethan the first. An opportunity that turned into a lucrative business for us. Her father, Edward Morris, the award-winning film-maker. And me, his wife, no more than a little old lady. The brains behind the operation.

Gwen.

Chapter 75

Cara sits in front of the old woman, silent, as she goes through her crimes. Gwen Morris refused to go to the police station, but said she would tell Cara everything, here. In the comfort of her own living room. One last time.

Cara switches her phone on, sets it to record. She gives the standard police caution, but Gwen barely acknowledges it. And Cara sits back, stunned, as Gwen tells all.

'You killed them,' Cara says, once Gwen's finished. 'You killed them all.'

'No more than they deserved, my dear.'

Her anger flares. 'What about my ex-husband?' she snaps. 'What about Griffin? They did nothing, and you tried to kill them.'

'Yes, I am sorry about that. I liked DS Griffin. How is he?'

'I don't know.' She stifles a sob, desperate to hear something, anything, about her brother's condition. 'Why did you do it?' she asks, her voice choked.

'Robbie. He insisted.'

'He said he paid you.'

'Not much. He didn't like that you were getting closer. To finding out who he really is.'

'But you knew?'

'Enough. He's a psychopath. A serial killer.'

'And you're not?'

'Those men, they were evil.' For the first time, Cara detects a snippet of emotion. Defiance, anger, behind her flat countenance. 'Not in the same way as Robbie, but evil all the same. They were murderers. Thieves. Rapists. And they all admitted their guilt, when the time came.' She looks at Cara, meets her gaze. 'Are you saying you disagree? Didn't Shauna Lloyd deserve revenge? Nicolas Rice? Baby Emma?'

Cara wants to argue, make the case that the justice system is the only avenue for retribution, but she can't. Every single one of the men on the tapes had got away scot-free. A trial in a court of law let those victims down.

'What I don't understand,' Cara says, 'is why you brought that disc in last Friday? You must have known we'd trace you.'

Gwen sighs. 'I'm sixty-one,' she says. 'No age by any estimation, but I'm tired. Psychic exhaustion, it's called. I read that somewhere. Tired of living a lie. I want to live out the rest of my years in peace, without this crap to contend with. When Siobhan died, the light went out of my life, and without Edward here to enjoy the spoils of our labour, what's the point? And that man. He scares me.'

'Who?'

'Robbie. He's a copper. A detective.' Cara nods. 'So you know. There's something in his eyes. I've always suspected, deep down, what he was capable of, but a few years ago we tried to stop. And he wouldn't let us. Told us who he was, who he'd killed. That Polaroid, the one you found in

Edward's safe, he gave that to us. Said we'd end up like that if we said no.' She shrugs, weakly. 'So we carried on.'

'How much of it was him, and how much was you?'

'Six and two threes, my dear. Why does it matter?'

'For me. I want to know.'

She shrugs. 'The initial idea, that was Robbie. He suggested the mechanic's pit at the old children's home, but I found the pub. Edward and I – we used to go there. The Wagon and Horses, beautiful place. I heard it had closed down, been abandoned. And it was remote, perfect for our purposes. A few repairs to the basement, a bit of tech, and it was good to go. Robbie found the potential customers, passed on their details, their phone numbers. And we messaged. Pointed them in the direction of the dark web, arranged the Bitcoin, contract agreed.' She meets Cara's gaze, her eyes sparkling with amusement. 'You think I'm too old, don't you? Too decrepit to get my head around the dark web?'

Cara smiles, despite herself. 'I'm learning not to underestimate you, Gwen.'

'And you'd be foolish to. It's not so hard, once you learn how.' She pauses, her eyes hardening again. 'Did you know him? We called him Robbie, but you'd know him as Shenton. The police officer.'

'Toby Shenton. He was an officer on my team.'

Gwen takes a quick breath in. 'Was? So he's dead?'

'Shot earlier today.'

The woman sags. 'Thank God for that. All my prayers have been answered. The devil himself,' she murmurs. And then she looks up. 'Oh, I'm so sorry. I've been wittering on and I've not offered you a cup of tea? Or coffee? Whatever you'd like.'

'I'm fine, thank you.'

'Biscuit? I might have a few digestives in a tin back there.'

'No. Thank you.'

The room settles, and in the silence, Cara appraises the woman in front of her. Her dress is dated and worn, her eyes bear the lines of more than her sixty-one years, but Cara misjudged her once, she's not going to do it again.

'You didn't have a clue, did you?' Gwen says, that twinkle back in her eye. 'That it was me?'

'Not until today,' Cara replies truthfully.

'And what gave it away?'

'The duck.' Cara remembers the photo on Shenton's wall. The road – with Ethan Davis's body. A photograph taken just minutes after his death, blood on the tarmac, the car's headlights blazing. And among it all, a single yellow rubber duck.

'That could have been Edward.'

'The ducks were your thing,' Cara replies. 'Yours and Siobhan's. You asked Shenton to place it there – something for your daughter, to mark the fact that Ethan killed her.'

'And that's why he had to die,' Gwen finishes with a resolute nod. She laughs, a quick cackle. 'I fooled you all. The poor old lady, invisible even in her own home. How old are you, detective?'

'I'm forty-two.'

'So you have a few good years in you yet. But your time will come. When the pretty boys don't flirt, when pregnant women will offer you a seat on the bus because you look so much worse off than them. When your eyesight will falter and the good health you've taken for granted will fail. That time will come, and you'll curse and rage, until you realise how wonderful invisibility can be. I'm underestimated,

394

ignored. I stood in front of two of your detectives as you searched my garden for dead bodies. Nobody gave me a second look.'

Gwen glances backwards, towards the living-room door. In the distance, Cara can hear the sirens. Coming for her. Coming for Gwen.

'Time's up,' Gwen says sadly. 'Any final requests?'

'Do you regret it?' Cara asks.

Gwen thinks for a moment, a hand pressed to her lips. 'No. And I would kill a hundred more if it meant getting my Siobhan back.'

'But this was never about getting her back. Siobhan was dead even before Robbie went after Ethan.'

'But you know what, my dear?' Gwen says. 'Knowing he died in agonising pain. Knowing he was scared and alone when he was killed. It gave me a lovely warm tingle inside. It made me feel better. And I wanted to do that for the others. Was that too much to ask?'

Cara doesn't reply, and in the silence, Gwen continues.

'Hell is empty,' she says. 'And all the devils are here.'

Chapter 76

The sirens heralded a cavalry of patrol cars, arresting both Cara and Gwen and driving them back to Southampton nick. Cara spent the night being interviewed by a grey-faced prick from Professional Standards, painstakingly explaining why shooting a crazed serial killer had been self-defence and the only option available. And, less convincingly, why she had to leave the scene straight after.

'Running doesn't usually suggest innocence,' he said, nasally.

'This hasn't exactly been my best week,' Cara replied, mastering the art of understatement.

But he'd let her go under investigation, deeming her no danger to the public, and now she sits on an uncomfortable chair in the emergency department, waiting for news on Griffin.

Other injured patients pass through the waiting room. Drunks with bloody noses; children with temperatures; an old lady with what's probably a broken wrist.

'Fell on the stairs,' she says, her voice wobbly. 'That'll be it now. My daughter will put me in a home.'

Cara gives her a wan smile, unable to muster the sympathy required.

'Who are you here for, love?' the lady asks.

'My brother.'

'Ill, is he?'

'Something like that.'

She taps Cara lightly on the arm. 'He'll be okay. These young men, they always are.'

And Griffin has been, up to now. Cara's visited him in hospital more times than she cares to count. First as a wayward teen, drinking and fighting and falling down. Then in the course of the job. Broken nose, busted hand. And everything that came after. With Mia, and the Echo Man.

Strange to think it's over.

Brody returns with two huge coffees, scalding hot and smelling like heaven in red branded cups. She passes one to Cara; she thanks her with a weak smile.

'Go home,' Cara says. 'Get some sleep.'

'I'll wait,' Brody replies. 'Any response from Charlie?'

'Nothing.'

'He'll come around.'

Cara nods, but knows that he might not. She's put her boyfriend through hell, ignoring his calls, shunning any comfort he offered. She wouldn't blame him if she never heard from him again.

But she can't think about Charlie now.

At nine a.m. a doctor in light blue scrubs and white trainers comes out. He speaks to the receptionist, who points to Cara.

Cara's legs turn to jelly as the doctor guides her and Brody to the side of the corridor. He's young, unshaven. Probably been here all night.

'Please,' Cara says. 'How is he?'

The doctor rubs his hand down his chin before speaking, his face grave. 'As you know, Nathanial arrived here in a bad way. Multiple stab wounds to his torso, bruising, broken ribs, contusions to his face and back. From what we can gather, he'd been suspended with his arms above his head, which holds him at risk for ischaemia in his limbs, and had taken multiple blows to his head. He'd lost a substantial amount of blood, and that's not even mentioning the fact he hadn't eaten or drunk anything for seventy-two hours. Our first priority was immediate stabilisation and damage control surgery.'

'How did that go?' Cara whispers. A hand creeps into hers; Cara takes unexpected comfort from having Brody by her side.

'The good news is we've got the bleeding under control and he doesn't seem to have any damage to his skull. The bad news is we've had to resect some of his small bowel, plus he's got four broken ribs, a broken maxilla and fractured mandible. Being suspended that way has dislocated both shoulders and restricted blood flow to his hands, but they look neurovascularly intact, so we're optimistic. We're still concerned about blood clots, and we'll be monitoring him closely over the next twenty-four hours.'

Cara swallows. 'Is he awake?'

'No, and we've got him intubated and sedated. For now. We'll try and hold the sedation in due course. See how he responds.'

'Can I see him?'

'I'll take you to him now. Just be prepared – he's not a pretty sight.'

'I know. Thank you, doctor.'

He gives her a weak smile and they leave Brody in the waiting room, walking down the corridor towards the ICU. He presses his keycard against the lock and they go inside.

It's a different ward to where Roo still lies, but Cara hates how this has become familiar. The hushed atmosphere, the nurses attending to their patients. The squeak of trainers on lino, the beep of monitors and equipment.

Roo's diagnosis is unchanged. His parents and Sarah rotate around his bedside; the kids have been in to see their father. Cara should visit, but can't face it. Griffin first. One at a time.

They reach the final bed.

'I'll keep in touch,' the doctor says, his voice little more than a whisper. 'He was in good shape, so he was lucky. He would have come out of this far worse had he not looked after himself before.'

Cara manages a smile. How Griffin would find that amusing – the fags, the late nights. Yet the doctor approves.

She makes her way down the side of the bed, getting a good look at her brother for the first time. And the doctor's not wrong – he's a mess.

His face is swollen out of all proportion, a mass of blues and reds and purples. Bandages and dressings cover his shoulders and his arms, the sheets pulled up to the top of his chest. An endotracheal tube is secured in his mouth, connected to a machine that wheezes and whines. Tubes protrude out of his arms, heading off to bags of clear fluid; others inch out from under the blankets, leading under the bed.

She sits down slowly and presses her hand lightly to her

lips. Tears creep down her cheeks and she lets them fall, too tired to hold them in. His wrists are bandaged, cuts and sores underneath; she reaches forward and touches his fingers gently with hers.

'Fuck, Nate,' she murmurs. 'I can't do this without you.' Her voice breaks and she lowers her head to the edge of his bed. 'I just can't.'

Cara loses track of time. She doesn't move, her head resting on the blankets, drifting in and out of sleep, her body exhausted.

A nurse disturbs her.

'I need to check on him, love,' she says, gently. 'You can come back after. Are you his sister?' Cara nods. 'I can tell.'

'But he . . .' Cara gestures to his battered face, the blood in his hair.

'It's not the looks,' she says with a smile. 'It's about the bond.'

Cara leaves as the curtain is pulled around. She heads back to the waiting area, and as she gets closer a man looks up from where he's been sitting, his head in his hands.

He stands as she walks closer.

'How is he?' Charlie asks.

'Not good,' Cara replies. She slumps in the nearest chair, Charlie sits next to her. He hands her a takeaway mug.

'It's cold. I'm sorry.'

'It's fine.' She opens the lid; it's still lukewarm and she takes a sip of the creamy coffee. 'Where's Brody?'

'Gone for food.' He hands her a paper bag. 'Here. Croissant. And a pain au chocolat. I thought you might need both.'

'Thank you.' Her stomach rumbles in response and for the first time in forty-eight hours, Cara's hungry. She takes the chocolate pastry out of the bag and eats it in large, hungry bites.

'Better?' Charlie says with a smile.

'You didn't have to come.'

'Of course I did.'

'I don't deserve you.' Charlie frowns. 'This past week, all I've done is push you away. I wouldn't blame you if you left and didn't come back.'

'That's not how this works.' He turns towards her in his seat. 'Cara, I knew this was never going to be easy. We both have demanding jobs, yours more so than mine. You have an ex-husband and two kids. Things . . . happened,' he concludes, 'in the past, and I was there, but I wasn't in the middle of it like you were. Your mother died. And all that before we even went near this awful case.'

'I'm sorry.'

'No, that's not my point. What I mean is, I love you. I've probably been in love with you from the first time I met you. When you were still married and you thought of me as little more than the tech nerd in the basement. I have waited. And I will always wait. I just need to know that you'll catch up.' He shakes his head quickly as she starts to talk. 'Not now,' he says. 'Not while Griffin is here. But one day.'

Cara nods, speechless. She's always got that feeling – that Charlie was more committed to this relationship than she was – but now he's articulated it she realises what a piece of shit she's been. Charlie has always been there for her. Never mentioning his own problems or worries, quietly getting on with the serious business of loving her. And what's she done? Pushed him away. Lied. Charlie deserves better. And she wants to be that person, she does.

But there is still a long way to go. Somebody to see. Decisions to make.

She just hopes that Charlie's still here when it's over.

Chapter 77

With the assurance from the doctors that nothing's going to change for at least a few hours, Cara leaves Brody with Griffin and crosses to HMP Winchester.

She's always thought it strange, the juxtaposition of the hospital and the prison on opposite sides of Romsey Road. One to preserve life, the other to punish.

Conversations have been had with the governor, and access is swift. She follows the normal procedures, leaving her phone and belongings, being shown into an old interview room on the West Wing. She glances up at the cameras in the corner of the room, at the recording equipment by her side. Her hands shake – lack of food, sleep, or something else. It seems strange to be nervous of him after all this time.

Locks rattle, and Noah is shown into the room. He was deemed well enough to leave hospital yesterday, although he walks carefully, bruises still mottling his face. The moment he sees her, he crumples with relief, collapsing in the seat opposite.

'You're okay,' he says. He runs his hands down his face, screws his eyes shut. 'I . . . I thought you might be . . .'

'Why wouldn't I be okay?' Cara asks, her voice hard. 'Is there something you want to tell me?'

He stares at her for a moment, then shakes his head.

'Would it help you open up if I told you that last night, I shot Toby Shenton in the head? That he's dead and lying in the mortuary across the road.'

Noah blinks. 'You . . .'

'I shot him. And it turns out that little Toby Shenton has been conducting some really nasty shit under our noses for the last two decades. That he's a fucking psychopath, and none of us knew. But you did, didn't you, Noah?' The bitterness spills out of her. 'If you'd just told us. Told me—'

'I couldn't. He said he'd kill you.'

'I'd have taken my chances.'

'That he'd kill Tilly and Josh. That he'd . . .'

Cara silences then. Swallows. 'And why would you care? Aren't you a sadistic serial killer?'

'Cara—'

'No, Noah. I don't know what happened back then, but I do know that you need to start being honest. Because, God help me, if you don't, I'm going to leave you to rot in here, despite what I know. Jamie Hoxton – one of my closest friends – was murdered. My brother nearly died.' She jabs a finger in the direction of the hospital. 'He was abducted, beaten, tortured. Shenton stabbed him, and he could still die – but I'm here, because I want to know the fucking truth. So talk. Now.'

Noah looks at her, then points at the recording equipment. 'Don't you want to turn that on?'

'No. This is me and you, Noah. You tell me what happened and I'll decide what I do next. I'm sick of behaving how I'm supposed to, obeying the rule of the law, when nobody else gives a shit. Not Shenton. Not my stupid brother. And not you. So talk.'

Noah nods. He swallows, clenches his jaw. Takes a deep breath in.

'I was at the children's home with Robert Keane. But you know that part.' Cara nods. 'He was my friend. My only friend. And back then I needed someone – anyone. Robbie didn't give a shit. He was reckless, dangerous – but he was also smart and fearless, and I needed some of that. So when he joined the Drug Squad after me we became friends again. And Christ, he did some fucked-up shit. But I was in awe, and terrified of him. The moment he killed that first girl, I knew. I knew he'd kill me too, if I ever did anything to stop him.'

'Why didn't you tell the police? You were a cop, Noah. A *detective*. You could have arrested him yourself.'

'But I didn't want to, don't you get that? Because who else did I have? All my life I've been alone, and the feeling that someone else is on your side – it's a drug. And then I transferred, and I met you. And for a while I forgot about Shenton, and I was happy. Because I had you.'

Cara's mouth is dry. She nods, quickly, willing him to continue.

'Then one day he turned up out of the blue. I hadn't seen him outside of work for ages, but there he was, at midnight. He drove me out to a house he'd broken in to. And I listened, stunned, as he raped a woman. As he killed her.'

'Mia.'

'Yes. I stood by, and I did nothing. Until he showed me into the room, and there was Griffin.'

'You beat him up.'

Noah nods. There are tears in his eyes. 'I don't know what came over me. Shenton was talking, and all I could feel

405

was this rage. So much fucking rage. At the world, at all the people who had called me nothing, useless, a waste of space. And the next thing I knew I had this log in my hand and Griffin was lying on the floor. I thought he was dead. And we ran. I knew then that you would never forgive me. And if that was the case, who cared about anything anymore? So I took the blame. I knew what Shenton had done, all the little details, because he told me. And that was the deal. He wouldn't touch you, and I would go to prison. And I would kill myself. Except I was too useless to even manage that.' Noah's crying now, tears falling to the tabletop. He doesn't look at her. Stares at his hands, tightly grasping one another. 'I tried. And last week, when I knew you were getting close, I tried again. Told them I was police, who I was, what I'd done. What I said I'd done,' he corrects. 'Knew that guy would try to kill me.'

He sniffs, wipes at his eyes with the sleeves of his grey jumper, then looks at the tabletop, working the cuffs around in his fingers. He looks so vulnerable, so young. Everything she knows about him now – she was never wrong about Noah. He was her friend. He wasn't a killer. And all she can think is, No more. No more lives will be ruined by Toby Shenton.

'Noah,' she says. 'Look at me.'

He hesitates for a moment, then does as she asks, meeting her gaze.

'I'm sick of this. Everything he did, the way he deceived us all – no more. In those last few moments, we were alone. Shenton and I. Griffin was out of it, he won't remember. I've got more interviews to come, and I'm going to say that Shenton confessed to it all. The Echo Man murders, that you had no part—'

'But Cara, I did. I killed a girl—'

'Who?'

'Her name was Abigail Young. She went missing in 2017. Shenton raped her, I strangled her, and she died and—' He lets out another sob. 'I puked in his car. He drove off without me. I don't know where he buried her.'

Cara remembers the case – Abigail was eighteen, walking home from college. The body buried in the woods, now too decomposed, no trace, no evidence. 'She was found last year,' Cara says, feeling sick. 'DCI Ryder hasn't made progress. No suspects.'

'That was me. I . . . I had to. I didn't want him to kill me. But I should have stopped him. He killed Mia, and I should have stopped him. I deserve all this.' He points up to the ceiling, the walls of the interview room in the prison. 'I deserve to be here.'

'No. No, you don't. Whatever you did, it was because of him. I will get your conviction overturned. Do you hear me? Keep your mouth shut and I will make sure you walk out of here a free man.'

Noah gapes for a moment.

'Do you hear me?'

'Yes. But why? You should hate me, for what I did.'

'I don't hate you. You were my best friend, and I should have realised what was going on. I should have helped you. I knew you were lying when you confessed. I should have fought harder. But I can do this. Now. Please. Let me do this.'

'And I'll walk free?'

His astonishment makes her smile. 'Yes. Go anywhere, do anything. Live next to some remote loch in Scotland. Or get a bar job in the middle of London. I don't care—'

'Come with me.'

His words stop her in her tracks. 'Sorry?'

'Come with me.' He leans forward, taking her hands. He grips them tightly. 'Cara, I love you. I always have. You should come with me. Quit your job—'

'I can't. Everything I've worked for—'

'It's killing you. The pressure. The stress. Don't you fancy it, just one tiny little bit?'

And, oh fuck, she does. She looks into his light brown eyes and she sees Noah. The man she spent every moment of every day with. The person who understood her better than anyone else. The man who risked his life for her, and would do it again.

'Tilly and Josh—'

'They can come with us. They'll be fine. You said yourself – Tilly is being bullied. She could start afresh. New school. What could be better? You and me, Cara. The way it should have been. In a different life. Without Shenton. This is the second chance we need. Please.'

She looks down at her hands – their fingers, tightly entwined on the table.

'Griffin . . .' she says quietly. 'He would never forgive me. He's all I have.'

'You're all *I* have,' Noah replies. He pulls his hands away. 'Don't decide now. I shouldn't have . . . it's a lot . . . I just . . .' He frowns. 'You're all I've ever wanted, Cara.'

Cara nods, feeling tears threaten. She pulls away, standing up and taking two steps backwards. She needs some distance. From this, from him.

'Keep yourself safe,' she says, her voice breaking, 'until I get you out. Please.'

And with that she turns and walks away. Quick steps,

desperate to put space between Noah and everything she feels when she is with him. Her brain whirrs, a confusing mess of indecision and worry. She escapes as quickly as she can, collecting her belongings and switching her phone on once she's clear of the prison walls. It beeps immediately. Messages. From Brody. From Charlie.

But before she can read them it rings, and she answers it.

'Cara, where are you?' Charlie says. 'Come now. It's Griffin. He's . . . he's not doing well.'

Chapter 78

They're not allowed near – Griffin out of bounds while the doctors assess and test. Cara paces outside the double doors to the ICU, Brody slumped in a chair next to her. Charlie, desperate for something useful to do, has left to fetch coffee.

'What did they say?' Cara asks her for the hundredth time.

'I don't know. Something about a chest infection. A reaction to the antibiotics.'

'What sort of reaction? I didn't know he's allergic. But they can treat that, right?'

'I don't know,' Brody repeats, wearily. She looks up with bloodshot eyes. 'They just said it wasn't good.'

Cara stops. Realises the spiral she's in, tries to contain her panic. She sits down next to the younger woman.

'I'm sorry,' Cara says. 'I—'

'I know. It's fine.' Brody drops her face to her hands and stays that way for a moment, silent.

'How are you doing?' Cara asks, gently.

Brody shrugs weakly, still staring at the floor. 'I'm okay. I . . . For the last few days I've been focusing on work.

Determined to catch this killer. To find Griffin. And then I got that man killed, not that I'm sorry about that, but . . .' She stops herself. 'I've not allowed myself to think about . . .' She gestures to the closed doors. 'This. And now he's here and I can't do anything to help, I just . . .' Her voice breaks and she starts to cry. 'I'm sorry. I shouldn't be crying. He's your brother and . . .'

'I've done my fair share of crying, I promise you.' Brody looks up and they share a sympathetic smile. 'Can I ask – you and Griffin. Are you together?'

'I think so. We went on a date. Before he went missing. Did he tell you that?' Cara shakes her head. 'It was nice. He was . . . I don't know. A different man to the cop I see at work. He was sweet, and affectionate.'

'He is. Behind that gruff exterior, he's all marshmallow.'

'I've been with some terrible men. Really awful. I had a type, couldn't stay away from them, so I swore off anything long term. I thought . . . Sex or nothing.' She colours. 'I'm sorry. You're my boss. I shouldn't be telling you this.'

'It's fine. I get it. And I'm not your boss here.'

'But I am sorry. Griffin said you knew about . . . what we've been doing.'

Cara gives her a wry smile. 'You didn't hide it well. And I'm not going to pretend I'm not pissed about it. Mainly because of the trouble you could get yourselves in.'

'We won't do it again.' Brody glances to the closed double doors. She angrily wipes the tears from her eyes. 'Fucking hell. He has to be okay. He has to.'

They sink into silence. Charlie arrives back with three coffees, handing them across wordlessly then moving a chair to Cara's side. Sitting down next to her.

'Any change?' he says.

But before she can reply, alarms sound inside the ICU. Frantic beeping, monitors going haywire. All three of them get to their feet as medical staff rush in, a mass of blue scrubs and shouted instructions. Through the open door, Cara watches as they crowd Griffin's bed, someone starting compressions while another preps a crash cart.

She feels Charlie's arm around her shoulders, pulling her close; she reaches out and grabs Brody's hand.

The worst has happened. Griffin is going to die.

Chapter 79

The day of the funeral is cool and crisp, bright sun pushing its way through the clouds. Cara watches as Charlie and Adam take their place next to the hearse as the back door is opened and the coffin is lifted.

Six pallbearers carry the glossy wooden coffin towards the church, the weight heavy on their shoulders. Cara follows, aware how many eyes are on her, how many people are watching this procession. The death of a police officer killed in the line of duty has attracted headlines across the country. As much as they tried to limit the coverage, there was no stopping the public lining the streets, the newspapers snapping pictures.

Cara attempts to blank her mind, concentrates on putting one foot after another as they shuffle into the church. She can't think about the body in the coffin. She can't, otherwise she'll lose it.

And she wants to do Jamie proud.

Inside, the light is dim, the air cold. She sees the chief constable in full dress uniform, the ACC and the rest of the chief officer group in the pew. Lines of PCs and sergeants in their tunics – Jamie touched a lot of lives.

She takes a seat next to Brody and Halstead, offers a weak smile. At the front, the coffin is gently lowered. She watches as Adam Bishop pauses, pressing his palm gently to the wood, his head bent, before he straightens, carefully correcting the angle of the blue shroud on the top, the police logo embroidered on the side.

Jamie wouldn't have wanted this fuss. Cara can almost hear him: *Just stick me in a cardboard box, boss. Bury me in the garden.* But his mother insisted, and Cara didn't want to make the old woman's day any worse. Besides, they should give him the best send-off possible. It is the least she can do.

In the darker hours, at two a.m., as Charlie lies sleeping next to her, Cara replays those last few days of the investigation. How, once again, she missed the killer in her team. Noah may have been innocent, but Shenton fooled them all. And the guilt of that. The fault lies squarely at her door, and Cara nurtures her self-hate, that burn of shame.

Charlie takes a seat in the pew next to her and he reaches out, taking her hand. She grips it tightly, a lifeboat in the swirling waves. Her steadying influence in the face of such death and destruction, and she wonders, again, why he puts up with her.

He's been with her at the hospital, swapping wards between her brother and her ex-husband. And miraculously, both are on the mend.

Once the anaphylaxis caused by the antibiotics for the chest infection was under control, Griffin's recovery was swift. The doctors warn him to take it easy, but he's desperate to be out of the hospital, begs Brody to wheel him outside in the chair. 'To see the sun,' he says, when Cara knows he's angling for a fag. Nobody lets him smoke, to his chagrin.

It's been the one bit of sunshine in an otherwise awful month.

Roo's prognosis is bleak, but he's awake. Substantial memory loss, confusion, nausea, fatigue, headaches, sensitivity to light and noise, the list goes on and on. They talk about rehab, about physiotherapy, and Cara tunes it out for the most part. Her priority has to lie with the kids. They're living with her, and that takes all her time. Taking them to visit Roo in the hospital, listening to their worries, that someone else they love will get injured, knowing she's the curse in all of this, that everyone close to her seems to pay the price.

Hymns are sung. Ones she remembers from her schooldays. She tries her best, but her mouth is dry, her brain mush.

Adam Bishop will speak first. Jamie's closest friend. Cara visited him and Romilly a week ago, cooed over baby Ivy, then together they went to Jamie's flat. They paused in the hallway. The place still smelled of him; his shoes lay discarded in the pile, his coat on the hook.

'I keep thinking he's going to come round,' Adam said to her. 'His key in the lock, calling out as he always used to do.' He looked at her, searching for understanding, and she nodded, a lump in her throat, knowing too well how many times she had gone to phone him, had looked for him in the corridors on the few times she's been back to the nick.

Adam opened the door into Jamie's bedroom, pausing.

'It's too much,' he whispered to the empty room, and Cara knew he wasn't talking to her anymore. 'I want to have a beer. Watch *Countryfile*. Without thinking about

415

you.' His shoulders sagged and he sat on the edge of the bed, covering his face in his hands as he shook under the weight of his grief. And as Cara gently closed the door, giving him the privacy to cry, she heard his last mumbled words. 'I just want to see you again.'

Because that's the heartache that knocks her for six, again and again. That void, the hole the dead leave in our lives. Her father first, then her mother. And now Jamie. Gone, leaving only grief and regret behind.

The vicar comes to the end of his eulogy and Cara realises she hasn't heard a single word. Adam gets to his feet.

He makes it to the pulpit, walking as if every step brings him pain. Once there, he grips the side, looking out into the congregation. Cara sees him lock eyes with Romilly, his wife giving him an encouraging nod.

His shoulders rise as he takes a deep breath.

'I first met Jamie when he joined my team in 2015. And it was love at first sight.' A ripple of laughter from the congregation. Adam smiles. 'He was a loveable teddy bear. At six foot two, he towered over me. Towered over most people, but he cried at anything – and I mean anything – and I wondered what I had done, recruiting him into our Major Crimes team, but there was something about Jamie. He was the good guy to my bad, the empathy to my arrogance. Apart, we were great coppers, but together we were brilliant. And, as many of you know, he came to live with us. Only for a few months, but while he was there, Jamie was the husband Romilly always wanted. He emptied the dishwasher. He cleaned. And he was a fantastic second father to Ivy.' Adam's voice cracks and he pushes his lips together, eyes closed as he tries to contain the emotion Cara knows must be bubbling in his chest. For a moment, he doesn't speak. He runs a finger around the neck of his shirt, then grips the pulpit so tightly his fingers turn white. He clears his throat. And this time manages to get the words out. 'He was my best friend. I loved him. He saved my life. And I don't know what I'm going to do without him.'

Cara blinks away tears as Adam hurries back to his seat, head down. Romilly whispers something to him, but he doesn't respond, and as the congregation stands for another hymn Adam remains seated, his shoulders heaving, silent, bent in two. Sobbing, his head in his hands.

Chapter 80

The service comes to an end. DCS Halstead does the final eulogy, talking about Jamie's unblemished record, his commitment to the job, his team. As she talks, Cara shoves her hands in her pocket, touching the screwed-up piece of A4 that holds her hastily written attempt. The last of many drafts, all discarded for being too insincere, too trite, not good enough. She's glad Halstead took over. Gave Cara a break, when Cara knows the real reason is Halstead doesn't want a high-profile suspended detective-slash murder suspect front and centre.

The organ plays and the congregation slowly moves from the church. The burial is later, close friends and family only, and Cara's still not sure if that includes her. She misses Griffin. He'd know what to do.

At home, Frank watches her from a distance. Reluctantly eating the food she provides with a haughty air, disgust that his lord and master hasn't been home. Griffin's bed in the hospital is surrounded by Get Well Soon cards, many adorned with images of black cats. He grumbles about the cards, accepts the chocolates, and Cara's reassured he's on the mend.

Charlie's been with her every step of the way. Stoic, capable. And fuck, how she loves him. She does, she realises now, looking at him in his smart, black suit. She loves how his hair falls in the mornings, messy, soft, and the way he looks at her, squinting, before his glasses go on. She loves how he is with the kids – patient, gentle – and their reliance on him, a source of stability in their lives. And how he makes her feel – cared for, respected. But also guilty – so incredibly guilty – that even after all of this, she can't stop thinking about Noah.

His acquittal has been slow in going through. Her statement was interrogated, cross-examined, and now, at last, the judge has agreed that the murders committed by the Echo Man were carried out by Toby Shenton, and any actions on the part of Noah Deakin were coercion, nothing more. But bureaucracy is slow, the CPS even more so. It could be weeks before he's released.

She still doesn't know what she's going to do. She loves Charlie, but her feelings for Noah are more complicated. He's a part of her soul, and the idea that she might never see him again fills her with dread. But it's not just that. The thought he articulated all those weeks ago thrills her. That she could just leave with him. Pack up her house, her kids, and walk away to some unknown place. Somewhere quiet, where they won't be disturbed. Maybe a camper van, travel the world. Put all of this behind them. That thought is intoxicating. And it nags at her, chewing at her brain when she lies next to Charlie at night.

Sunshine dazzles as they leave the church. She finds

herself walking next to Adam. He looks at her, gives a weak smile.

'How's Griffin?'

'Better every day. Thank you.'

Adam pauses, gestures her over to the side, while Romilly and Charlie walk on ahead. Close up, he looks awful. His eyes red-rimmed, exhaustion highlighting every pore. But she can't imagine she looks that great either.

'Are you sleeping?' she asks him.

'Not much. You?'

'Eight hours a night,' she jokes, and he snorts.

'Listen, I wanted to ask you – are you going back to work?'

'I don't know,' she answers truthfully. 'PSD have cleared me, with some help from the great British public,' she adds, remembering the op-ed pieces in the *Guardian* defending her actions, the screaming headlines about the detective who stopped the serial killer. 'But I haven't made my mind up.' She studies him carefully. 'Why?'

'I've been offered a job.' He pauses. 'Yours.' It doesn't surprise her. 'Temporary basis,' he adds quickly. 'Until you're back on your feet.'

'You should take it.'

'Really?'

'Yeah.' And now it's out of her mouth, she realises she means it. 'I need to be with the kids right now,' she continues. 'Not working twelve-hour days under artificial light. And it's a good opportunity for you. Build a team from scratch. Put your own stamp on it. Just make sure that DCI Ryder has a run for her money.'

'Fuck, that awful woman.' He laughs and they share a smile, united in mutual hatred of the only cop who emerged out of the last few months unscathed. 'Brody's coming back,' he continues. 'Did she say?'

'Yes. She's good. You'll like her.'

'As long as she doesn't kill any more paedophiles.'

'You know.'

'Jamie phoned me. Before he . . . He didn't know what to do.'

'And what did you say?'

'That he should talk to you. As his senior officer, the buck stopped there.'

'And now?'

'Nobody's investigating, are they? I think they have enough on their plate. Let it go.'

Cara glances to Charlie, waiting at the car. She turns back to Adam. 'Accept the job, DCI Bishop. And who knows, it might become permanent.'

Adam narrows his eyes, giving her a quizzical look. 'You'd never leave the force. You're like me. It's in your bones.'

'That's what I thought. But I don't know. Everything that's happened. Everything we've been through. At what point do we say, enough is enough?'

'You're a good cop, Cara. Besides, what else would you do?'

'Run a bar? Write a book?'

'Landlords and authors. Alcoholics the lot of them.' Adam smiles, turns towards the sound of his name as Romilly comes towards them. 'I'd better go. See you later – at the burial?'

'I'll be there,' Cara replies.

She watches Adam walk away, thinking about his words. What else would she do? Sleep. Eat. Cry. After the past month, she's numb, rendered exhausted and dazed by the events she's been forced to live through. So many dead. So many futures like Jamie's extinguished, and because of that, she knows one thing for sure.

She will live without fear, without regret, without looking over her shoulder. Because the Echo Man is dead. And she has her whole life ahead of her.

Chapter 81

At first, all Griffin felt was pain. When he lifted his head, when he spoke, when he breathed. He was reluctant to take the painkillers, knowing how addiction took control last time, but the doctors persuaded him.

'You need to rest,' they said. 'And you can't do that if you're in pain.'

So he let them do their worst.

Slowly, the fug cleared. He was moved from the ICU to a normal ward, where he flirted with the nurses, ate the terrible hospital food. Brody became a constant, bringing him grapes and chocolate, even smuggling him a burger, although he suspects she asked permission first.

He asks every day when he can go home. The doctors shake their heads, but he's noticed them changing. Checking his chart first, conferring with their colleagues. He misses Frank and mentions it to Brody; the next day a soft fluffy cat appears. Amber eyes made out of glass, a superior expression. He mocked at the time, but he finds himself sleeping with it in the crook of his arm. A comfort, when there's been so little.

Because he still imagines himself there. In the concrete pit, where he was cold and hungry and afraid. Where there was nothing but pain, and he wakes with a jolt, sucking in air as if he's drowning, tears wet on his cheeks.

He finds Brody next to him. Reaches out; she takes his hand.

'I dreamed about you,' he whispers. 'When I was down there.'

He hasn't talked about it much, and she squeezes his hand, presses her lips against it.

'Don't go,' he says. When all he means is *Don't leave me*. And she replies: 'I won't.'

Cara comes to see him after the sentencing. Gwen Morris confessed to it all.

'Whole life term,' Cara says. 'She'll never be released from prison.'

He worries about his sister. She'll not face charges for shooting Toby Shenton, but he sees dark clouds surrounding her. She's slow to smile, lost in her thoughts. She's always been resilient, but he wonders whether this is her limit. Whether she can take any more.

He's watching a film with Brody when Cara arrives. A cartoon, *Finding Nemo*, and he empathises with the fish. Memories are slow to fade, his brain stutters and jumps.

'You'll get better over time,' Cara says, when Griffin tells her about it. 'The doctors said to be patient.' She looks at Brody. 'Could you give us a minute?'

Brody smiles and gets up. 'I need to get going anyway. See you later?' She kisses Griffin on the cheek, still reserved in front of her former boss.

'You like her,' Cara says, once she's gone.

'I do.'

424

'I'm glad.' They share a smile, but Griffin's worried.

'What's up? Is Frank okay?'

'Frank is absolutely fine. Although the little bastard brought in a rat yesterday and I could have done without that. A live one.'

'That's nice. He's bringing you presents.'

'Perhaps he can show his love in other ways. Like not clawing me to death when I try to stroke him.' She pauses, her face downcast.

'Cara? What's going on?'

He's only seen that expression a few times before. When he was sixteen, and their father died. And later, when their mother went the same way.

'What is it, Cara? You're scaring me.'

'Nate, I need to tell you something. And it's going to be hard for you to hear, but I need you to listen.'

'Is this about Shenton? Related to the case?'

'Partly. But it's not to do with Shenton.' She pauses, and he knows, a ripple of hatred running through his bones.

'I need to talk to you about Noah.'

TWO WEEKS LATER

Epilogue

Noah Deakin never believed this would happen until he was stepping out of the main gates of HMP Winchester into the cool fresh April morning. The suit he wore to court hangs loose on his shoulders, his wallet and a pair of navy blue Converse rest in the bottom of a plastic bag, his only possessions. He has twenty-five pounds to his name.

He looks out to the car park. He hasn't spoken to Cara since her last visit, weeks ago now. Hasn't wanted to pressure her – she's gone through a lot. But a small part of him dares to hope. A shred of optimism, persisting, despite everything he's done.

In the distance, a blue Audi estate makes its way through the gates. He recognises it and his whole body buzzes, fizzing with apprehension. The car stops. The driver's door opens. But the person who gets out isn't who he expects.

Nate Griffin closes the door. He walks across to Noah, and any previous excitement fades in a millisecond. Griffin is wearing black jeans, black boots and a worn black jacket. From a distance, he looks the same, but every movement seems painful; as he gets closer Noah can make out the barely healed cuts on his face, the extra grey in his hair.

Griffin stops a few metres away. Noah doesn't move.

'You're out then,' he says.

'What do you want, Griffin?'

'Get in the car.'

Noah considers his options. He could run, and Griffin's in no fit state to give chase, but what would be the point? This is the ending he always expected. The one he deserves.

He opens the passenger's side and gets in. Griffin does the same.

He starts the engine without a word. They drive in silence. Out of Winchester, into a countryside of rolling fields, still bare and muddy from winter, bordered by high hedges of blackthorn. They drive for about half an hour; the roads get narrower, the traffic less frequent, until Griffin pulls into the gateway of a farmer's field. He cuts the engine.

'Get out.'

Noah does as he's told. Griffin pauses for a moment, his head down, and Noah wonders if Griffin's going to leave him here, until the door opens and he climbs out. The wind whips across the muddy field, and Noah wraps his arms around his body, shivering with cold and dread.

Griffin points to the gateway, and they both walk towards it, Noah in front.

They're alone. Nobody can see them now, visibility blocked by a high hedge, new leaves blooming, fresh and green.

'Are you going to beat the shit out of me?' Noah asks.

Griffin regards him from under lowered brows. 'Look at me. I've been out of hospital for a week. I can barely walk. Do I look like I'm able to beat the shit out of you?'

Griffin reaches into his pocket and pulls out a packet of cigarettes. He takes one out and lights it, cupping his hand around the flame, then offers them to Noah. Noah takes one, doing the same.

'I'm going to ask you some questions. I expect you to be honest.'

Noah frowns. Whatever he expected from Griffin, this isn't it. 'Okay?'

A long inhale on the cigarette, then an exhale. 'Did you kill my wife?'

'No.'

'Did you know what Shenton was going to do?'

'No.'

'Were you there?'

'I was in the bathroom. I could hear her.'

'And you did nothing.'

'Yes.'

Noah wants to say more, to explain his cowardice, but anything that comes to mind is insufficient.

'Did you try to kill me?' Griffin asks. His tone hasn't changed – serious, matter-of-fact.

'I . . . I wasn't trying to kill you. But I was angry.' Noah shakes his head, remembering that strange, half-existence.

'Angry at me?'

'Maybe, on some level. But mainly at the world. At Shenton. For the hold he had over me. For everything he made me do.'

'Okay.' Griffin lights a new cigarette from the old, stubs the butt under his boot. 'I probably would have kicked the shit out of you, back then. Given half the chance.'

'But you're not going to do that now?'

Griffin sighs. 'No.' He takes another long drag. 'When

Cara told me what she'd done, that she was going to get you out, I was furious. As far as I was concerned you should rot in prison, Shenton or otherwise. But she shared some things, about you, how you grew up, and she told me I need to forgive. Because all this hatred, this anger' – he thrusts a fist towards his chest – 'in here. It's not doing me any good. And if I'm going to move on. Be happy,' he adds, with a sarcastic curl of his lip, as if contentment were the most impossible thing in the world, 'then I need to forgive you. Otherwise, what do we do? We punch and we scream and we kill, but all we'll end up destroying is ourselves.'

Griffin laughs, then shakes his head. 'Look at me, spouting philosophical bullshit. Anyway, she said I should come and see you. So here I am.'

Griffin drops the cigarette in the mud and reaches out towards him. Noah recoils, then realises what he's doing – offering a handshake. And slowly Noah puts forward his own.

They shake hands, solemnly, carefully. Neither grip too strong, neither too weak, then Griffin pulls away. He reaches into his pocket and takes out what looks like a credit card. He holds it out to Noah.

'What's that?'

'What does it look like? A prepaid card. There's a few hundred on there. Enough to get you started. Find your feet.'

Noah's shocked. By this show of generosity more than anything else Griffin has done this morning. 'Thank you.'

'Don't thank me. Cara wanted you to have it. I just ask one thing.'

'Anything.'

'Stay away from my sister. From Cara. I know you two have always been . . . close. But no more. She's gone away with Charlie and the kids for a few weeks, and when she gets back I don't want you anywhere near her. Don't call. Don't make contact. Get as far away from Southampton as you can. They're going to move in together, and she has a real chance of happiness here. You are not to screw it up.'

Noah nods. He asked Cara the question, and with her absence she's given her reply. Whatever was between them, it's over. He has to respect that.

'You have my word.' He pauses. 'Charlie's a good guy?'

'The best. Better than me. Definitely worthier than you. He'll look after her. Now fuck off.'

Noah looks around. 'We're in the middle of nowhere.'

'You've got feet, haven't you? Fucking walk.'

And with that, Griffin strolls back to the gate.

'Griffin?' He doesn't stop. 'Nate?'

Griffin turns.

'I'm sorry. For what it's worth.'

Griffin looks as if he's going to reply, but instead just nods and gets into the car. Noah watches as the blue Audi drives away. He looks at the card in his hand, and the trainers in the plastic bag. He leans against the gate and unties the laces of the once smart black shoes, taking them off and putting the Converse on his feet. He looks down at the scuffed worn sneakers, and feels like himself again.

He leaves the other shoes in the mud and starts to walk. North, he guesses. To a railway station, maybe even hitch a lift. Head to Scotland. Glasgow, maybe, or Edinburgh. To somewhere he can be unknown. Just another drifter, running away from their past.

It was a ridiculous thought, that he and Cara could be together. She has a life here, a better one than he'd ever be able to provide. And he's glad she's happy. After everything

431

she's been through – that he's put her through – she deserves a nice man. Someone to love her and the kids, look after her and give her everything she wants.

She's given him his freedom, and that's all he needs.

And so Noah Deakin starts to walk. Towards a main road. Towards somewhere he can call home. And for the first time in his life, he's free.

Acknowledgements

It's been a long time since the death and destruction in *The Echo Man* and I've wanted to write the conclusion to Noah Deakin's story ever since. He's always been one of my favourite characters and his story seemed unfinished; it was so much fun to come back to him again. Him – and Shenton, of course!

Thank you so much to the wonderful Kathryn Cheshire at Hemlock/HarperCollins for letting me write this crazy story, and to Julia Wisdom, Maud Davies and the rest of the team – it's a joy to work with you all.

A huge thank you must go to my incredible agent Ed Wilson for knowing exactly the author I want to be and never getting in the way of pitching these insane stories. Thank you also to Hélène Butler for getting the books out to the growing collective of foreign publishers, and to Anna Dawson and the rest of the team at Johnson and Alcock for their unwavering support.

Thank you to Charlotte Webb for the copyedit (and

knowing that John McClane doesn't have an 'I') and to Sarah Bance for the proofread.

Thank you to Soraya Vink, Ellis Gielen, and the incredible team at HarperCollins Holland for making me so welcome.

Now to the ever-increasing rota of technical experts!

It's important to me to get the technical stuff right (or as much as I can), and it's down to these guys that I can even get close. Thank you to PC Dan Roberts and Charlie Roberts for answering the bulk of my questions on police procedure, and thank you to Graham Bartlett for filling in the gaps. Thank you to Sgt Jon Bates from the SCIU for providing the know-how behind Roo's car accident, and to Steph Fox for detailing how to get corpses out of concrete. There were a lot of dead and dying bodies in this one, so thank you to Dr Matt Evans for checking pages and pages of my terrible attempts at medical jargon and for discussing at length how to inflict the most pain on poor old Griffin without actually killing him. See also: how to kill someone with a dildo. Thank you, Matt, for not batting an eye at that one.

Thank you to Luke Snelling and Adam Southward for answering my questions about IP addresses and Bitcoin and webcams. And finally, thank you to Lauren Sprengel for providing much needed detail about life in HMP Nottingham.

I couldn't have done it without you all.

As always, any mistakes or errors, whether deliberate or otherwise, are mine and mine alone.

It would be impossible to get through all these lonely days at my desk without the entertainment, badgers, pincers and llamas from the hideously named New Criminal Minds group: Heather, Jo, Rachael, Niki, Kate, Liz, Elle, Dom,

Tim, Adam, Polly, Harriet, Victoria, Rob, Fliss, Simon, Susie, Natalie, and Barry. I dare you to find writers as supportive as these. Thank you to Dominic Nolan for the invaluable first read and feedback.

Thank you also to my Winchester partners-in-crime, Liv Matthews and Karen Hamilton. No city centre café is safe with us around.

A huge thank you must go to Teri Andrews for being my 'date' to The Noisy Lobster down at Avon beach in Christchurch – where Griffin and Brody go on their night out. It's a wonderful place to go if you ever fancy some good seafood, I wholly recommend it.

Endless gratitude must go to the amazing bookshops who get my bonkers novels into readers' hands. I am incredibly fortunate to have a number of bookshops supporting my journey – to mention a few (and I will forget some, sorry!), thank you to the teams at Waterstones Westquay, Romsey, Portsmouth, Whiteley, Salisbury, Winchester High Street and Brooks Shopping Centre. Thank you to Robyn and Daniel at Imaginarium Books in Lymington, Sarah and Jazz at The Book Shop in Lee-on-the-Solent, Steve at P&G Wells, and the team at October Books in Portswood.

Thank you to my family – to Chris and Ben and Max; to Dad; to Tom, Mel, Henry and Leo; and to Jon, Susan, Megan and Anwen. I love you.

And if you've got this far, thank you to you, the reader, for picking up my books out of the hundreds and thousands of other incredible crime thrillers out there. I love seeing your photos on social media and hearing all your comments and questions. Do keep in touch on social media (@samhollandbooks.)

Finally, thank you to Charlotte Griffin and Tom Deakin,

to whom this book is dedicated. When I first put your names to Nate and Noah, none of us could possibly know how it would turn out, and you've never shied away from this strange infamy. It is fitting that two of my favourite characters are named after two of my favourite people. Thank you.